FLIGHT OF THE SPARROW

FALLON DEMORNAY

All rights reserved. No part of this publication may be reproduced, stored in a retrieval system, or transmitted in any form or by any means electronic, mechanical, photocopying, recording, or otherwise without prior written permission from Podium Publishing.

This is a work of fiction. Names, characters, places, and incidents are either products of the author's imagination or used fictitiously. Any resemblance to actual events, locales, or persons, living, dead, or undead, is entirely coincidental.

Copyright © 2025 by Fallon MacLean

Cover design by M.S. Corley

ISBN: 978-1-0394-8282-1

Published in 2025 by Podium Publishing
www.podiumentertainment.com

FLIGHT
OF THE
SPARROW

To my grandmother: Laura Maude Maclean—I wasn't brave enough to reach you in time, and that will haunt me forever.

FLIGHT
OF THE
SPARROW

CHAPTER ONE

D*on't be afraid* . . .

Nimah Dabo-124 pressed a clammy hand to her brow as the whisper of ghosts rang between her ears like a vicious toothache. A distant echo from a past she struggled to forget.

Don't be afraid . . .

"You alright?" Cadet Liselle Namsara lingered by a food counter for spicy pad thai.

"Fine," Nimah lied, her eyes combing the busy slums of the Soot District, thusly named as, being this close to the spacity's generators, everything was coated in a filmy, chalky grease.

People pushed through overcrowded walkways crammed with vendor stalls and flashing neon holoverts stacked upon each other, disappearing into air traffic that whizzed overhead—a flurry of swooping single-passenger gliders, patchwork taxis, and refurbished cruisers filling the air with a heady aroma of exhaust. But the readout on her wristdeck showed the levels were at least twenty percent below hazardous.

"You're not seriously thinking about eating that, are you?" Nimah frowned as the robo-chef tossed miracle noodles into a wok and added cubes of something that was supposed to pass for meat. It was more plastic than protein but on this side of Tor12, a spacity with close to a hundred million inhabitants, it was impossible to find anything that wasn't recycled or lab-grown.

"I'm starving and we have at least three hours left on our rotation. Besides," Liselle laughed as she whisked through the menu, "add enough hot sauce and it might be alright."

"Waste of credits if you ask me. You're just going to puke it up when we thread back to base. But go ahead, it's your funeral." Hypertravel gates, all government owned, were round pools of plasma called Eyes, and when you dove into them—threading the eye of the needle as it were—in less than a breath, you were on the other side of the Inner Circle. Threading was hard even on the staunchest of agents, but if Nimah had it her way, it would be the only way she'd ever travel across the void.

"I'm good." Liselle tapped her flat stomach. "Perks of being retrofit."

Like all Inner Circle cadets, Liselle had been genetically enhanced after birth with synth-organs designed to outlast and outperform their traditionally grown counterparts. With routine maintenance, she'd live to be a hundred without breaking a sweat. A mark of privilege thanks to having SIGA government officials for parents. Of being born on the *right* side of the RIM.

"Tell me something, Nims." She tucked a twisted lock of black hair ringed with silver beads behind her ear. "Why do you want to be an agent so bad if you're afraid of the void?"

"I'm not afraid," she bristled.

Liselle leveled a stare. "I saw you when you came out of the simulation. I've never seen anyone so truly rattled. Especially not *you*."

Nimah cursed. If only she could erase the last six hours. Within the walls of the Academy, she was known as the girl without fear, and she'd worked damned hard to make sure everyone believed that. But now she could feel the carefully crafted facade crumbling around her like scorched paper, laying bare a truth she could no longer ignore.

She *was* afraid. Every single second of every single day, Nimah was terrified to the bone—of the void. The one weakness she hadn't been able to shake after a decade of training. Open space, the naked vastness of it and the terrifying spread of glittering black dropped her stomach into her bowels, tying it all up in knots until she puked. And even though all flight simulations were done virtually, it was designed to feel as close to the real thing as possible. So fucking real that several hours later, Nimah was still shaking. Still nauseated. Still on the brink of hopeless tears.

"Spare me the drag, alright? I'm fine." She had to be. *Because I have to belong somewhere.* Nimah smothered the fragile truth whispering inside of her; a truth she'd never dared admit to anyone. Not even Liselle.

The STARs were the elite of the elite and Nimah was determined to become one of them. Only the top three percent of the Academy would earn the honor of wearing the badge, and then be shipped out to SIGA, the Stars Intelligence and Government Authority operative headquarters. A floating spacity tasked with patrolling nearly fifteen hundred terraformed planets and moons. The most desirable of which comprised the Inner Circle and were populated by the prestigious members who held seats in government, military, and commerce, and inherited astronomical generational wealth. In essence, they held all the power and all the profit.

Next were the second-tier citizens who comprised the working class who occupied planets and moons known to have harsher climates or challenging terrains but were otherwise habitable and yielded significant profits in agriculture, mining, and lumber. They worked long days and longer hours to meet quarterly quotas to maintain their citizenship through the sweat of labor.

Third class was for the grunts of the workforce who earned credits through menial labor—cleaning toilets, clearing tables, driving taxis, and scrubbing floors. Third class was a tough life and within the last decade more were finding themselves out of work and struggling to compete against the rollout of synths that were not only far more efficient, able to work around the clock without rest, but also required no pay for employment. Some prophesized that synths would eventually replace the entire third-class workforce. A harrowing thought that Nimah pushed away with a heavy breath.

Third-class citizens who failed to earn enough to afford the levies and taxes that came at the end of each year had only one other place they could go. The RIM. A massive asteroid belt tucked at the fringe of the galaxy. Once little more than a dumping ground, it had been terraformed into reservation lands for non-class citizens displaced from the Integration Zone Wars that ended almost a century ago.

Nimah would never make it to SIGA if she couldn't stomach being voidborne, and as of today she was teetering on the edge. This was her third failed simulation exam. One more and her cadet status would be revoked. One more, and she'd be cast out to the RIM. *Again.*

"C'mon, Nims, don't be iced. I'm just trying to understand. I want to help."

"You can help by ordering your trash food so we can get back to our rotation. There's fourteen sectors we still need to scan."

"Loosen a button. Let your hair down. For *once*." To illustrate her point, Liselle tossed her locs, which she'd freed almost an hour ago, and punched the call icon to place her order.

Nimah instinctively smoothed a hand across her impeccably styled regulation bun. It was ruthlessly taut, smoothing her tight curls, but that was the code and Nimah *always* followed the code. Even if it meant suffering through splitting tension headaches.

It was so easy for the other cadets to relax when they were born with the right credentials and no numbers hitched to the end of their names. A minor infraction or two on Liselle's record wouldn't leave so much as a scratch, but for Nimah—a RIM-rat—every blemish became a scar. She had to be perfect. Pristine. Not only because everyone already expected her to fail, but because if she gave them a reason to look any closer or dig any deeper into her past . . .

Nimah clamped down on the bitter ache of memories and blamed the shock of her tenuous circumstances for jostling up old ghosts she had buried long ago. If there was ever a chance of being exposed as the granddaughter of the void's once-renowned space pirate, it would've happened during her induction into the Academy. Besides, Captain Indira Roscoe was gone, and after fifteen years there was no reason for Nimah to think about her now.

<*Order 02347—ready for pickup!*> The robo-chef slapped the steaming, greasy square carton onto the counter and Liselle seized it with giddy fingers. Tearing into a packet of chopsticks with her teeth, she swirled the metal utensils in her ninety-three-percent synthetic noodles and slurped down a sickening mouthful.

"Ugh, this is so razor. Like mad razor, Nims!"

FLIGHT OF THE SPARROW

"It's the chemicals tricking the synapses in your brain." Nimah's lip curled in disgust. "You know it's pure garbage with almost zero nutritional value."

"Don't care," Liselle mumbled around more food than her mouth should've been able to hold. "So. Good."

"I'm going to remind you of this conversation when you're begging me to put you out of your misery later." Sighing, Nimah shook a bemused head, eyes flicking across the busy street to a bustling bar with the windows rolled up so she could see straight inside. Instinct pulled her gaze to the far corner where a young man sat alone at a square table of weathered fiberboard.

A hood pulled over his head framed a stubbled jaw and sullen mouth, but it was the scar hooked across his chin and down the side of his neck, where it tore through the thick black lines of his glowing hologram tattoo, that gave him away.

Nimah blinked, narrowed her eyes, and when the sight didn't change, she snatched Liselle by the arm and hauled her back a step. "Please tell me I'm not hallucinating."

Liselle grumbled but followed Nimah's gaze, took a good, long look, then cursed. "It *can't* be him."

"It is." Nimah's heart skipped a manic beat. Maverick Ethos-333. Number seven on the STARs Most Wanted list. A list all cadets learned by rote. He'd become a criminal legend at twelve for stealing a third-class Z47 Dragonfly and outmaneuvering agents in a hyper-speed chase through one of the most insane, and skilled, flight paths ever documented. Later injured in a crash that left him wheelchair-bound at sixteen, the last known photos of him were at least five years out of date, but whatever had happened to him since had stripped all youthful softness for granite and steel.

And he was here, cozied up at a bar not twenty-five feet away.

"Call it in," Nimah whispered, not daring to lift her eyes from him for a moment lest he evaporate. "Tell dispatch to send all available units for backup."

"Dispatch? We're neck deep in the Soots—the signal is shit."

"Then get to higher ground." Nimah swatted Liselle's arm. "And give me the cuffs."

Liselle removed them from the pack she wore, then watched as Nimah activated the magnicuffs with a press of her thumb to the locking mechanism. "What are you going to do?"

"What I was trained to do." The only thing that would give her a hope in the void of graduating. She needed a career-making collar.

She *needed* Maverick.

"I don't like this, Mav." Boomer's voice vibrated between Maverick's ears like a stereo cranked to the edge of too high.

"I know." Maverick wiggled his jaw, lowering the volume. "You told me twice before I left the shuttle."

"Just want it on record, is all."

"Consider it recorded and thoroughly underscored."

"I'm telling you the greenie's a no-show."

"It's only been ten minutes."

"Late is late. Cut your damn losses and get your no-good ass back on the Banshee *so we can burn outta here."*

Maverick stroked a hand across the rubber surface of his wheels. The meet was supposed to have gone down ten minutes ago, but punctuality wasn't common among criminals. Sometimes a new client—a greenie—wanted to feel you out and kept you sitting while they watched to make sure you weren't packing extra heat or bringing any unexpected surprises like an agent tail.

After a few moments, his comms spiked with Boomer's heavy sigh. *"Seriously, Mav. We've got enough heat on us, and you decide to do a meet close enough to spit on the Academy? You're askin' to get collared. Or skinned if Hatchett finds out we're poaching his waters."*

"Which is why it'll work." Because no one would ever expect him to be that reckless.

Besides, there was a difference between guts and thick-headed stupidity, and it was easier to get lost in a crowd than a barely populated outpost. Tor12 was one of the busiest trading spacities in the Inner Circle, and he'd positioned this meeting where the vibrations from the generators killed most of their surveillance, plus he was wearing a thin mesh camo-mask to conceal his features from facial recognition scanning. Toss in the disruptor pulsing from the back of his chair and he could scramble any trace signals without tripping alarm sensors.

FLIGHT OF THE SPARROW 9

As for the bar itself, it was packed with off-the-clock workers, all too burnt out to give a soggy fuck about anything aside from disappearing into the bottom of a bottle. And while normally Maverick wouldn't have agreed to a face-to-face with a greenie so deep in the Inner Circle, this client had made a compelling offer. One that, if it all played out on the level, would be worth the risk. Prime was near impossible to boost, and this client had a solid lead on a shipment of freshly mined ore that would not only earn him enough credits to rival the most prestigious of the Inner Circle—but free him from Hatchett's yoke. Wiping his name from the blackbooks and allowing him to have a new life. A clean slate.

The chance to live for himself . . .

Restless hunger burst inside him anew, bright as a newborn star, but he'd never be free so long as he was bound to Hatchett, and no corner of the void was far enough to escape his wrath if Maverick failed.

"Twenty minutes, Booms, and we're out of here. Just make sure the *Banshee*'s running hot when I give the signal."

"Need I remind you that flying is your job," Boomer grumbled. *"Mine's just to punch people and blow shit up."*

Maverick rolled his eyes skyward and prayed for strength. "Killing comms. Call you if the greenie decides to vapor." Pressing a finger behind his ear, he sighed as Boomer's discourse vanished into the rumbling din of the bar.

Boomer hated being cut off, and Maverick imagined him beating a meaty fist against the shuttle's console right then. So long as he didn't break anything, Boomer was free to burn his temper as he pleased. If it were a first-class voidship the thought would've never crossed his mind, but the *Banshee*, so named because she screamed like a wailing bitch when you punched her throttle, was a rust bucket held together with magtape and a prayer.

Thankfully, for all her faults, she held true. A miracle considering Hatchett preferred to keep Maverick on a short leash. Very short. And it was starting to chafe his neck raw to the bone.

One day he'd have a ship of his own, sleek and capable of deep-void travel so he could hardburn past the RIM's barrier and fall completely off SIGA's radar with nothing around him but naked space and scattered stars. Each one a siren beckoning him to go deeper beyond the glittering horizon than any pilot had dared venture before.

That's where he belonged. That's where his heart truly soared.

Freedom.

A young girl plunked down into the seat across from him, scattering his thoughts like marbles. Maverick rolled the beer bottle between his hands. Definitely not the greenie. Scrubbed-clean face with large burnt-whiskey eyes, black hair tied in a slick bun, muted grey cadet uniform with pale gold buttons, running from neck to navel, polished as her shoes. He didn't need to look under the table to know. Everything about her screamed military.

"You're a long way from the Academy, Cadet." Raising his beer, he took a slow, steady sip, swallowing a mouthful of brew and suds.

"I'd like to see your identity tag, please."

"Why?"

"Because I am a cadet on duty and it's within my rights to make such a request of anyone I deem suspect." She raised her chin revealing a tiny silver nick in the skin, and held out a waiting hand, small with shortened, manicured nails, but her palms were calloused from rigorous workouts and Academy training. Even though she was petite, she'd been honed for combat. Hand to hand. Weapons. Endurance and distance. She wasn't a girl, she was a weapon.

And this was a problem.

"Identity tag. A third request will result in a citation against your record for noncompliance." She wiggled impatient fingers and the cuff of her jacket pulled back, revealing a slender wrist, the smooth, golden-brown skin marred with a faded purple scar. He had enough scars of his own to know that one went bone deep. And what it meant.

"Tell me something." He gestured with the neck of his bottle. "How'd a RIM-rat manage to wiggle her way out of the trash and into a cadet uniform?"

She visibly bristled at the term. The acid brands were given to cast-out orphans, a calling card that would identify the boarding house that she'd been shipped to. Once you were a RIM-rat that's all the Inner Circle would ever see, so for her to have made it into the illustrious halls of the SIGA Academy, she was either very talented, very lucky, or—somehow— very well connected.

FLIGHT OF THE SPARROW

None of which boded well for him.

The cadet tugged down the sleeve, hiding the telltale scar, her spine pulling impossibly straight as she boosted from her seat and pressed a pin on her lapel, activating the recorder. "Maverick Ethos-333, on behalf of SIGA authority, I am placing you under arrest. Please keep your hands where I can see them. Any attempts to resist or movements interpreted as aggression will be met with force—lethal if necessary. Do you understand?"

"I do," he said with a lazy drawl and took another slow sip from his beer. Pulse hammering at the base of his jaw.

"Your compliance is appreciated and will be documented for the presiding judge to take into consideration during your sentencing." She released magnicuffs from her belt. A coiled strip of steel that, once snapped around skin, wouldn't release without the arresting officer's thumbprint.

No locks to pick. No wires to short-circuit. Only other way out of those was to saw through the wrists, and Maverick happened to like his hands right where they were—attached to his body. "Sorry, Cadet. Never said I would comply." His timing had to be exact, and when she reached for his arm, he flashed a sucks-to-be-you grin as her fingers passed right through him before killing the transmission.

The world shuddered and pixelated into black.

Slumped in his chair, Maverick sucked in air, blinked away tears, forcing his head to settle and focus. Sliding out of a projection took time—time he didn't have—and killing a link without a proper shutdown sequence was like punching his guts into his ribs, making it hard to breathe. And his *teeth*! Every nerve screamed in arcing bullets of agony to his brain like a current across a malfunctioning motherboard.

Maverick ripped the camo-mask and electrodes from his face and wiggled his jaw, loosening the joint. This was too convenient to be an accident. Either the client got busted before the meeting or had set Maverick up to claim the reward. But as seventh on the STARs Most Wanted list, he had to be smarter—faster—than a man with his criminal record and two working legs.

Only an idiot would've wandered the streets to meet a greenie for the first time in the flesh. But a livestreamed full-body projection was complicated, and for it to hold full saturation he had to be within close proximity to the meet. Anything over ten feet would flicker, so he'd positioned himself in the back alley behind the bar, near the rusting waste bin that swallowed cubes of trash and carried them to the recycling plant. This was the only point within range that kept him away from foot and air traffic, but it also wedged him in on three sides. Only way out was up.

Get moving.

Swiping a finger behind his ear, he reactivated his comm. "Booms, I'm pinched. Get the *Banshee* hot. I'm burning rubber to you."

"Sonofa—How long?"

Maverick cast his gaze beyond the towering buildings to the distant spread of mooring mesh that cast across the digital sky like a web, obscuring the hanger where all vessels were docked. "Fifteen minutes, if I'm lucky." He'd studied the city schematics when pulling into Tor12 and had carved out two exit strategies. The fastest was a main thoroughfare that was illegal to fly through, but well—what was one more infraction to join his list of felonies?

"Make it ten," Boomer snapped. *"And don't be late, Mav. I'm iced enough as is."*

Despite himself, Maverick grinned. "Copy." He'd only just fired up his chair, engaging the hoverwheels, when the back door to the alley burst open and the cadet froze on the threshold. Haloed in billowing steam from the kitchens, murderous determination shattered the stoic calm of her face and shone in her eyes like dying stars.

"That was fast, Cadet." Maverick tightened the strap of his chest harness. "I'm impressed." And dammit, he was. "Nothing personal, but I don't do well in captivity." He pushed the throttle as she lunged into the alley, her fingertips swiping at empty air.

Scowling up at him before she bolted, she was quickly lost among the jutting waste pipes and mesh-covered walkways. Turning his focus on the airspace ahead of him, a grudging smile twisted his lips.

It had been a long time since he'd had a race to the finish line with a worthy adversary.

CHAPTER TWO

Nims, what's your twenty? I lost you," Liselle's voice fractured from interference.

Nimah cursed. Bastard was carrying a disruptor. Ignoring the burn in her legs, she kept her eyes on Maverick as he tore through the airways in a wheelchair he'd modified into an unlicensed hovercraft that broke at least twenty codes.

"In pursuit of suspect," she panted. "He's making a jump for the M14 tunnel. Where's my backup?"

"Agents are threading in less than five."

The M14 would take Maverick straight to the docks where all ships were moored, and in Tor12 the guards were low-level security grunts earning baseline credits and minimal comp benefits. Wanted felon or not, they'd never risk injury to stop him from entering his own ship. Probably even help the bastard unmoor from the dock. He could be voidborne in five minutes, and if Maverick slipped through her fingers— forget graduating, a disgrace like that on her file would be career suicide.

Losing him was not an option.

Hundreds of vehicles cluttered the airways, but she didn't bother picking through them to find Maverick. He was too far ahead, but now that she had a good idea as to where he was going, there was one sure way to cut him off.

Once across the bridge, she charged for the turbolift bank. "Send all units to the docks," she ordered while using her credentials to bypass the

14   **FALLON DEMORNAY**

lift controls and punched the button for the mooring dock, thirteen thousand feet above ground level.

<Override accepted. The main docks are at the summit of level one hundred and fifteen,> a bot spoke in crisp, blunted syllables of automation through the lift comms as the doors sealed, and within a moment, it rose with stomach-dropping speed. *<Our scans detect your vitals find the ascending velocity unpleasant; should you require a receptacle, one can be summoned for your convenience.>*

She'd rather swallow her tongue, and nearly did just that when the lift swept in an ascending arch, traveling as fast as blaserfire through the cylindrical tube. Turbolifts rarely malfunctioned within the Inner Circle, but she was all too aware that a single maglock glitch or a short in the current and she'd drop like a stone. And who's bright idea was it to make these things entirely of glass? Ears popping, bile in her throat, and panting, she pressed against the curved wall as the ground vanished from beneath her feet. Reminding herself to breathe through the panic, Nimah clamped her eyes shut. *It will all be over soon. Just a few more seconds.*

Don't be afraid . . .

"Miss?"

A dozen curious faces peered at her from the open lift doorway. "Move!" she bellowed as she bolted onto the landing and kicked her rubbery legs as fast as they would carry her across the platform. Nimah reached the hanger, panting and sweating, and scanned the docks for movement. Sentries and guards, but no sign of Maverick. She'd practically broken the sound barrier in an effort to beat him here, and thanks to the shocking speed of turbolifts compared to his illegal flying chair, she had.

Now to lay her trap. Nimah wove through the aisles. Ships sat in neat rows, anchored with mooring rods, but it was a shuttle with *Banshee* emblazoned across the side in glowing yellow neon that caught her attention. Perched on the runway, rear hatch open and waiting, thrusters vibrating less than three hundred yards out. It was hideous, all scorched hull metal and reclaimed glass, yellowed with age, but instinct warmed through Nimah. This was Maverick's boat.

Scaling up the service ladder into the rafters, Nimah waited and held her mark as a few minutes later Maverick's chair whizzed from the mouth of the tunnel that opened to the belly of the docks. Once he passed

FLIGHT OF THE SPARROW 15

beneath her, her shadow fell across him and he had a moment to glance up—to brace—before Nimah dropped on him like a sack of bricks.

"Fuck!" Maverick yanked hard on the throttle, trying to course correct before the chair slammed into the guardrail. "Are you *trying* to kill us both?" he snarled, ducking the swing of her elbow to his face as she grappled for control.

"Maverick Ethos-333, you are under *arrest!*"

"Not today." Swiveling around, he shot toward the guardrail and, unfastening his harness, slammed hard against it.

Nimah's teeth clenched at the heavy crunch of metal and together they launched out of the chair. Maverick hit the walkway first and sent her tumbling off him. Spilling over the edge, Nimah clawed at open air, fell, and before she could find the breath to scream, slammed to a jarring stop, nearly wrenching her soul from her body.

Cautiously, she opened her eyes to find herself sprawled on the security net. A thin mesh of steel that protected the airways from debris falling off the moored ships—as something as small and innocuous as a coin or a bolt could cause a lethal accident. Nimah groaned, shifting onto hands and knees—the mesh netting rattled and she froze. It was designed to catch small objects, not a body, and under her weight it wasn't going to hold for long.

"Suggest you get a move on, Cadet." Maverick's shout pulled her mind back into focus as he dragged himself on his elbows toward his chair hovering nearby, beaten but still flying. But as his eyes shot to her face, the laughter in him faded into hesitation.

"I . . . I can't move."

"All you have to do is climb up," he said, abandoning his earlier sarcasm. "Six feet. That's nothing after dropping almost twice that onto me."

Her eyes slid down and beneath the meshed steel, the tops of the Tor12 spacity buildings looked like pinpricks from this height, and the ground was so far gone it wasn't even visible anymore.

She shook her head. "I can't. Too high. Too high." Guards shouted at her from across the walkway but otherwise kept their distance, and her internal alarm told Nimah reinforcements were two minutes out. She wasn't going to make it another sixty seconds if she didn't move. Fast. But everything in her was frozen. Locked into place. "Please," she stammered as the mesh shuddered beneath her fingers. Fear ashen on her tongue. Dry as ground bones. "Help me . . ."

Muttering a curse, Maverick dragged himself to the edge of the walkway and shot down an arm. "This is the best I can do. You have to reach for me."

"I ca—"

"Look at me," he interrupted. Tone firm, but gentle. Secure. "Just at me, okay? I promise I won't let you fall, but you've gotta meet me halfway, Cadet. Now, get your feet under you. Nice and easy."

Hands shaking, she eased into a crouch and as the mesh warped, she swallowed her scream, launching her heart into her throat. A metal web, thin as thawing ice on a spring lake, was all that separated her from a thirteen-thousand-foot drop and the next move was going to punch her right through.

"Okay, on my mark, jump with everything you have. I'll catch you."

She gave the barest nod, cheeks damp. "You'd better."

Maverick gathered himself with a breath, and shouted, *"Now!"*

She barely got any power behind her push when the mesh tore. Their fingers grazed as Maverick swiped for her hand—a desperate grab—and held on as Nimah swayed from his wrist.

"I need my other hand free," he panted against the strain. Sweat dripped into his eyes as tremors ripped down his shoulder. Without his legs to help him it was entirely up to the strength of his upper body to haul her onto the walkway.

She nodded, her lips parted in shallow breaths. "Don't let go."

Maverick almost laughed. Adjusting his grip, he rolled onto his back and hooked his fingers in the joint of the walkway before he heaved with everything he had—roaring through ten struggling seconds that ended with what sounded like a sob of relief when she hooked a leg over the walkway and rolled over him.

For a moment they lay tangled together. Breathless and weak.

"Close call, Cadet." His hand patted her back limply. "You okay?"

She nodded. Her heart hammered through her chest, straight into him, and his hammered right back, just as fierce.

"Fuck me. Everything hurts," he grunted, but grinned despite it. "What are you, Cadet, a buck ten?"

"Twenty," she corrected, voice muffled against his shoulder.

FLIGHT OF THE SPARROW 17

"That's gotta be a new personal best." Now Maverick did laugh and tried to move his arm, but it snagged with a jolt. "What the—" His gaze rolled up to the wrist of his spent arm and stared at the glowing silver links fastening him to the rail, frozen in disbelief. It lasted only a moment before cold fury burned through his shock. "Didn't think playing the helpless damsel was part of STARs training."

Hands planted to his chest, she looked down at him and prayed he couldn't feel the tremors of terror still coursing through her bones. "Worked, didn't it?" In the distance she heard the wail of approaching sirens. The whir of propellers. The heavy stomp of boots. "I'm sorry," she whispered, sliding off him.

Resigned, Maverick closed his eyes.

CHAPTER THREE

In her dreams Nimah was falling.

An endless plummet as desperate hands clawed at naked air, the towers of Tor12 rising like spears eager to run her through. She woke with a violent jolt seconds before impact, shaken and sweaty, and cursed at the time displayed on her wristdeck. Unable to sleep, she'd tossed well into the predawn hours and somehow passed out cold and slept through her wakeup call for her final exam.

"There you are." Liselle stopped pacing as Nimah exited her cabin and quickly fell into step with her, matching Nimah's long stride.

"Sorry, I overslept." She'd rushed through a shower, yanked on her uniform, and barely tamed her curls into her regulation bun in three minutes, leaving only five for them to race to the simulation room in the next wing.

The Academy, nestled on the water planet Atreyes, was an architectural marvel of glass, white stone, and steel. Tunneled walkways spread from the core in a web, connecting and interconnecting, spiraling up and down in more levels than Nimah could count. Sunlight shone through the faceted dome overhead, infiltrating to the deepest foundation with holomirrors. A trick from the ancients of Earth-Prior, the home they'd once hailed from a thousand years ago before their planet gave way to the rot of climate change. Forcing them to eject what remained of humanity into deep space, hurtling through the void in search of a new place to call home.

"I get it." Liselle wiggled her brows. "Someone stayed up all night rewatching the newscasts of Maverick's arrest."

FLIGHT OF THE SPARROW

Nimah frowned. Someone had alerted the media within minutes of her slapping magnicuffs on Maverick and the press had clamored at the entrance of the tunnel, drones buzzing in the air, as a team of agents hauled Maverick and his accomplice away. Newscasts broke less than three hours later, but there'd been no mention of Nimah as the arresting cadet, and she tried not to sulk over the likelihood that credit for the collar might instead be given to the responding agents at the scene.

"Oh, stop it." Liselle waved a hand with a laugh when Nimah vocalized as much. "Of course they're going to give you the credit! Chief Commander will probably make a formal announcement at the press conference scheduled for later today. And I for one *can't wait* to see the look on everyone's faces when they do. My best friend collared Maverick Ethos-333—the boost is gonna be wild," she said, awed and proud.

So proud it made Nimah's insides ache with guilt. She should feel amazing. But instead all she could think about well into last night was the fact that rather than take off when he'd had the chance, Maverick chose to save her life. And she'd thanked him by putting him in magnicuffs.

Stop it, Nimah. One good deed did not erase a decade of crime. She was training to be an agent tasked with enforcing the law, it wasn't her job to determine who was or wasn't worthy of conviction. She knew this. Understood this. But it didn't make it any easier to swallow the betrayed anger she saw in his face as he was hauled away.

Perhaps if she stood before the judge at his trial and attested to his selflessness, her testimony might soften his sentencing, or at the very least have it noted on his record. She owed him that much.

They reached the exam room without a second to spare and joined a sea of one hundred and fifty senior cadets battling their way through the doors.

"Welcome, Cadets." Professor Nicholson pressed his palms together. His voice projecting cleanly across the cavernous room, large as a flight hangar and perfectly square, with hundred-foot ceilings and dim lighting. A massive holoscreen covered the entire back wall. Empty desks in theatre-style seating ran in neat rows on either side of the room and overhead fifty life-size simulation shuttles hung suspended by an array of wires and cables.

Passing beneath them, Nimah's heart immediately shot into the narrow walls of her throat and all thoughts of Maverick and her guilt gave way to the first yawning stretch of anxiety at what was to come. It slid down her arms and settled into her bones, wearing her skin like a costume.

"Today is your official exam, which will test your understanding of flight theory in simulation. Joining us are esteemed members of SIGA's operational divisions." Professor Nicholson gestured to the five proctors who stood in a neat line behind him.

There were three men and two women, all dressed in pristine white government suits stamped with gilded brocade that swept across their shoulders. Emphasizing their perfect posture, they stood like soldiers holding formation in the field of battle.

"They will monitor your performance and provide expert evaluation in accordance with examination guidelines, to ascertain your ability to navigate complicated flight coordinates and perform under stress. Your scores from this exam will determine which of the five operational divisions, if any, whose apprenticeship programs you qualify to apply for upon graduation. As for the exam itself, you've all been preassigned to your pods and we'll run simulations in batches of twenty. Please note that no two flight scenarios will be alike, that there is also a written component of this exam, and that you will also be required to assess and evaluate the performance of one of your peers. Are there any final questions before I begin calling names for the first round of simulations?" Professor Nicholson swept his gaze across the assembled faces of the cadets before clapping his hands together in approval. "Excellent. Then please find your seats; we'll begin shortly."

"Have you decided which apprenticeship program you want to apply for after graduation?" Liselle asked as she and Nimah made their way to the desks overlooking the simulation floor.

"Defense," Nimah answered without hesitation, opting for an empty desk positioned near the front row that offered clear visuals of the front of the class, but was also positioned near the doorway for clear entry and exit.

Liselle's eyes shifted as she struggled to pick her way through all the things she wanted to say but wouldn't.

FLIGHT OF THE SPARROW   21

Nimah already knew what was likely going through her mind. While landing the defense apprenticeship would allow Nimah to bypass ten years of fieldwork in the void and move straight into headquarters, putting her in the room with the greatest strategic minds of SIGA—she'd have to beat out just about everyone in her year to do it. Children of the most affluent families who'd been bred, in a very literal sense, to succeed in ways she couldn't even fathom.

It was not only difficult, it was likely impossible. But so was her even enrolling in the Academy in the first place.

"Defense?" A voice chortled from the row of seats behind Nimah, snapping her back to present. "You do realize less than one percent of the graduating body is ever accepted."

Nimah cut a glare over her shoulder to the owner of the voice. Cadet Manuel Ortega. One of the top five not only in their class, but in the entire senior year. "I'm aware."

"Good." He perched an elbow on the armrest of his chair as he leaned forward. "Then you're also aware that out of five hundred and fifty graduating cadets last year, only three were successful in applying for the defense program. To qualify, you'll have to clear the top three of our graduating class, and you've never reached higher than top ten."

"Not yet."

"You're good, Dabo." Manuel swept brown eyes over Nimah with a bemused smirk. "For a RIM-rat. But let's be honest, you don't have the brass to overtake me."

Nimah pushed up her chin. "Everyone thought that my first day," she retorted calmly. "And then again my first month. And again my first year. But over and over, I've run laps around you. All of you. And now here I am, six months away from graduating. So maybe it's time you stopped underestimating me."

"Cute speech." His smile went cold. "But everything you've done up to this point won't matter when you've failed every single practice flight sim for the past three months. And if you can't fly," he jerked a dismissive shoulder, "you'll never be a STAR."

His words struck like a blaser beam to the chest and Nimah bit down on the inside of her cheek until the burn behind her eyes cleared. She refused to let anyone see her cry—least of all the other cadets.

"Shut up, Trolltega," Liselle snarled through clenched teeth.

"Seriously?" Manuel rolled his eyes. "What are we, first-years?"

"Seeing as you still behave like one." Liselle cut him a lethal smirk, steering Nimah away. "Ignore him."

"I'm fine." But despite herself, his snide words echoed inside her like a dull toothache. In the Academy's entire history there had only ever been twelve cadets enrolled who weren't first-class citizens. Of those twelve, only two had graduated. If Nimah wanted to be the third, and earn an apprenticeship in defense, Manuel was right. Passing wasn't enough.

She'd have to excel.

Overhead the shuttles rattled, lowering to the simulation room floor to prepare for the first round of testing. For twelve years she'd studied until the point of extreme exhaustion, pushing her mind and her body beyond its limits just to keep up with her privileged cohort. Battling through every exam and test, sometimes by the skin of her teeth. The only thing that stopped her from quitting a hundred times over was fear. Fear of where she'd end up again if she washed out. Now that fear was staring her right in the face, and everything in Nimah went cold and empty with stark terror at the thought of what was to come.

Don't be afraid.

The promise of a fierce headache bloomed across the dome of her skull. Nimah pressed the flat of her hands against the throbbing pulse of her temples as things she'd long since buried surged relentlessly forward. Sharp fragments that violently juddered behind her eyes, engulfing her in a wave of nausea that weakened her knees and sent the ground beneath her to pitch.

Flames streaking across the viewport.

The wail of sirens splintering in her ears.

The strobing flash of navsystem lights signaling engine failure.

The violent jolt of thrusters rattling her teeth.

Don't be afraid.

Liselle leaned in to bump shoulder to shoulder. "You ready?"

Gathering herself, Nimah sucked in a bracing breath and gathered the frayed edges of her tormenting past in rough hands, cramming it like a big blanket into a small box. And then buried it all so deep inside of her she couldn't feel it anymore, until her heart rate slowed and the ringing between her ears thinned. "I have to be."

"Cadet Dabo-124."

FLIGHT OF THE SPARROW   23

Nimah rose from behind her exam desk at the authoritative sound of Commander Alan Nguyen's voice and raised her hand to her sweating brow in salute. "Sir."

"At ease." Alan tucked his hands behind his back. Long in the torso but shorter in the arms and legs with a furrowed brow and strong chin, he wore the official white of a commander, shoulders drawn with regal grace. Even though he was a foot shorter than Nimah's average five-three, there wasn't a single cadet in the entire STARs Academy, past or present, who would say that Commander Nguyen, as a thirty-year STARs veteran, was anything less than a force to be reckoned with. There was only one other agent she respected more.

"I'm sorry to interrupt your exam, but I've already informed Professor Nicholson that Chief Commander Wallace would like to speak with you," he said in the quiet, deep voice of someone accustomed to being listened to. Obeyed. "She has requested your presence in her office. Immediately."

Nimah's knees almost buckled from under her a second time. "Yes, Commander. Of course."

Alan angled his head and stepped to the side. "With me, Cadet." He marched off without a backward glance and Liselle's face broke into a silent open-mouthed smiling scream as she shoved Nimah after him.

Breathe. This was what she'd wanted. Hoped for. A private meeting with Chief Commander Kimora Wallace—after collaring Maverick Ethos-333—could only mean one thing.

She was getting her brass.

The Chief Commander's office was at the summit of the Academy. Fifteen minutes and three lifts later, they were outside her doors. A panel of stealth glass blocked out all light and sound on the other side unless disengaged by the Chief Commander. All doorways and windows were coded to her biometrics; no one could enter or leave her office without her direct authorization.

The identity screen flashed by the door and slid down the wall to adjust to Alan's eyelevel, scanning him for facial recognition, and within a half second the rounded door dissolved.

Chief Commander Wallace stood on the other side, her military jacket silver-white as her hair, cut in a biased bob and shaved low into a fade on the left side. Narrow shoulders were made broad with fringed epaulets, and elaborate gold passementerie, decorating neck to navel, capped with elegantly embossed brass bars. She was regal. Powerful. Iconic. Everything Nimah aspired to be, and for a moment she almost forgot to breathe.

"Cadet Dabo-124." Her gold HWKeyes, retrofitted for night vision, among other things, flickered to Nimah. "Welcome." Wallace nodded to Commander Nguyen, dismissing him.

Nimah crossed the threshold and the particle door solidified behind her. The Chief Commander swept out an inviting arm, ushering her inside the massive office, complete with a large conference and seating area, over to her desk perched before a wall of windows so vast, so pristine, it was like peering through open air.

"Would you like something to drink?"

"No, thank you," Nimah mumbled around a thick tongue and hated how clumsy she sounded. At Chief Commander's silent behest, she sat down, awed by the grandeur. The view overlooked the main training floor where all the cadets lined up in neat rows, from novice to advanced, and drilled for hours in sun, rain, or snow.

More than once, Nimah had caught sight of the Chief Commander watching them and often wondered if she was able to pick out faces from so high up. Could she see her? Would someone like Nimah ever measure up to warrant her attention amid Inner Circle cadets who were given every advantage and privilege to outshine her? And now here she was inside the Chief Commander's office. A space so sacrosanct only the topmost members of the Academy's hierarchy ever set foot.

"Thank you for coming straight to see me," Wallace said as she slid into the wingback chair behind her desk and crossed her legs. "I understand you had an eventful afternoon yesterday."

"To say the least." Nimah rubbed sweating palms against her thighs.

Chief Commander Wallace pressed a white-gloved finger to plum lips, gold eyes churning like liquid gold. They were both compelling and unsettling to behold this close. "Cadet, I'm going to be candid with you. I received an anonymous report earlier today, which, in light of certain disturbing events that are soon to break the newscasts, I wanted

FLIGHT OF THE SPARROW 25

to meet with you about so I can better ascertain the facts before I proceed."

Confused, Nimah swallowed deeply. ". . . Okay?"

"Are you or are you not the granddaughter of Captain Indira Roscoe?"

The ground dropped from beneath Nimah and sent her entire world into a dizzying spin. That name. She hadn't heard that name in almost fifteen years, and near as long since she'd last laid eyes on the woman who owned it.

"I . . ." Nimah struggled around thin, shallow breaths. "Yes."

"Thank you for your honesty. Now, can you tell me *what* this is?" Wallace removed a package from her top drawer and plunked it onto her desk. The parcel was small, and the privacy tape cut through as the contents would've been thoroughly inspected before being allowed onto Academy grounds. "It arrived for you this morning."

"Me?" Nimah never received anything, let alone packages. Beneath Wallace's scrutinizing glare, she opened the box and her breath snagged like a ragged fingernail inside her throat at the sight of the stone bird. Hand carved, given the chiseled, imperfect finish, and ashen black with flecks of soft blue trapped within. It was beautifully crafted, and lighter than she'd expected when she picked it up, weighing the bird in her hand.

Sparrow. The name rang inside of her, familiar and warm. That's what her grandmother had called Nimah as a child. She was the only person who would've given this to her. But why now—after all these years?

Nimah returned the bird to the box and clenched her hands into tight fists, her nails digging hard into her palms to keep herself grounded. Conscious. "What's this all about, Chief Commander? What are you not telling me?"

With a flick of Chief Commander Wallace's wrist, a holoscreen appeared before Nimah, showing the smoking wreckage of the UPN Forum. Once a proud structure, the hundred-story prism-shaped building now lay in a pile of rubble and ruin. "As you know, the millennial summit for United Planetary Nations leaders was set to gather two days ago, but the meeting was interrupted before it could begin. Nearly a hundred ambassadors and their attachés were killed," Wallace continued, swiping through an array of images captured from the ground. "Almost thrice that number were injured—some critically, but this is only the barest fraction of the damage that could've been caused if the bombs had blown *after* the assembly convened."

Nimah struggled to pick up her jaw, eyes watering at the display of catastrophic destruction. "That's not possible," she whispered. The Forum was one of the few spaces where key officials of government and diplomacy—including SIGA's president—gathered to meet in person rather than through commcasts, a gesture of good faith and trust. As a result, it was safeguarded by some of the most advanced security in all the Inner Circle.

By all intents and purposes, the Forum should've been impregnable. "Who could do such a thing?"

Wallace flicked a finger and an image pixelated onto the holoscreen of a masked figure striding into a SIGA base. "Thirty minutes ago, the terrorist insurgent turned herself in to custody."

Nimah knew that walk and the set of those proud shoulders even before the figure drew away the mask. Her grandmother stood, dressed head to toe in black, her dark hair in a long braid, amber eyes gleaming with defiance as she raised her arms high and sank to her knees before primed blasers.

Slumped forward, Nimah pressed a hand to her mouth, smothering a sob. No. It wasn't possible. For the last decade and a half, Captain Indira "La Voz" Roscoe had been a ghost. Mid-third year at the Academy, Nimah had succumbed to curiosity and snuck into the library to run a trace search, but all she'd been able to find were whispers that the last known sighting of the *Stormchaser* and her captain was of it sailing into a nebula storm, or that she'd been ripped apart by a starved kraken hunting for negsharks. No one knew for certain, only that she'd vanished from the void as well as Nimah's life. And now suddenly here she was. A little grayer at the temples and grim around the mouth, but very much alive.

"My grandmother wouldn't do this. She didn't do this."

"The footage shows otherwise."

"This? It isn't even stamped with holomarks, and there's no location tags or regulation codes . . . This didn't come from an official channel. Who sent it?"

"That's classified."

"It was leaked, wasn't it? By the same source who also exposed my familial history?"

Wallace didn't respond but Nimah didn't need her to in order to know she was right. "That doesn't seem odd to you, Chief Commander? This could've easily been forged by hacks in a lab. This is a setup!" Dizzy with adrenaline and desperation, Nimah braced the desk, holding her steady like a raft in a storm.

Wallace arched a brow. "If that were true, then why would Roscoe turn herself in?"

A snag to be sure, but Nimah waved it aside. "Maybe she wanted to set the record straight. Has she been questioned yet? When is her trial?"

"The Forum explosion has been deemed an act of extreme terrorism." Wallace cupped her hands together, linked her fingers. "As such it's been decided that a trial will be waived. Captain Indira Roscoe will be formally sentenced before the Crown Justice, and then transported to Hollow Point prison, where she will later be executed for her crimes."

Nimah knew what *decided* meant. There hadn't been an act of terrorism of this magnitude on an official gathering since the Zone Wars, and as such a show of immediate strength was necessary to pacify the public and quell further insurrection. This wasn't about justice, this was about sweeping the mess under a rug as quickly as possible.

"I don't understand . . . If she's to be executed, why are you transporting her to a prison?"

Wallace held the silence for a moment, finger tapping a steady beat against the surface of her desk in contemplation before she spoke. "It's also come to our attention that the son of IESO's founder was kidnapped from the Forum, where he was slated to present his latest energy research, moments before it was blown apart. He's yet to be located." Rising, Chief Commander Wallace circled her desk and reclined against it. The toes of her polished black boots in line with Nimah's now scuffed pair. "Cormack Shinoda is, understandably, distraught. After her trial and sentencing by the Council of SIGA Justice, Captain Indira Roscoe will undergo . . . extraction." Wallace wiped the screen from the air. "At the moment, we're keeping her arrest quiet as the health and safety of Jonothan Shinoda depends on her potential associates not being aware of her capture while we try to ascertain his whereabouts. But as news outlets will get wind of it soon, the clock is ticking. For La Voz, and anyone who may be helping her."

It was subtle, but something in the Chief Commander's tone made Nimah's head snap up so fast she almost blacked out. "Wait . . . you think *I* am one of her *accomplices*?"

"You wouldn't be the first renegade to try to breach our walls." Wallace turned over the box that contained the sparrow, and there, etched on the bottom, was a letter V made with two crossed swords. The sigil of La Voz and her Valkyries. "I would be remiss to ignore the possibility that, as a cadet, you'd be able to give her valuable insight and knowledge into our security protocols and procedures. And while you may not have full clearance yet, you're within reasonable proximity to agency-sealed schematics and floorplans for all government facilities, including the Forum. Hacking into our systems from the inside would be exceedingly difficult." Wallace's eyes narrowed. "But regrettably not impossible for a cadet with enough wherewithal or determination."

Nimah's jaw nearly unhinged from her skull. "I'm not—I would *never* . . . I barely even remember what she looks like."

"That last part was a lie, Dabo-124, but I'll forgive you for it, this once. Overall your distress readings make it clear you have not been compromised as I initially thought. And while given Captain Roscoe's previous military service records, we might've been willing to overlook your . . . family connections, we cannot overlook *this*."

"What are you saying?"

"The Academy is for the privileged. The *few*. We simply cannot condone or sanction the advancement of a cadet with ties to known terrorist organizations." Wallace firmed her shoulders. "SIGA is and must remain impenetrable; our policy is absolute in this regard."

"But I've done nothing wrong!" Nimah lurched out of her chair—a sudden move that could've been perceived as an act of aggression, but Wallace didn't even blink. Not that she'd expected her to. The Chief Commander could cripple Nimah before she even formed the thought to attack. Let alone follow through.

"On that score, at least, we can agree." Wallace lowered her chin in thought, before continuing with a nod. "I'll do what I can to keep your name out of the newscasts, in order to protect you from the backlash

FLIGHT OF THE SPARROW 29

and ridicule." Because if it did get out, forget Inner Circle, Nimah wouldn't be welcome anywhere. Work, housing, all of it would be impossible. She'd be a pariah with only one place to go. "Part of that effort means you won't be named as the cadet who collared Ethos-333, and the official notice regarding your departure will be that you were dismissed due to poor academic standing."

Nimah's mouth tumbled open, aghast. It was bad enough she had to face the risk of being outed as the granddaughter of a pirate turned terrorist, but this galled her to the core. "You can't be serious!"

"It's the best I can offer."

The best she could offer would've been to allow Nimah to stay. As Chief Commander it was well within her power to have fought for Nimah, but instead here was another woman she'd adored and worshiped casting her aside like a trash cube.

"Please don't do this. *Please.*" Tears blurred the Chief Commander's face into a soupy mess. There was no containing them, or the panic, as they spilled from Nimah, hot with grief that seared her to the marrow. "This isn't just about a career, the STARs Academy is my home," her voice broke, and she didn't give a damn. "It's all I have."

"I'm sorry, but it's out of my hands." Metallic gold eyes deepened with something akin to sympathy. "Effective immediately, you are no longer a cadet-in-training. Turn in your credentials, Citizen Dabo-124, and clear out your locker. You have an hour to pack and vacate the Academy grounds."

CHAPTER FOUR

Nimah floated like a ghost outside of her body as she left Wallace's office in a disoriented daze. By the time she reached the locker rooms, numbness spread from the points of her fingers across her hands, up her arms, and into her chest. Nimah couldn't feel. Couldn't think. Every movement was like floating outside of herself. Her body was a raw nerve exposed in a world where everything was jagged and sharp and far too *much*. Each breath, a serrated cut across her chest. Each exhale, a vicious burn through her mouth and nose. Each sound, brittle glass fracturing in her ears.

Gripping the stone sparrow, she tightened her fingers around the figurine until her palm screamed and fingers ached, an attempt to anchor herself in her body, but even that wasn't enough to slice through the brutal emptiness cleaving her apart as old wounds ripped open and Nimah struggled to breathe against the ache.

Years of schooling and training. An entire lifetime of work and effort—gone in a blink for something that wasn't even her fault. She'd never asked to be the granddaughter of a pirate. It wasn't fair.

This can't be happening. This can't be real.

Liselle slammed her locker shut. "This is bullshit," she seethed with venom but her eyes shone with misery. "You can't let them do this to you, Nims. You can't."

Slumped on the end of her bunk, Nimah hung her head. She'd packed her bag almost twenty minutes ago, and it had taken less than half that

FLIGHT OF THE SPARROW 31

to stow away what little she had by the way of personal effects, but the Chief Commander had given her one hour and she wanted to savor every precious second she had left.

The narrow cabin she shared with Liselle was the same one they'd checked into their first year, with twin lockers, a bunk bed fixed to the wall, and an oval window overlooking the jade sea. It shone like green turquoise in the sun, and at night, algae glowed pale purple and blue—so bright that it danced across the slate walls and ceiling—soothing her like a child afraid of the dark.

The ache of tears roared in her throat, but she swallowed them down. Not here. Not now. She wanted to leave with a measure of dignity, head high and eyes bright. She had nothing to be ashamed of. None of this was her fault.

"We can take this to court. I can hail my mom. She has to know someone who would be willing to adjudicate on your behalf," Liselle continued, wringing her hands.

Maybe if she had Liselle's family connections to the government, or Manuel's class ranking, the Academy would've pushed against protocol. But her? A middle-of-the-pack orphaned nobody?

"It won't make a difference."

"But—"

"Stop trying to boost me, Lis," Nimah snapped, then softened with a mournful sigh. "I always feared this would happen. That they'd find out." She stroked the brand seared into her left wrist. "It's why I've always worked so hard. I thought . . . if I was perfect, if I gave everything I had to this program, then if one day the terrible truth about my past ever did come to light, my accomplishments and integrity would speak for themselves." And maybe that would've been true . . . had her grandmother not allegedly blown up a building, killing dozens and injuring hundreds more. "But today I learned it doesn't matter what I've done. I'm just another RIM-rat." *And I don't belong anywhere.*

Liselle dropped to her knees before her, cheeks damp and chin stubborn. "It's not over. Do you hear me? We can fix this. *You* collared Maverick fucking Ethos-333. There are agents who have tried for a decade and failed. But you did that, Nimah. Alone. It's legendary."

Nimah pushed her lips into a watery smile. "I got lucky."

**"Fuck that." Liselle gathered Nimah's hands, her grip strong and assuring. "You're brilliant and badass. You deserve the chance to graduate. To fucking *try*."

Despite every effort, tears splashed the back of their joined hands. "Thank you for not giving up on me."

"We're family. You don't quit on family." Liselle squeezed back. "We started this together and we're finishing this together, too. Whatever it takes."

A sharp knock at the door interrupted them, and the particle surface dissolved as Commander Alan crossed the threshold. "Cadet." He nodded to Liselle. "Citizen," he said to Nimah—and that hurt like a kick to the teeth. She could almost taste blood. "I'm here to escort you off grounds."

"You?" Nimah gasped before she could swallow her surprise.

Commander Alan pressed a hand to his chest. "It would be my honor."

Nimah dissolved into fresh tears.

Alan retreated a horrified step.

"Two minutes, Commander." Liselle stood, shielding Nimah. "I'll have her cleaned up."

It took nearly ten, but Nimah emerged fresh-faced and calm. Liselle worked wonders with a bit of auto-correcting concealer that buffed the redness out of her cheeks and drops to brighten her bloodshot eyes.

It made walking the halls of the Academy less humiliating but did little to stave off the harrowing ache of despair gathering in her chest like a storm poised to break. A storm that howled and gnashed as Nimah passed a group of junior cadets gathered outside Professor Danbi's classroom, dressed in crisp soft blue uniforms that would be replaced with storm gray for those who advanced to senior cadets, and lastly a nanosuit of agent black upon graduation. Dark as the deepest parts of the void itself.

Nimah pushed up her chin with a sniffle and was grateful that most of the cadets in her year would already be in class at this time, allowing her a quiet exit unwitnessed by her peers who'd otherwise have made the ordeal far more traumatic than it already was. Ortega for sure would cackle when he learned of Nimah's disgrace. *Expulsion due to poor academic performance* . . . Recalling that detail alone almost made her break into a thousand fragile pieces. All those years of hard work and dedication—just to have it swept away for a crime she didn't even commit. The death of her dreams all by proxy of a grandmother who'd walked out of her life without a second thought or backward glance.

The main doors were towering panels of white-tinted steel etched with stars to commemorate those who'd graduated. Four thousand three hundred and eighty-seven. She'd counted them as a child while mopping the floors with the rest of the initiates scrubbing their way up from the bottom of the ladder.

She'd been awed by them, and a little terrified, but as they yawned open at her approach, Nimah's heart lunged into her throat and beat in the hollow just below her chin.

"This is where we part ways, Citizen." Commander Alan paused on the threshold. "Transport has been arranged to take you into Lysandis Megacity where temporary lodgings have been secured on your behalf."

Nimah held her breath to keep from crying all over again. "I'm indebted to you, Commander."

Alan held out a small hand but shook with a firm grip. "In all the years I've watched you grow, you've always landed on your feet. I'm confident you will do so now. Good luck to you, Nimah." Alan raised his hand in a salute then turned on a sharp heel and marched inside, a general to lead his troops, the doors whispering shut behind him.

Nimah shouldered her bag and the tears inside of her dried up into a fine dust that she expelled with a weary exhale as she crossed the paved courtyard to the waiting transport vehicle. A sleek black hovercraft with a robo-driver at the wheel. The door popped up as she approached, and she slung her rucksack into the backseat.

<Citizen Nimah Dabo-124, please confirm your identity,> the robo-driver droned in a static monotone through the grill speaker in lieu of a mouth.

"Yes, that's me."

<Buckle in, please. We will be cruising shortly.>

Lysandis Megacity was a sprawling landscape of pearlescent stone, vibrant greenery, and glowing neon holoverts that spun and danced like hummingbirds in a sun-drenched sky. She'd loved Atreyes the moment her ship had docked in the moor. All its warmth and light. This was one of the few megacities that was built with stone instead of steel, similar to the ancient structures of Earth-Prior, but there was no way she could afford to stay here for long. Not as a former RIM-rat with an incomplete education and no citizenship records. Atreyes, as one of the most desirable planets within the Inner Circle, was for the wealthy. The connected. Tomorrow she'd have to figure out where she might find a job and an affordable residence off-world. Maybe on one of the spacities in zones eight or nine.

Her accounts showed enough credits from her cadet stipend to see her through the month—maybe six weeks if she really pinched. After that she was in trouble.

Had she not been dismissed, Nimah might've been able to secure a transfer to a lesser facility. While the Academy trained agents who then would eventually migrate to senior intelligence, there were smaller, less prestigious schools for security personnel and on-world police where she, a senior cadet, would've been welcomed with a red carpet. But without references from the Chief Commander or a clean academic record to support her, and no financial assistance to cover tuition— opening those doors wasn't likely. Which meant if she wanted to secure employment, she'd have to look far lower than she cared to admit. And none of those options were going to be available within the more affluent zones.

Shouldering her bag, Nimah shoved the depressing thought aside as she entered the lobby of the hotel. High rounded ceilings with floating electrospheres offered light and warmth. People flowed in and out, some checking in at the reception counter and others with bags trailing behind them to where a line of black sedans hovered in standby. There were no human-operated taxis here. Only luxury robo-chauffeured cruisers with interiors of *real* leather.

Nimah slunk to the main counter.

"Can I help you?" The concierge smiled in welcome but the light tracks following the angles of her face and the adjusting rings in her eyes gave her away as synthetic.

"Nimah Dabo-124. I have a reservation."

The synth dropped her gaze and swiped her fingers cross the screen. "Yes. Here you are. Please scan in." She gestured to the camera. "Once

FLIGHT OF THE SPARROW

I record your retinal information into the system you will be able to access your suite and all lifts within the hotel. Your reservation is for a single bunk on the lowest level with access to reception and the fitness center only. Should you require an upgrade for access to more of our amenities, we will be happy to assist you for as little as five hundred and twenty-three credits a night."

"No, this is fine." Resting her chin in the cradle, Nimah stared into the round black orb.

"There. All registered. Our records show that you're paid in full until the end of the month. Your room is D47. Have a wonderful afternoon." Before Nimah could say thank you, the concierge was already casting her full-wattage smile on the next guest as if Nimah had evaporated on the spot.

No point in taking it personally. A synth was designed to be pleasant but efficient. Plucking up her bag, Nimah walked away to the turbolifts. She didn't even have to press the call button as sensors scanned her and brought her all the way to ground level. Her room was just big enough to accommodate a narrow bed, a wall-mounted holoscreen, a cabinet for her clothes, and a folding door that connected to a bathroom about the size of a broom closet with a standing shower, sink, and toilet tucked inside. But, despite its diminutive size the room's finishings were all premium. Strip lights in the wall winked on when she entered, as did the screen, projecting a holovert of a travel rep, eager to book her on the next tour of the golden Meriden Mountains or a day cruise along the jade waters of Alazar.

Snatching the remote, she shut the screen off and tossed her bag onto the bunk. In the silence she could almost hear the fragments of her life crumbling around her like a rock ricocheting down a deep, dark well on the way to rock bottom. Rooting through her bag, Nimah found the stone bird and held it in her trembling hand. Part of her wanted to smash it into dust just like her life, but before she could act on the impulse, something in her eased. Warmed.

Sparrow . . . The name whispered through her, deep and familiar, as the room shuddered away and for a moment, Nimah felt like she was falling. No, not falling. Flying . . . but a harsh knock at the door wrenched her back to solid ground.

36 FALLON DEMORNAY

"Housekeeping."

A little dazed, Nimah tucked the bird into her jacket pocket so she could shake out her tingling hands. "Um—the room's fine. I don't need anything."

"We have fresh towels. Won't take more than a second."

"Oh. Right. Okay." Opening the door, Nimah reached out for towels and instead found herself staring down the barrel of a gun. Held by a woman towering near six-five with bushy white hair haloing a stern face and eyes hidden behind round goggles capped in brass.

A second woman with long, straggly silver hair huddled close to her side beneath an ankle-length overcoat. She spoke, low and hushed, the words slurred and too messy for Nimah to make out.

"Yeah, she's the spit of her for sure," the first one answered, her red lips smeared at the corner from the drag of fingers pulling away a lit cigarette. "Inside, kid. We got some talking to do, heard?"

Instinct sent Nimah's heart racing, but her training kept her grounded and reminded her to assess before she reacted. "I don't have much." She walked backward, knuckling her eye with one hand while the other reached into her pocket and closed around the stone sparrow. A trinket and utterly worthless, yet for some reason she clung to it now like it was made of gold.

"That's cute." The woman chuckled. "We're not here to rob you, heard? Not today, at least."

Recognition shocked through Nimah, clear as a struck bell, but with it came the jolt of a memory of racing through the corridors of the *Stormchaser*. A brief glimmer, like sunlight flashing off hull metal, but enough for her to remember. These women were part of her grandmother's crew. They were *pirates*.

"Dobs?" Nimah whispered.

"Ah, good. Saves me a bit of tongue-wagging."

"Goody-hi." The other, Mumbles, cast Nimah a lopsided smile of chunky teeth and a shy wiggle of fingers, and Nimah's mind stripped away years of weathered skin and hard wrinkles. Her once-impish smile was now a gummy grin, flaxen hair still worn in pigtails, poorly braided and tied with bright ribbon, but those bright, wide eyes hadn't changed a bit, even if the rest of her had.

FLIGHT OF THE SPARROW

As for Dobs—Dorothy Dobrevnic—it was the gun that should've given her away immediately. An old-fashioned piece, all metal and gunpowder. Dobs was never without it.

"Must confess, I expected you to be a bit more frazzled-like at our little reunion."

Dobs pulled back her gun hand, then set the hammer before holstering her weapon. "Ain't you gonna ask why we're here?"

Nimah crossed her arms over her chest if only to keep from fidgeting. "If you wanted me to know then you'd tell me. Asking is pointless."

Dobs cracked a smile around surprisingly white, even teeth. "Fucking A." She swiped her hand across the wall and, as it opened, a couple of narrow chairs slid out. Dobs plopped down in one and her legs, comically long, pushed her knees almost as high as her shoulders. "Suppose you heard about Ro, eh?"

Nimah snorted and lowered to the edge of her bunk. "Who hasn't by now?"

Dobs anchored her elbows on her thighs and leaned forward. "Then let's skip pleasantries and get straight to it, shall we? The *Stormchaser*—your grandmother's ship—has been impounded in the Academy vault. We need your help to boost it and rescue her."

"That's impossible. The Academy is a *fortress.*"

"Yes, but you're a cadet."

"Not anymore. The Academy doesn't allow granddaughters of terrorists to graduate. I was expelled." She struggled to hold back the tears. Not here, not in front of these women.

"And did they erase your memory when they took your credentials?" Dobs arched a brow. "You have information, and that's all we need. Mumbles and I can handle the rest. Just gotta get us through the door."

Nimah laughed, but it came out more as a broken, bitter sob. Gathering herself, she took one deep breath before meeting Dobs's steady gaze. "I am not committing a felony so that you can boost my grandmother from her collar."

White brows flattened into a hard line. "Why not?"

"Because she *blew up* the Forum! People *died.*"

"Ro would never do this. Never."

"SIGA has footage that says otherwise."

"Those bureaucratic government assholes wouldn't know the truth if it kicked them in the teeth." Dobs bounced a fist against the wall. "Ro is a lot of things—a killer, sure, she's killed plenty, but not innocents. And bombs never were her style. Kidnapping, neither. Someone set her up."

"She turned herself in, Dobs. Why would she do that if she wasn't guilty?"

Dobs removed a cigarette from a crushed pack and sparked the end with a lighter. "Can't pretend I know her mind." She paused to suck in a thick stream of smoke. Fragrant and rich as ground coffee and summer rain. "Ro was always a closed book, heard? Even to me. But there's a bigger picture at play. We just gotta trust in her."

"Well, I don't. I'm not ruining my life for her."

"Look around you, kid." Dobs spread her hands, trailing ash. "What are you fighting so hard to protect? SIGA didn't give a soggy shit about you, did they? No. Soon as they found out you were kin to Ro, they kicked your skinny ass to the gutter. How long till you're shipped back to the RIM—five weeks? Six?"

A hard lump clogged the back of Nimah's throat. "Maybe once she's dead I can plead my case before a judge."

Cold disgust washed over Dobs like a storm. "You'd trade your blood for brass?"

"I'm looking out for myself." Nimah set her jaw. "Just like she did when she dumped me without warning or a second thought."

Dobs surged toward Nimah, looming over her like an angry giant. "You wanna know what kind of woman your grandmother is?" When Nimah recoiled, Dobs tugged the neckline of her cowl to reveal a hooked line of a deep serrated scar slicing across the left side of her throat. "A piece of a propeller blade lodged in my throat when we were SIGA infantry fighting in Illyrio. She carried me on her back for near twenty clicks. Kept me alive when most would've given up. And that ain't the first time. That's who you share blood with. That's the kind of heart that should be beating in your chest." Dobs leaned down and jabbed Nimah's chest with a finger that punched hard as a fist.

"And what if she is guilty? What then?"

"Don't care. I won't give up on her. Not now. Not when she needs me most."

FLIGHT OF THE SPARROW 39

You don't give up on family. Liselle's words echoed in the ferocity of Dobs's declaration.

"That's your prerogative." Nimah slapped her hand away. But the spot ached, and the ache sank bone deep. "Far as my grandmother is concerned, I think I'm entitled not to care."

"Then you don't deserve to call her kin." Dobs snatched up her coat and stalked to the door. "You wanna know why you were left?" she seethed from the doorway. "Maybe if you had the guts to face her, you'd find out. But that'll never happen if she's dead."

Nimah held herself together until they were gone before she slumped down on the bed. Shaken. Every emotion in her rising to the dome of her skull, threatening to explode. Head in her hands, she swallowed a vicious, frustrated scream. All she'd wanted was to be an agent. To belong somewhere after spending a lifetime as an outcast, without purpose or family, and she'd been so close, only to have it wrenched from her grasp.

She owed her grandmother nothing. Not love or loyalty, even if her heart yearned for both. So why did standing her ground and wanting to protect her boundaries make her the villain?

The screen flashed on the wall. The remote was tucked half under her thigh and her weight had activated the newscast. It swirled before her, replaying footage of the explosion. Pulling the remote from under her, she turned on the audio.

"*—Roscoe, detained for questioning regarding the disappearance of Jonothan Shinoda. Authorities have—*" Nimah froze the newscast on the holoimage of her grandmother. Captain Roscoe rendered in a seven-inch, three-dimensional projection. Her face proud, despite the magnicuffs glowing on her wrists.

Guilty, her head screamed, but something deep in her gut refused to accept it.

There was a reason Captain Indira Roscoe was the most renowned pirate to sail the void and why she'd been given the name La Voz. The voice of the people. She'd carved out her legacy by completing impossible heists and dispersing the wealth not only with her crew, but to the impoverished outcasts on the RIM. Always giving more than taking.

Destroying the Forum made no sense. There was no benefit, and nothing of value to steal, except the teenage son of a trillionaire prime ore mining executive. But ransom was not a pirate's game. Too messy. Too many variables. And why kidnap Jonothan Shinoda only to turn herself over to authorities less than two days later?

It wasn't adding up.

Why did she even care? Irritated, Nimah threw the remote at the wall and it shattered. Raining glass shards like the tears she refused to shed. Fifteen *years* of never seeing her grandmother's face and now she couldn't escape it. Gripping the sparrow, she whimpered as the ghost of memories slithered over her, slick as oil. Coating her skin and suffocating her senses so nothing else could permeate.

Like the feeling of the scars criss-crossed over her grandmother's calloused palm, or the grip of her blunt fingers holding Nimah's hand tight as she led her down the ramp of the *Stormchaser* and into the dusty terrain of an outpost. The light of an amplifier carrying the sun's warmth to the Outer RIM haloed her face, making it harder for Nimah to discern her features, and shone blood-red in the threads of silver weaving through a midnight-black braid long enough to graze her hip. She'd handed Nimah over to a warden—the woman responsible for tending to cast-out orphans—then, without a word, returned to her ship. And no matter how loudly Nimah had screamed for her, or how hard she'd wept, Ro never turned around. She never came back.

Maybe if you had the guts to face her, you'd find out. But that'll never happen if she's dead. Dobs's words circled back like a roundhouse kick to the head and Nimah swayed, staggered by their truth. She'd always been terrified of the void for as long as she could remember. Her grandmother might argue it was because she'd spent too long with her feet on the ground, but floating out there, in silence and stars, made you feel your own insignificance. There was no escaping—you were alone. Yet Nimah had never felt more alone than she did right now.

What if she's innocent? The thought, sparked in the darkness of her fears and depression, burst like a flare to rain fire in an empty sky. She knew how the justice system worked. Even if there was some other explanation, they'd never stop to consider the possibility that her grandmother was anything other than guilty. Not after she'd turned herself in and claimed ownership of the crime. Captain Roscoe would be put to death, and Nimah's dreams of becoming an agent would be lost to her forever. But if she could uncover the truth, maybe she'd save a woman's life *and* earn her way back into the Academy.

A dangerous act of desperation to be sure, but she was desperate. Either she'd free a terrorist and become a fugitive herself for the rest of her days, or she'd abandon an innocent woman—and the only family she had left—to the gallows. Whichever way Nimah looked at it, the stakes were high and the consequences dire, but there was only one way to find out.

And she'd have to cross the void to do it.

CHAPTER FIVE

I f she was going to break into the Academy, she needed to be tactical.

After a long shower, Nimah dressed in civilian attire: black pants, fitted black shirt, flat-soled boots, and hair tied back in a bun. She'd only stepped off the lift when she spotted Dobs and Mumbles tucked at the large circular lobby bar. Surrounded by bright white walls, chrome and pale blue glass, the pair of them stuck out like a sore thumb. Patched and dirty as they were, it was a wonder synth guards hadn't rolled by to pitch them off the landing. No way could they afford to be guests in a place like this, not even in the ground-level cabins where Nimah was squirreled away.

Dobs swiveled around on the barstool as she approached, while Mumbles blew bubbles into a glass of chocolate oat milk.

Nimah sighed. "I wasn't sure you'd still be here."

"Figured an hour or two of stewing in your own piss and vinegar would change your mind." The synth-tender plunked down a tumbler of whiskey in front of Dobs. Neat. Two fingers.

Nimah couldn't mask her surprise. Premium alcohol didn't come cheap. She skimmed her gaze across the bar and though it was quiet for a Wednesday evening, a few eyes slipped across to them, shining with disdain. "You know the bar is reserved for guests only?"

Dobs hooked her elbows on the bar top and chuckled darkly. "I got a knack for getting around things." Raising her hands, she flipped from front to back to show they were empty, then with a surprisingly

FLIGHT OF THE SPARROW 43

dexterous twist of her wrist, she flashed a glowing silver orb before rolling it back up her baggy sleeve. "Call it the Blind-Eye. Mumbles's specialty. Could order a forty-ounce first-grade Wagyu dripping in real butter without breaking a sweat."

Mumbles giggled while twirling her straw in her glass. "Nimsy come fly."

"Yes." Dobs lifted her tumbler and kicked back the glass. "She finally gained a set."

"Shouldn't we go somewhere else?"

"Why would we do that?"

"Because . . ." She whisked her eyes left and right to emphasize the lobby brimming with nearly a hundred guests. Some tucked into wide, comfortable chairs reading on screens or watching the newscasts, others gathered in winding rows for check-in. "As marked associates of a terrorist, don't you think it's bad to be so exposed?"

"First lesson of pirating, kid: When you're this deep in the Inner Circle, the more public, the better, heard? No one expects you to stand still when the sirens are wailing. They expect you to run. And running is how you get collared. Sit." Dobs patted the barstool to her right. "All the staff here are synths that won't give a damn long as we don't trigger their sensors. And the guests? Well, they're too posh to sit too close or to question the hotel's system. We're golden."

Hiking up onto the barstool, Nimah planted her elbows to polished cloned mahogany, the surface diamond-lacquered to prevent scratches and ensure longevity. Someone could pop a sonic grenade in the hotel lobby, and it wouldn't even make a dent. "Alright, so what's your plan?"

"You already heard it." Removing a flask from her breast pocket, Dobs poured liquid into her empty tumbler. "Steal the *Stormchaser*, reunite with the old crew, and save the day. Not much more to it." Dobs cracked a grin, smoke and fire on her breath.

"So, basically, you don't have one."

"Look, kid, Ro was always the brains of our 'fit. I just shoot and steal."

Nimah rolled her eyes, pinched the bridge of her nose. Wonderful. That she'd expected anything more from a couple of elderly space pirates was laughable. "You said reunite with the crew." Nimah arched a brow. "Does that mean you have them onboard? They've all agreed to this?"

Lowering her eyes, Dobs sipped from her tumbler. "Sure do."

"Well, that's something at least. Because no way are we going to be able to pull this off with just the two of us."

"Three, kid."

Nimah arched a brow at Mumbles, busy blowing bubbles wildly into her glass, chocolate milk sloshing over the rim.

"Ah, don't let her gobbledygook fool you none." Dobs tapped a blunt finger to her temple. "Wires may be crossed, and the lights may flicker some, but they're on, heard? Besides, you'd be surprised what Mumbles can do with a bit of old bubble gum, some spare tubing, and a broken microchip. What she lacks in conversation she makes up for with her penchant for gadgets and gizmos."

Nimah closed her eyes with an aggrieved sigh. "If we do this, we do it my way." She raised a warning finger. "No guns. No casualties. And we do it *tonight*." The heads of staff would be tied up with the events at the Forum wreckage for at least the next twelve hours. Anything after that window would be too risky. Impossible, even.

"Ay, ay." Dobs raised a hand to mimic the STARs salute. "But before we go kicking in doors, we gotta suss out a pilot. *Stormchaser*'s a two-seater. I've got some experience in second chair, but we'll need a first to get us off the ground." She arched a brow at Nimah. "You must've had some flight training by now. You any good, kid?"

"Not enough for first. But I have someone in mind." And because she could hardly believe the insanity of what she was about to embark on, Nimah snatched the tumbler from Dobs.

"I wouldn't, if I were you," Dobs cautioned, but Nimah had already downed the fiery liquor in one swallow.

It hit her gut like a roundhouse kick. Eyes watering, lungs burning, Nimah wheezed around an exploding, smoky cough. "What *is* this?"

"Call it the Devil's Seawater."

"I think it's melting my intestines!"

Dobs slapped her knee with a cackle. "Drink up, me hearties, yo-ho!"

The STARs Academy was a veritable fortress of glass and stone and steel, with towers and spires connected by webs of arching bridges. It housed

FLIGHT OF THE SPARROW

twelve thousand eight hundred and twenty-four cadets with less than six hundred administrative staff to oversee them—all retired agents at that—but there were ways to slip attention.

When she'd first been brought to the Academy, it was immediately obvious that Nimah hadn't fit in with the other kids. They were all stronger, faster, and smarter than her, making it a constant struggle for her to keep up. But it was the RIM-brand that had truly set her apart, earning her nothing but snide remarks and sneers from the Inner Circle kids who'd grown up believing anyone from outside was trash. Unworthy. Expendable.

It wasn't until her third year when she'd heard the whispered stories of older cadets sneaking out to go swimming in the lagoon that she got an idea. Half the challenge—and the fun, apparently—was in not getting caught and returning with a prize to prove you'd made it to the Black Pearl Lagoon. Those who were discovered faced expulsion, but if you pulled it off, then you were part of the club. A rite of passage she had to complete if she was ever going to truly belong.

Determined to win the approval of the cadets every bit as much as that of her teachers, after months of planning and endless hours of combing the Academy archives to study the massive facility, she'd found a way out through the basement air ducts. A treacherous journey through pristine steel pipework riddled with sensors and snares, but she'd slipped through and made the swim. She returned with her trophy, a black stone, round and glossy as a pearl, plucked from the bed of the shimmering incandescent waters, making her the youngest cadet to complete the pearl run at ten. Word spread among the older cadets, and after that she was in. She was one of them. No longer shoved into corners, tripped in the halls, or sneered at from across the cafeteria tables where she sat mostly alone. That was the day her life at the Academy had changed for the better. She'd found her home—her purpose—and Nimah was prepared to do anything to get back to it.

Whatever the cost.

Stooping in the shallow iridescent lagoon waters hugging the base of the Academy's foundational wall, Nimah assessed the grate covering the mouth of an airshaft. "It looks like it's still unmonitored." Gripping the grate, she planted a boot to the wall and tugged hard, wrenching it free after several straining seconds.

46   FALLON DEMORNAY

"Aren't you worried about sentries?" Dobs asked while Nimah deposited the grate to the side. Mumbles, too afraid to get her feet wet, rode piggyback.

"There weren't any when I first found this way out. I doubt that's changed in the years since. So long as we move quickly, we should be fine."

Adjusting Mumbles's weight on her back, Dobs peered into the black mouth of the vent. "What's down there?"

"Maintenance corridor. Ventilation shafts run all along the perimeter. Hundreds of them. We'll slide in on our backs. But wait until I reach the bottom before you come in after me, and make sure you lie flat, keeping your head low." Nimah hooked her legs over the edge, arms planted on either side. "Unless you want a haircut."

"Heard." Dobs braced the open shaft and scanned the dark tunnel of steel. "You sure this is the right one? We ain't about to shoot ourselves into no furnace or such?"

Nimah tapped the side of the grating where a carving was etched. ND124. "Marked it myself so I wouldn't forget." Hooking her legs into the shaft, Nimah crossed her arms over her chest, and let gravity take her.

It was a solid fifty feet before the shaft leveled out, and at the bottom Nimah spread her feet wide to stop her from shooting out like a bullet. The airshaft was tighter than she remembered, but she wasn't a child anymore, so Nimah slithered the rest of the way on her back to avoid triggering the sensors. If activated, mesh lasers would slice through her like a sieve through water. She'd be cubed so fine that the maintenance bots would have to scoop her up and mop away the rest.

"Wow, it's hot." Nimah pressed her brow against her forearm. Found it slicked in sweat. "Why am I so damn hot?"

"*Have you cleared the vent shaft?*" Dobs's voice rattled between her ears through the comms.

"Almost." Nimah rolled her forehead against cool steel, desperate for relief. "Just need a minute."

"*We ain't got one. Quit dragging and clear the way so Mumbles can follow you down.*"

FLIGHT OF THE SPARROW 47

"Let's see how fast you move when you're the one inching a mile on your back."

"This was your plan, don't snap at me for keeping you on schedule, heard?"

"Shudap," she slurred around a thickening tongue. Snorted. *"Shudaaaaaap."* The comms hummed as a soggy giggle trickled out of her, quickly chased by another. Why was that so funny?

"Damn, kid, you barely gargled a mouthful of Seawater and now you're three sheets to the wind."

Starfished on her back, Nimah smothered a booze-soaked laugh. "M'fine. 'Kay?" Even though she lay perfectly still, the vent walls swayed like she was floating in the lagoon, gazing up at milky splashes of stars. It would almost be soothing if her stomach wasn't swaying right along with it. Strange to think she was busting into the Academy like a traitorous thief, yet she felt light, almost effervescent, and more confident than she could remember feeling in a very long time. "I could get used to this."

"Move your skinny ass unless you want to taste my boot when I come down there."

Dobs was right. Time was against her. With a kick of her feet and a push of her rubbery arms, she scooted one giggling inch at a time with Dobs cursing her the entire way, her back and arms screaming through the slog until at long last she reached the grate. Unfastening the bolts with a pair of pliers she'd boosted from a toolkit in the maintenance wing of the hotel, she refused to blink until the screws came out clean and she'd hooked her fingers in the slats so it wouldn't clatter to the ground.

Tucking the grate into the vent, she poured herself like sloshed rum from a bottle into the corridor of the basement service wing where all the synths and bots were stored when not activated for service, along with cleaning supplies, servers, and electricity panels. And was pleased to see, as she'd told no one about how she'd managed to slip the grounds, not much had changed in a decade.

Concrete walls met industrial strip lights that flickered but otherwise didn't activate. Only robo-techs worked down here and required little more than low-level illumination for their sensors to navigate. Thank the stars. She didn't think she could handle any bright glare right now, but the pulsing beams emphasized the churning momentum gathering behind her skull.

Dobs slithered out into the corridor with Mumbles wiggling out ass-backward behind her. "Which way, kid?"

"I . . ." Nimah swayed as a hot flash rolled through, bright as a solar flare. Bracing the wall so she wouldn't pitch over, the corridor wobbled like heat waves off scorched hull metal. "Can't focus."

Dobs slapped Nimah across the face. Hard. Then held her steady until the ground stopped pitching beneath her feet like a rickety ship caught in a storm.

"There." She stooped so they were nearly nose to nose. "How's that?"

"Better." Nimah blinked up at Dobs, her vision suddenly and alarmingly clear. "You hit me!"

"Adrenaline tempers the effects a bit." Dobs winced. "But it'll come back all the more foul before too long. So we best move. Which way?"

"The barracks are to the right, and the left leads to the maintenance lifts. They're not coded for clearance, so we can ride them undetected." Nimah nodded. "How much time do we have left on the Blind-Eye?"

"Twosy twenty," Mumbles grunted with a wiggle of fingers and brows, the silver luminescent orb hovering over her shoulder, disrupting and distorting the visual space around them with refractive light that masked their movements to cameras and heat sensors.

"That means we're good for at least forty," Dobs translated. "Can't guarantee it'll hold beyond that."

"That's not a lot of time." Nimah did the math in her foggy head. The ship would need half that window to warm the thrusters, and it would take at least ten minutes to reach Liselle's cabin and perhaps another twenty to bust out Maverick. "We need to split up to cover more ground. You and Mumbles head to the vault hangar to prep the ship. I'll get our pilot."

Dobs assessed Nimah with a scrutinizing gaze. "Maybe you should take Mumbles to the vault while I do the heavy lift, kid."

FLIGHT OF THE SPARROW 49

"I know every inch of this place, how to dodge camera angles, sentry rotations, and where to locate the holding cells. We don't have time for me to walk you through it. Just trust me. Go."

"Heard. Oh, and if you feel yourself going slanty again, another hard knock should do it. But go for the left next, unless you want your right cheek red as the Devil's arse." She winked, and the three of them pushed off in opposite directions.

Opening a maintenance locker, Nimah lifted out an oversized, filthy service uniform and quickly tugged it on. No one would look twice at her. Legs somewhere between steel and jelly, Nimah ran down the maintenance corridor, and by the time she reached the door to her former cabin, she'd worked up a fine sweat. She knocked, rather than ring the bell, and bounced on the spot until the particle door dissolved and Liselle gaped in disbelief on the other side. Nimah shoved her back and spilled in after her, swatting the locks to seal the door.

"Slap me."

"Are you *drunk?*"

"Just do it!" Nimah blinked feverishly. Everything was turning purple and with three Liselles standing before her, she couldn't tell which to focus on. "Left side. Hard!" Liselle's hand cracked across her cheek and Nimah shook off the burn as her eyes settled in her skull. "Ah. Better."

"Are you out of your mind, Nims? If someone sees you—"

"I don't have a lot of time, so listen closely and don't interrupt." She paused with a deep burp and shuddered against the rise of Seawater at the back of her throat, then rushed through everything as quickly as her thickening tongue could manage.

Seated on the edge of her bunk, Liselle blinked at her twice. Long and slow as a navsystem struggling not to short circuit over faulty coordinates. "Are you kidding me? No. No! You must be out your damn—"

"You said you'd help me," Nimah pressed. "*Whatever* it takes."

"I was thinking more along the lines of drafting a petition or . . . organizing a cadet walkout. Y'know, something less *illegal.*" Liselle's features crumbled into a defeated frown. "Forget being expelled, if we're caught this is a death sentence. You understand that, right?"

Nimah nodded, tremors scoring up her legs. "For me, yes. Only if I fail. But when the Chief Commander questions you, you're going to tell her I held you at blaserpoint and you had no choice but to comply."

"They'll never believe it. Everyone knows I'd give my left arm for you."

"They will when you activate the alarms once we reach the vault."

Liselle's eyes widened. "But that will alert not only the Academy personnel, but SIGA headquarters, too."

"I know." Nimah offered a thin smile. Every agent within a hundred-mile radius would be hailed, but it was the only way to protect her best friend, and Nimah hoped when the time came Liselle's parents could insulate her from the rest.

"You'll never make it out of the sky, let alone the Inner Circle," she whispered.

"With the right pilot, yes, we will."

It took only a fraction of a second, but her mouth tumbled open. "Nims, you've really gone off the deep end."

"Tell me about it." Stepping away from the wall, Nimah rubbed her hands together. "Now, I need you to open the vault so my crew can get inside."

"*Crew?*" Liselle shook her head. "You already sound like a damn pirate." Sighing, she whisked at the air and a trio of holoscreens spread around her. Glowing panels with scrolling network scans. Cadet credentials were made to mimic the clearance and authority of a STARs agent. The higher your class ranking, the more access privileges you were given. Liselle was third in their year and could go just about anywhere but the Chief Commander's wing.

Focused, Liselle swiped and flicked and swirled while Nimah stripped off sweat-dampened clothes and shimmied into Liselle's spare cadet uniform. Because the legs were several inches too long, she cuffed the ankles with clumsy fingers and stuffed them inside her black boots. Uniforms were tailored to individual measurements, so every inch of her had to look pristine if this was going to work.

Rising too quickly, Nimah swayed and leaned against the wall. Facing the mirror, she focused on her reflection. Her eyes were glassy, her cheeks flushed, and her hair was damp with sweat. Wisps of curls escaped and fired in all directions. She looked about as drunk as she felt. Lifting a

FLIGHT OF THE SPARROW

cap off its hook, she tugged it over her head and adjusted the brim so only the lower half of her face was visible. At first glance anyone would see just another cadet working her rotation. If they looked closer . . .

"There." Liselle flicked the screens away, jaw set at a furious angle. "I've committed a felony."

"You can strangle me later. Come on," she said, snatching Liselle's hand. "We're not finished yet."

CHAPTER SIX

Maverick didn't do well in cages.

Dumped in a high-grade cell made of carbide steel. Nothing short of a sonic grenade—twelve of them—was going to bust him and Boomer out, but at least the magnicuffs were off. It was barely eight feet across in any direction, with two bunks hinged to the wall and a single toilet with a floating sink between them. The faded patch on the wall where the mirror had once been made him smirk.

Didn't trust them with broken glass, apparently. Or blankets and pillows. Each bed was stripped to the thin foam mattress. It had only been a handful of hours since his arrest and already his skin was starting to chafe beneath the jumpsuit. The air was stagnant. The walls were narrow. The light—so fucking bright—was really pissing him off.

Maverick adjusted his legs, stretching across his naked bunk while Boomer paced, steam shooting from his ears.

"Sit down, Booms." But only when Boomer continued his restless pacing did he remember they'd taken his hearing aids, both of them, along with the rest of their personal effects. Maverick clenched his teeth. Boomer hated being without them about as much as Maverick hated being without his chair.

A vulnerable skinner was a dead skinner.

Ripping a button from the cuff of his orange jumpsuit with his teeth, Maverick chucked it at the back of his head, and Boomer turned with a snarl—eyes blazing. "You're not going to wear a hole through the floor so quit trying," Maverick spoke carefully so Boomer could read his lips.

FLIGHT OF THE SPARROW 53

Fuck you! Boomer shot back with a hard flick of his hands.

"Okay. I deserve that."

Fucking yes you do. This is all your fault!

Maverick opened his mouth, and promptly shut it. Yeah. It was. No point denying it. He'd let himself get collared all because he'd got it in his head that saving the cadet was the noble course of action when the smart move would've been to hop back in his chair and leave her to her fate. And thanks to his actions, not only was Maverick in deep waters with Hatchett, but after ten years of spinning circles around STARs agents it was a *cadet* who got the better of him.

The humiliation was absolute.

Boomer snapped his thick fingers and the sound cracked in the cell like a shot. *If you'd listened to me, we'd be voidborne right now. But no. You had to get your damn wires crossed over a straw deal,* he went on, hands moving so fast Maverick struggled to keep up. Although he was fairly fluent in RIM-SL, Boomer in a snit was like trying to follow a drunken rant.

Each gesture was sloppy, and punctuated with fucks.

"It wasn't a trap."

Don't ice me, Mav! You think a cadet showing up was coincidence?

"Yes." Because if SIGA had really been onto him, they would send their best. Not a cadet on training wheels. And fuck, it rankled him to know she was somewhere in this building right now—getting all kinds of accolades for his collar.

In one small moment he'd destroyed his reputation and established hers.

Then I guess you've got shit for luck and me right along with you. Boomer plunked down next to him, the weight of all his muscle and rage threatening to rip the bunk off its hinges. *We ain't got long, Mav. Once Hatchett hears, he'll send for our heads. The fuck we gonna do?*

A good question. One Maverick didn't readily have an answer to.

As the time dragged, Boomer's anger gave way to exhaustion. After returning to his bunk, he passed out in a matter of minutes and snored deeply into his foam mattress, his body so long in the leg that his feet hung well off the end and his shoulders so wide across that his left arm dropped to the floor. How he slept in such conditions baffled the mind. Unable to rest, Maverick hauled himself upright, using the bracket.

He'd escaped worse than this, he reminded himself. After stowing aboard the *Bright Fang* to steal a shipment of prime, he'd been caught in the cargo hold thanks to a series of new motion sensors his source had failed to include in the ship's schematics he'd sold him for a hefty purse. To punish his arrogance, pirate Captain Tien Feng-Lo had ordered her crew to keel haul him. Tied to the thrusters and dragged a hundred yards behind the ship for a parsec, if his tether didn't snap, he'd have been roped back in and dumped on some outpost. If it did . . . he'd have been left to float until his suit ran out of oxygen.

Shoved into the airlock, the countdown throbbing in his skull, Maverick had tripped the system, confusing the ship's security into thinking there was a fire on the main bridge, locking Captain Feng-Lo and her crew in while he slipped the airlock and relieved her of her cache. A boost had tipped the scales in Maverick's favor with Hatchett, ignominious bastard that he was.

As long as Maverick kept his head, he could think his way out of this box.

Knowing SIGA, they wouldn't risk transporting them until ready for trial. Lots of things went wrong when it came to prisoner relocation. The Academy was essentially unbreachable. Not even Hatchett could slither his way through. Maverick and Boomer could be pent up for weeks, maybe even months, but that gave him time to plan, and there was nothing like living on borrowed time to inspire creativity.

Sensors chimed and as the particle wall dissolved, cold dread washed across him. Normally a collar sat for at least twenty-four hours before they were dragged into an interview room to be grilled within an inch of their sanity. Someone upstairs wasn't wasting any time.

"Interrogation time already?" Maverick sneered and flicked his eyes to the pair of cadets. A tall Black girl with thin dreads and the other, shorter by several inches. Even with the brim of a boxed cap pulled down almost to her nose, he'd know that scarred chin and stubborn mouth a mile away.

Anger sparked in his gut, fueled by humiliation and betrayal, which he crushed to dust inside himself. To be betrayed would've meant there had been trust and friendship. He and Nimah Dabo-124 had exchanged neither, but his gut screamed it all the same.

"Come to gloat, Cadet?"

FLIGHT OF THE SPARROW   55

Nimah yanked off her cap and long, damp hair tumbled around a flushed face with glassy eyes. "Hardly." She swayed and planted an arm to the wall to keep from pitching over.

Maverick's brows lowered in scrutiny. "Been celebrating hard, eh?"

"Sah—shu . . . shhhhut it," she snapped, then shook her head once as if to gather herself. "I've come to get you out of here."

Maverick cocked his head to the side and bobbed it three times as if to dislodge water from his ear canal. "Sorry, I think I misheard you. Say that one more time and with less bullshit."

Nimah frowned. "Bullshit?"

"You just made a collar of a lifetime and now wanna bust out the man who put your name on the map?"

"Guess you haven't seen the newscasts."

Maverick spread his hand, indicating the barren walls.

"Right." Nimah brushed a hand across her sweating face and told him in garbled words about a terrorist attack on the Forum and the richest kid to breathe air being kidnapped.

Maverick whistled, long and low. "No shit."

"They've collared Captain Roscoe for it. My grandmother."

The second part slipped out of her so soft Maverick had to strain to catch it at all. He'd heard the name Captain Indira Roscoe more times than he cared to count. Hatchett despised the woman, and it always gave Maverick a measure of perverse joy to hear the tales of when La Voz and her Valkyries swiped a shipment Hatchett had been eyeballing for weeks.

She was ruthless, and elegant. She was a legend. And he was supposed to believe this straightlaced RIM-rat was the granddaughter of one of the most infamous space pirates ever to sail the void?

A snort ripped from his chest, quickly chased by a bone-rattling laugh that beat the walls like a fist. He laughed until his lungs seized and throat constricted in gut-burning rasps. "Stop, stop. Please, it's too much." He dabbed tears from his eyes.

"S'not a joke."

"Yeah, yeah." Maverick tucked his hands behind his head. "And my mother is the president of SIGA."

"I'm not lying. I've been expelled because of her."

56 FALLON DEMORNAY

"Oh?" Now that caught his attention and his interest. Within a handful of hours of collaring him, instead of rising up in the ranks, she'd lost it all and now was not only a civilian, but a fledgling criminal. He cut her a scathing grin. "Thank the stars for small comforts."

"I'm being serious, Maverick."

"I bet you are." He raised his hands in a slow clap. "Rousing performance, Cadet, truly a consummate actress to the end, but I'm really not in the mood for games." Like a damn fool he'd played right into her trap once already. No way was he going to fall for it again.

"Tell me about it." The second cadet grumbled.

But it was her seriousness that gave him pause. "You're not fucking with me, are you?"

"Nope." Nimah smiled, but it was shaky as a newborn lamb. "So get up. And let's go."

Maverick ran his tongue along the edge of his teeth, then sat up and adjusted his legs so they hung off the side of the bunk. "Why?"

"Why, what?"

"Why should I go with you?"

Nimah blinked, eyes shifting as if she was seeing two of him. "Um. Because?"

"Not an answer."

"Do you really wanna spend your life in a cell?"

"They can't hold me for long. I'm far too slippery. I'll be gone in a week or two. A month at most. What you're offering is a chance to slip the noose quicker. Or choke myself with it. So if I'm gonna take this gamble," Maverick rubbed his fingers together, "then what's in it for me?"

"Isn't freedom enough?"

"Considering you're the reason I'm in here, no," he answered darkly. "Not nearly enough to make us square."

"Can you please sort this out later?" the second cadet snapped.

"Liselle, please."

"What? We don't have the luxury of time on our hands."

"I do." Maverick jerked a shoulder. "I've got plenty. It's you who's on the clock." And it was that little detail that gave him leverage even if he, too, was on borrowed time. She'd waltzed in offering him the perfect escape on a platter but when it came to skinning a mark, you never took

FLIGHT OF THE SPARROW   57

the first offer. You always pushed for more and cut as close to the bone as possible.

"Fine. I'll make sure you're compensated."

"How much?"

"Ten thousand credits."

Likely every last cent she had. Maverick leaned back with a grin. "You couldn't convince me to do your laundry for that."

"A hundred thou—"

He interrupted her with a yawn and dashed a hand, closing his eyes. "See yourself out. Make sure you lock up when you go."

"One million credits!"

Maverick cocked open an eye. "Now that's more like it. But tossing numbers is easy. How are you gonna deliver?"

Nimah chewed her bottom lip, scraping away a thin layer of skin. "That's the reward Cormack Shinoda is offering for the return of his son. I'll let you claim it when we save my grandmother and discover the identity of the true terrorists responsible for kidnapping him and blowing up the Forum."

"Even if we could do all that, Cormack'll never pay a reward to a skinner."

"He will if SIGA officials Lennox and Isabeau Namsara vouch for you."

The second cadet—Liselle—sputtered with a gasp. "You expect my parents to do what now?"

Maverick arched a brow. "I'll also need collateral."

Nimah's chest rose in shallow, panting breaths. "The *Stormchaser*. If I can't get you the money, then I'll give you my grandmother's ship."

Maverick clenched his hands, then rolled his wrists in slow, methodical circles. The ship itself wouldn't be worth anywhere near a million credits, but the infamy attached to it was priceless, not to mention Hatchett would cut off his left testicle to get his hands on the vessel. The man held a bitter grudge as tenderly as a mother did her newborn. He'd break the *Stormchaser* down to the studs, but at the very least it might be enough to soothe Hatchett's ire.

The reward, however, would free Maverick of his debt and he could buy out the rest of Hatchett's skinners. An army of kids holed up in steel bunks with mattresses thin as a slice of synth-bread. Dirty. Scared. Angry. Bearing scars from beatings or fights amongst each other. Kids who deserved to taste innocence and love, not the hard edge of Hatchett's whip. He plucked his skinners young, desperate, and needy. Gave them clothes, food, education, and training—all at a cost amounting to an impossible debt with rising interest, and then put them to work to burn it off. Infiltrating rich households, corporate empires, or even rival ships, reaping the rewards of their efforts. You skinned a mark and gave Hatchett his pound of flesh for the rest of your life. There was no one to protect RIM-rats from men like him. A monster in a thousand-credit suit with a soul black as the farthest edges of the void.

With a million credits, Maverick could change all that.

He sat up, held out a hand. "Deal."

Nimah clasped his, shook briskly. "How are we for time?"

"Not good." Liselle gestured to Maverick. "And he can't run."

"I don't have to." He nodded to Boomer's hulking mass, snoring against the wall.

"Whoa!" Liselle flashed her hands. "The agreement was to bust you out. Not him, too."

"I'm not leaving Booms." Maverick set his jaw. "And you're not strong enough to carry me."

"He's right," Nimah conceded, tugging at the neckline of her uniform. Sweat soaked the material, turning it almost black. "Wake him."

Liselle rolled her eyes so hard her entire head followed, then kicked the edge of the bunk. It rattled hard and Boomer shot out of sleep like a devil, swinging furious fists. A reflex all kids in Hatchett's employ shared.

You slept with one eye open, or else you might not wake at all.

Maverick waved his arm and Boomer blinked at him like a bull set to charge. "Get up, big guy, we're making a run for it."

It was degrading as all fuck, being carried about like a child, but pride wasn't a luxury Maverick could afford. Not if he wanted his freedom, and as soon as they were in the air, he'd settle things with Cadet Dabo-124. No. Not a cadet anymore. She was a civilian and now a budding criminal. He clung to that soul-warming kernel of karma as Liselle led the way, moving quickly while Nimah hurried after her, knees buckling every few strides like she was stumbling across a storm-ridden ship from the days of yore.

FLIGHT OF THE SPARROW

"Been drinking Seawater, eh?"

She glared up at him, eyes bloodshot and glassy. "How'd you know?"

"Every skinner dances with the Devil." Maverick winked. "How much you take?"

"Half a glass."

His brows winged up in surprise. "A whiff is enough to put most on their asses. Surprised you're still standing."

"You really need to stop talking."

"And you're going to get worse before you get better." He remembered his first hit all too well. How it rolled on him in relentless waves, each one growing stronger. Sharper. Until he was just a boy caught in a hurricane, dragged to the depths by the Devil himself. He woke in a puddle of vomit a day later, sick as a dog on his deathbed. The mere memory of it turned him green, and to this day he still didn't have the stomach for hard booze.

Liselle flattened against the corridor and peered around. Cursed. "The sentries are back." She shot dark eyes to Nimah and then to Maverick, lips pressed into a sneering line. "Thanks to your little lovers' quarrel we're seconds away from being pinched."

"Isn't there another way to the hanger?" Maverick asked as Boomer adjusted his hold, bouncing him like a toddler, and the burn of shame in his cheeks was beyond his control. Soon as they reached the hangar, he'd get his chair back. Impatience for the stability of his own wheels beneath him made him almost frantic.

"No." Nimah set both hands to her cheeks as if trying to hold her head steady on a boneless neck.

"Shit!" Liselle whipped around. "They're coming this way."

Maverick heard the encroaching clomp of boots. Sentries were retired agents and if they rounded the corner, there was nowhere for Boomer and him to hide. Everything was about to go sideways, real quick.

"We have to go back," Liselle protested. "Abort mission."

"Not an option." Taking Liselle by the arm, Nimah pulled her aside. "Remember Professor Blake's lesson on diversion tactics?"

"Whatever you've been drinking, I think I'll need some when this is over." Liselle shook out her neck, wiggled her shoulders, and then shoved Nimah hard, launching her into the corridor. "You stupid bitch!"

"Don't call me that!" Nimah roared. "You're the moron who just *had* to see the infamous Maverick for yourself." She shot out a kick, but Liselle deflected it easily and retaliated with a punch, pulling back just enough so it glanced off Nimah's chin. The barest kiss of knuckles, but she rocked with it, feigning the impact of a solid blow.

The sentries charged forward, ripping them apart. Their backs to him and Boomer. But if one of them turned even the slightest . . .

"Stand down," the older man snapped. "What are you both doing down here? All cadets should be in quarters at this hour."

"Sir, I swear I had nothing to do with it. *Nothing*." Liselle shot out an arm as if aiming to strike Nimah again, forcing the second sentry to blockade her efforts while Nimah slumped on her knees and sobbed loudly into her hands.

"Nothing to do with *what*?" he demanded, irritation thick in his voice. "Speak quickly or else I'll haul you both into isolation to cool your damn heads."

"It was your idea!" Nimah shouted, tears cascading.

"Yes, but *you* opened the door," Liselle tossed back, shoving against the sentry in her way. She kept moving. Pacing. Drawing eyes and attention to her. "Now he's out! Escaped. And it's all your fault!"

"Escaped?" the man demanded, horrified. His hand shot to his lapel for his comm, but his fingers met bare cloth.

"Looking for this?" Nimah stomped a foot, crushing the pin, and before he could pick up his jaw, she lunged.

And, admittedly, Maverick wouldn't have seen it coming either.

She was a cyclone of arms and legs, spinning between the sentries, knocking the first one down, and while he dropped, she tangled with the other. A hand-strike to the throat to silence his screams, a vicious jab of curled knuckles into his solar plexus, and his eyes rolled up as her hand practically disappeared into the cavity of his ribs.

The older sentry on the ground freed his weapon and Nimah dodged the fire of a blaser that would've burned through her skull. She dove to the ground. Springing from hands to knees, rolling over him, she hooked his arm around his neck, snapped on the magnicuffs Maverick hadn't seen her remove from his own belt, and latched the other link to his foot. Twisting him into a human pretzel. The sentry sputtered, cursed, struggled. Picking up his discarded blaser, she

FLIGHT OF THE SPARROW   61

knocked a sharp elbow to his face, and he tumbled back, twisted up and motionless.

This wasn't smooth, articulated cadet training. This was something else.

Where in the void had she learned to fight like that?

"Someone will have heard that," Maverick cautioned as Nimah collected his discarded weapon.

"I know." The adrenaline had cleared some of the fog out of her eyes, easing the color in her cheeks.

It struck him with a shock that she'd been three sheets to the wind and disabled *two* retired agents. If she could do that drunk . . . the hell was she capable of when sober?

Nimah turned to Liselle. "Hit the alarm."

"But we're not at the—?"

"Do it!" Terror flashed across her face—the same kind of terror he'd seen in her when she was frozen on the net and seconds from plummeting to death. She was scared. Scared to the bone for her friend.

Cursing, Liselle slammed the panic button with her elbow and the lights switched from pale white to red with pulsing strobes. "Now what?" she shouted over the pitch of the wailing alarm.

"I'm sorry," Nimah answered. And lashed out with a sharp roundhouse kick to the head. Liselle spun like a roulette wheel and dropped, unconscious.

Stooping over her friend, Nimah looked up at both him and Boomer, stark eyes bathed in flashing red and shouted, "Run!"

CHAPTER SEVEN

The hangar wasn't far, but the alarm's activation made getting there a challenge. All entrances and exits would be sealed, but Nimah had to trust that Dobs and Mumbles had the ship primed for flight.

Outside the hangar door, Nimah fired the blaser and the panel erupted in sparks. Messy but efficient. The door parted an inch and Nimah used the barrel to pry it open the rest of the way to find Dobs smiling with Mumbles on the other side.

"Smooth as real butter in a hot skillet, kid." She stubbed out a cigarette. "I'm impressed."

"Butta." Mumbles raised her hands and wiggled both pinkies like rabbit ears. "Smoothy-like."

Boomer's elbow punched into Nimah's shoulder.

"Where's the vault, Cadet?"

"What?" She blinked at Maverick. "Why?"

"Not leaving without what's mine."

"To the left," Nimah answered. "Here, you'll need this." She handed Boomer her blaser.

Dobs's eyes bounced from Nimah to Boomer, then fell on Maverick. Her steel brows flatlined over blue eyes as Boomer carried him off. "You didn't say the pilot was a skinbag," she uttered once they were out of earshot.

"Have you got another option up your sleeve?" Nimah demanded. "Because it's him or we're not getting off the ground."

Dobs raised her hands. "Just saying my piece."

"The ship hot?"

"Like hellfire."

"Then get aboard. We'll be moving in two minutes." Nimah kicked into a run and reached the storage vault as Boomer fired a shot to the deadbolt, melting it clean off. "You were the last to be processed, so your gear will be near the front," she said, wrenching the door open so they could duck inside.

"There!" Maverick pointed to the folded shape of his chair. It had been collapsed, tagged, and wedged between the wall and shelving. Boomer lowered him to the floor, and while he wrestled with his chair, Boomer snapped on the silver disks behind his ears. They glowed when activated, light webbing that raced down the side of his scalp and into his skull.

He stretched his jaw, wiggled it as a high-pitched whine sounded, the tone climbing until it vanished. "Razor." He smiled. "S'more like it."

Maverick fastened his harness and punched a thumb on the control panel. His chair grumbled to life. Wheezing like a sick lamb. "Baby," he crooned. "What did they do to you?"

"We don't have time for you to change. You can get out of those jumpsuits once we're on the *Stormchaser.*" It was hard to imagine after a decade and a half Nimah was about to set foot on her again. A void-craft, old enough to be considered a classic, with a streamlined body fashioned from stealth steel, diamond glass, and rotating thrusters. Every inch of her was sleek and dangerous, which was why her grandmother had given her a warrior's name. Fierce and proud, the *Stormchaser* was so much more than a ship. She was home . . . once upon a time.

Grabbing their clothes, Nimah stuffed them into a rucksack. "Are you ready?"

"Ready as I'll ever be."

Rising to her feet, she yanked open the door. "Get moving." They didn't get more than two paces beyond the vault when a wave of blaser-fire rained, peppering the wall mere feet away. The three of them ducked behind a towering stack of crates. "Go!" Nimah popped a fresh cartridge into her blaser. "Break for the ship, I'll keep them busy."

Boomer bobbed a nod. "Razor."

Maverick hesitated. "What about you?"

64   **FALLON DEMORNAY**

"Go!" she shouted again. Popping up, eyes scanning above the top of the stack, she homed in on the barrel and swept the room for sentries. Two emerged and she took aim, giving Boomer cover while he and Maverick hustled for the *Stormchaser*. Over the barrage of shots, she heard the wakening whirl of engines, the rumble of thrusters.

"We're loaded, kid." Dobs's voice crackled across comms. *"Get a move on."*

The air above her opened with fire. "There's too many of them." Back pressed to the wall, she had three feet of cover and no escape route but through the sentries shouting for her to surrender. "I'm pinned and low on ammo."

"Get creative," Dobs answered. *"Three minutes for engines to engage. You've got two."*

Blaserfire splintered chunks of concrete, and Nimah bounced the end of her blaser against her thigh. Dobs was a pirate to the bone. Now that she had the *Stormchaser*, and a pilot for first chair, as far as purpose went Nimah's was tapped out. Even Maverick had no reason to stay behind. Panic kicked her heart and head into action. Part of training involved using the environment to your advantage. Nimah eyed the crates before her containing confiscated contraband. Everything from drugs to stolen artifacts to illegal weapons . . .

"Please have something useful." Taking aim, she fired three clean shots at the locks, emptying her clip, and ducked the return shots before prying the first lock from the top crate. It was stuffed with contraband clothing and merchandise, all totally fucking useless in a gunfight. Whispering a prayer, she snapped off the second lock and almost fainted with relief.

Sonic grenades. Designed to release a blast of energy, they were deadly in the void, but on land it would knock out a crowd if set properly. And kill them, if she didn't. Twisting the dial to what she hoped was reasonable, Nimah waited for the pause of reload before pulling the safety and tossing the grenade.

"Sonic!" someone shouted.

The hard blast of energy drowned out the scattered cries and toppled crates. Nimah smacked against the wall from the force of the wave. Ears ringing, she shook her head clear.

FLIGHT OF THE SPARROW

"Nice," Maverick's voice floated between her ears, and she could hear the approving smile in his words. *"Move your ass, Cadet. Boomer's got your six."*

"Copy." Leaping from cover she ran like her life depended on it, because it did. Over the staggered rows of crates, the *Stormchaser* hovered. And when her path cleared, the gangway lifted from the dock, and the gap between the edge of the moor and the ship widened. Boomer was positioned by the open hatch, a canon-sized blaser strapped to his shoulder.

"Gotta jump for it!" he shouted.

I'll never make it. Her feet wanted to cement to the ground, her body wanted to drop and surrender. Instead, arms pumping, legs screaming, she shoved the doubt aside, and pushed harder. Faster.

The whiz of blaserfire zinged past her head from behind. One sliced across her thigh, a searing burn that cauterized in an instant, but she didn't stop. Didn't look back. Didn't doubt. And—screaming—she dove.

Air rushed over her skin. A moment of weightlessness before gravity clawed at her waist, hungry to pull her down in the sickening drop of freefall as she clawed for the unspooled length of mooring line and gripped. Palms seared as she slid to a stop and swung like a pendulum with barely a foot to spare.

Eyes shut and heart racing, Nimah swallowed a sickening rise of vomit.

"Hold on!" Boomer shouted, his voice punctuated with the roar of fire.

That's all she could do. Hold on and pray. Hands screaming and fingers on fire as inch by inch he heaved and hauled. A strong hand snatched her by the arm and picked her up like she weighed no more than a feather. Jelly-legged, Nimah slid to the floor and released a sob of relief. She did it. They were in the air.

Boomer punched the button on a control panel swaying from a length of cable, and the hatch whined shut. Blaserfire hammered against the hull, too thick to penetrate.

"Thank you." Rising to her feet, Nimah held out a hand.

"No worries." Boomer bounced a fist against Nimah's shoulder. "Can you walk or do I gotta carry you, too?"

66   FALLON DEMORNAY

"No, I can manage."

"Razor."

The ship was larger on the inside than she appeared from without, but Nimah knew every turn and doorway. Her feet followed with memories of youth, racing from the cargo hold, she led the way past the engineering deck and the living quarters to the stairs of the main bridge, bilevel with piloting up top and navigation below, separated by grated flooring.

Boomer swung left and down the polished brass pole to the second level. Opposite it on the right was a narrow-stacked ladder to scale quickly back to the first. Diving into the gun cage, he yanked on the weapon's helm that would allow him to see a three-sixty view from the rear guns. Maverick was already strapped into the pilot's chair, taking control of the yoke.

At his side, Dobs, aviator goggles pulled over her eyes, cast a grim smile over her shoulder. "Glad you could make it, kid. Strap in."

Nimah leapt into an empty passenger seat. She'd barely locked the harness and fastened the buckles when the ship shuddered and pitched viciously to the right, then ripped violently to the left. Her stomach tangled with her guts into a messy knot of terror as she gripped the padded harness so hard her knuckles screamed.

"Ma!" Dobs shouted for the navsystem. "Give us a full diagnostic of all fuel cells and shield levels."

The navsystem hummed thoughtfully before responding in a smooth, clipped voice of an older woman. *<Prime cells at eighty-four percent capacity. Shield integrity—optimal.>*

"Agents have broken atmo," Maverick grunted at the helm. "We're in for a bumpy ride." He jerked the yoke as cruisers filled the sky, sleek single or duo passenger fighter jets designed for lethal maneuverability and packed enough firepower to take down vessels ten times their size.

Like the *Stormchaser*.

"I count twelve very angry, first-class fighters about to chew us apart," Boomer called up from below.

"We got weapons lock," Dobs chimed in. "At least nine—ten! Dial back. Get us out of range."

"No. That's what they want us to do." Maverick drove the *Stormchaser* head on until STARs jets filled the viewport. Blue streams of light erupted from the swarm, lancing toward them, and he corkscrewed out of the way and slid under their formation before punching through their center. He kept them whizzing and whirling, struggling to keep up and catching each other in crossfire all while dodging unscathed with brutal finesse.

Nimah would've been impressed if her heart wasn't trying to escape from her throat. Beneath her feet Boomer roared, the sound tangled with a laugh, as he met fire with fire. The shriek of chewed-up metal and the force of an explosion threw her forward in her harness as Maverick spun and swiveled the *Stormchaser* in a dance with the wind, hurtling dangerously close to the Academy. And the fighters followed in a wicked chase as he wove around the intricate web of arching bridges and spires, then tore aside into a stomach-churning maneuver that almost had Nimah vomiting over herself as he shot for the horizon leading out over open water.

"One of the stabilizers is off." Dobs punched at buttons and knobs. "Diverting power across the grid to compensate, but can't hold for long. The strain will pop the rest like sonics, heard?"

"Forget the stabilizers." Maverick grunted and rolled them into a sweeping barrel turn, dodging a spray of blue light. "They're flanking us to take out the launch thrusters so we can't break atmo. Get down and man the starboard gun cage with Boomer," his words vibrated with each shuddering jolt. "Get 'em off me."

"Heard." Dobs unfastened her harness and moved with the ease of someone accustomed to holding her ground amidst a hurricane as she swung a leg around the brass pole and shot down to the second level.

"Cadet! Get up here. I need you in second chair."

Ice shot through her bowels and Nimah opened her mouth to answer but another weak cry tore from her throat as the ship rattled hard through the dense clouds. Turbulence and dodging blaserfire was a terrible combination.

"*Cadet!*"

"I can't!" she croaked. Cold spiked down her spine, fire blasted her skin. She was freezing and burning all at once as terror cinched tight as a noose at what they were about to do. She'd known they'd have to break atmo—launch straight into the void—but the imminent reality suddenly rendered her immobile with panic.

"You will if you want to live." Maverick seared her with a glare over his shoulder. "You're the only one with free hands and flight training. I need you!"

Visible through the metal grating, Dobs and Boomer, visors down, rained curses and blaserfire across the naked sky. Across from Nimah, Mumbles jammed a thumb into her mouth, eyes wide as a fascinated child's watching her morning cartoons. She might be capable of making a stealth camera from a tin can, but she was useless in a gunfight or behind a yolk.

He was right. There was no one else, and she'd come too far to die now.

Nimah clutched the buckle, and it took several limp attempts before she managed to uncouple it. Spilling out of her seat, she battled to the flight console, weak as a baby, and strapped in. The ship jostled, bouncing hard, and Nimah swallowed the rise of terrified bile in the back of her throat. "Okay," she panted, blinking through tears. "Now what?"

"Brace yourself." Maverick pushed hard on the yoke and the ship pitched into a moment of heart-stopping weightlessness—before dropping into a sheer nosedive.

Now Nimah did scream, high and loud, as the blue of the sky was replaced with the dazzling stretch of turquoise water below, barreling toward them at an alarming speed. Pushed back in her chair, Nimah planted a foot against the console. *"What are you doing!?"*

"What I do best," Maverick shouted back. Sweat on his brow, jaw grim with focus.

Close your eyes, Sparrow, a voice rose within her, but fear spread like an infection. Overtaking all reason.

Rising over the hum of engines and the scream burning through her chest, the ship's alarm surged.

<Proximity warning—nine hundred feet to impact.>

Sparks rained from behind them, striking the water and emitting white clouds of steam.

"Divert seventy percent power to forward thrusters and engage the reverse pistons," Maverick ordered. "When I tell you to," he gestured to a lever wedged between them, "pull this. Only on my mark."

FLIGHT OF THE SPARROW 69

Nimah sprang to action with shaking hands and shallow breaths. Blood roared in her ears. Her heart pounded in her throat. Focusing on the task kept her from passing out, but her thoughts were scattered, her movements jittery, and it took far too long for her to comply.

"Hurry up!"

"I'm trying!"

<Proximity warning—five hundred feet to impact.>

Her hand hovered over the switch. The water was so close she could make out the ripples breaking the surface. See the shape of the *Stormchaser*—a violent black shadow—against a glittering jade canvas. In a matter of seconds they'd strike and, at this breakneck speed, the impact would shatter the ship like it was made of glass instead of sophisticated carbide steel.

<Seventy-five feet to impact.>

"Now!"

Nimah punched the lever and the ship slammed to a sudden stop— the harness cinching so tight Nimah swore every rib cracked as the ship's helm kissed the water before snapping into a sharp one-hundred-and-eighty-degree spin. Nose up, the reverse thrusters engaged as fighters whipped past them, unable to break in time. Popping explosions rattled the *Stormchaser* as she rose, belching plumes of white smoke, and charging ahead to break the atmosphere. Launching so hard, so fast— swallowing hundreds of feet per second—Nimah was nearly smothered under the dragging force.

Maverick strained against it, pushing hard on the yoke and the engines howled at maximum throttle as he struggled to keep her steady. "Come on, baby."

Pressure. Nimah's ribs screamed under it. Her lungs collapsed. Her skull whined. The weight bearing down was too much. The ship groaned under the strain, the wings trembled, resisting the violent exit like a moth caught in a hurricane.

"Come on," Maverick roared.

The ship rattled and groaned. Alarms blared as the navigation system cautioned against the load. He was pushing the ship too hard. If the engines failed, they'd either drop eighty thousand feet or bounce off the ozone and shatter like a glass bubble.

"She's too heavy," Maverick groaned, "Nimah, take the second yoke. Help me."

Terror pinned Nimah in her seat like a butterfly to a board.

"What's wrong with you?" A shot struck them from behind. The ship rattled. Maverick swore. "If I can't keep her in position we won't break atmo. Cadet!"

Tears streamed from her eyes, fractured sobs wrenched from her throat, lost in the violent turbulence as flames flashed across the glass, engulfing the hull. And beyond the sizzling waves of red, the bright-blue sky deepened to reedy black. Stretching like a grinning mouth that yawned wide to swallow them whole.

The void.

Someone might've called her name, or maybe she'd imagined it. Either way, Nimah couldn't see. Couldn't breathe. Couldn't feel or think. Every sense had gone numb to everything except the furious storm of panic in her head. This wasn't like being launched in the virtual pod— this was worse. So much worse because this wasn't a simulation.

This was real.

And she was going to die.

Something snapped. A violent scream of tearing metal. Pouring heat flashed across her, and wailing alarms gave way to a dark chasm as Nimah slipped into that endless black. Into nothing.

Nothing but silence broken by the echo of a child's screams . . .

CHAPTER EIGHT

Liselle adjusted the pack of ice on her jaw so that the medtech could inject her with a dose of something to numb the pain. It wasn't broken, but fuck if it didn't feel like it. Nimah had knocked her out cold while miraculously causing little harm aside from a blackening bruise.

Good. Because if she'd woken to a wired jaw—and eating through a straw for the next two weeks while the nanites embedded under her skin stitched back bone—Nimah would've had a serious ass whooping to look forward to if she ever came home after her stint on the Most Wanted list.

No. Not if. *When.* Because Nimah was going to be alright. She would make it. She had to. And Liselle refused to let her mind wander to the very real possibility that she wouldn't. Then, when the dust settled and things went back to normal—void have mercy—she was going to strangle the dumb bitch.

Chief Commander Wallace sailed into the medbay and Liselle almost swallowed her tongue. Livid couldn't even begin to describe the waves of fury emanating from the Chief Commander like gamma radiation. Her white hair a stark wave against the flush of rage bright in her gold HWKeyes that sparked like live wires the moment they pinned to Liselle.

Commander Nguyen scuttled in after her, chest high and shoulders drawn, but there was a hint of color in his tawny face. Either a result of exertion from his short legs having to keep up with Wallace's gaping stride or strained emotion, Liselle didn't have time to settle on which.

"How did this happen?" Wallace demanded, hands fisted and chin high.

"My repo—"

"I read your statement, Cadet Namsara, thoroughly, and find it remarkable that while I was away holding a press conference at SIGA base—frantically trying to clean up the Forum mess—Citizen Dabo-124 somehow managed to blithely stroll into the Academy and *free* both Maverick Ethos-333 and Djimon 'Boomer' Omunye from containment within less than an hour. The *Stormchaser* stolen. Agents swatted from the sky like flies. All because of *you*."

Liselle squirmed. Even though she was sitting on a medbay bed and not a steel chair in a containment room, this was an interrogation all the same. "I hit the alarm."

"*After* she'd already removed Maverick and his accomplice from custody. You also released the locks on the gate of the hangar, and you helped her subdue a pair of sentries." Wallace leaned forward, until they were almost nose to nose. "You're fortunate our cameras were blinded by rogue tech so I can't confirm the latter most especially, otherwise you'd be in magnicuffs right now, but my gut knows you're more involved than you're letting on."

Liselle measured her breathing. She'd been trained to withstand this and worse, but something about Kimora Wallace tested the brass of even the most senior of agents.

"Chief Commander," Commander Nguyen cleared his throat, "our sensors indicated that Cadet Namsara was truthful in her statement. She was not a willing participant."

"No, I fucking wasn't." And she'd clung to that little nugget of truth like a raft in a hurricane while they'd strapped all kinds of wires and sensors to various pressure points before grilling her for an hour.

"Our medical exam further corroborates this," the medtech spoke up. A slender guy with hair tinted electric green at the temples. "Her injuries are consistent with a violent assault. Computer simulations, based on dermoscans, show that this wasn't a staged blow. There's no indication of hesitation or flinching, even on a microscopic level, before contact was made. She never saw it coming."

Wallace waved a dismissive hand, but her expression wavered as rage thinned to doubt. As Chief Commander, given the assault on the Forum,

FLIGHT OF THE SPARROW

it was her responsibility to speak alongside the SIGA board regarding the terrorist attack and subsequent arrest. STARs agents were supposed to be untouchable. Beyond perfection. And this assault had fractured that image.

If having SIGA officials for parents taught Liselle anything it was that in a crisis of this magnitude, damage control was an imperative, because if word of what happened got out to news outlets—there would be no recovery from the nosedive. SIGA would be harpooned, and Chief Commander Wallace stripped of her brass. Her only hope now to save herself, and the reputation of the Academy, would be to find Nimah and the escaped felons as quickly and quietly as possible. And off-the-books ops only had one outcome . . .

Liselle scooted off the bed. "I'd like to formally request to join the taskforce."

Wallace turned. HWKeyes bright with disbelief. "Out of the question."

"You need me." Liselle crossed her arms. "I'm guessing they made a clean escape? Otherwise you wouldn't be so livid right now. They deployed decoys, right?"

"Ion tracers picked up at least a dozen of them," Commander Nguyen confirmed, and to his credit didn't so much as flinch when Wallace swung her eyes on him and glared. "More than we've ever seen. More than should be possible. All pulling in different directions. There's no telling which escape route was theirs."

And only an idiot would spread SIGA resources across such a wide radius. Even if SIGA's reach was vast, there was still paperwork and plenty of red tape to navigate, all of which would cost precious time and increase the risk of news leaking to the press. If Wallace wanted to move quickly, and quietly, she'd have to make strategic guesses as to which trails could possibly be theirs, two or three at most, and cross her fingers.

"That's classic Maverick," Liselle continued. "By now they've vanished into the void, and every second spent guessing where they went is valuable time lost in recovery." The first twenty-four hours were the most crucial. After that, the chance of apprehension declined drastically. Throwing her shoulders back, Liselle held her ground. "Nimah is—*was*—my best friend. We've spent every day at the Academy together since we were seven. No one knows her like I do. I can be an asset in apprehending her."

Commander Nguyen tensed and something like disappointment set in the lines of his long face, but it was gone by the time he turned to Chief Commander Wallace. "Cadet Namsara raises an excellent point."

Wallace ground her teeth so hard Liselle could almost hear enamel crack, but her subtle nod loosened the knot in Liselle's chest enough for her to breathe. "Very well. Soon as Medtech Sato has cleared you for duty, report to the command room."

Liselle pressed her fingers to her brow in a stiff salute. "Yes, Chief Commander."

"I will notify the SIGA board of our unfortunate . . . circumstances, but we must keep this contained from the public *until* we have remanded the suspects to custody."

"Understood." Liselle bobbed a nod.

"Good." Wallace turned elegantly, like a snow leopard studded in polished brass, black heeled boots clicking in a lethal melody of claws about to rake Liselle to the bone. And hadn't made it more than twelve paces before the entryway to the medbay pixelated open and a man strode in. A man who needed no introduction. Everyone within the Inner Circle and Outer RIM knew Cormack Shinoda.

A glorified legacy chief executive officer of IESO, he owned the largest and most prolific prime ore mining company in the void. A position he'd inherited from a long line of Shinodas before him, like a prince ascending a throne. Unlike other mining corporations, Shinoda's family owned a majority stake in shares, which gave him inexhaustible wealth and the infamy of a God. Given the way he carried himself, the rumors hadn't been exaggerated in the least.

Flanked by what Liselle pegged as a personal security team given their tactile suits—strong enough to stop a blaser-bullet, and tensile enough for ease of movement—Shinoda sliced through the center of the room as if entering an IESO board meeting instead of the Academy medbay.

So much for keeping it quiet.

"Mr. Shinoda, civilians aren't permitted within—"

Shinoda raised a hand. Just a casual lift, and Chief Commander Wallace went silent. Liselle could hardly believe what she was witnessing.

FLIGHT OF THE SPARROW

"Chief Commander Wallace, I won't waste your time with dick measuring. I'm here because my security team has been alerted to the events that transpired nearly two hours ago. As there have been no public announcements, I assume you will be primarily responsible for putting together a task force to retrieve these fugitives quietly. So tell me—what is your plan for apprehension?"

"That's classified."

"Nothing is classified when it pertains to my *son*," Shinoda's tone hardened along with the tension in his shoulders. "You know how things work." He angled himself square with Chief Commander Wallace. "Who I am. Who I am connected to. The SIGA board has given my presence special consideration, therefore, effective immediately, your directives will come from me." Removing a holocard from his breast pocket, he offered it to Wallace to review.

Which she did. Thoroughly. She took several long minutes to comb the document, then sighed in resignation, returning the holocard to him. "How can I be of service, Mr. Shinoda?"

Light curved over the dome of Shinoda's bald head, smooth and round as an egg, and refracted in his eyes. Both shone silver—FLCN-grade retrofits that were given to him as a young man after a radiation accident at one of the company's principal mines.

Everyone knew the story. Pirates had attempted to raid the installation, seeking to boost a prime ore shipment—a catastrophic failure that resulted in nearly two dozen deaths, including Shinoda senior who died shielding his son from a blast from a ruptured ore container. The young Shinoda emerged alive, as medtechs were able to get to him quickly, and though they'd been able to regenerate his badly burned skin to near-pristine condition, his eyes, as a result of exposure to unrefined prime, had melted from his skull. Leaving no other recourse but to replace them.

FLCN retrofits were nowhere near as advanced as the Chief Commander's sixth-generation HWK, but it was said that his retrofit surgeries, performed at a low-grade facility aboard a spacity close to the assault, had been so painful Cormack Shinoda swore off all future retrofits. Any and all examinations since then were rumored to take place at his home, and were limited to only once a year.

"You can start by clearing the room," Shinoda demanded. "I'd like a word with you, Chief Commander. And with you." He wiggled a summoning finger at Liselle as Commander Nguyen and Medtech Sato were ushered out by his personal security.

Sliding off the medtable, Liselle stood at attention.

"My security team tells me that the former cadet, Nimah Dabo-124, was your best friend, correct?"

Surprise washed over her, but training had taught Liselle there was no point puzzling over how he knew. Point is he did. "Yes, sir."

"And you're the daughter of Counselor Lennox Namsara, correct?"

"Yes, sir."

Shinoda tipped his chin. "I know your father well. We've completed many business transactions together. Good man. Unfortunate taste in friends notwithstanding, I'm sure you are a testament to his great name."

Liselle struggled not to clench her jaw and to keep her voice light even if his very presence made her skin crawl. "Thank you, sir."

"I find it interesting," he continued, now addressing Wallace, "that a non-class citizen came to such a place, known for its integrity and uncompromising standards, yet no one flagged her familial connection to an infamous pirate captain until earlier today. Curious, even."

Chief Commander Wallace tucked her hands behind her back in an official stance. "I wasn't there for her initial assessment and as her recruitment records were sealed, I can't speak on that matter, but she was always a model cadet during the entirety of her training at the Academy. Smart and determined to excel, which makes her recent actions extremely . . . alarming."

"Indeed. Now, what are your plans to apprehend her?"

"Based on critical analysis of the situation, our intelligence team has given us forty-eight hours from time of departure to apprehend all fugitives. If in that time we fail to do so, I'll activate cybers to execute Blackout Protocol."

Liselle's heart seized. Blackout Protocol was reserved for the most dangerous offenders to be returned to SIGA base not in magnicuffs, but in body bags. Cybers were off-the-books operatives; retrofitted until they were more metal than flesh—and trained to succeed at near-suicidal missions as government-sanctioned assassins stripped of fear, empathy, and remorse.

"Do you think that's wise, Chief Commander?"

FLIGHT OF THE SPARROW

"As their intent, so far as we can assume, is to rescue a confessed terrorist—absolutely."

"And what of my son?"

"Of course all efforts will be made to secure Jonothan and return him safely, but our immediate concern is neutralizing an intergalactic threat by ensuring that Captain Indira Roscoe does not escape custody."

Shinoda's smile sharpened. "You know why IESO has remained ahead of our peers? Legacy. For three hundred years, a Shinoda has always maintained authority and active control—we have never changed hands. You see, legacy equates to stability, and stability promises growth. A future. But since news has leaked of Jonothan missing, share prices have declined steadily, and the longer he is gone, the more anxious investors will get. I cannot allow that to continue."

"I understand."

"Excellent." Shinoda's smile sharpened. "My risk advisors have projected a seventy-two-hour window before we enter a critical tailspin from which we won't recover. Therefore, in an attempt to stop the hemorrhaging, I will be hosting a massive gala that will be broadcast live across the entirety of the Inner Circle, where I will announce a groundbreaking development in IESO's future ahead of our fiscal year end, but I can't do that without my son, the future of my company—my *legacy*—by my side. I expect you to deliver Jonothan in perfect health *before* the gala. That gives you less than three days."

"I'll endeavor to do all I can, sir, but there are no guarantees."

"I suggest you get in the habit of making them, Chief Commander, and once Jonothan has been safely located I would also like Captain Roscoe delivered to me." Shinoda smiled a thin, predatory grin. "Discreetly."

"I can't sanction that."

"Your reputation as an honorable woman precedes you, Chief Commander. Sterling brass to the bone." Shinoda raised an unbothered chin. Even then, he was still several inches shorter than Wallace. "But I do understand how proper incentivization can inspire action; therefore, allow me to present you with *this*." He keyed a new code into the holodeck and returned the sheet of glass to Wallace. "It's a commendation, already signed by President Doja, as you can see, stating that upon successful completion of this mission, pending my complete satisfaction, you will be promoted—immediately—to admiral."

Liselle barely held back her gasp. *Admiral.* There were only six in SIGA history since Earth-Prior, and none had ever been younger than fifty, let alone women. Shinoda was offering not only a chance for Wallace to undo this mess, but rise above it. And make history.

Chief Commander Wallace's lips parted with a soft exhalation of breath. "Yes, sir."

"Wonderful. I expect frequent updates."

As Cormack Shinoda strode from the room with Wallace not far behind, Liselle closed her eyes. Her thoughts and heart reeled with shock and uncertainty, and she pressed a steadying hand to her stomach.

Nimah, her heart whispered, *I hope you know what you're doing.*

Don't be afraid.

Nimah shook awake like she'd plummeted a thousand feet in a second, and swallowed the burn of a chilling scream that threatened to split open scar tissue in its wake. Tearing her clean in half so that the terrified child she'd buried deep inside of her bones could emerge, blood-soaked and tearstained.

Cold. So cold . . .

"Hey, easy, kid. Easy."

A damp cloth clamped over her mouth and Nimah tried to fight it off, but hands—freakishly strong—held her fast until the pungent medicinal vapors soaked into her lungs. Each drugging inhale, spicy and fragrant, cleared the fog a little more until Dobs came into focus. Dense curls, some white, some ash gray, framed her weathered face, and a rolled and unlit cigarette hung between red painted lips.

"There, there you go. Deep breaths. Get your legs back under you."

She wasn't hurtling through the void, spinning in the dark. She was on the *Stormchaser.* The gentle hum of the ship was steady as a heartbeat, and Nimah latched onto that, pushing the ghosts of her nightmares away. "What happened?" her craggy voice came out raw and rough as skin scraping against concrete.

"We punched outta there by our teeth." Dobs snorted as she pried open Nimah's eyes, waving a penlight in one then moved on to the next.

FLIGHT OF THE SPARROW 79

"Skinbag flew like a damn prodigy. In all my years sailing, never seen the like. Doubt I will again. You, on the other hand, passed out like a greenie who's never broken atmo a day out the womb."

Spots danced around her vision and Nimah struggled to blink them away. "I . . . I just—"

"Don't worry." Dobs lowered the penlight and tucked it away in the breast pocket of her jumpsuit. "Seawater fucks with the best of us."

Relief cooled the scorch of heat beneath Nimah's skin, grateful that she wouldn't have to explain herself. No one would understand the truth. Especially not a pirate.

"How's the head?"

"I feel like I was put through a carbide steel wall."

Dobs snorted. "Sounds about right." With a clap of her hands, the overhead lighting dimmed from bright gold to soothing amber. "And the hand?"

Confused, Nimah raised her bandaged right hand to her face. "What happened?"

"You were gripping this when you passed out." Dobs removed the stone sparrow from her pocket, a length of twine looped around its neck so it dangled like a body at the end of a rope. "Held it so tight the wings gouged into your skin. Damn near had to break your fingers to pry it loose." She put it down on the bedside table and admittedly, something in Nimah eased. "Can you sit up?"

"I think so." Weak as a newborn, Nimah pushed upright in the bed and the protesting muscles of her neck sent vicious bolts of pain across her shoulders and down her back. Whiplash. Wonderful. Black dots of unconsciousness loomed in the edges of her vision and Nimah breathed through the dizzying spin before, finally, her gaze settled. Sharpened. Taking in her surroundings, her stomach clenched with a fresh wave of despair. "This is my grandmother's cabin."

"Seemed fitting."

"I don't want to be here." It was bad enough she was on the *Stormchaser* at all, but this? This was too much. "You take the captain's quarters. I'll settle somewhere else."

"Suit yourself. Hold it down," Dobs cautioned as nausea kicked Nimah's stomach into her ribs. "Stuff does more damage on the way up, heard? Here." She pressed a cup to Nimah's mouth and poured a warm salted broth down her throat.

The first swallow was hard, but the next brought welcomed relief and she guzzled it all, quenching the fire in her belly. "Thank you." Nimah sighed.

"Ro never had a taste for Seawater, either, but the night your mom died, she got pissed." Her brows furrowed. "She was never the sort you'd call maternal, but losing Zory tore her up deep."

"I'm not in the mood to go down memory lane right now."

"Easy kid, didn't mean no foul."

"I'm fine," Nimah answered, but the waver in her voice belied her weakness, as did the prickling of emotion in her eyes that said she was still hurt. Still cared. *She left me.* Anger bubbled through her veins, a dark and vicious poison that made her want to throw the mug and watch it shatter like her heart. *She left me and never once looked back.*

"Now that you've got some color back in those cheeks, about our pilot."

"Are we going to argue about this again?" Nimah sighed, though grateful for the abrupt change in topic.

"That skinbag is connected to Hatchett—the worst possible gobshite in the void."

"Pirates, skinners—what's the difference? You both wear the same shade of black." Nimah shrugged but her breath snagged at Dobs's penetrating glare.

"No we don't. Pirates follow a code, kid. We have honor. Integrity. Skinners look after themselves, and'll strip you to the bone the first chance they get. He'll betray us."

Like how my grandmother betrayed me? Nimah didn't say it aloud, but the words burned through her with conviction. Whatever Dobs would have her believe, neither could be trusted and both were everything she aspired not to be. Thieves and cutthroats, they took what they wanted without care for the harm they caused to those around them, and represented everything Nimah had worked so hard to overcome and stood against.

"There's no point in arguing semantics," Nimah continued, filling the silence. "Neither of us can fly first chair, so we need him." And

FLIGHT OF THE SPARROW   81

Maverick needed them just as much if he expected to claim the reward—or the ship, but Nimah kept that detail to herself. The less Dobs knew about her arrangement with Maverick, the better.

Dobs clucked her tongue. "Just speaking my mind on the matter, is all." She tapped her brow. "Keep a weather eye open, heard?"

Nimah kicked up her chin. "Are we done here?"

"Yeah, kid, we're done." Slapping her hands to her thighs, Dobs stretched into a stand. "Drink. Eat." She gestured to the side table, where a tray of bread and a thermos of more steaming broth sat. "Effects will wear off soon with a full belly and lots of fluids."

"Dobs . . ." Nimah skimmed her nails along the beveled surface of the mug. "Would you have really done it? Left me behind?"

Leaning against the jamb, Dobs sparked her lighter, hand cupped around the flame, and sucked hard until the end of the cigarette glowed hellfire red. "Nah, kid. You're one of us," she said after a long, smoky inhale, then touched a faded tattoo etched inside her left wrist of a pair of wings framing a sword. "To the void or Valhalla, heard? Valkyries fly for life."

That statement should have soothed, but instead it scored deeper, sawing past scar tissue into raw, naked flesh. Because if that were true, her grandmother would've never abandoned her in the first place, which meant Nimah had never been a Valkyrie in her eyes.

She hadn't mattered at all.

An hour later the broth and bread had settled her stomach, enough for Nimah to climb out of the bunk to shower. Pounding hot water leveled her head on her shoulders and she emerged finally feeling like herself.

Wrapped in a towel, Nimah explored her grandmother's cabin. Closest to the bridge, it was the largest of all crew quarters and split into two levels with its own private gym, lounge, and retractable kitchenette that disappeared into riveted steel walls interrupted only by a single shaded viewport. Across from the wide bunk made from plate metal was a desk of real wood—oak, if memory served—and above it a few plyboard shelves laden with photographs printed on glass.

Nimah picked up the oldest of the collection: her grandmother smiling with Dobs at her side, arm hooked over her shoulder, and Mumbles

82   FALLON DEMORNAY

visible behind them, seated in the open hatch of a ship. They couldn't have been more than Nimah's age, taken long before they'd become pirates.

Setting the framed image onto the shelf, Nimah stopped by the foot of the bunk. The cadet uniform lay in a heap, stinking of sweat and Seawater. There was no way she could wear it even if she wanted to. Sighing, she stalked to the closet, wrenched it open, and rummaged through hangers of white tanks and several pairs of high-waisted camo pants. Captain Ro was a woman of simple taste and preferred a stream-lined wardrobe with little variation.

Like grandmother, like granddaughter, apparently.

And buried in the back, a full-length coat. Brown leather, scarred and rough. Nimah struggled to breathe around the hard lump in her throat as she traced a hand along a weather-beaten sleeve. She'd never forgotten it. The smell. The feel. And strapped at the waist was a sheathed sword.

Her grandmother's cutlass. Nimah weighed the sword, the blade made of triple-folded carbide with a lasered edge hot enough to cut through diamond glass. How many times had she seen this weapon on her grandmother's hip? Been awed by its beauty and danger and strength? Few pirates carried a cutlass, styled to emulate those from the golden years of Earth-Prior when they sailed on water in vessels made of wood with cannons and canvas sails.

The old days might be gone, but this little bit of history remained.

Her grandmother had once told Nimah wielding a sword took met-tle. It meant you had the skill to get in close, beneath an opponent's energy shields or past their wall of blaserfire. A sword meant you weren't afraid to look them in the eyes as they died, stained in their own blood and piss. As a symbol of captaincy, the fact that she'd left the sword aboard the ship before being collared . . . was disconcerting.

Feelings rose in her, and the memories she'd buried deep inside of her roared to the surface of her heart. Nimah reeled back into her body, out of the murky waters of the past where she had no desire to swim. The past was behind her, and everything she was doing right now was only a means to an end. Her true home was the Academy, her true family Liselle—and getting back to both was all that mattered. Yanking out a shirt and pair of pants, she eyed the coat and blade, both

FLIGHT OF THE SPARROW

beckoning, before shutting the door, sealing away the ghosts in the past where they belonged.

Dressing quickly, the clothes far too big, Nimah cuffed and rolled them as much as possible, then slipped back into her black knee-high boots and yanked the sparrow pendant over her head. Soon as it fell against her chest, a wave of dizziness sent Nimah swaying. Glimpses shot through her—a towering city hewn into massive trunks of trees, unfamiliar laughter, rich as damp soil, spiraling through her head, and the sweeping wave of awe as she shot up, weightless, into a cloudless lavender sky to watch a world burn—Nimah yanked her hand away from the stone bird like she'd been singed. And just as suddenly, she was back on the ship.

Stumbling into the bathroom, she vomited into the sink. What the fuck was that? *Seawater.* Clearly she was still battling the hallucinatory effects, but a tremor deep in the pit of her stomach said it was something else. Something more.

Nimah rinsed out her mouth, wiped her face clean on the towel, and exited the cabin. She heard the clash of voices long before she reached the bridge, and found Dobs, Mumbles, Maverick, and Boomer huddled around the navigation console. Beyond them the void pressed in against the viewport and she swayed into a stumble but recovered her footing with a slap of her hand to the jamb.

All eyes flashed to her.

"The princess had enough beauty rest?" Boomer crossed his arms, muscles bunching and bulging.

"Good to see you're on your feet." Dobs said around a lit cigarette, flicking ash with each syllable. "Pull up a chair."

Nimah wove around the console and positioned herself with the viewport to her back. Not that it helped much. She could *feel* the void like a hungry beast salivating for her throat, and barely repressed a shudder.

"You still drunk?" Boomer sneered.

"I'm fine." Nimah pushed into her spine, drawing straight. "Where are we? Why aren't we moving?"

Dobs stubbed out her cigarette with a smoky exhale. "We thought it best to hold in a cold zone until we could agree on a clear plan of action."

"That plan include how to stay alive?"

"Shut up, Booms." Maverick jabbed him in the hip with an elbow.

"What?" Boomer jabbed Maverick back, catching him in the shoulder. "We're seconds from stalled, thanks to *her*."

"We're also free of our collars because of her."

"Would never have been collared in the first place if not for her, either." Boomer thrust out his angular jaw—thick as a cinderblock and likely as tough. "Not if you'd listened when I said this was a fucking *tra*—"

"Settle down, children, or else I'll start knocking heads together." Dobs arched a scathing brow. "Unfortunately, Boomer touched a sore point we can't move past. We got us a breached hull. The area's sealed off for now, but our biggest concern is life support. Coolant levels are low, which means temp regulation is shot and we're bleeding oxygen like a stuck artery."

"And you're only telling me this now?" Nimah gasped.

Dobs lit a fresh cigarette and sucked hard. "Didn't think it best to rile you up till you had a clear head."

Nimah's thoughts spun like the winds of a solar storm. A cold zone meant they were off the known grid in a quadrant heavily riddled with space debris or radiation, which made it unlikely they'd be crossed by anyone. Pirate, agent, or otherwise.

It also meant if the ship stalled, they were in deep, deep water. Her heart stuttered at the thought, shocking her with an icy lick of fear. Adrenaline surged, carrying panic with it. *Not again. Not again. Not again.* But losing her head to an anxiety attack wouldn't help any of them get out of this. She'd done enough damage already.

Nimah gathered her breath.

Five things you can see. The stain of lipstick on Dobs's fingers. Blue lights in the console. Stubble on Boomer's chin. Rubber bands on Mumbles's left wrist. Green in Maverick's eyes.

"She's in rough shape, but she'll sail as far as Sahara9, I'm sure of it," Dobs continued. "We'll dock there for a full twenty-four and then—"

"What? No!" Nimah jolted into action. "We can't stop. Not with SIGA sending every agent in the Inner Circle to hunt us down!" Criminals who stopped to catch their breath were always the first to get caught. Once you were running, you had to keep running even if your lungs exploded. It was the only hope they had of pulling this mission off.

FLIGHT OF THE SPARROW

Four things you can touch. Rough denim. Smooth metal. A curled bit of plastic peeling off the console. The end of her braid skimming against her lower back.

"Don't have much of a choice, kid. Mumbles's done what she can to stem the bleed, but if we don't get this boat patched up proper, we're dead in the void outside of six hours."

"Bang-bang no goody." Mumbles spread her hands with an apologetic head tilt, confirming Dobs's dire prognosis.

Three things you can hear. The hum of the engines. The creak of Dobs's kneecap. Maverick's wheels against the grated floor.

"Why not Helio12 or even Retico2?" Nimah gestured to the nano-map, as it shifted in real time to show a direct charted course to two much closer outposts. "Both are off-world spacities within reasonable range, and a hell of a lot safer than turning our rudder *back* in the direction we just fired from."

Dobs clucked her tongue. "Even if there wasn't a gobshite on either who would give their eye teeth to turn us in, the only engineer who can make this heap voidworthy again is on Sahara9." She rose onto long legs and flicked her Zippo, sparking a flame she used to light a fresh cigarette. "Chu practically put the *Stormchaser* together with her bare hands. Without her, we'll never make the hardburn to Tortuga to rope in the rest of the old crew by tomorrow, and without them, Ro's as good as dead."

"Why do we have to go to Sahara9 when I thought all the crew was meeting us at Tortuga?"

"Chu is eighty and obstreperous on her best day." Dobs jerked a shoulder and blew a steady stream of pale blue smoke. "If we want her on board, we'll need to go to her and plead our case."

Nimah narrowed her gaze, adrenaline pounding in her temples. "You said everyone was already in agreement."

"I may have finessed the truth a bit."

"You mean you lied."

"Pirate." Dobs wiggled a thumb at her face. "You wouldn't have agreed to this otherwise, so—shoot me."

Nimah tossed her hands with a snarl.

Two things you can smell. Tobacco spreading in a musty cloud of ash, and beneath it, the licorice candy Mumbles unwrapped and popped into her mouth.

Every instinct she had railed against the plan, but beneath it she heard the foggy echo of her grandmother's voice. *You won't get far with a boat taking on water, Sparrow.* Dobs was right. They were hemorrhaging and it was *her* fault. A dense, hard lump of terror enveloped Nimah at the thought of being trapped on a stalled ship. No power. Thinning oxygen. The cold creep of death slithering ever closer. She'd tasted it once before and could almost feel it slicking her skin now like a wet, frozen coat.

One thing you can taste. Nimah licked at the salty residue of sweat on her lips.

"Sahara9." She shook out numb, tingling hands. "We'll stop there."

CHAPTER NINE

The *Stormchaser* rattled and groaned in a halting, choppy descent that had Nimah grinding her molars. Weak and sweaty, she limped off the ship last and pitched over the rail to vomit, swiping the evidence from her lips before rejoining the others at the end of the gangway.

She got her first good look at the *Stormchaser* in the searing sunlight. Like most pirate ships, she was a fusion of scavenged parts jerry-rigged together in a patchwork design that should never have been able to get off the ground, the hull covered in scum from decades of condensation and dirt, riddled with dents and scrapes, but she flew true anyway and could run down a freighter, outmaneuver a STARs fighter jet, and go deepvoid with the best of them.

She was a warrior.

"Get her shields up," Dobs warned. "We got a bit of a hike, and a tin can is gonna cook in this heat."

Heat was too gentle a word. Barely two minutes out of the airlock and sweat was sliding across Nimah's skin like the stroke of fingers, running from collarbone to hip, dampening her shirt as angry waves seared across her skin from the vicious glare of the distant sun, on its own too far away for its warmth to reach this planet. But the amplifier was set like an oven to roast, a silver blue orb that hung in a cobalt sky with brackets that spun and twisted around it, like coils in a lightbulb, spiraling out waves of collected energy. Properly maintained, Sahara9 would've been no different than the balmy temperatures of Atreyes. But this was a third-class world, and out here, funding for planetary maintenance was scarce.

"This place makes the ice-lands of Antial seem like paradise." Boomer swiped at his brow and scattered drops with a snap of his wrist. "Where are we?"

Maverick tapped his wheels. "The devil's asshole, feels like."

"Wait." Nimah squinted off into the distance. "Is that a house?" It was little more than a flat gray blip against a sheet of reddish canyon wall threaded with ribbons of white, but heat waves breaking around it implied an independent structure, and if she shifted a quarter inch there was a flash of sunlight reflecting off glass.

"That speck in the distant yonder?" Boomer croaked, sweat rolling in sheets down his face. "Couldn't land us any closer, Mav?"

"Any closer," Dobs yanked a wide-brim hat onto her head, "and we'd've been gunned down like clay pigeons. Only thing Chu hates more than uninvited guests is company. C'mon." She trudged into a hike, long legs eating up ground. "It's only two miles."

Those two miles stretched like twenty over hot sand studded with rocks.

"How does anyone live all the way out here?" Nimah panted, struggling to keep up with Dobs's gaping stride. Aside from the sweat raining from her chin and spreading across the canvas of her back, it was near impossible to tell that Dobs felt the heat at all. The *Stormchaser*'s system had announced as they touched down that the entire dusty planet boasted a working population of four thousand and twelve—why any of them elected to live such a lonely, desolate existence was beyond comprehension.

"Chu's always been a keep-to-herself sort. More comfortable with machines than people. And dogs. Always had a thing for them, too."

"I thought her name was Magaly? Magaly Estevez."

"It is."

"What is Chu short for?" she asked, throat thickening with thirst.

Ignoring her question, Dobs kicked up the pace. The house, a dozen yards away at most, was a short, hipshot structure that had a hard lean to the left like a tree near blown over. A tin roof sizzled overtop wind- and sand-bleached walls. The front door was ajar, screen slapping with each drag and pull of breeze. At first glance you'd think the place was abandoned, but Nimah's eyes traced over the fine details. The porch was clean—recently swept. The windows, sparkling. In a place this dusty, they'd be filthy within a day.

"This way." Dobs cocked her head, leading them around the wide porch to the back of the house. Nimah sighed as the sun disappeared behind the canyon wall, towering well over fifty feet, and the cooling relief of shade fell across them.

"Water!" Boomer rushed forward, stuck his hand into the rain barrel and scooped up greedy palmfuls. "Razor, it's *cold*!"

Nimah and Maverick joined him, and she almost whimpered at the first fresh taste sliding in a cooling kiss down her parched throat. The barrel, stamped with a SIGA crest, was made with steel designed to hold the contents at a set temperature regardless of environmental conditions—and reserved for government transport containers. No way could a mechanic living in a nearly deserted outpost afford such a thing. She traced her fingers across the welding marks with an impressed smile. Or should have had the skill to break it apart.

"You kids done?" Dobs cocked a hip.

"How are you not dying of thirst?" Maverick swiped a wet hand across his face, spiking dampened hair.

"I'd tell you," she winked, "but then I'd have to kill you. C'mon. She's in her garage."

"How d'you know?"

"Because I do," Dobs shot back, already leaving them in her dust.

Sure enough, Dobs was right. The garage was three times the size of the farmhouse and set into the canyon wall, bracketed with beams made of more SIGA-grade steel. There, tangled up in the guts of a scrap heap, stood a woman, small as a child, in an oversized jumpsuit splotched with engine grease like an artist's with paint. Hunched over, blowtorch in hand, she sliced through a carbide metal plate with surgical precision while a dog, buried under black shaggy fur, lounged a few feet away. Its head popped up as they entered, and it let out a soft, deep *woof.*

The blowtorch snapped off and Chu kicked up her visor, revealing a wrinkled face puckered into a sour expression. "*Puta madre.*"

"Say my name," Dobs spread her hands, "and I will appear. Been what—fourteen years?"

"And change." Climbing down from the heap, Chu ambled over to her workbench and tossed down her torch. "What brings you to the ass crack of nowhere?"

Dobs slid her hands into the back pockets of her cargos. "Ro's been collared."

Chu eased back around. "*Mentirosa.*"

"Wish I was lying."

"When?"

Dobs clicked her tongue. "'Bout thirty-six hours ago."

"I'll be damned. Never thought I'd live to see the day Captain Ro was . . ." Chu dragged the welding visor from her head and ruffled a hand through rough-chopped gray hair salted with black. "The void will be a darker place without her spark to light the horizon."

"You make it sound like she's already dead," Nimah interjected, and was surprised by the defensiveness lacing her tone.

"Ain't she though? A collar's good as a noose for a pirate." Chu cleaned her greasy hands on an oil-stained rag tucked into her waistband before rooting out a pair of bifocals from her chest pocket and slipping them on. Beady eyes blown up to twice their normal size behind thick glass snapped to Nimah. Softened. "Ah, hell." Chu shuffled to her and gathered Nimah's hands. Her grip strong, despite gnarled knuckles. "Last time I saw you, you were lanky as a puppy growing into her paws. Always racing about the bridge, or coloring the hull with your crayons. *Ooooh,* Ro used to get so mad every time she came across one of your doodles."

Despite herself Nimah smiled. "Please, Chu. Help us save her."

Wrinkled lips pressed into a thin line. "No."

"No?"

"Look around you." Chu dropped Nimah's hands. Stepped back. "I live off-grid in the hottest hell-bitch there is for a reason. Isn't a holo-screen or a soul for a thousand clicks in any which direction, and plan to keep it that way. I'm too old and too tired to be shooting rigs into the void and chasing after the next score. Thinking I was making a damn. *Ha!*" She spat a phlegmy wad and it sizzled when it struck the compact dirt. "I'm done with fighting."

"You turn yellow?" Dobs sighed, all dreary disappointment. "This is Ro we're talking about."

FLIGHT OF THE SPARROW 91

"Not my problem. Not anymore. If you thought to send a wave, I would've said as much and spared you the wasted breath." Chu wiped grease off her hands and nodded toward her towering heap of scrap. "I've likely got the parts to get you void-worthy by morning." She shuffled forward until she and Dobs bumped boots, and tipped her chin so high it was a wonder she didn't topple backward. "After that, you put Sahara9 to your rudder until this lump of burning coal is but a speck in your memory."

Dobs sliced her tongue across the edge of her teeth. "Heard."

Nimah released a breath as Chu shuffled off toward her rickety house. "Why do you look so morose? She's agreed to fix the ship—isn't that what we wanted? What we came here for?"

"Sure." Dobs stuffed her hands into her trouser pockets. "But if you think our little snafu at the Academy will be the last storm in the water we face—think again, kid. We're going canon to canon with SIGA." She shook a bereaved head. "How long you think we'll last out there without an engineer onboard?"

Dobs was right. If they were lucky maybe they'd find one on Tortuga, but the *Stormchaser* wasn't manufactured on an assembly line—she was a patchwork vessel with fully customized rigging, and the only one who knew her down to the last bolt was Chu.

"What are we going to do?"

"Give her the night to cool her jets; Chu'll hear reason in the morning."

"And if she doesn't?"

Dobs dusted her hands, scowling into the distance. "Then Captain Roscoe is gonna dance the Tyburn Jig."

Wind whispered around Nimah like ghosts of memory creeping around the edges of her skull, lurking in twilight shadows. She didn't want to remember. Didn't want to feel. But it all spiraled back, a ball of twine rolling down a hill, and she couldn't spool it back fast enough.

Don't be afraid . . .

Tears blistered her throat, her eyes, and she sniffed them away as Maverick rolled toward her, a plate of food in his lap.

"You missed dinner." He nodded down to the tin plate of soupy beans and imitation bacon ribboning across it. "Tastes about as bad as it looks, but you need to eat."

"I'm fine."

Tapping the edge of the plate, a staticky wave snapped across it, sealing the plate before he set it aside on the slope of the sandy dune. Nimah snorted. More stolen and repurposed SIGA tech.

"You keep saying 'I'm fine' like you've got a point to prove," he said, sliding out of his chair to join her on the sand.

Nimah scowled into the distance, eyes fixed on the setting sun—still blistering white and hot, unlike a true sun, which would've glowed deep-orange-tinged as it died on the horizon. The sky above deepened to darkest indigo with stars spread wide and vast, almost like they were sailing through the void instead of hunkered down on a dune surrounded by canyon walls. She shivered against the sudden creep of cold.

"Here." Maverick shucked off his jacket and tossed it into her lap.

"I'm fine." He arched a brow and, despite herself, Nimah laughed. Truly laughed as she shrugged it on. "Won't you be cold without it?"

"Not for a while yet, I think. Spent all day roasting, feels good to catch a breeze."

The jacket, made from twice-recycled leather, swam over her narrow frame, but it was warmed from the heat of Maverick's skin and she sighed into it. It smelled of him, too. His sweat—not entirely unpleasant—and the richness of his soap. Simple and clean. Slumping back in the sand, Nimah folded her hands beneath her head. Maverick reclined with her, mimicking her pose.

"I never liked stargazing," she confessed. "They're so beautiful, that's all anyone sees. Beauty. But me? I look up and see nothing but the empty space between them. I see the truth."

"What truth?"

"That the void isn't beautiful. It's dangerous. A dark, cavernous hole that swallows up everything it sinks its greedy teeth into, chewing up your bones. The void takes and takes and takes until you have nothing. Until you're alone."

"That's real grim, Cadet." Rolling to his side, Maverick propped himself up onto his elbow. "Ask any pirate, or skinner for that matter,

FLIGHT OF THE SPARROW   93

and they'll tell you the void is hope. It's freedom. Escape. It's a million questions waiting to be answered. The chance for adventure. Discovery. Fortune."

Nimah's brows furrowed. "That's because you haven't seen what I've seen." *Not yet.*

Deep green eyes sliced to her, and in the quiet dark they were almost black. Penetrating. "That little bit on Tor12 wasn't an act, was it?"

A simple question, but still a dangerous one for her to answer. Nimah buried her nose in the collar and gave a gentle shake of her head. "No. It wasn't."

"How can a kid who grew up with pirates be afraid of the void? Space is in your blood. And now you're training to become part of a system all pirates are fighting against. Why?"

"You wouldn't understand."

"Try me." Maverick rolled his wrist, bare without his jacket to cover, and showed her a branded scar burned deep into his tawny skin. Three crescents linked up, each one smaller than the last, and a six-digit number running right through it.

A RIM-rat brand.

Nimah chewed her lip, needing the pain to keep tears from sliding up and out of her. A flood she didn't want to set free. Not now. Not ever. "If you grew up on the RIM, then you know what it's like out there, so I don't have to tell you." The poverty. The sickness. Children outnumbering adults ten to one. Filthy and starving. Living on streets cleaved through stacked mounds of cubed trash, digging for scraps. She'd only been cast out there for a couple of years, but that was more than enough. Nimah would die before she ended up there again.

"No, you don't," Maverick agreed. "How old were you?"

"My grandmother dumped me when I was seven. No warning," she whispered. "No explanation. One day I had a home, a family, a reason to wake every day with joy and love, and the next—" She shook her head, eyes closed against the bright, bitter wash of heartbreak. *Gone.* Ripped away like a scab, left to bleed and bleed until it finally became a scar. "About three years later I was sold with half a dozen others by the boarding house warden to fill a workorder."

Maverick cursed. "It's illegal to sell kids to mining corporations for labor."

"Doesn't stop it from happening." No one cared about RIM-rats—undesirable, unwanted. As the minority populace, deemed non-class citizens after the Integration Zone Wars, there was no protection to stop the vultures from swooping in and stripping the carcass clean.

Prime ore mining was dangerous work. The radioactive mineral was hard to get to and resulted in a constant need for fresh bodies to dig it up. The largest corporations picked through prisons for strong backs, but the smaller ones resorted to getting workers wherever they could find them. Legally, or otherwise.

"But something went wrong with the ship's navigation system, and we must've veered way off course," Nimah continued. "Thrusting the crew plus two hundred and eighty-four *passengers* into a dead zone, where we stalled."

"How long were you stuck out there?"

"Almost two months. Half died within the first six weeks—ejected into the void by a desperate crew trying to stretch rations. Fighting and sheer panic whittled down the numbers from there." And she could still hear it. The screaming. "I hid in a vent until it stopped. Hands pressed hard over my eyes, but I could smell the blood. Hear the dying. I wept alone in the dark until she found me."

"Who?"

Nimah glanced across her shoulder at Maverick, deep into his penetrating eyes. "Miranda Zhang. She was the ship's nurse. She put a pink dotted bandage on my knee after I'd skinned it while boarding. I was shaken after being snatched, and far too weepy-eyed to see the gap in the gangway. My toe caught and I tumbled over. Miranda picked me up with a smile, carried me to the medbay, then told me stories that made me laugh while she applied the bandage. Kissed it." And though the ache hadn't stopped, she had felt better.

Don't be afraid, Miranda whispered, clutching at her side. Blood poured from between her fingers and splattered like paint as she led Nimah by the hand down to the lifeboats and helped her climb inside one before sealing it shut.

Tears in her eyes, Miranda pressed a bloody palm to the glass. *Don't be afraid*, she said again, then released the valve and launched Nimah screaming into the void, where she spiraled and spun amidst the black and

FLIGHT OF THE SPARROW   95

stars and silence until she lost all sense of direction and time. Until cold snuck in like a thief, pressing in all around her and squeezed like a fist.

"I don't remember when they found me. Don't remember being pulled from the lifeboat and rushed into the medbay at Hollow Point." It was all lost to an endless chasm of dark and cold and Miranda's bloody handprint, frozen on the glass like a broken butterfly that haunted her nightmares for years to come. "A few days later I was brought to the Academy for an assessment, and by the end of the week, enrolled." And how she remembered that instant of walking into the Academy for the first time! A palace of white stone and glass on a planet so full of *life*. So lush and green and dazzling in its beauty. "I thought STARs agents were superheroes, you know? Like something out of the flash comics I dug out of trash heaps, so sleek and fierce in their nanosuits. I looked at them and saw purpose, safety, and family. Everything I'd lost and hoped to find again."

"You've been through a hell of a ride," Maverick said, breaking the silence between them. "A cadet on the rise, pushed out onto the streets, and now a hunted fugitive trying to save her grandmother from the noose." He drummed restless fingers on his thigh. "I was raised by my mom before . . . well, before," he said, a fringe of dark hair falling into his eyes. Shielding them from her. "She was what you'd call a rebel, I suppose. My grandparents fought in the Zone Wars, and later were cast to the RIM. Out there . . . you had to latch onto anything to keep your spirit kicking, and my mom wasn't impressed by much, but she worshiped Captain Roscoe—tales of her fearlessness and her righteous wrath against SIGA. Your grandmother's a legend to many."

"Legends are rarely built on truth."

"And what's your truth, Cadet?" Maverick arched a brow. "As a skinner, I'm used to extreme risks for a score. Fear of death holds no sway over me. But you're a cadet, and I find it surprising you'd go against everything you believe in to save a woman you clearly despise."

"I think I've answered enough of your questions."

A smirk tugged at his lips, pleased he'd found a soft spot to burrow beneath her skin. "Don't you trust me?"

After what she'd done to him—how could she? Even if she'd handed him the keys to his freedom a few hours after collaring him, a skinner would never let such a grievance lie. So long as their interests were aligned, she had little to fear, but once the scales tipped—Nimah was certain retribution would fall on her shoulders, swiftly and without remorse. Few things were more dangerous than a pirate or a skinner scorned.

"Only as far as I can throw you," she answered. Which Nimah gathered wouldn't be more than three feet, at best.

"C'mon. We're playing for the same team." Smiling, Maverick reached between them, and tugged on a stray curl behind Nimah's left ear. "Tell me why?" His hand didn't fall away. Instead he rubbed that tendril of hair. Rough fingertips met smooth skin and sent sparks shooting down to her toes. Something inside her burned like liftoff, the tug-of-war between gravity and the thrusters, with her caught in between his easy touch and his damned eyes.

"Because." She sat up, pulling away. "I worked so hard for so long to have a place to belong, and I was almost there. But now . . . Who am I now?" Orphaned again, lost, and spiraling in the dark. "I want my life back." The odds were stacked against them, and they'd likely die trying, but if she didn't—might as well be dead, anyway.

Maverick jolted up, his hand closing tight around her bicep.

"Hey!" Nimah snapped, wrenching out of his grip.

"Shut up, Cadet." His gaze tore across the sky, head swiveling like an owl's.

Disgusted, her mouth tumbled open—and she promptly ate a mouthful of sand, kicked up by a vicious blast of whirring engines as something ripped across the canyon, banked hard, then shot back around. Spearing them in a blinding spotlight. Ships.

SIGA ships.

CHAPTER TEN

G et down!" Maverick wrenched Nimah against him and rolled them behind the dune as light swept overhead and across the canyon walls.

"Did they see us?" Nimah panted beneath him.

"Yup."

"Perfect." Nimah pushed up and peered over the rise of the sand-bank. Two ships had landed near where they'd touched down with the *Stormchaser* that morning.

Chu had shown them where to move the *Stormchaser* to both keep it out of sight and get her close enough to the garage so she could work on the repairs. But there were clear landing tracks any first-year cadet could easily follow, which they must've seen from above and then circled in for a closer inspection.

"It's a scouting party," she said as Maverick slithered next to her and gestured to the two narrow ships as the wings collapsed, hugging the sleek body stamped with SIGA crests. They were designed for stealth, and she hadn't caught the whisper of their engines until far too late. "Each craft holds six, seven tops," she worried, her bottom lip between her teeth. "Knowing Chief Commander Wallace, she'd have kept her taskforce small in order to keep a low profile. But for her to have found us this quickly . . . Wallace must be *furious*."

"Did you expect anything less?"

"Not really," she sighed. "But I had hoped we'd get farther than this." This was fast. Almost *too* fast, but there was no time to dwell on that detail. They needed to move, and quickly.

"We've got twenty minutes before they're on us," she said, shuffling back. If the damn sun were still out, it would take them considerably longer.

Maverick slithered across cool sand and hauled himself up and into his chair. "Booms." He activated his comms speaker while strapping in. "Boomer—dammit, answer me." When only silence answered, he spun the comms dial on his wrist and a pixelated holo of Boomer sitting down half hidden behind a trifold Inner Circle newspaper bloomed above the liquid black disk. "Booms!" At the snap of Maverick's voice, Boomer jolted with a squeal that shot three octaves higher than a man his size should've been able to muster.

"*What, Mav? Can't a guy get five minutes of peace to take a—?*"

"STARs have landed."

"*Shit,*" Boomer's raspy groan shuddered like static.

"Pull your pants up and get to the hangar to warn the others. We're coming to you," Maverick ordered. As the holo of Boomer winked out, he punched the keys on his armrest and his chair trembled beneath him. "Fuck."

"What's wrong?"

"I need to conserve energy. My last recharge was two days ago, and with the *Stormchaser* limping all the way to Sahara9 I didn't want to put extra strain on her power cells. Run," he said to Nimah, pushing hard on his wheels, kicking up sand. "Go. I'm right behind you."

"But . . ." Nimah's eyes skipped from him to his chair. "What about—?"

"I said *go*, Cadet!"

Hunched low, Nimah took off at a sprint and ignored the urge to turn back and help him. If Maverick was confident he could manage on his own without her, then she intended to trust his word. She reached the garage within minutes to find Chu squaring off with Dobs, Boomer beside them. And given the tension in the air, he'd already delivered the news.

"They wouldn't be chasing you unless you did somethin' stupid," Chu snapped, waving a wrench like a weapon in Dobs's face. "Now you've led 'em straight to me."

"Can we fight about this later?" Nimah pressed a hand to her side. "How long until the *Stormchaser* can get voidborne?"

FLIGHT OF THE SPARROW 99

Chu ruffled her hair. "The patch on the hull could use another hour to set and the fuel cells likely ain't past eighty."

That was a problem. "How long until they're at capacity?"

"Fifteen minutes. Might be able to punch it to ten if I divert my energy cache to the refueling grid."

"Do it. We'll never hardburn out of this quad without a full charge behind us. The rest can be done on the fly." Nimah activated comms. "Maverick, where are you?"

"Here," he shouted back as he rolled into the garage with the dog close behind him.

"'Bout damn time," Boomer grumbled, but his face shone with relief before he rounded on Chu. "Got any weapons in this dump?"

Swiveling the toothpick between her teeth, Chu stalked to a swaying control panel and angrily punched buttons. Several feet away, the floor groaned and two metal doors swung open revealing racks that rose up on hinges bearing a cache of weapons large enough to rival a SIGA stronghold.

Gatling blaser guns, sonic grenades, repeaters, and armored vests.

Doe-eyed, Boomer sniffled and dashed away a tear. "Never seen anything so beautiful."

"Those days are gone and behind you, eh?" Dobs rattled a dry laugh, dusty as the terrain.

"Shut your hole." Chu snatched a blaser, military grade, popped a cell clip into the gun, and primed the charger. "And grab something that goes *pow!*"

"Don't mind if I do." Boomer skipped over, giddy as an Inner Circle citizen about to go on an ultra-credit shopping spree.

"Mumbles, get topside and warm the throttle for Maverick," Nimah ordered, helping herself to a sawed-off repeater. "I want her loose and limber. Boomer, go with her and protect the *Stormchaser* in case SIGA has anyone circling above. We can't let her get clipped again. Flag us when the charge is done."

"Razor," he answered and pounded his fist to Maverick's shoulder, strapped like a one-man army. Mumbles mimed a salute and skipped away, a pink unicorn rucksack slung over one shoulder. The pair of them headed for a spiral iron staircase at the backend of the garage that led up to the landing pad atop the canyon, where the *Stormchaser* was charging.

Sirens whirred loudly. "Perimeter's breached." Chu staggered into a run, favoring her left hip, and barely hit ten feet out onto the sand when a blast rent the air—a wall of heat that morphed into a wave of fire—knocking her back as the farmhouse exploded.

Rushing out into the storm of smoke, Dobs hooked an arm around Chu and hauled her across the sand into the garage while Maverick and Nimah gave cover fire. Debris rained in splintered wood and frags of smoking tin.

"You alright?" she shouted over the chaos.

Chu shook her head and blinked, bifocals askance on her upturned nose. "My home. They . . ." Her puckered lips peeled back into a grimace as she struggled to stand. Whistling for her dog, she stalked for the rack and disappeared from sight.

"C'mon, Cadet." Maverick nodded toward the sand bowl. "We'll take the right flank."

Nimah cocked the sawed-off repeater. A close-range weapon with a vicious kick. Not strong enough to punch through a nanosuit, but a direct hit would take an agent clean off their feet. The kind of weapon meant to disable and disarm. Not kill.

They hovered near the entrance and waited for a gap in the blaserfire for reload before dashing out. Nimah fired off shots in the distance, covering Maverick as he pumped his wheels, racing out into the sand bowl. A fresh barrage of blaserfire opened up around them, coming from the direction of the smoking wreckage. Only precision explosives could do that kind of damage, allowing control over the directionality of the blast to ensure offensive forces would be unscathed upon detonation. They'd wanted Chu to see—and to feel—the destruction of her home.

They'd made it personal.

A shot struck Maverick hard in the ribs, almost tipping his chair over as he shot behind a jagged outcrop of stone, and he wheezed through the burn. "Shit, I felt that through the vest."

"How bad?" Nimah demanded, popping off a few cover shots before ducking down to assess him as he traced the smoking hole with his finger. There was a bit of blood, but not much.

FLIGHT OF THE SPARROW 101

"Surface wound, I think."

Blaserfire seared overhead, breaking off chunks of rock from the canyon with each strike. Nimah hunched over him, shielding him from the debris. "We can't hold here for long. This canyon has us pinned." And the only way out was up. Nimah shucked bullets from a belt looped across her chest, slammed them into the barrel, then cocked the trigger, pumping one into the chamber. She had ten rounds before she'd have to do another reload.

"Shoot and keep shooting." Maverick took position and found a clear line of sight along the left.

Nimah settled next to him. Worry firmed the line of her mouth as she scanned the basin. And when an agent rushed out from cover, Nimah hesitated.

Maverick released three shots. Knee. Hip. Chest. "She's not out there, Cadet. Your friend."

"How could you know that?" Nimah demanded without pulling her gaze from the field.

"Because I do." He popped off a couple more, catching another agent in the thigh. The man dropped, rolling onto his side with a shout.

Nimah swept for another target, when Chu sauntered out into the center of the fray strapped into a harness bearing twin Gatling guns perched on her shoulders.

Face grim and eyes narrowed, Chu faced the enemy and roared, "Eat lead, *pendejos!*" She squeezed the trigger, raining fire and fury in her wake. Answering shots that hit her disrupter shield and sputtered like zapped insects. She caught a charging agent in her strafe of blaserfire and sent his torso one way, his legs another, before she swung for a four-ton boulder and chewed through stone in a matter of seconds to obliterate her targets cowering behind it. Her maniacal laugh rang almost as loud as the chaos she wrought.

Maverick tapped Nimah's shoulder. "Boomer says the ship's primed. Get on."

"Get on *what?*" When Maverick gestured to his lap, Nimah blanched. Her eyes shot to the canyon wall, and crept up to the edge, fifty feet off the ground. "Will it carry us both?"

"I designed her myself," Maverick assured. "She can haul a rhino and still have plenty of kick. Now get on! No, facing me," he amended. Taking away the repeater, Maverick tossed it aside and handed her one of his pistols. "I steer, you shoot."

Muttering a curse, Nimah swung a leg across, straddling his lap. "Please tell me you've done this before."

"With Boomer. Twice."

She laughed, a nervous, anxious sound as he dropped the armrests and flipped a few switches. The thrusters engaged as the wheels slanted beneath them, spinning like propeller blades.

"Hold on tight," he ordered, then pushed the throttle.

Nimah's scream was swallowed in the roar of his chair, driving hard from beyond the shelter of the rock and Chu's raging gunfire. Her arm cinched so tight around his shoulders it was a wonder he could breathe.

"Start shooting!" he ordered.

Nimah squeezed the trigger, the punch kicked her hard, and he held her fast against him. At thirty-five feet up the chair whined and groaned, shuddered and dipped. "I thought you said it could handle the weight!" she squeaked. A row of lights on his armrest flashed in warning. Twenty percent and fading rapidly. And when it gave a stomach-plummeting jolt, Nimah's fingers went limp. "Oh no!"

"What?"

"I . . . I dropped your gun." Both arms closed around him now. "I'm sorry. I'm sorry."

"Forget it." His body vibrated with the strain of the chair and Nimah's gaze remained glued to the edge of the canyon. Three feet to go. Fifteen percent. His front wheels kissed the ledge as it slithered to twelve and, using what little momentum he could manage, pushed forward—hard— and dropped the back wheels into place.

Perched outside the hatch, Boomer held an enormous laser rifle and a crosshair lens over his right eye. "Where're the others?" he demanded, but his question was obliterated by the blast of a sonic grenade in the sand bowl. A *massive* one.

If the *Stormchaser* had been ground-level, it would've obliterated her fuel cells to zero.

"Shit." Boomer peered down but clouds of sand made visibility impossible. "Was that us or them?"

"Let's hope us," Maverick answered.

FLIGHT OF THE SPARROW

"Fuck's wrong with her?" Boomer scowled, gesturing to Nimah still in his lap and clinging to him like a shaking stone.

"Shut up, Booms. Cover the stairs in case agents are on their way up instead of Dobs and Chu." Maverick pumped his wheels, driving his chair up the ramp of the *Stormchaser*, and rolled to a stop in the cargo hold.

"Hey," he whispered, soft and easy, stroking hands across her shoulders. "You alright, Cadet?" A tremble scored through her as she drew back one halting inch at a time.

Trembling arms still banded around his shoulders, her fingers locked behind his neck. Drawing close. So close they shared a breath. They'd been like this before, hell—he'd been on top of her more than once—but something about it now staggered her to the core.

Sharp voices rose in the distance, a haze, a fog—but Nimah pulled away and was on her feet seconds before Boomer reemerged, carrying Chu's hobbling weight as blood bloomed from beneath her hand.

"You've been hit!" Chu winced as Nimah lifted her small hand, covered in a saggy layer of wrinkled skin, splotched and sun-browned. "Bleeding is slow. I don't think you've damaged anything internally."

"Still hurts like being kicked by a mule in spiked shoes."

"Stop!" Everyone froze at the forceful command, and Nimah's heart plummeted at the sight of Liselle standing in the entryway of the hatch, blaser primed and shaking.

"Liselle," Nimah whispered. "What are you doing?"

Dried blood matted the black hair by her right temple, and her wide brown eyes scanned the hold before ending on Nimah. "Saving you from yourself." Removing magnicuffs from her belt, Liselle tossed them at Nimah's feet. "Put them on. I'm taking you with me."

"I can't do that."

"Nims, I'm not arguing with you, alright? You're in over your head—that's why I joined this stupid taskforce. This is for the best. Trust me." Liselle ground the last part of her statement between clenched teeth, enunciating her words in a way that hinted at an underscored meaning. "My dad can help you." Her eyes brightened, desperate with hope. "He can represent you at trial and ensure you get the lowest possible sentencing, but you have to come with me *right now*."

Nimah shifted on hesitant feet, her mind spiraling far too fast with adrenaline, but before she could speak, a sharp click cut through the tension, and Dobs, six-shooter in hand, jabbed Liselle from behind with the muzzle, kicking her head forward.

"Drop the piece."

"Dobs!" Nimah snapped as Liselle released her blaser, and it clattered loudly off the grating. "Don't!"

"Sorry, kid. We tried it your way, now we're doing it mine." Dobs swaggered in from Liselle's left to stand before her. A giant in stature. Liselle's eyes swung up . . . and kept going.

"Dobs—" Nimah swept in, fury and fear shaking her down to her toes. "You're not going to kill her. That's an order."

"That all depends on this one." Dobs kissed her teeth. "I admire a girl with grit," she said directly to Liselle. "Any other old day, I'd offer you a drink for it. Unfortunately, you have the supreme misfortune of being in my way, heard? Now before you go and say something clever, I know what you're thinking. *I'm retrofit. Do your worst.* But this ain't a fancy bit of SIGA tech." Dobs wiggled her gun, then sharp as a cobra strike, she snatched Liselle by the throat, and, to Nimah's horror, fed the barrel between Liselle's teeth.

"This is old school. Seventeen inches of steel that kicks like a mule strapped to a proton cannon. Swallowing a bullet ain't like getting struck by a blaser, it punches a hole out the back of your skull the size of a grapefruit. Nanites'll have nothing to put back together. This is permanent. So I'm gonna ask you once, kindly. Step off this ship, and do it quicklike." Angling the gun, Dobs pushed up hard against the top of Liselle's mouth. "Or I'll give you a sunroof."

Liselle's eyes watered. She answered with a stiff nod.

"Smart choice." Dobs retracted the gun and released her. Liselle dropped an inch, settling firmly on her feet instead of being perched on her toes. "Shoo."

Liselle raked a furious gaze across them, hands raised as she backed up slowly.

"Wait!" Nimah rushed forward. "Liselle, I'm sorry. I'm so sorry."

"All you had to do was come with me." Liselle eased down the gangway until her boots hit dirt. "You're making a mistake, Nims."

FLIGHT OF THE SPARROW 105

Dobs pressed a thumb to a flat, gray button and with a grumble the hatch doors slid shut, followed by the hiss of air decompressing in the airlock.

"Did you have to do that?"

Dobs swatted Nimah's shoulder, almost launching her off her feet. "Better to ask forgiveness than beg for permission, heard? Now let's get this damn boat in the air. And you . . ." She blocked Boomer's path to the stairway, Chu still slumped in his arms. "No room on this boat for anyone who ain't crew."

"Are you kidding?" Nimah gasped. "Chu needs medical attention."

"I'm a pirate. Not a comedian, kid." Dobs hooked her tongue over her teeth and sucked hard. "Decide now, Chulita. You with us? You in?"

Chu winced, her wrinkled skin pale from blood loss but a determined glare in her beady eyes, amplified behind bifocals. "Those *pendejos* destroyed my home. I've been shot, and they almost killed my dog." She stiffened her upper lip. "Fuck yeah, I'm in."

Liselle stepped out from the cover of the canyon wall as the shuttle set down. She cupped a hand to her eyes to shield against the hard rays of a false sun rippling on a horizon of dust and stone. Each second layered on degree after sweltering degree. In ten minutes, she'd be broiling.

The airlock opened and Chief Commander Wallace sauntered out, a team of armed agents at her back. She stalked to Liselle, the rings in her gold eyes adjusting to the wakening light.

"What happened, Cadet?"

Chaos and debris littered the sand basin. The blackened, ruined husk of a house splattered about like a concaved skull. Bodies of agents lay across the edge of the canyon wall where she'd dragged them one by one into the shade. Some concussed, a few injured and bleeding, but otherwise no loss of life. A miracle.

Liselle blew out a hard breath. "Pretty much what it looks like."

"Where is Magaly Estevez?"

"She was taken aboard the *Stormchaser*. Wounded, but alive."

Wallace snarled a vicious curse below her breath. "Get our survivors aboard the shuttle, alert medtechs to be on standby." Her white-gloved hand fisted so tight it trembled against her hip. "And send a wave to base. I want the Blackout Protocol enacted immediately."

"Commander!" Liselle snatched her arm in a moment of haste, then quickly retracted her hand before she was robbed of it. "Shinoda gave the taskforce seventy-two hours. There's still ti—"

"I don't care." Wallace whipped around. Her white wing of hair slashing hard across her face so that only a single gold eye burned hot as the rising false sun. "More agents are injured, and now the *Stormchaser* has gained another wanted felon and pirate. I'm done playing nice."

"We can still catch them. I struck Maverick Ethos-333 in the side with a hijacker." Liselle pushed up her sleeve to show the biometric data still uploading from the TICK, extracting vitals from Maverick that she would be able to read on a display embedded in her wrist. The hijacker was newer tech, too small—too sophisticated—to be detected by any sensor a ship like the *Stormchaser* might have onboard, and very difficult to trace given its long-range capabilities, allowing them to follow for as long as they needed to without triggering the *Stormchaser*'s radar.

Wallace's head tilted. "I can't seem to access your feed."

"It's encrypted."

"Why?"

"Because I have a plan." And she'd spent the last forty minutes working it all out as she waited for the Chief Commander to touch ground. A last-ditch effort to save Nimah from herself.

"Give me the encryption code."

"No." Liselle hugged her arm to her chest. "Not until you hear me out," she amended quickly. "If we fail in apprehending Nim—"

"We won't fail, Cadet."

"The first lesson we're taught is to anticipate failure so that we can better plan for success. Right now, we're looking at two possible scenarios. Return empty-handed, and you'll be fired—or at the very least, demoted, for what happened at the Academy. And if we do succeed, yes, you'll make Admiral, but even if Cormack Shinoda does keep to his word how many will whisper that you're a puppet in his pocket and question your integrity? Capability? Your merit?"

Liselle paused to let the weight of her words resonate and settle, and knew she'd found her mark in the heavy rise and fall of the chief commander's chest. "The next stop they're likely to make is Tortuga."

FLIGHT OF THE SPARROW 107

Wallace crossed her arms. "Why do you think they'll go there?"

"We acted pre-emptively by striking at them on Sahara9. Now Nimah will assume we know where the rest of the Valkyrie crew are positioned and won't dare risk another meet anywhere on the known grid. Tortuga is the largest and most infamous pirate stronghold in the void—yet no pirate has ever betrayed its location, therefore its the only place they can go to ensure they won't be ambushed a second time. If I'm right, they'll lead us to it and then you, Chief Commander, can do what no one else has done before . . . end the scourge of piracy once and for all. After that, you'll be so much more than an admiral. You'll be a legend."

Wallace's narrow chin shifted with the grate of her clenched teeth. "How do you suggest we proceed?"

"Turn a member of the *Stormchaser* to our side." Liselle edged closer, heart in her throat. "Nimah wants to come back to the Academy. She wants to come home. Give her that and she'll turn. She'll *help* us."

"Out of the question. Given her recent actions, that bridge is burnt to cinder."

"But—"

"It's a good plan," Wallace cut her off, "but you're concentrating on the wrong person. It'll take two hours for us to get back to the ship and sorted. I suggest you use that time to find something to leverage against Maverick." She turned on her heel, stalking for the shuttle. "Otherwise, I'll enact Blackout Protocol."

"I don't need two hours. There's only one thing Maverick wants more than anything in the void. One thing he'd sell his soul for." As the chief commander halted and spun back around, Liselle swallowed the rise of bile, and whispered a silent apology to the stars. "Freedom."

CHAPTER ELEVEN

Bleeding donkey piss! Quit jabbing me like a pincushion!"

"Not her fault you've got paper for skin," Dobs retorted. "The sutures won't hold unless she goes deep enough to give 'em something to hang on to."

Chu snarled as Nimah tied off the last stitch. "There. All done." She wiped blood off her hands and tossed the sodden rag into a shallow steel bowl piled with red-soaked gauze and medical implements.

Chu swung her legs down from the exam table and winced. A small, wrinkled hand pressed to her side, patched up with a plasma bandage.

"Nice handiwork, kid." Dobs uncapped her flask and took a long, healthy swallow. "Couldn't have done it better myself."

"As our resident medtech, maybe you should have."

Dobs winked. "Doesn't hurt to learn a new skill, kid. Besides, Chu would never let me near her with a feather, let alone a needle. Ain't that right?"

"I'd rather chew glass," Chu grunted.

A fluffy tail wagged from under the table, startling Nimah at first. "I didn't see you under there." She scratched the shaggy dog under the chin. "Such a good, quiet boy."

Chu leaned over, her glasses sliding down to the rounded tip of her nose. "He's taken a shine to you."

"Hard not to like him, too." Nimah smiled as a pink and grey tongue slipped out the barest fraction. He had warm black eyes, glossy as polished marble, but in them she saw wisdom.

"Found the mutt in a scrap heap. Just a pup, all skin and bone—thought he was dead till I caught a faint whimper and realized he was still breathing. Barely. Took me two long months to bring him back from three paws in the grave. Been by my side ever since."

"What's his name?"

"Dog." At Nimah's blank stare Chu dashed a hand in the air. "Don't got time or 'clination to be sweating over a name. He don't mind it, do ya?" Dog woofed a short, soft bark and Chu's features warmed with something Nimah couldn't imagine as anything other than true love. It lasted only for a second before she seized with a sharp curse. "Bleeding void, get me something to dull the pain!"

Dobs wiggled her flask and hitched a thumb over her shoulder. "Got more Seawater in my cabin."

Chu's head popped up like she smelled a fresh steak. "Why we sitting here gabbing for? Lead the way."

While the pair of them took off, Dog trotting close behind, Nimah slumped against the operating table and swallowed bitter memories of bile and Seawater as the floor wobbled beneath her—or maybe it was her knees.

"You alright, Cadet? If I didn't know any better, I'd think you're still seasick."

"I'm fine." Nimah straightened as Maverick whisked into the room. His chair glided smoothly and silently—primed by a fresh charge. "We broke from hardburn already?" She'd been so focused on stitching up Chu she hadn't felt the throttle shift.

"'Bout two minutes ago. Sahara9 is two parsecs to our rudder, and you'll be happy to hear radius scans are clear in all directions. Looks like we've dodged SIGA a second time."

Nimah released an unsteady breath. "Good. Great. How's the wound?"

"Twinges," he said, "but not much else."

"I should still take a look at it." Nimah gestured to the table. "Can you get up here?"

Maverick skimmed his tongue along the edge of his smile. "Yeah. I can manage." Scooting close to the foot of the table, he unfastened his harness, and, anchoring his grip, heaved up. His legs wobbled beneath him, but they held true thanks to a set of braces she hadn't seen him wearing before.

"What is this?" she asked, touching the curved bracket that hugged his thigh. Four more ringed his legs down to his ankle, and beneath it she could feel the contraction and release of his muscles shocked by electrical pulses.

"Keeps them from atrophying." Boosting onto the table, Maverick sat back and propped himself against the wall. "Don't plan on being in this chair forever, Cadet."

Nimah cleared her throat, uncertain what to say to that. Retrofitting was astronomically expensive, and extraordinarily painful. No way could a skinner afford such a procedure. Even one who worked for the notorious Hatchett, leader of the largest crime syndicate in the Inner Circle. He'd carved out a large territory, occupying three zones where most were lucky if they could hold onto the borders of one.

"Raise your left arm," Nimah instructed. Gathering the hem of his shirt, she rolled it up and over his shoulder, baring his entire left side. Hard, packed golden muscle was marred by a vicious purple welt that spread from armpit to hip with a weeping red eye at the center. "You're lucky. The vest took the worst of it." Leaning closer, she prodded gently. "Does that hurt?"

"Only when you poke." She arched a brow. He smirked. "Hey, you asked."

Smart ass. She didn't say the words out loud, but Maverick chuckled like he'd heard it all the same. "Something punctured the skin, but I don't see anything in the wound. I should scan it for traces of foreign matter. Organic and non-organic." She tapped an authoritative hand to his thigh. "Lie down."

Maverick did as instructed, pulling up one leg at a time by his cuffs before reclining with a grimace. "I see those gears grinding, Cadet. What's going on in that head of yours?"

"Nothing."

"You're a shit liar."

Her eyes flickered to his, narrowed. "I'll have you know I scored top eighth percentile in deceptive tactics to withstand cross-interrogation."

Maverick snorted. "Child's play."

And for a skinner, it would be. Con artists as well as thieves, they were trained to lie with the ease of truth. That was the only way to play

FLIGHT OF THE SPARROW

the skingame. They infiltrated companies, gangs, and households to earn trust and gain access to secrets, then used both to strip their mark of everything they had. You rarely saw them coming, and that's what made them so dangerous.

Keep a weather eye open, heard? Dobs was right. Nimah had to be careful.

Nimah took a breath to gather herself before she turned around and pressed the probe to his side. He winced through a shallow breath and closed his eyes while the machine hummed and pulsed.

"Why were you at Tor12?"

"Why do you want to know?"

"Because it was a colossal risk," Nimah answered. "You had to know every spacity within radius would be heavily patrolled after the UPN assault."

Maverick rolled his bottom lip between his teeth. "Was supposed to meet a greenie selling details on a shipment, but they never showed."

"Shipment of what?"

"Prime."

Aghast, Nimah shook her head. Prime was the void's most valuable resource. Even more precious than fresh water or air, given it was the single greatest power source in existence, enabling not only the capacity for interstellar travel—it was the only reason they'd successfully terraformed half a galaxy, allowing the Inner Circle to become all that it was today. As a result, all mining corporations were required by law to ensure the mineral was under SIGA protection at all stages of mining and extraction. Shipment theft—even in the smallest amount—came with an automatic death sentence. No trial. No chance to appeal.

Nimah set her hands to the table and leaned over him to meet his shifting gaze. "You'd risk certain death for credits?"

Maverick set his jaw. "You wouldn't understand."

"You're right. I don't." Nimah removed the probe. "All clear."

"Got any bandages?" Maverick brushed a hand over the planes of his stomach, fingers gliding across every notch and muscled groove. "I'm partial to pink with polka dots."

Despite herself, Nimah smiled. "Fresh out, sorry."

"Then a kiss'll do." Maverick boosted onto his elbows, bringing them suddenly very, very close. He tapped a blunt fingertip to his cheek.

Heat seared up the back of her neck like the lick of a tongue, wakening nerves, and a wild desperate urge singed her belly, just as it had when she'd straddled him. The memory flooded her—the way she'd been so nearly drawn in by tangled breaths and the searing burn in his eyes, the hard grip of his hands dragging her forward, grinding heat against heat. Need against need.

Nimah rocked back, putting distance between them before she did something very, very stupid. "I think you're forgetting yourself."

"Hey, relax, I was just joking, Cadet."

"Yes." Nimah wiped off her already clean hands on a micro cloth, needing something to occupy them to mask their shaking. "I'm a cadet. One day I will be an agent, and you are a felon. A *career* felon." He was a skinner for one of the worst gangs in the void. Kissing him would be more than a mistake, it was dangerous. Stupid. They were opposite sides of the law and she couldn't afford to blur the lines any more than they already had.

"We were both born on the wrong side of the RIM." His eyes hardened. "But you think you're better than me because you got scooped up by luck?"

"No one forced your hand, Maverick. You chose this life."

Maverick scoffed with a disbelieving laugh. "Do you even know how skinners are made? We're children, stolen or sold, that get dumped in a concrete bunker where we're starved and deprived of light or interaction until we break. By the time we're let out, we don't know how long we've been in there but we're fucking grateful to be free of it. Grateful to be served scraps for dinner, or to sleep on a worn-out foam mattress in a mildewy cabin. We'll take anything, *do* anything." His eyes narrowed to vicious slits. "You think you're the only one who knows darkness, Cadet? Who knows terror?"

"I . . ." Nimah's heart sank in her chest. "I'm sorry. I shouldn't have—"

"Save your bullshit apology." Sitting up, Maverick shimmied from the table and into his chair, and with a disgusted shake of his head, rolled

FLIGHT OF THE SPARROW

briskly from the room. Only when he was gone did Nimah slump back, weak-kneed—breathless with relief.

And regret.

Several hours of faster-than-light flying later, thrusters disengaged with a lurch, and Nimah took in her first breathless view of Tortuga, the fabled pirate stronghold. A crescent-shaped spacity, complete with hyperdrive thrusters and distortion shields, which explained why it had never been found or stumbled upon. Large as a small planet, or moon, it shimmered like an uncut jewel cocooned by a bay of bioluminescent void dust that hugged it like ocean water along a sandy shore.

Crossing the barrier, the ship taxied into the dock like a boat making berth. Dockworkers tossed heavy lines to secure the *Stormchaser* while steam hissed from the thrusters, hot from flight. A multitude of ships were tethered along the dock, each splashed with paint. Some were bold and fierce in their design, others bright and artful. Nimah recognized more than a few. The *Wind Rats* and *Bone Dogs*, *Three Skulls*, *Kingsmen*, and *Jade Fire Swords*. Just about every pirate worth knowing was here.

At the end of the dock a bustling harbor surged, rife with people and structures made of reclaimed foam board, steel, and plastic. Each of them as slanted as a drunk pirate's swagger on a storm-ridden deck. Overhead an artificial sky shone beneath atmo-netting that acted as a shield between them and the void, dazzling and clear with digital gulls circling across it, winging through gilded sunbeams of a projected sun.

Sand shifted beneath her boots and even the air somehow smelled of sea and sweat. If she closed her eyes, Nimah could almost believe this was a terraformed island instead of an illegal stronghold in the heart of a rogue sector, bustling with pirates.

There wasn't a single cadet in the Academy who wouldn't kill to get their hands on the coordinates. Coordinates that now resided in the *Stormchaser*'s navsystem . . . If all went sideways, bartering those wouldn't get her back into the Academy but it might be enough to lessen whatever sentence would fall on her head. And though Nimah hoped it wouldn't have to come to that, she filed the thought away as a possible contingency.

Dobs tipped up her head, breathed in slow and deep. "Feels good to be back."

"How long's it been?" A sidecar, pocked with rust and peeling paint, rumbled past them, drunken pirates crammed inside or hanging off the back end, and all singing loudly.

"Too long," Dobs answered, weaving with practiced ease around the jostling bodies. "The conclave will assemble there." She gestured to a towering spire surrounded by three floating concentric rings. "I hailed Sigourney and Gertrude yesterday. With any luck, we'll be ready to go by day's end."

"Wait, if the conclave is *that* way," Nimah grunted and cursed around the knocks of many impatient elbows as Dobs pushed deeper into the throng, "then *why* are we heading deeper into the market?"

"Gotta grab a few things first. *Ah*—perfect." Dobs halted by a booth bearing a variety of trinkets made with precious metals.

"We don't have time to *shop*."

Dobs lifted a bull skull enrobed in gold, chiseled with intricate detailing and studded in jewels. It was tacky and completely ridiculous. "Pirates got a code, kid, and on our turf we best keep to it." She wiggled the skull. "Queen demands tribute, heard?"

"Queen?" Nimah wrinkled her nose. "I thought the whole point of piracy was to rebel against authority?"

"Only the wrong kind." Dobs shucked a credit card from her pocket and waved it at the vendor, a dour-faced man covered in metallic tattoos lining the smooth dome of his sun-beaten head and a craggy gray beard, threaded with turquoise, that swallowed him from nose to chin. He wiggled fingers—what was left of them, blunted by a knuckle or two.

"Fuck you, I'm not paying *that*," Dobs scoffed. "What you take me for? A swab?" The man grunted and repeated the gesture. "Go on, kid." Dobs planted her feet, scowled. "This is gonna take a minute."

Nimah rolled her eyes and pushed her way to rejoin the rest of the crew loitering by the large fountain shaped like a topless mermaid sunbathing on a sundial.

"What's Dobs up to?" Maverick asked.

"Haggling." Nimah curled tentative fingertips around the sparrow pendant. The stone was surprisingly warm to the touch, almost like it

FLIGHT OF THE SPARROW 115

had been basking in the sunlight rather than tucked away in the lining of her temperature-regulating leather jacket. No, this wasn't *her* jacket. It was her grandmother's. Evident in how it hung wide on her shoulders with a hem that would've cut just below her grandmother's knees but now occasionally kissed the ground when Nimah walked. She'd donned it only at Dobs's insistence that it was necessary to blend in, here of all places, and nothing screamed pirate like scarred leather. But soon as she was aboard the *Stormchaser* she intended to be free of the damn thing. If only she could shake off this mess she'd landed in just as easily.

"Well, since we've got time to burn, I'll meet you back at the ship in an hour. You've got babysitting duty." He jerked a thumb at Mumbles—looping around the circumference of the fountain, arms spread for balance, not that it helped much. She teetered and swayed with every step.

"What? Why?"

"Need a few things for repairs." Maverick tapped the armrest of his chair. "And this place is as good as any to find them. Otherwise I'd've stayed aboard the ship with Booms."

"We can't split up."

"An hour."

Nimah scowled as Maverick was quickly swallowed in the seething crowd of the market. She plunked down on the chiseled stone edge of the fountain beneath the shadow of the clock tower, a hard sweat rolling into her eyes. Perched on her knees, Mumbles hummed a cheerful, off-tune melody, a wax crayon clamped tight in her fist. Lank, graying hair, twisted into badly formed pigtails tied off with knotted pink ribbon, swayed while she whisked back and forth over stone with concentrated focus.

Nimah crouched at her side. "Hey, Mumbles."

"Goody-hi."

"What are you doing?"

She ceased in her rocking and faced Nimah with a sloppy smile. "Draweding." And went back to work etching into the smooth sandstone a crude picture of a stick figure with red lips and a cap of white curly hair.

"Looks just like Dobs."

Mumbles jowls wobbled with a nod. "Yup, yup. Dobby-like."

She settled in closer and the sparrow pendant swayed against Nimah's chest, the stone bird swinging as if in wild flight.

Mumbles stilled at the sight of it. "Burd." Reaching out, she raised it between them, twisting and turning the pendant in her trembling arthritic fingers. "Capsy. Capsy burd. Halla. Halla . . ." Her eyes faded and went distant, as if she wasn't seeing Nimah anymore—but something beyond her. Suddenly, she seized with a gasp, and dropped the sparrow as if it had burned her.

"Keep it gone, Nimsy." Seizing the collar of Nimah's shirt, those vacant eyes focused, clearing away the fog of memory for clarity. "Keep it gone!"

"What?" Nimah croaked. "What are you—keep *what* gone?"

"Listen! Listen, with ears and eyes, yes?" Taking Nimah's hands, she cupped them around the sparrow, crushing it in their melded grip. "Fly the way home. Fly the way *home.*" Mumbles grimaced, mouth open, and bounced the heel of her hand against the dome of her head, fingers flexing and twisting with frustration as if trying to push something out of her brain and into her mouth. "Buttons two and six. Send the wave. Hail stars and make them fall!" Her voice grew louder, on the edge of frantic. "Hail stars and make them fall. Make them fall. Make them fall!" Yanking away from Nimah, she tore off into the crowd, shrieking those words.

"Mumbles, wait!" Boosting to her feet, Nimah prepared to give chase when a hand caught her by the arm, nearly yanking her off the ground.

"Leave her be, kid."

"But . . . what if she gets hurt? Lost?"

"Only one place she'll go."

Nimah glared up at Dobs. Haloed in harsh sunlight, she was little more than an ashen smear, a rucksack hooked over her right shoulder. "What took you so long?"

"Bartering can't be rushed." Dobs swiveled her gaze. "Where's the skinbag?"

"He left. Something about repairing his chair."

"That so?" Dobs sucked hard on the edge of her teeth. "Well, best get moving." She pressed the comms behind her right ear. "Chu? You ready to stretch those sticks you call legs?"

"Kiss my bony ass, Sasquatch. These sticks'll run circles around you."

FLIGHT OF THE SPARROW   **117**

Dobs cracked a grin. "Tell Boomer to keep an eye open for Mumbles. The kid and I are heading for the conclave. Let's see who gets there first."

"Copy."

The heart of Tortuga was a hive of towers shaped like jagged combs from all the docking bays disgorging a wide variety of transport vessels. They rode in a transport shuttle up to the conclave, a circular outdoor pavilion at the top of the uppermost tower, with swaths of red and black fabric ribboning across to diffuse the harsh sun.

Chu flashed chunky teeth in a smug grin as they entered the courtyard and, always several strides ahead of them with legs that ate up miles in seconds, Dobs knelt at the center of a sixteen-point compass laid into the stone of the round courtyard, made of brass, silver, and gold.

At the northernmost point, Sigourney, the Bone Queen, sat on a black lacquered throne. One leg draped casually over the armrest. She was dressed in latex, metal, and—yes—bones, beneath a blood-red cape. Matted locks and twists of soot-gray hair fell in various lengths. Some as short as her chin and others well past her hips.

"Dorothy," she purred. Kohl-blackened eyes, made luminescent as a wolf's in moonlight, dominated an aged face, heavily lined and sagging around midnight lips. "It has been forever and a day."

"Siggy. Quite the getup you've got here." Dobs straightened to her feet and hooked her thumbs in her belt loops, stance easy with casual confidence Nimah couldn't imitate. Not in this darkened den of gothic despair.

Skulls, some old and beaten, others gleaming and fresh, were staked along the perimeter in concentric rings running up along the sides of the curved walls. Hundreds of them with the arm bones crossed beneath them, an homage to the ancient pirate's sigil.

"Our vanquished enemies." Sigourney leaned forward so knobby elbows rested on lean thighs wrapped in liquid black. "I collect their bones."

"Speaking of," Dobs said with a grin, and shucked her satchel from her shoulder. "A gift."

The queen nodded and a burly man with retrofit blue eyes stepped forward, his ghostly white skin covered in blood-red tattoos. He plucked up the satchel and fished out the gleaming bull skull. A beam of sunlight brightened the yellow gold and made the embedded gems shine like stars.

"Precious," Sigourney crooned, tenderly stroking the skull as a mother would an infant, fingertips decorated with claw-like rings.

"We're here—" The crunch of metal piercing the gilded skull stopped Nimah cold as Sigourney anchored it on one of the points jutting from atop her throne like spires in a wicked crown.

"I know what has brought you to my shores." Satisfied it would hold true, Sigourney turned and whisked the air by her ear as if summoning a stray whisper. "'Terrorist,' says the wind. 'Destined for the gallows,' says the rain." She lowered that hand, and stroked the black lacquered armrest like a cat itching to scratch. "You've come for *her*."

"I have," Dobs answered.

A gong sounded as the doors parted, and in stalked a woman wearing a gauzy gown of cobalt and amethyst, bold against rich brown skin dusted in a glimmering powder.

"Theydies and gentlethem," she said with a delicate roll of her hand before sinking into a curtsy. "Gertrude, the minx of Sparta3, dame of seduction and breaker of hearts, has arrived."

Nimah didn't have a single memory of Gertrude in dresses or silks, but somehow the warrior who'd wielded the ferocity of a goddess was just as fierce and powerful in a dress as she had been in boots and leather. Though she was all muscle and strength, her movements were sleek as a cat's and sensual as a full moon.

"This isn't a stage." Dobs rolled her eyes. "Cut the performance shit."

"The world's a stage, darling, and I am but a sun destined to shine upon it." Gertrude shimmied broad shoulders. "I'd say it's good to see you, Dobs, but that's a lie even I don't have the skill to pull off."

"You know you've missed me."

"Like a flare-up of herpes." But her teasing smile belied the harsh words.

Both women burst into laughter, and Dobs clasped her into a fast hug. "I forgot what a rude-ass bitch you are."

"Don't see how, it's conveniently listed right there in my name." Gertrude withdrew from the embrace with an arch look. "Darling, in all seriousness, who is hacking at your hair? We must find them and cut off their villainous hands immediately."

"Don't start."

FLIGHT OF THE SPARROW

"Listen, if your goal is to walk around looking like a connie fresh out the cellblock, well then you've hit the mark." Gertrude adjusted her shawl with a smirk that fell to Nimah. "And who is this adorable creature? My, she does have the look of . . . of . . . no. Could it be?" Crossing to Nimah, she pressed a soft hand against her cheek, eyes shining. "Little Sparrow, is that you?"

"Hello, Auntie G."

Gertrude burst out a booming laugh, drawing Nimah against her full chest and lifting her onto her toes. Warmth flooded Nimah as she sank into that embrace of spiced perfume and summer sun—a scent she knew and remembered well, and for a moment, she was a child again.

"Oh, my darling. My sweet little darling, how you've *grown!*" Sweeping away, Gertrude rounded her in a wide circle. "And in all the right places, too."

"Touching as this is, can we please refocus?" Dobs interrupted. "Captain Ro needs us."

Gertrude adjusted her shawl. "And you want our help?"

"Wouldn't dream of doing this without the old crew."

Sigourney swung a leg back across the arm of her throne. "Why should I go dashing about the void? I'm queen of Tortuga."

"The Sigourney I knew lived to taste gunmetal and blood, laughing as she blew STARs from the void."

"The devil in you speaks true." Midnight lips parted with a grin, her split tongue twisting in delight across canines filed to fanged points. "I shall call upon the Generals of Black to preside in my absence." Sigourney thumped a fist against her chest. "I will fly with you."

"Really?" Nimah tried to hold back the desperation, but it surged out of her like oxygen through a breached hull.

"I owe the captain my throne and every precious bone upon it."

Gertrude snorted and cut a glare to Sigourney. "You realize what Dobs is suggesting will result in all of us getting killed, yeah?"

"Better to die with a roar in our throats than a whimper on our lips." Sigourney spread her hands, flexed lithe muscle. "I was born into this world screaming and bloody—I shall go out the same."

"*Oi*, not everyone here has a burning death wish, Siggy." Gertrude adjusted her shawl. "I've got at least a dozen good years left in me, thank you very much, and I'd like to live them in relative style and comfort."

"To what end? Should Ro hang, the horns of war will sound across the void, howling for pirate blood." Sigourney set her hands on her narrow hips. "I wear the crown, but Ro is our true queen. It is she they have always feared. 'Tis not a matter of principle, but survival. We face our foe in the field, or be burnt to ashes in our ships."

"Fucking A." Dobs hiked a boot to the seat of the throne. "This isn't a storm we can wait to dry up and blow over. STARs landed on Sahara9 mere hours after we got to Chu."

"Blew up my house," Chu chimed in. "Shot me, for fuck's sake. Nearly killed my dog."

"And they'll come for the rest of us soon enough," Dobs finished.

"I have a business to run!" Gertrude snapped open a fan edged in lace, waved it imperiously. "A lucrative business with mouths that depend on me."

"I think your cogs can manage the devastating loss of your company for a few days."

Gertrude cut her eyes. "I'm talking about my *staff*, Dobs. I'm *needed* here."

"Captain needs you more." Dobs crossed her arms. "We owe her this. We all do."

"It's been fifteen years. *Fifteen*. What you're asking me to do is impossible."

"Far as I know only Gertrude can turn impossible into 'I'm possible.'" Dobs rounded on her with a cunning grin. "You're the void-whisperer. No one can read the stars like you. We need you to lead the way."

The proud line of Gertrude's stubborn shoulders wavered. She worked a nail between her teeth, then waved an airy hand. "Sod it. Yellow was never my color anyway. But if I'm going to drop my knickers and get dry shagged by the likes of you," she wagged an accusing finger at Dobs, "I won't do it for *free*."

"Fair." Dobs bounced a fist off her knee. "State your price."

"The boy."

"I would accept similar tribute," Sigourney purred. "Beautiful and broken, most preferred."

FLIGHT OF THE SPARROW   121

"I'm talking about the *reward*," Gertrude clarified with a disgusted shake of her head. "I've heard whispers that Cormack Shinoda's son was snatched by whomever blew up the Forum. A man like that will offer a staggering sum for the safe return of his son. We save Ro, and then turn our efforts to track down the boy—at which point *I*," she pressed a hand to her chest, "claim the entirety of the bounty."

"What's a licensed companion need with that many credits?"

"For starters, a ship. First-class, SIGA-grade, which will let me expand my clientele across the void. Named her *Lola*." She winked at Nimah. "Long story short, I've got a month to pay off my debts to the blackbooks. So if you want me, that's what it'll cost you."

All eyes bounced to Nimah.

"I'll make sure you get the money when this is over. I promise." A problem to be sure, considering Nimah had promised Maverick the same thing. But he wasn't here, and thankfully, no one else aside from Liselle was in the room when she made the arrangement. When the time came, she'd deal with the fallout. For now, they had to get up in the air, no matter the cost.

"All of it, little sparrow, on your word." Gertrude dropped her chin and arched a brow.

"All of it," Nimah agreed. "If . . . the queen doesn't object?"

Sigourney shrugged. "What need have I with the promise of gold? I am queen. 'Tis glory and bones I'm after."

"Then we're in accord." Dobs clapped her hands together. Pleased with the outcome.

Sigourney leapt atop her throne, one foot planted to the armrest, and loosed a cry, her fanged smile wide and fist thumping a hard beat against her chest. "Lo! Warriors of old, arise, arise and take to wing! Lo, do we charge, with shield to splinter and sword to sing. For wrath. For glory. Hail, Valkyries!" Fist raised high, she swept her red cape back from her shoulders, varnished bones rattling into a bloody puddle at her feet.

"To the void or Valhalla, only the brave may live forever!"

CHAPTER TWELVE

Apprehension pricked across Maverick's skin like the buzz of electricity, a sense of foreboding. You didn't survive a decade under a man like Hatchett without developing a keen sense of danger. Hatchett didn't suffer fools or forgive traitors kindly, and by now there was no way his capture had gone unreported. Maverick was on borrowed time; just how much remained to be seen, and he knew of only one clear way to find out.

The whisper network. Twelve links in a chain that stretched across the Inner Circle. As the eyes and ears of the void, little escaped their notice.

Maverick stopped outside a bar. Simple and ineffectual, that was the essence of the whispers' code. To go unnoticed. Except to those who knew where to look and how to find them. Maverick activated the black light on his wristdeck and waved it before him. A logo flashed across rust-colored brick. Three spikes linked at the base.

A soundwave.

Pushing open the teal door, paint weathered and flaking at the lightest touch, he rolled across the threshold and held up his hands as a pair of synth-guards stepped forward. "I'm unarmed," he said and waited patiently for them to run a body scan to confirm the statement true.

"Clear," the first one said, blank faced with only a single swiveling blue orb acting as an eye. The pair returned to their posts as a girl straightened from the counter, her brilliant pink eyes wide in a slender face, framed by the folds of her loose hijab.

"Oh, Mav—you stupid bastard."

"Good to see you, too, Neon."

The whispers were completely anonymous—their entire histories wiped clean by the best hackers in the void. Neon had been one of Hatchett's skinners, back when they were barely kids, but unlike the rest of them, she'd found a way out. She'd escaped.

Maverick was perhaps the only person in all the void who knew who she *really* was, and more importantly, what she'd run from.

"You really shouldn't have surfaced here." She rounded the bar top, hands on her hips, "And riding in the *Stormchaser*, no less."

"Heard about Tor12, eh?"

"Who fucking hasn't?" She tossed her hands. "Did you really think you could pull a job like that and he *wouldn't* find out? *You?* The kid he groomed to take over? That kind of insult can't stand. Hatchett's calling for your hide."

"Well, it was a straw deal," Maverick drummed his thumbs on his wheels. "He can have fifty percent of zero and we'll call it square."

Neon crossed her arms. "That's not how it works with skinners, Mav, and you know it."

"It was a setup," Maverick repeated, a little slower this time because apparently Neon had a hard time understanding. "No trade, no cut, no profit. Can't give him something I don't have."

"Doesn't change facts. The man is pure greed wrapped in flesh, but he's sparing no expense. There's serious credits on the table for whoever brings you to him still kicking."

Leaning forward, Maverick took Neon's hand. Squeezed. "Put a hold on the bounty. Bury it, Neon. All I need is two days, three tops, and then I'll have something he's always wanted."

"Giving him the *Stormchaser* won't be enough to pacify him. Not now." Neon retracted her hand. "I wish I could help you . . ."

The tingle of warning sharpened, itching down the back of Maverick's neck. A fuse running low. "You burning me, Neon?"

Neon scored her teeth across her bottom lip. "I'm sorry. You did this to yourself."

The beaded curtain swayed and Maverick had his gun drawn as a woman stepped out. Her military white jacket with navy slacks gave her away as upper brass, but it was her slanted bob of silver white hair highlighting the pulsing glow of HWKeyes that told Maverick who he was dealing with, and he was in deep shit. She arched a brow at Neon. "You were supposed to scan him for weapons."

Neon swallowed hard. "I did."

Amused, she pursed her lips. "Impressive."

"Chief Commander Wallace." Maverick raised his chin, lowered his gun.

"You know who I am, good. That saves us from wasting time with introductions." Her gaze narrowed on him with laser focus. Gauging his vitals and reflexes. She'd know his moves a half second before the signals in his brain reached his body to carry them out.

But he didn't need retrofits to know that even though she'd entered alone, there was bound to be an agent or two close by. Probably had him in thermal crosshairs. Even if he could somehow outmaneuver the chief commander, no way was he busting out past a team of STARs gone dark.

Relax. If she wanted you collared you would be. So if this wasn't a snare, then it had to be a negotiation, which meant she wanted something from him. The question was, what?

Wallace dragged out the chair facing him and sat down. "I want to make you a deal, Maverick. One I expect you won't walk away from."

"That supposed to be funny?"

Her eyes dipped to his wheels. "Poor choice of words. I apologize."

"How did you find us?" Maverick demanded. "This is a stronghold. Ruthlessly safeguarded."

"Hm." Wallace nodded. "You were tagged on Sahara9 with a hijacker called a TICK. It's part of our newgen line. Highly untraceable."

Maverick pressed a hand to his side and cursed. Of course. Nimah had scanned the wound, but newgen SIGA tech was too sophisticated for anything aboard the *Stormchaser*.

"Now." Wallace linked her hands, threading her gloved fingers. "Before I begin, you should know I have several ships, just out of range so your navsystem wouldn't detect them, waiting for my signal. I could take you all down right now, but that won't help me get what I need."

FLIGHT OF THE SPARROW 125

"Nimah," he answered. "You want to stop her from rescuing her grandmother."

Wallace laughed. "If it was that simple, I'd have swooped in the moment you docked in Tortuga. No, I'm not here to stop you. In fact, I want you to succeed."

Maverick frowned. *Now this just got interesting.* "Why?"

Wallace weighed the question carefully. "Captain Rosco was military once. She knows our methods and was trained to withstand them, therefore interrogation won't work. Not fast enough, at least. Unfortunately my superiors disagree with my assessment. Only she knows the whereabouts of Jonothan Shinoda, and you're a skinner." Her golden eyes brightened. "You've been trained to earn trust and extract highly sensitive information with ease. Therefore, after she's rescued, I need you to get her to reveal his location and report back to me as soon as you have it. Once I have him secured, we will then collar the entire Valkyrie crew."

"Why would I do that?"

"Because we both want something not easily obtained, and I see no reason why we can't mutually benefit from an alliance." She smiled. "Facial reconstruction, cornea replacement. Cyberspine. Risky procedures."

Maverick tried to loosen the muscles in his jaw and neck, but they locked tight as a bed of hardened concrete. There was only one sure way to disappear off the grid—it took more than identity tags and records. You actually had to become someone else.

No one knew of his plans, not even Boomer, but there was no point asking how she figured it out, or lying. Even with all his training, she'd see right through him. "So what?"

"Painful," she commented, "even with the best of Inner Circle surgeons. Can't imagine how much agony a blackbook hack-job might cause, but that will fall second to the agony you'll endure at Hatchett's hands."

"Your concern for my welfare is touching."

"I'm not your mother, Maverick. I don't have a concerned bone in my body when it comes to you. What I do have is a vested interest in a possible ally. Help me get Jonothan Shinoda, and not only will I expunge your record and give you a clean slate with new identity tags—the works—but I'll personally guarantee you walk again. With your *own* legs. Let's call it a bonus."

126   FALLON DEMORNAY

That shut him up cold. For the first three years after his accident, Maverick had chased down every lead he could to get his hands on a blackbook cyberspine. Not only were they insanely expensive, they also came with the risk of death during surgery and even then, most transplants spent a lifetime in pain, relying heavily on opiates just to cope.

Wallace was offering a brand-new identity *and* premium-grade restoration, healing every broken bone, every damaged cell. The process was expensive and even the wealthy were limited to two rounds—extending their lifespan by fifty years. The closest they'd come to achieving immortality.

Forget cyberspines. He'd be as good as new. Better. So why was he hesitating? A lifetime in the ass end of the void had taught him to do whatever it took to survive, but apprehension gnawed on him all the same.

"What happens to Nimah?"

Wallace scored her tongue along the edge of her teeth. "She made her choices. My offer extends only to you."

"And if I say no?"

"Then I collar everyone right now and ship you to Hatchett myself." Wallace tilted her head, white hair swinging gently. "So. Do I have your assurance of cooperation?"

Maverick swallowed a rough lump of glass and guilt. ". . . Yes."

Nimah stood at the edge of the mooring dock flanked by a sea of clouds stretched like a soft blanket of golden tipped cotton. And while nauseating panic wanted her to whirl away to the safety of walls, something else almost urged her to take another step forward, to surrender to oblivion and fall. But it was the weight of the pendant around her throat that drew her back to the solid structure of her body and pushed her away from that precarious edge until she'd retreated to a comfortable distance. One where she no longer felt the sickness of terror coiling through her belly, turning the bones in her legs to water.

Nimah had quite seriously for a moment imagined herself plummeting, arms spread, a bird about to take flight. A startling thought, given everyone had finally agreed to join in this foolish venture to rescue her grandmother, most of them for nothing. She should be elated right now.

Brimming with joy, with positivity and hope. So why wasn't she? Why did she feel the cool kiss of despair sealing her fate with doom?

"You alright, kid?"

"Yeah. I'm great."

"Coulda fooled me." Widening her stance, Dobs clapped a hand to Nimah's shoulder. "Ah. 'Bout fucking time."

Breaking the surface of clouds, the *Stormchaser* shone in the sky, hull metal brightened by the glare of the late-day sun as she swooped in to moor at the Queen of Bones' private dock.

Hatch opening, Boomer ambled out with a devil-may-care grin, brawny arms crossed over his chest. "That was some razor flying if I do say so myself."

"Razor? Try dull as hundred-year-old driftwood." Dobs cackled. "You circled the mooring thrice like you needed keys to see three feet in front of you."

"Sun was in my eye."

"You got eyes at the back of your skull? Sun's at your six. Not your twelve."

Boomer thrust out an affronted bottom lip. "Yeah, well I ain't no damn pilot, am I?"

"Fucking A. Speaking of the devil, any word from our *actual* pilot?"

Boomer clapped a hand to the back of his neck and rubbed hard. "Uh—on his way. Got tied up some at a hack-shop scouting for parts for his chair."

"Hm." Dobs nodded, but the pinched lines around her mouth said everything Nimah already suspected—she didn't buy it for shit.

"Mumbles make it back to the ship okay?" Nimah asked, changing the subject.

Boomer stiffened his bottom lip with a nod. "Yeah, got her watching toons on a holoscreen."

"Good, well we got some gear to board." Dobs waved toward the stack of crates offloaded from the dock sidecar. "You can help load the cargo while we wait for our pilot." Boomer scowled but otherwise marched off to do as instructed. "You ain't concerned about that?"

"Everything's fine."

"He's been gone longer than an hour, kid."

"I said everything's fine."

Dobs paused to take a long, deep drag of smoke before dropping her cigarette and crushing it under the toe of her boot. "You know how a skinbag skins their mark?" She removed the flask from inside her cropped jacket, same faded green as her jumpsuit, and unscrewed the cap to guzzle. "They don't swoop in like a ghost—they become your best friend," she continued, fumes of Seawater and ash wafting off her breath. Even outside it was strong enough to make Nimah's eyes water and her stomach flip in a dizzy knot. "Get real close-like. Smile with devilish charm, and to earn your trust they give and give until that's all you can see, but while they give with one hand—they take with the other. And they take it all." Capping the flask, Dobs tapped her nose and winked. "Weather eye, kid."

Nimah shook her head, clearing it of the hazy doubt as she followed Dobs aboard the ship, settling her focus only as far as she could see. One step after the other, as her grandmother would say, and never set a foot in the unknown without keeping the other firmly rooted in the familiar. Be present, be grounded, focus on what is in your control.

That's all she could do.

"Piss and vinegar." Chu planted her hands on her hips and scowled at the pile of crates and chests growing in the center of the cargo hold like a stacked mountain. "We rob a brothel? What's all this being hauled on deck for?"

"These are my personal effects." Gertrude sashayed up the gangway and into the cargo hold, waving an iridescent fan of feathers that matched the neon tips of her curls.

"Effects?" Chu scowled. "We're off to rescue our captain, not stage an Inner Circle burlesque tour."

"We all have our weapons for war." Gertrude swatted her fan in Chu's face. "These happen to be mine."

Wedging herself between the bickering pair, Dobs caught Chu by the scruff of her neck before she could pounce like a snapping Chihuahua. All swinging elbows and colorful curses. "D'you really have to push her buttons before we're even voidborne?"

"Can't help it when she makes it so easy. Oi! Careful, darling, careful, that one has my delicates," she called out as Boomer heaved down a trunk, nearly dropping it on Nimah's toe.

"Delicates?" He grunted. "Weighs like you packed a body. Not silks."

FLIGHT OF THE SPARROW 129

Gertrude's eyes glimmered with seductive mystery. "Maybe I have, darling."

"Are we about ready to take off?" Nimah asked, assessing the timer on her wristdeck. The delay on Sahara9 had cost them any buffer she'd allocated for contingency. From here on out, there was no margin for error, and a cold sweat gathered at the base of her neck.

"Just about." Chu scratched at the protruding line of her collarbone. "As soon as we get this mountain of crap secured. Figure we can have it moved over to crew quarters once we're voidborne."

"Heard." Dobs jerked a thumb over her shoulder. "Then let's get this strapped and convene on the bridge."

Twenty minutes later, the crew gathered around the navigation console just as Maverick whisked onto the bridge. At his approach, Sigourney bared gleaming fangs. "You lost, boy?"

"He's not lost, Siggy. He's our pilot." Dobs snapped the cap on her zippo and sucked hard on a fresh cigarette. "Took you long enough. Was 'bout to send out a search party."

"Dense crowds make for slow maneuvering," he offered by way of explanation, fingers tapping the sides of his wheels in a lazy, unaffected rhythm.

If there was anything to hide, his expression gave absolutely nothing away, and Nimah couldn't tell if that fact calmed or unsettled her.

"What are you, twenty if a day?" Gertrude skimmed an appraising gaze from head to toe. "Barely old enough to shave and already riding first chair."

"I'm Maverick." His smile took on the cutting edge of scored pride.

"Well, now. Quite the little rebel. Top eight of the most wanted, was it?"

"Seven."

"And what about this darling chap?" Gertrude turned dark brown eyes to Boomer and to Nimah's surprise, he glowed like a smitten cog.

"Uh, they call me Boomer, ma'am. Munitions. And number fourteen last I checked."

"Lovely." Gertrude slapped the length of her closed fan against Dobs's forearm. "Just what we need to fly under the radar."

Dobs boosted from her seat. "Well, since we're all getting acquainted, shall we continue with introductions, ladies?"

"Nah, we're good," Boomer answered. "Ya'll are fucking billies!" Boomer cast dreamy eyes around the console. Even Maverick had a tempered expression of awe beneath his stoic exterior.

Not surprising, given they would've been weaned on the grand tales of the Valkyries. And now here they stood, fully assembled for the first time in fifteen years, weathered and wrinkled and more than a decade past their prime. The sight of them should've been little more than a hilarious tableau, but Nimah was hard pressed to admit that despite their baffling extremes, a vibrating current of strength and ferocity clung to each of the women. They were legendary, still.

Chu blinked up at Dobs. "Fuck's a billy?"

"Y'know." Boomer rolled his eyes with a grin as Mumbles spun in her chair, chanting "billies" under her breath, buzzing her *b*s the way some would roll their *r*s. "Billies. Like goats."

Chu bristled. "Did he really just call me a—?"

"He means 'greatest of all time,' darling." Gertrude tapped her arm. "The youth are bringing back some choice relics."

"Enough." Dobs clapped her hands. "You're up, kid."

Sighing, Nimah ran her hands over her tightly coiffed hair drawn in a regulation bun—the same as every other day. Determined to remain a cadet to the core, even if the uniform she'd boarded the vessel with now fit like a shrunken sock. "According to newscasts, Captain Roscoe's trial is delayed while the Crown Justice is reviewing the case—but that's not true." Nimah bounced a fist against the console. "The verdict's already been rendered by SIGA, who are transporting her to Hollow Point."

"How can you be sure?" Gertrude asked.

"Because I was told as much by the chief commander before I was expelled." And saying those words brought back the bitter sting of the axe resting on her neck. "SIGA wants this dealt with quickly," Nimah continued, "but misdirecting the public allows for a clear transport window so if anyone wanted to interfere, they'd be too late. But more importantly, this gives them time to extract information surrounding the whereabouts of Jonothan Shinoda without causing public upset."

Dobs kissed her teeth. "What's our deficit?"

FLIGHT OF THE SPARROW 131

"She was likely shipped out at least twelve hours before her capture statement was issued to the press," Nimah answered.

"Long enough for the ion trail to fade, making their course impossible to detect. And without the origin point," Gertrude crossed her arms with a grimace, "that complicates matters significantly."

"We don't need the origin, just the destination," Nimah interjected.

"Only STARs agents and SIGA defense officials know where Hollow Point is situated, Sparrow." Gertrude scoffed. "Surely you don't think we have the ability to hack into a tightly encrypted defense network from this old boat?"

"We don't need to. I've been there."

All heads swiveled to Nimah.

"When?" Dobs demanded.

"When I was a child." Nimah took a sobering breath, gathering herself, before she told them her story—about the *Avenger* stalling in deepvoid, and her nearly dying in the lifeboat. "I was revived at Hollow Point and held there until fully recovered. A major general happened to be touring the facility and assessed me. That's how I was brought to the Academy."

Chu's lips spread from a pucker to a grin. "You got the keys?"

"I memorized them," Nimah confessed. "I thought . . . well, I'd already been snatched once and at the time I didn't know who these people were, where I was going, or what they wanted from me. And Grandmother always said never set a foot in the unknown—"

"—Without leaving the other rooted in the familiar," Dobs finished, stubbing out her cigarette.

"The STARship will take the long way around. It's time lost in travel, but they won't transport her across main thoroughfares. Not with us in the wind."

"Why not thread?" Chu worked her chin between her thumb and forefinger. "Seems a wasted effort when you can spit her across the circle in half a second."

"There's no Eye at any military stronghold," Nimah answered. "While they do make for expeditious travel, breach one and all are compromised. Hollow Point, much like Tortuga, remains the fortress that it is because its coordinates are so closely guarded. Our best point of interception is here." She swiped her finger, marking the holomap.

Gertrude eased forward and her dark eyes, haloed in glittering gold shadow, narrowed. "Plenty of cover amidst the castoff asteroid debris from the RIM, and any lingering radiation from the abandoned mines should throw off their radar."

"Exactly. Once we're in position, we come in underneath and fly in tandem, provided Chu can manage to put the *Stormchaser* in stealth. Then we breach the base stabilizers."

"How are we supposed to do that with its shields up?" Chu commented.

"By wearing STARs-authenticated nanosuits. All nanites are replications of a single organism, like cells in a body—so that they all recognize each other. It's how agents avoid friendly fire in the field, and it allows ejected agents to bypass shields for their safety. We can't fake them. It's got to be real or the plan won't work."

"These are not items we can pluck off the blackbooks," Sigourney commented. "Alas, even Tortuga has its limits."

"I know. Which is why we need to stop here." Nimah touched the holoscreen and it whipped back in full zoom on a lunar outpost in quad nine of zone seven. "This outpost is manned by a small base. Everything we'll need is there. Electronics. Weapons. Ammo. And of course, nanosuits."

"Good thing we've got a pair of skinners on hand." Dobs winked at Maverick and Boomer. "This should be child's play for you."

"If we had a month to study specs and gain a point of access—sure," Maverick agreed. "Not a few hours."

Dobs clapped a hand on his shoulder. "I have faith you'll pull through."

"Hold on, Sparrow." Gertrude leaned over the console. "If your keys are accurate, based on time of departure, even if we took off right this second—we can't catch them. The math isn't mathing."

"If we were to follow from behind, yes, you're right." Nimah swiped the screen and the holomap scaled back, showing the entire Inner Circle with two glowing triangles marking the *Stormchaser* and the projected location of the STARship. "But if we take a straight path across, we will reach this point several hours ahead of them."

"Across? Are you daft?" Gertrude scoffed. "The circle is rife with void traffic *and* SIGA voidship sensors. Far too many variables and points of

FLIGHT OF THE SPARROW 133

impact for anyone to chart a course clean through. Pirates sail deep for a reason, Sparrow."

Nimah knew it was a complicated run, one Gertrude had every right to be concerned about. Hardburning required a very specific chain of coordinates to be approved by the ship's navsystem before it could be launched, and even if accepted there was always a risk of contingency error. To make matters worse, their flight plan would have to be unregistered by void-traffic control, so the possibility of cross-impact with another ship was high.

She'd seen a phenomenon once in a virtual museum, of two bullets fired from enemy guns during an ancient war that had struck mid-air, one bullet impaling the other. A freak oddity. If the *Stormchaser* was off a fraction of a degree in one of a thousand different directions—with minimal opportunity to stop or course-correct—the results could be catastrophic.

Maverick's instincts would not only have to be good, they'd have to be flawless.

"It's crazy. But the kid's right." Dobs puffed a thick stream of smoke from a cigarette she nearly sucked down to the filter in one drag. "What's our window?"

"Sixteen hours." Nimah swiped away the thick ashen cloud with a cough. "Eighteen, max."

"How many of those to get to the outpost?"

Gertrude worked her thumb in a slow, hard circle across her palm. "Six, give or take."

"Heard. Gertrude, plot the course. The rest of you," Dobs clapped her hands, "best get some sleep while you can."

CHAPTER THIRTEEN

Even though she was exhausted, sleep refused to come easy when every shudder and groan of the *Stormchaser* gliding through the void woke Nimah from dreams where haunting memories lurked in distant shadows, waiting to pull her in like hands from the grave.

Don't be afraid . . .

Changing into workout thermals, Nimah went for a run, weaving through the *Stormchaser*'s passages and corridors like the track at the Academy. The track lights in the grated floor pulsed like a heartbeat and it soothed her own to match that steady rhythm.

So much had changed in less than a day. With each minute that ticked by, her old life ran through her fingers like sand, and the more she struggled to hold onto it, the faster it slipped away. Soon it would be gone. Soon there would be no coming back—not unless she located Jonothan Shinoda and the true culprits responsible for the Forum attack. And the conflict of it warred inside her head, battering against the delicate nerves of her temples until she thought she was going to fracture from the anxiety and stress. So much at stake . . . could she really see this through? And even if she did, could such sins ever truly be forgiven?

It all sounded insurmountable, but it was too late to turn back now.

The only way out was forward.

On her third lap, she eased from a jog into a cooling walk. Rounding the corner, she entered the kitchen and found Chu scowling at some fixed point on the wall. Her shoulders were hunched and the notches of her spine pressed against the thin material of her white tank. Cargos were

FLIGHT OF THE SPARROW 135

belted high on her narrow waist, sagged around boxy hips and cuffed over matchstick ankles.

Uncapping a canister of water, Nimah guzzled deeply and did a quick look around for the shaggy mop of black and white. Loyal and faithful as a shadow, and never more than a pace away from Chu's side since they left Sahara9. "Where's Dog?"

"Left him behind." Chu's lips vanished into a thin line. "Some shop-keep took a shine to 'im and well . . . it's for the best. Got no place for a flea-bitten bonebag 'board this boat," she finished with a watery sniff, and whisked her bifocals atop her head so she could slice her fingers beneath the bags of her eyes.

Lowering the canister to the counter, Nimah reached for her shoulder. "You alright?"

"Just a bit of grit. *Ahhh!*" Chu swatted her away. "Fuck it." Stalking from the kitchen, she disappeared into the corridor with a grunt, knees creaking about as loudly as the rest of her.

Finished with her water, Nimah was about to kick back into a run when the crackle of a punchy song caught her ear, and she followed it toward the crew quarters where it streamed from an open cabin.

Dobs sat at the foot of her ruthlessly made bunk, privacy screen raised so that streams of light bled across the viewport like rain. Eyes closed as if meditating, a cigarette hung from her lips with an inch of ash that tumbled into her lap. "Something I can do for you, kid?" She cracked open an eye.

"How did you know I was standing here?"

Dobs tapped a finger to her temple. "You think too damn loud."

"Can't sleep?"

"Never do before a job. Guess you can't either."

"Not really, no."

Dobs gestured to the table. "Come. Sit."

A snore rent the air and Nimah hesitated as Mumbles, curled up on the top bunk, swung onto her side, knees tucked to her chest like a small child.

"Don't worry. She won't wake. Gave her a sedative to help her rest after all the recent excitement."

Nimah eased a hip onto the edge of the table. "I'm glad she's alright. The way she freaked out on Tortuga worried me."

"Been happening more frequent these days. Was on her own in the ward for so long sometimes she can't tell reality from delusion. They weren't treating her, heard? Just left her to rot with her broken memories. That's why I got her out." Dobs paused to sip from her flask between drags of smoke. "Soon as I touched ground again." Her head swayed, weighing her thoughts before she added, "After Ro disbanded us, Mumbles and I stuck together for a spell, but then I had to go deep-void for a job for a few years, and then it took a couple more for me to track where she'd been cast off to while I was gone."

"Why?" Nimah circled her arms around her knees, intrigued.

Soot-gray brows flattened over shocking blue eyes. "Why didn't I leave her in a padded room, arms and legs tied down with only fragmented memories for company? Because no one deserves that sort of hell. Least of all her." Dobs skimmed her teeth across her bottom lip, then lifted her gaze to the slumbering rise and fall of Mumbles's back, snoring face down into the pillow. "She's still in there, kid, and one day I'm gonna help her find her way back out."

A sharp jolt rocked the ship, pitching it hard to one side before deftly righting itself—too fast for the gravity stabilizers to react and hold the *Stormchaser* steady.

If Nimah hadn't caught herself in time the jarring momentum would've pitched her head over heels out the door. "What was that?" But her startled question was quickly answered as a glowing body swam outside the length of the viewport, at least twenty feet long.

"Negsharks." Dobs blew out a sharp stream of smoke. "A pod's been following us for the last hour, riding our thermals."

"Negs?" Glowing beasts that shimmered like iridescent stardust with six fathomless black eyes on either side of their flat heads. They were plentiful once, this side of the void, but their numbers had faded over the years. She'd never seen any this close before, outside of a simulation. And simulations didn't do them justice. "What are they doing?"

"Not sure." Dobs tapped the unlit end of a fresh cigarette against her thigh. "Don't usually catch them this far out of their waters. Drawn to prime, heard? It's how mining companies used to know where to dig back in the day. But when their habitats are bled dry, they tend to wander. Maybe they sensed the prime in our fuel

FLIGHT OF THE SPARROW 137

cells and came sniffing, though can't say we're carrying enough to be of interest."

Another glistening body slithered by, and Nimah caught the slow passing of eyes and a jagged smile. "Should we be worried?"

"Nah. Pretty harmless, unless you went for a spacewalk." Dobs smirked up at Nimah. "Just be thankful it ain't a kraken. Now there's a beast of the seas born of a foul mood. Saw one large enough to tear the *Stormchaser* apart as if it were made of paper." A soft cackle eked out of her, and Nimah couldn't tell if Dobs was spinning tales to freak her out, or if she was being serious. "Don't worry. We'll lose them soon enough. Negs don't have stamina for the long haul."

"I'm not worried." But another jostling bang to the hull betrayed the lie, shooting her stomach into her throat and her heart to her knees as Nimah squeezed her eyes shut with a panicked breath. Her hand clutched the pendant tucked under her bodysuit.

"Heard Gertrude's gonna get you all gussied up," Dobs tossed out. "Make you into a bona fide companion."

"Yeah." Nimah bounced the toe of her boot to the metal leg of the table, hard enough for the blunt pain to spike across her nerves, and tried to focus her breathing back to a normal rate. Dobs was distracting her, and she was grateful for it. "She's putting together disguises for me and Maverick—part of the plan he's worked out."

Ash tumbled into a chalky anthill on the roughened material of Dobs's jumpsuit. "Just . . . don't let your guard down with him. No matter what you might think, skinbags can't be trusted. 'Specially not one of Hatchett's." She went silent as she lit a fresh cigarette.

"So you keep telling me." Nimah waited for her to continue, but more didn't come. "What's the history there? Between him and my grandmother?"

Dobs exhaled long and slow. "You sure you wanna know?"

Nodding, Nimah settled in closer, hands on her knees. "It's relevant information."

"Well, guess it started back when we were given our first run deep-void. Met Ro back in training, and she was barely a day older than you when we joined our platoon, but even then Ro had a way about her, heard? Just bred for command and control. More than a few senior officers were saluting *her*, by the end." A snuffling laugh leaked from Dobs, and the sound brought a tender smile to Nimah's lips.

There was love there. Strong and steadfast. And it warmed her just as much as it hurt.

"After eighteen months' hard sailing, we got caught in a nebula storm that pushed us off course and forced us to shelter on a rogue—a planet not governed by SIGA. Damage sustained in the emergency landing kept us grounded and we'd only just set up a base when the locals captured us. Ro had managed to send out an SOS before our capture, but the response . . . well, apparently we weren't worth the effort."

"Locals?" Nimah frowned. "The planet was . . . inhabited?"

"Yeah. By a humanoid society far more advanced than ours." Dobs grinned. "Fucking wild."

"How long were you stuck there?" Nimah whispered, still trying to take it all in. They'd seen alien life in the void—from negsharks to krakens—but a world-inhabiting civilization? Not so much. Not yet. Until now, apparently.

"Six years." Dobs cleared her throat with a bitter grunt. "Not gonna lie, almost gave up thinking we'd ever sail the void again. But never underestimate the greed of bureaucratic assholes out to deepen their pockets. Guess SIGA decided to take a closer look at the planet, ran specs or whatever, and realized it was a rich cache of resources. In particular a mineral that proved to be a remarkable energy source unlike anything we'd ever seen. Stronger than prime. A battalion was sent under the guise of trade negotiations, but Ro saw through it. SIGA doesn't ask, heard? They *take*. She knew it was an extermination coming, so she rallied the indigenous. They might've lived peacefully, but they had the skills and weapons to fight back. To *win*, even."

"So what happened?"

Dobs angled her cigarette, stared at the line of smoke dancing above the blazing end. "Not sure. Somehow the planet's defenses failed and SIGA launched a pre-emptive assault. Came in hot. Real hot. We held strong for as long as we could, but when it became apparent the war was lost, the indigenous leaders—knowing what their tech was capable of in the wrong hands—did the only thing they could and deployed a devastating weapon, leaving nothing for SIGA to come in and reap. Just like

FLIGHT OF THE SPARROW 139

that." Dobs snapped her fingers and the sound shot like blaser-fire between Nimah's ears. "Planet destroyed and an entire civilization eradicated in minutes. A hollow victory. We barely got off-world in time, and Mumbles never spoke straight after that."

"From the shock?"

"Nah." Dobs sucked hard on the final dregs of tobacco. "She took a hard knock to the head. Fell nearly three stories during the assault. Miracle she survived at all." Stubbing out her cigarette against the sole of her boot, Dobs flicked the butt across the room and it bounced off the riveted wall and into the growing mountain of the ashtray.

"Stripped of his brass, Hatchett turned to the underbelly of crime, where he'd already been slithering about. As for Ro, while gazing out over the desiccated remains of what was once a brilliant people—it struck her the planet didn't have a name. Indigenous just called it home. So she gave it one. Valhalla. That was the day we turned our backs on SIGA. That was the day we became Valkyries. But it was RIMers who dubbed her La Voz, because she was a warrior and no one could tell her shit. When Ro spoke, everyone listened. That's power. That's respect. The voice of the people, kid."

Restless fingers beat against Nimah's thigh, an impatient tattoo that accelerated with her rising temper. "I know I should be proud. All her great deeds. Heroic efforts. Indira Rosco—a brave woman who cared about the welfare of others but didn't think twice before abandoning her own blood? And here I am shooting across the void with a motley crew of geriatric pirates and skinner fugitives—I've blown up my whole life to save someone who didn't even want me." Nimah scoffed with a bitter laugh. "I must be a complete moron."

Eyeing her coolly, Dobs exhaled in a heavy stream of smoke and irritation. "This endless pity parade of yours is getting real tired, heard?"

Nimah sputtered around an affronted gasp. "Excuse me?"

"So you got left. You ain't the only one," Dobs retaliated, her tone forceful as a slap. "Ro shucked us all, and believe me it hurt just as much. We were family, too."

Guilt boiled through her like acid and Nimah wanted to melt into the floor, to disappear. Dobs was right, and it was stupidly selfish for

140 FALLON DEMORNAY

her to think she was the only one who'd been hurt by her grand-mother's actions.

"You know what your problem is?" Dobs jabbed two fingers at her, fresh cigarette wedged between chipped, red-painted nails. "You're too busy worrying whether the glass is half empty or half full when you should just be fucking grateful you got a glass to drink from. Make your peace with the past, kid, and move on."

Nimah's eyes dipped to the toes of her boots, and she struggled to hold back the cold wash of shame threatening to spill out of her in tears. "I've been so angry for so long . . ." A whispered confession. "I don't know who I'll be without it. I don't know how to let it go."

"Like this." Dobs raised her hands gently toward the sky as if cradling a baby bird that tumbled out of the nest. "Go," she crooned. "Fly away. You're free."

Blinking her eyes clear, Nimah swiped at her nose. "What are you doing?"

"Letting go of my last fuck." Sparking a lighter with a cagey grin, Dobs lit her third cigarette. "You should try it, kid. Life's easier when you got none left in you to give."

"Thought you said you weren't a comedian?"

"Fucking A," Dobs cackled, but the laugh faded into a wheeze—exploded into a cough. She stiffened, eyes wide as it punched through her chest, and was quickly chased by another—and another. On her knees, Dobs pitched over, red-faced and hacking behind cupped hands, so hard and fast she couldn't catch a breath before the next one seized her.

"Dobs!" Nimah caught her before she face-planted and helped lower Dobs to the ground. "What do I do? You're turning *purple!*"

Dobs slapped at her chest, but the fit was too violent for her to get a grip. Understanding, Nimah rummaged through her breast pockets until she found a slender pipe. Bringing it to her lips, she activated a button and Dobs sucked hard, inhaling a vaporized shot that fired three times.

Dobs jerked straight, like a fish yanked on a line, head up and back arched, twitching violently—mouth agape and eyes wheeling for what felt like a year before a gasp tore out of her. Loud as a scream. But with each haggard breath that followed, the color in her cheeks eased from a vicious red to a livid pink.

FLIGHT OF THE SPARROW 141

"Fuck . . ." Dobs reclined against the wall, shoulders shaking, and swiped a hand across her mouth, smearing red across her chin—too wet to be lipstick. "That was a bad one."

"What is it?" Nimah asked, still perched on her knees. Almost too afraid to move. "What's wrong? What do you need? Please . . . tell me what to do?"

Overhead, Mumbles sighed and rough snores wafted from the top bunk.

"Nothing." She patted Nimah's trembling hand, resolute. "I'm dying, kid. Got a few months left in me. Likely less, the way I've been smoking this shit." Withdrawing another cigarette from a crushed pack, she placed the filtered end between her lips and sparked the lighter with an unsteady hand.

"Maybe—you should stop?"

"Won't make a lick of difference at this point. Damage done. Seawater does a pretty good job of keepin' the worst of it at bay." She wiggled the flask Nimah never saw her without. "Clears my esophagus and helps with the migraines. At least I can enjoy a buzz before I'm drowning in blood and phlegm." Dobs sucked hard and the tip flared orange—a dying sun slowly fading out in a blaze of glory.

"That's what this is." Nimah slumped next to Dobs, hands folded uselessly in her lap. "This is your swan song. Your last adventure."

Narrowed eyes swiveled to her, and after a beat, Dobs nodded gently. "Didn't want to lay up in a bed watching death creep toward me like a fucking ghost. This is how I'm meant to go." She gestured around them. "Guns blazing in a final fuck you before I'm stuffed in an incinerator and reduced to an ounce of cubed ash. Few pirates live to see their graying years, heard? It's a hard life. The void ain't for the weak."

No, it wasn't. Which was perhaps why Nimah always struggled to find her place in it.

"Mumbles will need someone when I'm . . . The crew is the only family she's got."

"I'll take care of her."

"And it's best if we don't . . ."

"They won't know. This stays with us."

Dobs gave a terse nod. Tears gleamed, trapped in the corners of stubborn eyes, sharp as broken glass, but before they could betray her and

142 **FALLON DEMORNAY**

fall, she boosted to her feet. "Gonna put the boot to Gertrude's ass. See what's taking so damn long," she muttered and stomped away, not with temper but with a purpose Nimah came to recognize as innately her. It was just the way she moved. Heavy and rough.

A pirate to the bone.

A Valkyrie to the end.

"You really need to sit still, darling, unless you want to look like an abstract painting."

Nimah's eyes watered beneath the glare of a hovering ring light. Tucked away on the communal deck, the lounge had been commandeered into Gertrude's "studio," given it had room to accommodate her racks of costumes and clothing, but also the best lighting—which, according to Gertrude, was *essential* for makeup.

Here, metal flooring gave way to hardwood against riveted alloy walls, with a long trestle table—also made of wood—surrounded by ad-hoc chairs overtop a woven rug and a swaying pendant light. Beyond the table, a length of viewport overlooked the stern of the ship, and opposite it, a seating area of plush couches and sectionals with cases of books—some made with *real* paper.

"Don't mind me." Chu scuttled into the kitchen and yanked a sealed cube from the fridge as Mumbles twirled the room in stomping circles with swaths of silk and ropes of gold necklaces, but for all her glee, she was surprisingly gentle with Gertrude's treasures. And Nimah caught the steady way Gertrude watched her, the corners of her lips lifting in a tender smile.

"What was she like before her accident?"

"Mumbles? Shockingly reticent."

"Which is why she and Dobs got along like pigs in shit," Chu scoffed.

"Indeed, darling. Though she also took a shine to our dear captain, not surprisingly. Don't think there's a soul alive who wasn't half in love with Indira Roscoe."

It took every ounce of Nimah's self-control not to roll her eyes. Overhead, Boomer grunted as he yanked an axe from a target on the wall. He and Sigourney had been at it for hours, throwing knives, darts, and now axes with her coaching him along the way, guiding his

FLIGHT OF THE SPARROW 143

technique. And Boomer, if his raucous laughter and shouting were any indication, was in his absolute glory.

Gertrude swept more color across Nimah's cheeks. "There. I think we're on to something now." And, with a flick of her wrist, a holomirror appeared between them.

Nimah scowled at a face she barely recognized. Sapphire shadow weighed down her eyes, smoked in black and framed with obscenely long lashes that were liable to start a hurricane and winking with lights at the tips. Shimmering powder, pale as moondust, accented the curve of bronzed cheeks and the fullness of her lips saturated in glossy plum.

"Well?"

"It's too *much.*"

"Dear, sweet, clueless child. I'll have you know that this is a *daytime* look."

Scrunching the length of a gossamer sleeve, Nimah raised it to her cheek. "Can't I just wipe some—?"

"*Oi!*" Gertrude brandished a warning finger like a sword. "Touch my masterpiece and risk losing the offending hand."

Defeated, Nimah dropped her hands into her lap. "I don't see why I have to be a companion."

"Because thanks to the Our Bodies, Our Choice Reparations Act of '099, companion licenses aren't regulated by any governing faction, and given our recent escapades we don't want them looking too closely at you or your documentation." Gertrude preened before the holomirror, extended to full-length with a snap. "Cheer up, little Sparrow, sex workers are well-received, even at official outposts. You'll be treated like a queen."

"But why do *I* have to go?"

"I can't very well travel alone. An experienced courtesan *always* has a coven."

"Can't Dobs or Chu—?"

"Dobs would have to be strangled first, and don't think the notion didn't tempt me," Gertrude interrupted, earning a smirk from Nimah. "And as for Chu . . ." She flounced her cap of dark curls—wide fat ringlets tipped with vibrant pink that matched her corset and heels. "I'm good, darling, but no amount of polish could ever account for her lack of refinement."

FALLON DEMORNAY

Perched at the table, Chu burped around a mouthful of rehydrated rice and stewed lumps of processed protein.

"See? Now stop making that face. You'll be as wrinkled as Chu's left tit before you're forty if you keep it up."

"Go pose in front o' the mirror some more, ya duck-kneed dung-munchin' crap sack!"

"Do you always have to be so mean to each other?"

"Oh, pay us no mind, darling. Insults are our love language." Gertrude dabbed more shimmer at the corners of her eyes. "Chu isn't happy unless she's miserable."

That should've made her smile, laugh even, but nothing was wrenching Nimah from her dark mood. How could it, when every second brought her closer to a line she didn't want to cross?

A strong finger hooked under her chin, notching it up until she was met with a pair of discerning brown eyes. "What's the matter, Sparrow?"

"You wouldn't understand."

"Oh, I think I might surprise you." Gertrude lowered to the stool, crossed a leg, and propped her chin on her fist. "Try me."

Nimah sighed. Shifted in her seat. "I've trained for years to protect and serve. This base . . . it's the sort of outpost I would've been deployed to after graduating. It's hard to accept that in order to protect my dreams, I have to defy everything I know and believe in."

"Guess it never occurred to you that to get what you want, you'd have to get your hands dirty." Chu glared at them from across the table, bifocals resting on the tip of her nose.

Nimah skimmed a hand across her arm. "Not this dirty. No." Not when she was traveling with a ship full of women who made their livelihood spitting in the face of SIGA authority.

"Typical." Finished with her food, Chu wiped her hands on her cargos and shrugged. "Quit bellyaching and woman up. Everyone's got a part to play. You do yours."

"Chulita!"

"Don't snap at me for saying what you were thinking."

"Why don't you go back to degreasing engines and leave the pep talk to me, yeah? Pay her no mind, Sparrow," Gertrude added as Chu waddled out without another word.

"She's not wrong."

FLIGHT OF THE SPARROW 145

"She's not right, either." Gertrude settled closer. "This is all new to you. Two days ago, you stood on one side of a line with a future full of goals and dreams. Now you're stuck on the other, wondering if you'll ever get to cross it again. Of course you're conflicted. Scared, too, I imagine." Nimah stifled a sniffle, and Gertrude's hand closed over hers. Squeezed. "I've run hundreds of jobs. This will be easy in and out, Sparrow. You'll see."

Easy? Thievery and lying might be second nature for pirates, but everything inside of her screamed in protest. However noble the cause, some lines should never be crossed. How many wrongs was it going to take to set things right?

"There's more ruffling those feathers," Gertrude murmured.

"Did you know?" Nimah asked, lifting her gaze. "That she was leaving me?"

Gertrude sighed a moment before shaking her head. "Not until it was already done. Your grandmother wasn't one for seeking council, and we didn't ask questions. We trusted her lead. When she returned after dropping you off, she announced we were disbanded. Divvied up our take—leaving nothing for herself—and that was it. We were Valkyries no more." Gertrude swept a hand down Nimah's arm. "Piracy is a hard life. Fraught with danger and struggle. We'd sail for months sometimes with skeleton rations, struggling to find our next score. After Zoraida's death . . . I can understand why she wanted better for you."

"You really believe that?"

"I have to." Gertrude answered with a soft, hesitant smile. "I have to believe that's what she wanted for all of us."

Unconsciously, Nimah's hand lifted, fingers closing around the sparrow. Wearing it was stupid, but she couldn't bring herself to remove the bird. The weight of it around her neck was both comforting and unsettling. Far as disguises went, it didn't belong, and anything to detract from the façade, however small, could be the single detail that broke the illusion. *I should take it off.* But as soon as the idea translated into movement, her stomach twisted and she stopped. Hesitated.

Don't, something deep inside her echoed. *Safe. Safe, Nimah . . .*

Nimah blinked at the sound of her name, and the sensation slipped away, a forgotten dream, as Maverick rolled into the cabin. If it weren't for the chair, she'd never have recognized him. Gertrude had dressed his face—the parts she could see—with a bit of gold leaf and shimmer, but the rest was hidden behind a long cobalt beard, woven into an intricate lattice threaded with gold beads that hung to his waist, and a solo-visor used by the visually impaired.

Thanks to her extensive wardrobe, equal parts carnal and theater, Gertrude had every guise possible to transform them from wanted fugitives into merchant and illustrious courtesan.

"Aren't you a handsome sight?" Gertrude clapped her hands together and hugged them to her ample chest. "I do think the pair of you are my best work yet."

"Dobs sent me to see if you're both ready."

"As ever." Sighing, Nimah rose and turned. Gossamer aquamarine fabric, designed to ripple and flow continuously, cascaded like water across her body. The neckline plunged to the point of obscenity but a heavy, ornate necklace circling her throat hung low enough that at least some of her modesty was preserved.

Maverick lurched to a stop at the sight of her.

"What?" she demanded.

He shook his head. "Nothing." Lips vanishing in a sea of blue, he whisked around with a sharp turn and rolled briskly out into the corridor.

"Definitely some of my best work." Smirking, Gertrude handed Nimah a pair of golden strappy heels.

Nimah rolled her eyes with an aggrieved grumble and stomped after him. Barefoot, as the grating would be impossible to walk across in icepicks.

Reclined against the entry hatch of the shuttle, Dobs stubbed out the cigarette as they approached. "'Bout time." She swiped a hand through the air, dispelling the wispy blue-gray cloud that followed her like a second shadow, and unfastened the cap on her flask. "How long does it take to paint a bit of glitter and gloss?"

"Two things should never be rushed," Gertrude sang out. "Makeup and seduction."

Dobs twirled a finger, and Nimah grudgingly spun on the spot. "Guess it was worth it. They'll be tripping over themselves for your attention."

Nimah's scowl deepened. That was the plan. She was the shiny distraction while Maverick slithered behind the scenes and stole what they needed from the outpost armory. Nanosuits and ammo, along with some upgraded tech for Gertrude and Chu to implement into the navsystem for a stealth hardburn. Yet no matter how vital this part of the mission, she couldn't help but feel like an idiot. Or guilty.

"Careful, that's authentic Zynisian silk," Gertrude barked as Dobs rubbed the length of Nimah's sleeve between her fingers. "A yard costs more than you'd steal in a year."

Dropping the fabric, Dobs whistled low. "Then how'd a nag like you ever afford it?"

"It was a gift from a very prestigious cog."

"A *blind* cog?"

Gertrude cast Dobs a lethal smirk. "Green always was a fabulous color for you, darling." Looping an arm through Nimah's, she sashayed into the shuttle.

The *Stormchaser* had ports for two but as far as Nimah could recall, her grandmother had ejected both. Extra weight made it cumbersome to maneuver in moments that required . . . finesse. Sigourney had managed to pluck one from Tortuga's market in half the time it took for Gertrude to transform them into a courtesan's quarters.

"Chu punched holes where she could without compromising integrity. Scrubbed her clean so radars won't get a lock on you until you're hot on 'em. Remember you got less than an hour to grab what we need and get off-moon." Dobs tapped the riveted wall with a hard slap, fresh cigarette dangling from between her lips. "To the void or Valhalla." She punched the airlock, sealing the hatch.

Once the inner door engaged, the shuttle rumbled awake. Maverick, already in position at the console, went to work warming the thrusters.

"Strap in, Cadet," he instructed, punching, twisting, and flipping buttons and switches.

She did, yanking down the overhead harness and pressing a hand to the hull behind her as the rumbling intensified. Gertrude, opposite Nimah, reclined into her seat, eyes closed and hands spread at her side as if in prayer. An actress quieting the mind.

Gravity slipped away as they disengaged from the *Stormchaser*'s stabilizers, and weightlessness swam around her. Unsettling in its buoyancy.

Her body lifted against the restraints, bile searing the back of Nimah's throat and nostrils. She clamped her lips together, breathed harshly from her nose and winced against the acrid burn, but didn't trust herself not to vomit.

Taking the yoke, Maverick toggled the shuttle into a gentle glide and the outpost swam into the viewport. It would be a short flight down, but the rippled surface of the artificial atmo told her it wasn't going to be a pleasant landing.

"Hold on." Maverick pushed the yoke forward—hard. Nimah sucked in a gasp as the shuttle twisted and swayed. Simulating a struggling ship so they could land under the guise of distress, and it wasn't long before a voice pushed through the shuttle's comms.

"Attention, unidentified vessel. You're about to enter heavily regulated airspace. Please provide your authorization code."

The flare of dazzling blue flames flashed across the viewport. The shuttle rattled and roared. Nimah tensed in the seat, knuckles white and eyes clamped so tight she worried she might've dislodged her false lashes.

Thunderous jolts slammed into them as they broke atmo. *It's only turbulence—air and pressure. Gravity and resistance.* The shuttle hit a thermal air pocket and bounced, hard enough to make her teeth slam together and her ears ring.

"Almost there."

Nimah answered with a hum meant to sound like *okay* but instead came out more like a tortured whine. Sweat bloomed across her skin, and her heart, lodged high in her throat, pulsed fast and unsteady as their descent. She didn't dare open her eyes until the shuttle's landing gear made hard contact with the ground and rolled to a lurching stop.

"Cadet." Maverick uncoupled his harness. "We're here."

"One minute."

"We don't have a minute."

"Indeed," Gertrude agreed. "Time to get into character, Sparrow."

Nimah sucked in a deep breath and opened her eyes. Yellowish light washed through the main viewport and she blinked against it—spotlights, from the walls of the base. There was no sun—false or otherwise—near this moon, and thick particle clouds, shimmering with waves of green and purple, blotted out the stars.

FLIGHT OF THE SPARROW 149

Unfastening her harness, Nimah rose, weak-kneed, trailing behind Gertrude while Maverick popped the hatch and lowered the gangway.

Agents swept in, three of them, blasers pinned to their chests. Dressed in SIGA blue—visors up, concealing their faces behind a glossy pane of smooth black glass. Given height, width of shoulders and hips, stance, and hand placement, Nimah ascertained two of the approaching agents were male and the third, closest to the shuttle, was female.

"Identify," the woman snapped.

Gertrude swept forward, shoulders drawn with regal grace, and held up her hands—not in supplication, but as if to command an audience. "I am Licensed Companion Madam Hildegarde, and this is my protégé, Brys Namsara. We—"

"You've landed without authorization on a military base." The female agent closed in. "Why did you refuse to respond to our hails?"

"The shuttle, as you can see, is in rough shape," Gertrude answered. "We barely escaped from pirates with our gowns, much less our lives."

"Disembark," the female agent commanded. "Slowly. Hands visible at all times. Forest—secure them in magnicuffs until we sort out their documentation. If they have any."

"Belay that order and stand down." The one behind her removed his helm. White-blond hair tumbled around a boyish face but fine lines around his eyes and mouth belied his age.

The female agent whirled around, her posture aghast. "But sir!"

"Pull the stick out of your rear, Mix," another teased, slapping her shoulder congenially. "When are we ever going to have a courtesan grace our doorstep this far into the ass end of quad nine?"

"I don't care." She released her own helm so she could snarl in his face. "They landed in an unclassified aircraft *without* authorization. *Without* a permit. *Without—*"

"What are they gonna do? Sing us to death?" Ignoring his highly outraged colleague, the agent offered Nimah a warm smile that showed a gap in his front teeth. "I'm Agent Forest. And this is Senior Agent Gallani." He gestured to the white-blond gentleman and then nodded to the scowling woman. "You've already had the misfortune of meeting Mix."

"Eat shit."

"You said you were attacked?" Gallani stepped forward, ignoring the surly temper of the junior agent.

"Yes, it was terrible." Gertrude pressed a hand to her cheek. "My consort managed to whisk me and my protégé to safety, but we lost many of my coven." She paused, allowing tears to gather in her eyes. "Forgive me. I've never seen such . . . violence."

"And yet not a scratch on any of you." Mix tapped a foot. "But your shuttle looks like she's been through a warzone. Amazing."

Forest sighed. "Ignore her. She's been stationed for three years. Longest run of our base. Made her a bit . . ." He spun a finger by his temple and whistled low.

Mix punched him in his shoulder.

"Come, let's get you inside the base. You can tell us all about your misadventures." Senior Agent Gallani offered a hand and Gertrude nudged Nimah forward to take it.

"At the very least you should run them through the bodyscan." Mix huffed after them, blaser still in hand.

"Why?" Forest swiped his card to disengage the lock. "Afraid she's got a bomb hidden in her skirts?"

Nimah pushed her lips into a steady smile. *If you only knew.*

CHAPTER FOURTEEN

Maverick slid into the role of skinner with ease, and hated how effortless it was, a casual observation of gestures and details telling him everything he needed to know about his marks. Like the subtle tic in Gallani's left hand. Nerve damage.

Given his age and rank, an outpost position like this meant he'd served his time during the Zone Wars but hadn't earned outstanding accreditations. Between that and his injuries, Gallani was evidently a good soldier, but one who got lost in the shuffle, and Maverick gathered he was more than happy to be forgotten. Moon outposts, with less than two dozen bodies occupying it, weren't often targeted for theft or attack. Being stationed here was a quiet, solitary existence and, for a man who'd seen more than his fair share of death and bloodshed, likely a welcomed reprieve.

Forest, however, had the spark of a fresh recruit still bright in his eyes. So fresh that he didn't realize a position on a moon outpost was hardly anything to smile about. Probably a month into his term and still too dazzled by his newly appointed agent status to see straight. The shine would wear off after the first year. Meanwhile both he and Gallani were too enamored with Gertrude and Nimah to pay him much attention. But Agent Mix was a problem, and watched the three of them with keen awareness. Slipping her wasn't going to be easy.

Maverick whisked his wheels, lagging behind the retinue as they brought Nimah and Gertrude into the community hall—and it was *packed*.

152   **FALLON DEMORNAY**

"Oh, it looks like we've interrupted a party." Gertrude pressed a coquettish hand to Forest's arm but her flickered glance toward Maverick was filled with alarm. This wasn't what they'd expected or prepared for.

"We've called in all rangers to the base. Regulators will be landing within the hour," Gallani answered. "Nothing to be concerned about. They're moving en masse to assess various outposts for possible breach."

"From what? Whom?" Nimah asked.

"That's classified," Mix snapped.

"What Mix means is we couldn't tell you even if we wanted to," Forest added. "Only first-tier brass have that intel. They give orders, we snap to—simple as that."

Maverick swallowed stiffly. *They're looking for us.* But the higher-ups were keeping the details contained, which meant they weren't boiling in hot water. Not yet. But this complicated things.

"If you'll excuse me for a moment." Gallani offered a nod before departing.

"There's too many bodies here," Gertrude muttered under her breath once they were alone. Mostly. Mix and Forest hadn't gone far, and the other agents were quickly taking notice of the colorful outsiders in their midst.

"We need to divide and conquer," Maverick grunted back.

"Let's start with *him*." Gertrude's gaze fixed on Gallani, deep in conversation with a member of his staff who was carting blankets. She leaned into Nimah. "He fancies you."

"What? How do you know?"

"Men are one third of my specialty, darling, and he's had eyes only for you since we landed." Gertrude's fingers prodded Nimah's back. "Find a way to get him alone and keep him occupied."

Nimah's skin shocked white. "What?"

"Mind out of the gutter. Unless you want to, then go off and spare no juicy details." She winked.

Nimah swiped a finger behind her ear, activating the comms. "What about you?"

"I'll manage this lot."

"How?"

FLIGHT OF THE SPARROW

"By doing what I do best." Gertrude tossed up a dramatic hand with a wide, showgirl grin. "*Performing*."

Gallani returned with a couple of blankets and hooked the first one around Nimah's shoulders. "Sorry we don't have anything finer, but the base gets chilly at night. This should keep you warm."

"Thank you." Nimah hugged it tighter to her shoulders and her smile dazzled with such sincerity it was hard not to think she was actually taking a shine to the senior agent. She slid into character easily, it seemed, while Maverick sweated in silence, scowling beneath a pound of makeup, adhesive, and bright blue facial hair.

Maverick had an easy face to recognize but Gertrude had a gift for forgery—a gift he put to the test in the way agent eyes rolled off him. Smooth as water off a polished hull, without a trace of recognition.

Even Maverick was taken aback by the transformation when he caught a glimpse of himself in the holomirror aboard the *Stormchaser*. The identity tag was of equally remarkable craftsmanship. He wore it around his neck—as did all merchants out on a trade route—saving the bother of pockets and purses that were easy to pilfer.

Lost credits were a minor inconvenience but a lost tag was an expensive setback that took time to replace and could disrupt both trade and transportation for months. Which led to a significant loss in income. No merchant worth his salt would ever dare leave his tag out of sight.

"Mix, go to the kitchens and prepare a couple of plates for our guests." Maverick perked up in his chair.

"Me?" Mix gaped in disbelief. "*Kitchen* duty?"

Senior Agent Gallani turned on his heel, every inch of him drawing upon the authority of his command. "The cooks have scrubbed down for the night and I won't see them hauled out of bed when you have a set of perfectly good hands. I suggest you make use of them."

Just a little closer . . .

"They're courtesans. Not foreign dignitaries or royalty."

"They are citizens of the Inner Circle—ones we are duty-bound to serve and protect—and you will remember who you are speaking to, Agent Mix, or I'll have your star for it."

Mix snapped her lips together and stalked off before Maverick could swipe her access card.

Shit.

"I dunno if that decision was razor, sir." Forest laughed. "She might put crushed glass in the stew."

"I'll be sure to make her sample it first." Gallani reached out and stroked a hand down Nimah's arm. "Please excuse the actions of Agent Mix. She will be reprimanded appropriately, I assure you. Come the morning, once we are realigned with communication satellites, we will hail a local transport ship to take you to the nearest spacity. From there I trust you'll be able to reconnect with the embassy."

"You are exceedingly kind. We're so grateful for your generous hospitality."

Maverick flashed eyes to Nimah, and mouthed the word *faint*. Understanding, Nimah fluttered a hand before her face and Gallani caught her before she dropped more than an inch.

"Oh my," she sighed against him. "I'm so terribly sorry. I don't know what came over me."

"Perhaps we should see our guests settled for the night. Mix can leave a tray with your meals outside your door so as not to disturb you. I'm sure you're exhausted after your ordeal."

"Actually, the poor child *has* been ship-bound for several weeks," Gertrude interjected. "Haven't you, darling? Perhaps a bit of fresh air would be better?"

"Oh, yes. I think a walk about would be wonderful." Nimah pressed a hand to Gallani's chest. "And company, if you can spare it."

Pink flushed on the high, sharp bones of his cheeks. "I'd be happy to."

Nimah looped a hand through his proffered arm, and as the man led her away, Maverick tried, really tried, not to hate him down to the edges of his perfect teeth.

"Little Sparrow, you do learn quickly," Gertrude murmured with an impressed shake of her head.

Too damn quickly.

"Easy, love." She rested her hand on his shoulder, squeezed. "Now, has anyone got any music?" Gertrude sashayed forward, arms spread for show—capturing the attention of her audience. "Because I feel a *song* coming on."

One jaunty showtune later and Maverick was able to make the slip. For all her posturing, Gertrude truly did have a voice—not entirely

FLIGHT OF THE SPARROW 155

beautiful or delicate—but commanding in its presence. All drama and flair, she'd rallied the eyes and ears of everyone in the room, working the polished table as if it were a stage in a grand arena.

It wasn't hard to understand how she had amassed such notoriety, but it *was* hard to pull away once she got going, but Maverick was here for one purpose and one purpose only. This part of the mission rested entirely on his shoulders—no way was he going to botch it.

He'd only just eased out of the community hall when his comms chimed.

"Hello?" Nimah whispered. "Maverick . . . can you hear me?"

"Finished with Gallani so soon?"

Maverick could almost hear her scowl. "I don't have long. He stepped away to receive a wave from the Regulators and . . . what's that noise?"

"Distraction." Maverick eased the door shut behind him as Gertrude belted through a chorus met with an onslaught of howling whistles. "The pups are eating it up."

"Wonderful. Did you get it?"

"Yup." He held the agent's access card before him. Forest's grinning face smiled on the plexiglass, bearing his credentials. The smarter move would've been to swipe Gallani's, as he was the ranking officer for the outpost—unfortunately it was the silver fox who'd swooped in to catch Nimah and not the eager youth, as he'd hoped.

"You're sure he didn't feel you?"

"You're doubting me, now? No, he didn't notice a thing." And as Forest was currently front row, belting along with the rest of his squad mates, he likely wouldn't notice for quite some time. "I'm about to make for the armory."

"Pretty sure we passed it when exiting the hangar."

"Then I'll start there," he agreed, recalling the thick nanite door and glowing access panel. "Here's hoping Forest has sufficient clearance."

"He will. All agents store their gear inside. Be quick. Be safe."

Warmth spread in his chest. "Always am, Cadet."

CHAPTER FIFTEEN

Gallani brought Nimah down a broad stairway, etched into the moonstone, to a wide terrace with a skillfully manicured garden of short hedges and rioting flowers. Situated on an open, flat shelf, the base overlooked a rippling stretch of terrain that glistened like cut diamonds, the way sunlight reflected gently off lapping water. Haunting and beautiful. In the distance, smoking spires from rehabilitation plants speared the horizon, where workers toiled away to recycle everything from plastic to food scraps.

Overhead the atmo bubble shimmered like the nacre of a shell. There was a stillness to the night that was unlike anything she'd experienced before. Almost like being underwater where the senses were muted and heavy, but without the oppressive weight in her ears or searing burn in her lungs—or the terrifying emptiness of zero gravity in the void.

She'd never moonwalked in her life, but as Nimah strolled across the soft chalky terrain with Gallani at her side, she wondered why she'd never thought to try it until now.

"What happened here?" She touched his forearm where his rolled sleeve exposed a deep, terrible scar on his right arm. The puckered tissue a livid purple, webbed with aged silver. It looked to be the result of an in-the-field job that had never been properly tended in a medbay, and a young soldier without proper insurance could never afford cosmetic repair. Given the brutal way it cleaved through muscle, from elbow to wrist, it was a marvel he had any use in his hand at all.

FLIGHT OF THE SPARROW 157

Gallani sighed. "Got snagged in the wreckage after being shot down during the Siege of Graywater on Atari6."

The Siege of Graywater, fought nearly twenty-two years ago, was a horrible three-day slaughter with SIGA recruits surrounded by rebel insurgents trying to take control of the base. It had been brutal and bloody but in the end the insurgents were fought off.

"How long have you been stationed here?"

"Eleven years." Her surprise must've shown as Senior Agent Gallani chuckled. "I know. Quite a tenure. I can assure you it hasn't always been easy but there are worse places to be." He cast his gaze away from her to the distant flat horizon limned in silver. "I don't expect a courtesan to understand."

"I think I do," she answered. The moon glowed with shimmering specks in the ash-gray dust. "It's beautiful, in a cold and desolate sort of way that I find almost endearing. This quiet and steady peace—I'd imagine that would be welcomed after all you've seen." She glanced up to see him staring at her. Assessing.

"Yes, precisely."

Heat flooded her chest. A kindred kind of warmth, born of admiration that brought with it the cold burn of shame. He was good. Decent. And she was lying straight to his face. What would he think of her when this was all over? When he realized she'd played a role for no other reason but to steal from under his nose and betray his trust?

"This is a curious trinket." His finger stroked the dangling sparrow and something shocked through her.

A sensation. A *feeling* . . . Similar to what she'd felt while swaying in her cabin after recovering from the Seawater, but stronger. And much sharper.

"Foolish childhood fancy. Can't seem to part with the hideous thing." Nimah tucked it away. The second his skin had met stone, a jolt ricocheted across every nerve like lightning trapped in a bottle. In that split moment, as unthinkable as it was to understand, she'd been inside his head and what she'd discovered in there made her heartbeat rise in alarm.

He knows.

Knows who you are.

Knows you're playing him.

He knows.

FALLON DEMORNAY

Those words reverberated inside of her, an echo that wouldn't dissipate.

"Sir." An agent she hadn't heard approach stopped at the base of the stairs and inclined his head. "It's time."

The hairs on Nimah's arms prickled. Training had taught her to spot trouble. To sense danger. And—if her instincts weren't already roused in alarm—everything from his tight shoulders to the sheen of sweat on his skin, as if he'd come sprinting in search of his commanding officer, screamed a warning as loud as Sigourney's battle cry.

"Apparently it is a night filled with excitement." Gallani extended his hand. "I'm sorry but I must cut this tour short. If you'd please, Ms. Nimara."

"Namsara," she corrected, accepting his proffered arm as any courtesan would a respectable gentleman.

"My apologies." He smiled as he led the way but there wasn't an ounce of apology in his eyes. "Any relation to Lennox Namsara?"

She tried to laugh ineffectually but it came out limp. The best lies were always grounded in truth, but this hadn't been a smart play. The Namsaras had gained a bit of notoriety for their political efforts after Liselle's father had run for presidency six years ago, but she hadn't banked on his name having reached this far from the Inner Circle.

"No, not that I'm aware of." Nimah caught the shift in his eyes, his stance. *Doubt. Suspicion.* Her cover was definitely blown.

When they reached the last step, she caught the steady and soft tread of the accompanying agent's footfalls in the moondust as he fell into stride behind them. Keeping pace but trying to be discreet about flanking her.

Nimah's stomach clenched into an apprehensive knot. When scrapping together the outline for this plan, she'd accounted for more time than this, and by her estimate Maverick had only been off comms for fifteen minutes, at best. She had to hope it was enough.

Gallani's hand tightened on her arm and Nimah knew as soon as they entered the base she was in trouble. If he didn't already have men in position waiting to slap her in magnicuffs, then he would do so himself—and fast.

Nimah had to act quickly.

FLIGHT OF THE SPARROW 159

She waited for Gallani to reach for the handle—and struck. The flat of her hand swung high into the apple of his throat, hard enough to stun. Kicking off the wall for momentum, she tackled the second agent clean around the waist and they tumbled together. Arms and legs. He was quick, but Nimah was desperate, and freeing the stunner hidden under her cuff bracelet, she jabbed the needlepoint into his neck and compressed the button to release a potent sedative. His eyes widened with shock before quickly rolling back as he slumped unconscious.

Nimah disentangled herself with a huff. Rising, she turned to face Gallani, leaning against the compound wall, barely recovered from a fit of coughing.

"You're trained," he rasped, voice rough and eyes watering. "One of *us*."

Nimah exhaled gently. "I'm sorry."

Gallani raised his fists, ready for her. They clashed, like twin comets, and it took two sharp blows for Nimah to realize she was in trouble. He wasn't just a senior agent. He was a war veteran. His instincts were sharper, his experience more rounded. She'd never beat him in a fair fight.

So don't fight fair, a distant echo rolled inside her. She dove beneath a flurry of haymakers and tucked into a roll. Seizing a fistful of moondust, she spun on her knees and launched it at his face. Gallani roared against the sting of chalky grit. Blinded for only a moment, but it was all she needed to swing his legs out from under him.

Arcing, rolling, she caught his arm in a hold, legs locked around his neck. Gray dust smeared into streaking tears, painting lines across his reddening face as he battled against her hold, struggling to break free. But he wouldn't relent. He wouldn't give up. No senior agent could. To reach for a stunner in her brace she'd have to break the hold, but if she released him now she'd never get the drop on him again. Not with the anger she saw in his eyes. The betrayed disbelief. If she broke the hold, he'd take her down. If she broke the hold, all would be lost.

Don't let go.
Don't let go.
Don't let go.

Nimah compressed her thighs. Squeezing harder, reducing oxygen and blood flow to his head until his eyes bulged, but he was strong, far too strong, and her own strength was failing her. In a writhing twist, he pried her legs apart enough to slip away and pin her down.

Nimah bucked but it was no use. He was too heavy. Too solid. And now he had the advantage of high ground. His fist caught her clean and fast—sweeping her into a daze that almost rendered her unconscious.

Fight.

A second blow and the moon spun in a violent whirl. "Can't . . ." Nimah croaked around a mouthful of blood.

Let me.

Let us.

Bleary, Nimah gazed up at Gallani . . . and then past him to an iridescent figure looming like a specter made of starlight. It reached out toward her as Gallani's fist drew back, slow as cold oil.

That fingertip tapped Nimah's brow—the center point between her eyes—and it snapped—this thing stirring awake inside of her.

She caught Gallani's fist inches from crashing into her face. Gallani grunted, cursed as her fingers closed tighter around his knuckles. With a quick jerk, she wrenched him forward and smashed her brow into the bridge of his nose.

Bone and cartilage cracked, spraying blood. Gallani reared back, just enough for her to wiggle free and pounce. Back on her feet, her next punch landed and the third had him shaking it off in a daze, throwing erratic swings to maintain distance. Catching him by the throat, she wrenched him back against the wall. His skull gave a firm *smack* against carbide steel.

Sweeping his arms aside with the flat of her palms, Nimah closed in and her fingers punched a series of points on either side of his neck. Three sharp moves that made his entire body lock and seize as bright terror flashed through his eyes before rolling back.

Gallani dropped at her feet.

The haze roared in her ears like a chant—a spell—and when it broke, she gasped in disbelief. He was limp. Too limp. No. *No!* Quickly, she rolled him onto his back, fingers pressing at the side of his throat.

FLIGHT OF THE SPARROW

"Please." Where was the pulse? "Please." She prodded and searched. Her own roared in her ears, pounded in the pads of her fingertips making it hard to feel, to know . . . there! *Still alive. Still alive.* Weakened with relief and adrenaline, Nimah slumped to the ground as the reality of what had just happened settled in. *What have I done? And what the hell was* that?

In the moment she hadn't questioned it. There hadn't been enough time. But now? She'd taken him down with moves she'd never used before and with a vicious fury she didn't recognize or understand. Somehow as natural as drawing breath, but it hadn't *felt* like her. More like something had moved through her. Something feral and wild and . . . *beyond.* Too sharp, too bright, too sudden to be mere instinct. It felt *older.* Separate from and yet part of her all the same, as her movements took on a life of their own.

"Stop it, Nimah." Nimah shook herself back into focus. This was not the time to think or dwell. She had to find Maverick and finish the job. Freeing another stunner from her brace, Nimah jabbed Gallani in the thigh. It would take a little longer for the sedative to circulate from there, which would hopefully allow his body more time to steady itself after the assault. Both agents would be unconscious for at least an hour, allowing for plenty of time for them to clear the zone. But if anyone stumbled across them—the alarms would sound and they'd be in big trouble. As she removed Gallani's access card from his belt, the door swung open and a dark head popped out.

"Easy, darling, I come in peace."

"Gertrude . . ." Nimah lowered her fists. "How did you find me?"

"Your comms. Figured when I couldn't reach you or Maverick it was my cue." Gertrude propped a hand on her hip as she assessed the two unconscious figures. "Seems we've worn out our welcome." Her gaze fell on Nimah and sharpened with concern. "Are you alright, Sparrow?"

"I . . ." Was she? Her skin seared like she'd been on fire, all heat but without the flame, and deeper still, crackling in her bones, was something else. An echo of what had taken hold of her like a demon, compelling her to act and move and do things she had never done before. But Nimah pushed it all down. Even if she somehow could find the words to

162 FALLON DEMORNAY

explain what had just happened, they were on borrowed time. "We need to get off-moon *immediately.*"

"I'm inclined to agree." Holding the door open, she swept Nimah in ahead of her, re-entering the base, before smashing the access panel with the blunt end of a blaser. The screen cracked. No one was getting in or out through that doorway without serious effort.

"Did you get eyes on Maverick?"

Gertrude shook her head as she took off in long strides. Even in heels she was unnervingly quiet. "His comms are down, so I came to find you first."

"Maverick." Nimah jogged down the corridor toward the base hangar. "Maverick—*dammit*—answer me." Nothing. No response. No whisper of connection. Only one reason he'd kill comms. Maverick was in trouble. And if he wasn't—he was *gonna* be.

Thankfully Senior Agent Gallani's pass gave her full clearance, so she was able to bypass the barracks and head straight to the hangar, where she almost collided head-on with Maverick as he waited by the entry. Seemingly without a care in the world.

"You . . ." She blinked twice, not quite believing her eyes. "You're alright."

Maverick shrugged. "Why wouldn't I be?"

Nimah's anxious heart climbed down from her throat but still beat wildly in her chest. "Gertrude said she couldn't reach you on comms."

"Walls in here are thick." Maverick rapped a knuckle to the steel plating above his shoulder. "Must've canceled out reception while I loaded the shuttle. Rather than draw attention, figured it best to wait for you both to rendezvous here. You look like you've been tussling, though."

"Cover's blown. Gallani isn't nearly as gullible as we'd hoped."

"Then let's get off-moon before we have any more surprises."

"I second that," Gertrude agreed. "Shall we, darlings?"

Maverick led the way with sharp pumps of his arms, pushing his chair in a smooth and brisk glide. Nimah and Gertrude swept the hangar with blasers, but it was empty of bodies—including sentries on duty. No outpost would leave a hanger unguarded.

"What's wrong?" Gertrude asked, catching Nimah's scowl as they boarded the shuttle.

"This is too easy." And as if to answer her concerns, the hangar swelled with the wail of alarms.

"That better, darling?" Gertrude tossed a hand. "The whole base will be on us soon."

"Already took care of it." Maverick tossed a ring of metal pins with a smirk as they boarded the shuttle.

Nimah lifted it, her fingers twisted and turning. "Grenades?" As the shuttle roared to life, the first one popped behind them, answering her question, and a fighter jet at the back of the hangar ignited with a blech of blue flames.

"One down, twenty to go!" Maverick cackled, and—blasting the hangar doors open with a pulse beam—he punched hard on the throttle. Tearing down the runway as the hangar erupted in a dazzling display of exploding sparks.

CHAPTER SIXTEEN

S omeone pass the lo mein."

Nimah frowned as Sigourney whisked a blue ceramic bowl under her nose. She'd dropped it when she was three, and her grandmother had welded it back together with yellow gold. Transforming the cracks into a thing of beauty rather than garish scars. It struck her now how easy it had been to turn an impossible mess into a work of art, not only restored but somehow better than it was before. But life wasn't pottery, and the fragments were far too many—once the pieces of a life were shattered, was it truly possible to weld them back together?

"Easy, Sparrow, unless you'd rather be called Crow." Gertrude spun a finger before her face. "Fine lines quickly become trenches."

"I prefer a face marred with the poetry of wisdom and age," Sigourney purred.

"Damn straight." Chu dumped rehydrated noodles and vegetables onto Mumbles's plate. "Tells the world you lived a life worth living."

"Is that how you justify your sagging jowls?"

"Not everyone wants to blink with their lips. Who's got them pickled eggs?"

Irritated by their bickering, Nimah boosted from the table and stalked toward the holoscreen streaming all newscasts across three zones covering everything *but* the incident out in quad nine.

"What's got your knickers in a knot?" Gertrude sang out. "Food's getting cold, come eat."

FLIGHT OF THE SPARROW 165

"It's been two hours." Frustrated, she tugged her hair from her bun and shook it loose with aggravated fingers. "It doesn't make sense."

"What's she going on about?" Chu muttered around a mouthful of greasy noodles.

"An assault on a base—even a lunar outpost—wouldn't go unreported. The satellite would've come into orbit by now, but *look*!" Nimah flung her hands toward the screen and waved at it like a gameshow assistant trying to highlight the obvious to an oblivious crowd. "Nothing! Not a whisper across fifty-seven channels."

"If they're smart, they won't." Chu huffed. "Makes 'em look weak."

"Gallani is a *senior* agent. No way he'd shirk his responsibility to save his pride."

"You'd be surprised what men'll do to preserve their egos." Dobs puffed lazy smoke circles. "Fragile as soap bubbles, heard?"

"Hey." Boomer wiggled a thumb between him and Maverick. "Couple of dudes right here resent that statement."

Dobs stuck a finger in her mouth and snapped the inside of her cheek with a loud *pop*, then winked at Nimah. "See what I mean?"

"You didn't see the look in his eyes." But Nimah had, and that look would haunt her. As would that glistening specter who somehow had inhabited her body and saved her life. Even now she could almost feel that surge of energy in her veins. The dazzling burst of raw power. The primal knowing as her body moved and responded in ways she couldn't explain, let alone comprehend why it had all felt so achingly familiar. But there wasn't room in her swirling, chaotic mind to chew on both issues. She had to focus on what was most important, and relevant. A ghost of stardust would have to take a back seat to much bigger issues. "I just think—"

"Can't you let it go, Cadet?" Maverick snapped, voice brittle with irritation. "We got away clean."

"Too clean!" Nimah planted her hands on her hips. "Something's *off*."

"The only thing off is your attitude." He tossed his fork to his barely touched plate. "We caught a break—you should be thrilled."

"It's not often I'll agree with a skinbag, but he's right." Dobs hooked an ankle across her knee and stubbed out her finished cigarette in a bit of pickled egg white. "Almost sounds like you're disappointed we *didn't* get pinched."

Nimah clamped her lips together. Was that it? Did some quiet part of her pray for self-sabotage? Maybe she did. Maybe the cowardly truth was, she wanted to fail because the next step was by far the worst. Launching her off a cliff from which there was no coming back. Not without the safe return of Jonothan Shinoda and a terrorist insurgent in a collar—proving her grandmother's innocence.

Because if she failed, then Nimah was completely and thoroughly ruined. Worse than a pirate, or a skinner, she was a traitor to her government. To her own beliefs and morals. If not, then Nimah had single-handedly destroyed any hope of a future with the STARs. Casting her dreams into a cavernous black hole, never to be seen again.

"If you're finished having a tantrum, why don't you come take a seat and we can discuss our next steps like proper pirates." Reclined casually in her chair, Dobs wiped grease from her hands but smeared more on her cheeks and chin. "Soon as Chu is finished making adjustments on the radiator, we can break outta this quad. Gertrude's found us a heading."

"Found is a funny way of putting it." Gertrude rolled her eyes. "But there was an interesting little note in your *extensive* file, Maverick, that got me thinking." She dropped her chin. "You ran the gauntlet back in '192."

Maverick's cheeks paled.

"What's the gauntlet?" Nimah asked as the table fell silent.

"You've never heard of the—?" Dobs scoffed. "What kind of cadet are you?"

"It's what we renegades call the Grimoire Channel," Gertrude explained. "Ma, pull up a holoscreen, give us a full spec grid of the Grimoire Channel."

The ship's navsystem hummed a steady beat while Sigourney cleared away empty plates and bowls for better line of sight to the holo-projection that spread across the length of the table. A rippling canvas of black pixels that would shift like metallic sand at the sound of her voice, taking shape in a three-dimensional mold of the complex asteroid system that sliced from one segment of the Inner Circle straight across to the Outer RIM.

"Okay. What about it?"

FLIGHT OF THE SPARROW 167

"The gauntlet is densely occupied by asteroid debris and space junk, which makes for a tricky run and even harder area for a STARship to patrol. All those moving bits—scanners can't know what is what. It's a veritable obstacle course."

"Flying through that sounds dangerous. And stupid."

"Oh, it definitely is both, Sparrow, I'll grant you that, but the *Challenger*—that's the ship transporting Ro—will have no choice but to break out of hardburn *here*." Gertrude tapped the edge of zone four. "The channel is too chaotic with debris to safely blitz through, even for a ship of her size. Which means—"

"You have to pilot by line of sight," Maverick finished through teeth clenched as tight as his fist. "It's a death trap."

"One that many have tried to run before and failed," Gertrude continued, then nodded at Maverick. "Yet you succeeded. Three times, before the age of *sixteen*."

"Yeah. And my last run put me in this chair." Maverick scrubbed a hand across the back of his neck. "You're also forgetting the *Challenger* will have shields far more sophisticated than ours. She can push through the worst of it with ease, but the *Stormchaser* is a hundredth of her size and far less equipped. If we get caught in the backdraft . . . her shields will hurl rock at us like blaserfire and pound us to dust."

"So if I get the gist . . ." Chu scratched sparse white hairs on her chin, "we're gonna die."

"Easy, darling. Be positive, yeah?"

"Fine." She banded skinny arms across her skinnier chest. "I'm *positive* we're gonna die."

"Risk is the name of the game, ladies and gents." Dobs clapped her hands together, calluses grating. "So, strap in because it's about to go balls to the wall when we get to the next part of the plan. Kid?"

Nimah leaned forward. "Gertrude, bring up the sim. Home in on the target."

Gertrude's fingers whisked at the air, swiping and sweeping until the pixelated image of the *Challenger* took shape in all her authoritative glory. Nimah's heart quickened at the sight of the class-4 Supreme X38 voidship, made for interstellar travel and large enough to carry a thousand occupants. Only the most proficient of agents would ever command such a vessel.

"Once we reach our arrival marker," she began, "this is where things will get interesting. *Challenger* is a powerful ship, but she's a megalodon with a weak spot we can play to our advantage."

"Supreme X38s don't have a weak spot," Chu balked. "That's why they're called *supreme*."

Dobs hiked a boot onto the seat of a chair and pressed an elbow to her knee. "Yes, she does. Right here. The underbelly." Reaching across, she tickled her fingers across the bottom of the ship, and Gertrude expanded focus for a clearer visual.

"What about the sensors, triggered by both thermal and motion?" Boomer interjected.

"Sensors," Nimah agreed. "But no *cameras*."

Boomer sputtered into silence. Maverick frowned. "Only because having them would be redundant. Sensors are *far* more efficient and powerful."

"So they thought." Nimah raised a finger. "Once the *Challenger* has rolled past, Mumbles will use one of her self-made gadgets to mimic an echo."

"A what?" Chu craned forward.

"An echo," Nimah repeated. "Plenty of them happen when you've got that much debris clustered together—the soundwave will distort their sensors long enough for Maverick to boost engines and get us into position *beneath* them to fly in tandem."

"Tan-what-now? What're we doing, exactly?"

"Speak slower, Sparrow, and use smaller words," Gertrude said loudly from behind the flat of her hand. "Some of us don't have all our faculties."

Chu pinned her with a bifocaled bug-eyed glare. "Go sit on a sonic grenade."

"I had no idea you were so kinky, darling."

"Focus, girls." Dobs clapped her hands but couldn't contain her smile.

"Once beneath the *Challenger*," Nimah continued, "it's up to Maverick to lock in at the same speed. Same thrust. An ounce of drag and they'll know. When the anchor is in place, our team will climb aboard through the landing gear here." She tapped the back end of the ship where the docking thrusters were disengaged. "Any motion from the nanotech suits will be dismissed by the system as part of the ship, rendering us virtually invisible."

The shields were designed to recognize and respond to the nano-suits, letting ejected agents breach defenses and climb aboard a new vessel safely in times of battle. Getting onboard should prove to be fairly easy, but freeing her grandmother, and detaching without alerting STARs agents that anything was amiss—would be a different matter.

Boomer swiped a hand over the dome of his head, mussing short black curls. "What's the plan once we've breached this whale?"

Dobs jerked a shoulder. "That's Nimah's territory."

"Me?" Heat drained from her cheeks. "Why *me*?"

"Oh, I'm sorry." Dobs smacked a hand to her brow. "Must've mistaken you with the *other* cadet on board."

"I . . ." Nimah sputtered, mouth flapping in silent horror. "But you're the pirates. This is what you do. Surely you can lead this without me. Or perhaps Boomer—"

"Boomer doesn't know STARship procedure and protocol. None of us do. Not like you. And call me crazy, but I don't think he has the skill-set required to lead a stealth op. No offense."

Shoveling food into his mouth, Boomer waved his fork. "Razor."

"There has to be someone else. Anyone!" The floor opened under-neath her—the world staggered. She'd put together the plan—but to execute it? "I can't . . . I *can't*—"

"I don't know what ghosts you're running from, and personally, I don't care." Dobs anchored her hands to the table and leaned forward until they were almost nose to nose. "If we had a month this would be a slice without you, but fact is you're our best and only resource to pull this off clean. So if I have to launch you into the void myself, I won't hesitate, heard?"

Don't be afraid.
  I can't do this.
  Don't be afraid.
  I can't do this.

Nimah braced the door to her cabin as those words looped around her skull, an endless refrain. Tears seared the back of her eyes at what she was expected to do. Cold terror raked down her back with sharp claws, popping nerves like seams until she unraveled. Came undone.

In a matter of hours she was going to be vaulting into naked space with nothing to keep her anchored—her knees buckled at the thought, and she struggled to breathe around the violent rise of vomit until she heaved into a corner. Emptying her stomach clean to the lining.

How? How could she pull this off when everything seemed too great. Too impossible. There was no going to Dobs and begging her to reconsider—the woman was fearless. A pirate wouldn't hesitate to make the leap. Nimah was no pirate. But there was no turning back now. If she failed it wouldn't be a prison cell waiting for her, but a body bag. Death called to her on both sides, and she was trapped in the middle of the impossible.

"You alright, Cadet?"

Nimah spat lumpy bile from her mouth and wiped tears from her eyes. "Just perfect." Straightening, she steadied her breathing before turning around. "How are you not terrified right now?"

"Why would I be?"

"The gauntlet. Aren't you scared to run it again? After . . ." She gestured vaguely.

Maverick tapped restless fingers against his wheels in a steady, punctuated rhythm. "Course I am. I'm not a moron. But I am the master of my fear, Cadet. It doesn't master me."

"How did you escape it?"

"By becoming stronger than it."

"*How?*"

"You sit in that darkness and you let it teach you what it needs to in order to move past it. You can't run from fear, Cadet. It's inside you and you can't escape what's inside you. You're fast," he added with a smirk, "but no one can outrun their demons."

He was right. Her entire life had been about running. From her past. From her fears. Maybe now it was time to stand and face it, once and for all. "Okay. Show me."

FLIGHT OF THE SPARROW

Understanding stretched between them. Maverick sighed. "I'm not the right guy."

"You're the only one who knows . . . who *knows*. Please. I'm out of options. I'm out of time."

Maverick exhaled a heavy breath as he shook away a burgeoning argument she saw rising in his eyes. "You're not going to like what I'm about to suggest." He cocked his head. "Follow me." Turning, he whisked past her and veered left.

She did. All the way to the medbay, where he slipped in to grab a case before venturing onward to her cabin. Nimah lingered on the threshold, more than a little confused. "What are we doing here?"

"Facing your fears." He spun around. "This was your grandmother's cabin, right?"

Nimah bristled. "What does this have to do with the void?"

"The void isn't the root of what's eating you. Not by a long shot. What you're most afraid of is loss of control. Complete vulnerability. That's why you're crossing the Inner Circle to rescue a woman you supposedly despise." Maverick dropped the case at the foot of the bed. "Because you're afraid of what life will mean when she's gone. Her death makes you more than an orphan—you'll be alone. Completely. You'll have lost everyone you ever loved and cared for. Sure, you have friends, maybe even a few as near as family—but it's not the same. Nowhere near the same as the thought of being the last. The only."

"I . . ." she stammered into silence. "And how am I supposed to face *that*?"

Maverick tapped the bunk. "Climb in and I'll show you." He snapped open the locks on the case. Inside was a neurocrown made from a circlet of steel with glowing electrodes and a dome of wires webbed across. Next to it, nestled in the black lining, were a series of syringes that contained powerful drugs designed to expand the mind and sharpen synapses. Whatever he had planned, he wasn't taking her out—he was taking her *in*.

Into her own mind. Into her subconscious self.

Suddenly the thought of vaulting into black space with nothing but a nanosuit didn't sound so terrible.

"You're right. I'm really not going to like this."

Maverick chuckled. "Told you."

"Hold on," Nimah whispered. Crossing the cabin, she slipped into the bathroom and staggered to the sink. Activating the faucet, she cupped cool water to splash across her face before rinsing the taste of bile from her mouth. She'd gone into neuro-stasis before—many times for fight simulations and training exercises—but it had always been about encoding and layering in the new, not revisiting the old. She glared at her reflection. Water streamed in beads from her cheeks and chin like silver pearls.

Face your past. Face your pain.

"You ready, Cadet?"

Nimah swallowed the searing burn of tears. "Ready as I'll ever be," she answered.

Joining him at the bunk, she sat down and pressed trembling hands to her bouncing thighs. Maverick went to work, feeding a needle into the central vein on the back of her left hand, connected wires and sensors to her inner elbow, wrist, and across the surface of her chest. Maverick reached for the crown last, and set it on her head, adjusting straps and anchors until it was snug but not too tight. Strobing lights tinted her vision blue.

Finished, he sat back in his chair, assessing his work. "There. That should do it."

"What now?"

"You go under. Whatever you find in there, Nimah, the important thing is to stop running from what you're afraid of. You've gotta charge toward it. Again, and again, as many times as it takes. Slam into that wall until you bring it down."

"What if I can't?"

"I've seen you do it a hundred times already. You charge in, even if your heart is in your throat, you don't let it stop you when it counts. You are a force to reckon with, Nimah. Don't you dare convince yourself otherwise."

A tremor coursed up her spine, spiking through nerves and out through the fine hairs on her arms and neck. *I've come too far to quit now.* Nimah reclined in the bunk. Resolute. Terrified. "Okay. Do it."

FLIGHT OF THE SPARROW 173

"This isn't going to be fun," he said, reaching for the first syringe. "Normally these are administered over the course of hours. We have minutes. It'll feel . . . unsettling."

Nimah tugged up her sleeve and offered her left arm. "Just do it."

The needle punched into the IV port and she winced against the burn of barbiturates flushing through the tubing in her hand and into her bloodstream, hot as a blowtorch. Her eyes swam, her ears rang. The ship trembled—or maybe it was only her—a violent course that rattled her teeth and made the air vibrate with light and sound.

Maverick rubbed away the sting in her arm, and lifted the second syringe. "Ready?"

Nimah could only manage a jerking nod. And pitched her head back into a silent cry as the second jolt spiked into her bones. Electric. Searing. This one brought whispers that swam inside of her head, distant and foggy, but she could hear them funneling like water circling a drain. All saying the same thing.

Don't be afraid.

Don't be afraid.

Don't be afraid.

"Last one," Maverick called out—miles away. The barest echo over the rising storm.

She couldn't find her tongue or her breath as the third—unfelt—flowed thick and slow, hollowing her out. Nimah slumped back on the bunk. Her chest heaving, a cold sweat broke across her skin.

Maverick loomed over her, his hands holding her face, his eyes trained on her fading gaze. "Let it take you," he said. "Don't fight it. Don't resist."

I'm not—she tried to speak, but her tongue wouldn't move.

It wasn't supposed to be like this. Not like this.

Slipping into neuro-stasis was normally a lot like sliding into a warm bath. It started with her fingers and toes, moving up until she was submerged in comfort and warmth, until her lungs rolled into a rhythm she could no longer feel, but still somehow sensed.

But this?

This was like lying naked across thin ice, waiting for it to break from beneath her, and she could feel the cracks spreading. Each fracture rang like thunder. The icy black about to envelop her whole.

This was like dying.

"Don't . . . don . . ." she struggled, fought, but the words wouldn't come. Her hand wouldn't move. Neither would her legs or feet.

"Never," Maverick answered as the trembling walls of the cabin faded at the edges behind him, pixelating into nothing. "I'm right here with you, Cadet. I'm not going anywhere."

The ice broke, with a final gasp, she vanished. And woke in the dark. Endless pitch.

Panic gripped her, but there was no kick of her heart into her throat, no heavy expanding of her lungs. She was incorporeal, still taking shape in the mindspace. But this wasn't a simulation, there wasn't a preset recording for her to enter or a prefabricated stage to make her forget this was all in her head. This was empty, vast subconsciousness. Nothing would exist without her painfully recreating it.

Easy, Cadet. Maverick's voice folded around her, soft and reassuring. Tangible in this stark nothingness. An embrace.

"I can't see."

You will soon. A hand settled on her shoulder and Nimah jerked around. But there was nothing. *I'm here. I'm here with you,* he said, as if reading her mind. Perhaps he was—in cojoined stasis, he more or less would share her thoughts. Her feelings. Her pain. All while skimming the surface of unconsciousness—nowhere near as deep as she was. Instructors often cojoined to ensure cadets were taking to the implanted training procedures and behavior modification. But this felt far more . . . intimate than she could remember it ever being.

Let your mind guide you to where you need to be.

"Where?"

Wherever it hurts the most.

How the hell was she supposed to know that? But Nimah closed her eyes—or tried to—and that quiet darkness thickened. Where it hurts the most. Inward, she had to go inward. She reached deep, and deeper still, and weeping swelled in the silence. Soft and distant.

Childlike.

"No." She pressed her hands to her ears. Straining to block it all out.

Nimah. You can do this.

"I can't go back there. Not *there*. Not again. Please."

The absence of tears running down her cheeks didn't diminish the fact that Nimah knew she was crying. Shaking with sobs. With cold. The dark flickered with a wash of midnight blue chased by the hard glare of blinking red. The scene rapidly took shape, despite her protests, despite her fear—or perhaps because of it. Sharpening into brutal clarity until it was fresh and real and tangible.

A backlit door emerged and swept toward her—drawn in by her terror.

Open it, he urged. *Whatever it is you need to face is on the other side.*

Nimah trembled, cowering in on herself. She'd wanted to forget. To let it all fade away and focus on him instead of those cries. Those screams.

Nimah, stay calm.

But she couldn't. In the wake of escalating terror, the door to the shuttle opened and the halls of the *Avenger* yawned wide, towering over her. No. It didn't grow. She shrank. Her hands, small as a child, stained in blood and stinging from open wounds.

A faint croak emerged from her in a weak, terrified little voice.

"Nimah. Calm yourself." It wasn't Maverick speaking to her now, or who shook her violently, but a crew member on the ship, clutching her in desperation. Blood like an oil-slick on his face, his eyes shining like dark moons and his fingers like clamps of iron on her skin.

"Come back. Nimah, come back!"

Around her the walls tore open with blood gushing from the seams like raw wounds. This wasn't realistic. This wasn't possible. But through the eyes of a child, she couldn't make sense of the chaos as blood rained down upon them in sheets and screams rang in her ears so loud that Maverick's voice drowned in the symphony of death.

Nimah tore away from the corridor and ran, her legs churning furiously, but the bodies snagged at her feet, and hands snatched at her legs until she was stuck. Rooted.

"Let me go!" she cried, struggling to wrench herself free, but those hands held her as a figure emerged from the darkness, rising from the

176   **FALLON DEMORNAY**

pile of twisted corpses. A gleaming silvery figure haloed in strobing red and blue. The same figure she'd seen on the outpost.

Frozen, Nimah could only gape in horror as it loomed closer, hand outstretched, moving with a preternatural grace, and pressed a finger to a point between her eyes.

Everything inside of her shocked bright—and scorched to the bone. "*Nimah!*"

She woke with a leaden jolt like she'd been shocked back into her body, ripped from blood-soaked nightmares into the steady calm of the cabin. Her name rang in her ears. Was it Maverick's voice that had called her back?

"I'm sorry, but you were freaking out and I had to pull you out fast." Maverick removed the IV from her elbow, then massaged the joint, and to her alarm she felt *nothing*. Panic fired through her head and must've shone in her eyes as he hunched over her and waved a hand inches from her face. "Try to breathe."

The moment he issued the command her chest gave a shuddering gulp followed by a series of wet pants. "Can't move."

"It's mild submersion paralysis." He brushed away tears from her cheeks and sensation sparked within her at that simple touch, tingling along her extremities—firing across each nerve like a string of lights. The press of the bunk at her back, the hum of the ship gliding through space.

"How many fingers," he asked, flashing a couple before her eyes.

"Three."

"Good."

Removing her neuro-crown, he tossed it to the foot of the bunk. "Dilation looks good. Color's back in your cheeks. How do you feel?"

How *did* she feel? Battered and beaten. Her arms ached with the burning echo of where the crewmember's crushing grip still singed. "Arm," she grumbled.

Understanding, Maverick rolled up her sleeve and Nimah watched as the blackening marks emerged on her skin.

"Heightened anxiety can draw out trauma from the mindspace into the real. I should get a compress for these."

FLIGHT OF THE SPARROW 177

Nimah frowned. She'd worn those bruises on her skin for nearly a month after her rescue. How long would these fresh welts linger? But as much as they hurt, they paled in comparison to the sear of her brow. "What about my head?" Why did it hurt so much? She could scarcely remember . . .

His eyes danced across her face. "I don't see anything. Could be the start of a migraine. C'mon. I need to sit you up. Get your circulation flowing." His hands hooked behind her shoulders. "Are you ready?"

She nodded, and with a deft jerk she was up and against him. Everything spun. Swayed.

"Steady," he said, holding her until her cheek settled against his shoulder.

"Why do I feel so weak?"

"You've been in stasis for several hours," he answered.

"Felt like minutes."

"Time moves differently when submerged. Deep breaths. Oxygen will purge the serum from your system. The more air you take in the faster you'll regain mobility."

"Don't think I can." Not when each breath felt like trying to lift a fighter jet.

"Here." He pressed her hand over his heart. "Breathe with me. Follow me."

Sighing against him, the warmth of his breath whisked against her ear. His heart pulsed against her palm—pushing through and into her. Each expansion and release of his lungs drew her closer. Deeper.

Did he always smell like leather soaked in sunshine? Or were the drugs fading from her system making her loopy? It felt good, holding him. Too good. Nimah wanted to linger in this moment. To steep herself in it like a warm bath. Floating in a cotton candy ether with Maverick as her anchor, holding her steady and slowly reeling her in.

"You doing alright? Still with me?"

"*Hmmm*," she answered, nuzzling closer, and that steady heart of his rippled.

Drawing back an inch, he tipped up her chin with the crook of his finger. Liquid eyes of brown and molten gold fixed to hers, bright as a waking star. "I know you don't think so," he tucked a curl behind her ear, "but you did amazing, Cadet. Truly."

Kiss me. She wanted to say the words. To breathe them into the finite space between their lips. To give them shape and sound and life. To make them real. But before she could manage to loosen her still-heavy tongue, Maverick eased away. Lowered his arms.

"I should get you a compress for those bruises."

CHAPTER SEVENTEEN

Maverick tugged the IV from his hand and shook out the numbness, his back resting against the headboard as Nimah pressed in against him. It was then he took in how close they were. Too close. The bunk was narrow, and he was wedged against the wall, leaving no way for him to escape.

Something had passed between them at the end, there. Something primal and deep—an urge and a longing. It wasn't hard to know exactly what she'd been thinking. What she'd wanted, and yet . . . His eyes fell from her to his hands in his lap. To the scarred knuckles from years of training in Hatchett's scrapyard with the other skinners. To the days of kill or be killed. Each mark lay like a tombstone in a graveyard of misery, and sank bone deep. He knew about trauma.

He knew about ghosts.

"Attention all passengers, we are pleased to announce that system upgrades and engine repairs have been completed. We are now ready to set course for our final destination," Dobs's voice rattled through the system speakers— bright and perky as a transport hostess before the launch of a cross-planetary flight mixed with the sharp, smoky edge of a pirate. *"Kindly report to the bridge to strap in as we prepare for hardburn in T-minus ten minutes—or be splattered to the walls of your cabins."*

"Maverick . . ."

"We're on the clock, Cadet. Time to get our game faces back on."

Nimah released a short breath. Nodded. "Right." Climbing out of bed, she gathered her mass of curls into a tight bun. "I'll head to the

180   **FALLON DEMORNAY**

bridge and let them know you're on your way," she said, and was gone before he managed to even shimmy into his chair.

Maverick pressed a hand to his side. To the healing stitches where beneath the skin a tracer pulsed, betraying him with every second. He'd been conditioned to feel nothing—no loyalty or honor or compassion to anyone except Hatchett. She was just a girl and this was just a job, but he'd made the vital mistake of letting himself feel for her. She was inside of him now, both head and heart. Messing him up. Making him forget what mattered most. His freedom. Everything he'd strived for over the last decade suddenly felt diminished. Selfish and unimportant.

The fuck was happening to him?

Maverick smacked his hands over his eyes. "Get a grip, for fuck's sake."

Chief Commander Wallace had made it clear what was on the line if he didn't follow through with their agreement. Hatchett wasn't a forgiving sort. There was no negotiating or buying his way out of the cross-hairs; once he'd set his mind on getting his pound of flesh, Hatchett would chase him to the ends of the void. Not that he'd have to, as Wallace vowed to personally deliver Maverick in magnicuffs without an ounce of pity or hesitation if he betrayed her. He'd seen the truth swirling in the metallic gold rings of her HWKeyes.

Turning against her was tantamount to suicide.

And yet . . .

Reaching across to the bedside table, Maverick dug around in the case for one of the used syringes, then sucked in a breath before punching the pointed head beneath the sutures, and went to work popping each one. The skin had already started to knit but quickly gave way. Eyes clamped shut, sweat bloomed on his chest and brow as he dug and searched with shaking fingers until he felt it—the slender pellet. Small as a grain of rice made of carbide steel and top-secret SIGA-grade tech, the ends strobed with a steady blue light.

He sat there for a moment and watched the tracker flicker and dance. Such a tiny thing. So innocuous and yet it held the power to destroy lives. His or Nimah's, depending on which way the pendulum of uncertainty within him swayed.

Closing his fingers around it, he rattled it like a game die and took one last moment to steel himself for the shitstorm about to rain on his head before he dropped the tracker and, with a hard jerk, rolled his wheel over it. The delicate snap roared in his head and chest, deafening as a blast of thrusters breaking atmo.

"Fuck me," he laughed and swiped an unsteady hand through his hair. No going back now. Maverick deposited the needle on the bunk and dressed quickly, taking care to wrap his now-open wound, which he'd have to close himself at some point. His future held only two possible certainties: Freedom. Or a body bag.

But if Wallace and Hatchett wanted him—they'd have to catch him first and no one flew like Maverick Ethos-333. He'd give them the chase of their lives.

He'd give them hell.

The nanosuit hung on the end of a hook in the fitting room near the airlock. Glistening, sleek, and black, threaded with tracks that glowed blue when activated, the light told the agent the status of their suit's integrity. Blue for fully operational. Green for localized damage, yellow for breach, and white for deceased.

She'd dreamed so often of wearing one, the nanites gliding over her body like a second skin, shifting and reshaping. Adapting to her unique physiology. Over time the suit bonded with the agent—learning to interpret and understand their individual needs and react accordingly.

Soon as a cadet was admitted into the Academy, nanites were bred to ensure there would be a suit waiting at the close of their graduation, presented by the chief commander along with the STARs badge.

Lifting it from the hook, she ran the thin and cool leather-like material between her fingers before slipping in one foot after the other and shimmying it up and over her hips. As soon as she fastened the neck, it hummed awake and vibrated—reading, recording, and mapping her various outputs. Standing before the full body holomirror, Nimah faced her reflection.

She looked like an agent, and though it was wrong, the sight made her smile. Made her hope that all wasn't lost. That this reflection would one day still become her reality.

Rescue Jonothan Shinoda. Find the true terrorists. And then she would have what her heart wanted most. Nimah pressed her palms together, damp with sweat, and a little cold. The fear was still there, the bone-deep terror that had haunted her for the last decade and would not be so easily vanquished.

Once, when she'd been barely four—maybe younger—she'd woken in the middle of the night screaming for "Nana." Her grandmother had come rushing into the cabin, thick black hair in a long single braid and eyes bright with alarm to find Nimah cowering beneath the covers. Terrified of the monsters she believed lived under her bunk, waiting to drag her below.

Sitting on the edge of the bunk, when Nimah had tried to climb weeping into her lap, Ro had held her in place and faced her sternly.

Fear means two things. Forget everything and run, or face everything and rise. There will always be something to be afraid of, Sparrow. There will always be monsters waiting to steal you away into the night—and I won't always be there to save you from them. One day you'll have to be brave.

One day, you'll have to save yourself.

At the time Nimah had thought she'd done something wrong to make her grandmother upset, but thinking back on it now—she had been preparing Nimah by not pacifying her with cuddles and hugs. Those would've made her feel safe in the moment, but after she would've been the same little girl cowering under her blankets from the monsters.

And in a way she had been—because she'd let herself forget that important lesson, along with so many others her grandmother had tried to instill in her tender mind. Maybe it was the shock of stasis, but they seeped into her now like water through paper. If she couldn't change being afraid, then what had to change was her response to fear.

So what will you do, Sparrow? Which one will you choose?

"I'll rise," she said to herself. As many times as she had to. As many times as it took.

"Ah, good, you're ready," Dobs said as she entered the fitting room. "Everyone's on the bridge, just came to fetch you myself. Make sure your head is on straight."

Nimah faced Dobs, the nanosuit hugging her like a glove, and the pulsing hum in the woven carbon fabric made her feel steady. Calm. She knew what this suit could do under pressure, and wearing it—she felt like a superhero.

A warrior.

Planted before her, Dobs swung her gaze from head to toe. "You look the part, at least."

FLIGHT OF THE SPARROW 183

Nimah raised her chin. "Let's hope I can act the part, too."

Dobs sighed deeply. "Fell off a ship once, when I was thirteen. The kind that floats." She winked down at Nimah. "It was a nighttime storm—winds knocked me over, and over I went. Blinded by salt and sea, in that briny pitch up is down, down is up. Nearly drowned."

"What happened?"

"Fought my way to the surface. Just had to trust it was the right way. Then I grabbed hold of a towline and hauled myself on board." Dobs spread her hands and looked down at her palms as if seeing old wounds that had long since healed. Those long fingers curled, tightening into fists. "Life casts you out to sea and it's up to you to decide what happens next. You live, or you drown. Heard? I know you're scared. Ain't nothing wrong with fear. But letting it hold you back—letting it control you—that's cowardice. You a coward?"

"I don't think so." Nimah shook her head. "I keep telling myself to be brave like my grandmother. I know what she did at my age. She was . . . fearless."

"More like reckless," Dobs corrected with a laugh and a wink. "But can't be brave unless you've got some kind of stupid in you, too. Maybe this'll help." Reaching behind her, Dobs thrust a sheathed blade at Nimah. Her grandmother's cutlass. "Ro never charged into a job without it. Said it put steel into her blood."

Accepting the blade, Nimah held the weight in her hands and something inside of her . . . glowed. *Home,* it whispered. *The way home . . .*

Dobs slapped her shoulder, jarring her back. "C'mon, kid. We've got a pirate to rescue."

Sword belted to her waist, Nimah followed Dobs. They rounded a corner just as Boomer sauntered out of the ship's compact weapons locker strapped with more explosives and guns than a man even his size should be able to carry and keep standing.

Maverick, waiting from him outside the locker, scowled at the sight of his friend. "What're you doing, Booms?"

Boomer inspected himself with a quizzical frown. "What?"

"Leave the repeater and the bazooka and, for the last time, *no* grenades."

Boomer released a harrowing gasp, as if Maverick had demanded he part with a beloved child. "But . . . ?"

"Quiet, Booms. I know that's not a word you're overly familiar with, but we gotta go soft on this one."

"Can't I take just *one*?" He pressed beseeching hands together. "A small one. Like this here Polly Pocket?" Rummaging in his vest, he plucked out a metal cylinder shaped like a tube of lipstick.

"No."

Frown lines deepened into trenches between his brow, and in a flurry of hands and facial movements, he launched into a furious barrage of RIM-SL that Nimah struggled to follow.

"What's he saying?" Dobs leaned in and whispered.

"Nothing good," Nimah said.

Maverick responded with a withering stare and a rush of gestures that had Boomer's expression darkening. "When'd you go and get all fucking boring on me?" he spat.

"Yeah, yeah. Cry into your pillow later."

Boomer grumbled as Maverick whisked away in the direction of the bridge. "Who died and made him cap?"

"Mav's right," Nimah offered gently, and was struck by his fierce scowl. "The whole point of this is to get in and out without a scene or casualties. The plan—"

"Plans rarely go as planned," Boomer tossed back. But after a long, frustrated growl, he swiveled on his heel and re-entered the weapons locker where he discarded each item with a salty curse. Some in English and others in languages she didn't recognize. "There," he stepped back out, armed with little more than a blaser and a couple of throwing knives. Hands spread, he turned full circle before her. "Do I pass inspection?"

Nimah tried not to smile—really tried—but his utterly dejected and bitter pout was priceless. "At ease, Cadet."

Hand to chest, Boomer jerked with a wide-eyed, affronted gasp before stalking off toward the bridge.

"I think you hurt his feelings." Smirking, Dobs nudged her with an elbow. "But he raised a solid point," she added as they climbed the stairs. "Plans go sideways all the time." She stopped outside the main entrance to the bridge and faced her. "You prepared to do what has to be done? No matter how messy? No matter how . . . difficult?"

FLIGHT OF THE SPARROW

Nimah didn't have to ask what she meant. Was she ready to get her hands dirty? Was she prepared to kill? "I'll do what needs to be done," she assured. "Whatever that entails."

"Then say the words, kid."

"What?"

"*The* words." Dobs set a hand on her shoulder. Squeezed. "You may dream of being an agent one day, but as of right now you're a pirate and we're your crew. We're counting on you to have our backs. Can't have you teetering on the line, on this. Time to cross it. Commit."

"Oh." Nimah skimmed her teeth across her bottom lip. "To the void or Valhalla—I'm a Valkyrie for life."

"Fucking A you are." Dobs grinned. "Alright, ladies, you know the drill." She clapped her hands as they entered the bridge.

The team strapped in and Nimah found an empty seat. She yanked down the harness, fastening the latches and tightened the straps until she could scarcely draw in a breath as the ship gave a trembling shudder like a lion coiling to pounce.

<Hardburn to commence in ten seconds.>

Maverick caught her gaze, inclined his chin with a subtle nod.

<Six seconds.>

"You ready, Cadet?"

<Two seconds.>

"To the void or Valhalla," Nimah whispered.

The stars went to liquid, streaking across the viewport, and like an arrow plucked from a bow, *Stormchaser* shot into the dark.

CHAPTER EIGHTEEN

The force sucked her back. Tears blistered her eyes. She'd hard-burned in simulation but this was so much more—the drag compressed against Nimah's chest.

Heavy and searing.

On a STARship the buffers would've been first-grade, the ride as smooth as falling into a gentle sleep, but the *Stormchaser* was slapped together with spare or stolen parts, and apparently not all of them gelled as seamlessly. G-force pressure seeped through cracks and looped around Nimah's throat, cinching tight until her vision blackened around the edges.

"Almost there," Maverick strained against the pull of unconsciousness.

Someone groaned thickly in response.

Maybe Boomer.

Maybe Dobs.

A hard jerk and jolt snapped through them as the *Stormchaser* lurched to a violent and sudden stop that wrenched Nimah forward in the harness. Muscles screamed in her neck and shoulders at that jarring transition.

"Fucking . . . Chu—I thought you said you had her ready for hard-burn?" Dobs spat, head hanging forward. "Feel like I've been stomped on by a herd of spooked orlephants."

"I'm a mechanic, not a magician."

Uncoupling her harness, Gertrude ambled over to the console, graceful as a dancer. "We're in position," she confirmed, "and the *Challenger* is almost within range. Time to kill all engines and blast the echo."

Maverick punched the power switch and the *Stormchaser* rumbled into silence, all main lights flickering out, leaving only the ones on the console to whirl and dance. *Challenger* was designed to pick up on large energy signals and prime ore emissions, even those hidden behind the most sophisticated of shields.

Only way to go dark on their radar was to go *dark*.

Sweat bloomed on Nimah's skin in alternating waves of hot and cold as they sat in the pitch black without a stray sound to cut through the eerie silence.

Two minutes was all they had to sync to the course trajectory: to go from cold engines, match speed, and maintain for the entire duration they were aboard the vessel. Even for the most advanced ships with a powerful prime ore engine—that was a big ask. The *Stormchaser* was about as old and weathered as her crew. It would be like Chu running a marathon against a retrofit cadet, but if they couldn't catch the *Challenger* before she broke the barrier to hardburn, Captain Ro was lost to them. And with it, all hope for Nimah's future.

"Steady." Dobs closed a hand over Maverick's shoulder.

A tremor shook through Nimah as the *Challenger* emerged, shaped like a battle axe, and sliced through the void above them. Smooth, graceful, and vicious as a glowing negshark. A half-million tons of voidship with nanites woven into the carbide steel body that rippled like quivering muscles, much like an agent's suit. Sentient. It allowed for the ship to adapt and react more succinctly. To fly and command such a beast, you had to have nerves of steel.

Hidden amidst clusters of debris, they waited as the *Challenger* sailed toward them. Its powerful shields swatted hunks of stone and ore from its path, and as those bits collided with the *Stormchaser*, fractured stone rang against hull metal like breaking bones.

"Mumbles," Dobs called out over her shoulder. "Your time to shine."

Tucking her length of pigtails behind her large ears, Mumbles wiggled her fingers and hooked her tongue at the corner of her wrinkled lips. "Pop-pop-pop!" She giggled, then pressed a button on a small, homemade trigger connected with a length of cable to what looked like a plastic bottle filled with Styrofoam balls and copper wire. The *Stormchaser* shuddered from the burst of a shockwave and the crew watched with bated breath as the wave scored across the navgrid in an expanding arch, racing toward the *Challenger.*

"Ten seconds until in position," Gertrude uttered gently. "Seven."

Maverick's hand flexed over the throttle.

"Four."

"We have one shot." Dobs leaned into his ear. "Don't fuck this up, boy—"

"Two."

"—or I'll have your guts for garters."

"Now!"

Maverick punched the power, and the ship roared swiftly to life. The *Stormchaser*'s thrusters engaged with a hard kick, punching Nimah back into her seat, and she clenched her teeth against the strain until it eased off her chest. Jaw grim, eyes focused, Maverick worked the yoke with skilled finesse, weaving and twisting around jagged bits of fractured ore as the *Challenger* swam ahead. Its powerful thrusters sent shockwaves to rattle the tiny ship and the *Stormchaser* strained to catch up.

"She's too fast."

"Push harder," Dobs ordered. "We can't lose her!"

"Any faster and I lose maneuverability. We'll hit *something*."

And out here there was plenty to hit. Nimah's fingers clenched the armrest of her seat, knuckles screaming, her nails cut into recycled leather until they met steel. "I have an idea." The ship rattled her teeth so hard she thought they'd drop from her head. "Gertrude, you know anything about skipping stones?"

Gertrude swiveled around in her seat and cast Nimah a surprised grin. "Girl, you're the right mix of crazy and style. I like it."

"Fuck is a skipping stone?" Chu scowled. "Don't like the sound of it much."

"You won't like the feel of it, either." Gertrude chuckled, her fingers whisking and moving with furious intent on the holoscreen. "Maverick, coordinates coming your way, darling."

He cursed as they popped on screen. "Have you lost your mind?"

"Just do it." Nimah braced herself. "It's our only play now."

FLIGHT OF THE SPARROW 189

"Fuck my life. Prepare for hardburn."

"Thought you said you couldn't burn through this minefield?" Boomer bellowed, the whites of his eyes bright against his dark skin. "Thought you said it was suicide to fly blind?"

"It is."

"We're only doing small pulses," Nimah explained. "Just far enough ahead to see."

"Yeah," Maverick snorted, "except what's empty now might not be when we get there."

He was right. Given the *Challenger's* hard sail, chunks of rock and ore spun and danced like dust motes in a stray sunbeam. Once Maverick was tucked beneath her and inside the safety of her flight path it would be smoother sailing. The *Stormchaser* could coast like an eagle catching thermals, or a turtle gliding the undertow of a strong current. But they had to catch her *first*.

<Error—system cannot accept coordinates. Structural integrity—>

"Ma, override to manual, on my authority," Dobs interceded, "Dorothy Dobrevnic, Valkyrie SIC, voice access code: aces over kings."

The system hummed to a pause, much like a woman sighing while rolling her eyes mid-argument.

<Override accepted. Hardburn to commence.>

Pulsing through hardburn was a lot like being swung repeatedly into a wall. Each violent stop had the edges of Nimah's vision blackening with the threat of unconsciousness. For Maverick to stay awake—focused— was a breathtaking skill.

"Hold on!" he shouted, veering hard right into evasive flying with a fraction of a second to react, yanking the *Stormchaser* from colliding nose-first with a swirling chunk of ore half their size. It was a close call but the smooth glide into position beneath the *Challenger* loosened the clench of Nimah's jaw.

"Well," Chu wheezed, mouth askance and hand across her flat chest like she was a breath away from a heart attack. "I think that put some hair on my tits."

"Now you'll have something to match your beard, darling."

Popping the buckle on her harness, Dobs slapped Maverick hard on the back with a guffaw. "That was some ace flying for a skinbag. Maybe you got a little pirate in you, after all."

190   FALLON DEMORNAY

Maverick shot her a dark smile. "That's sweet. Are we becoming friends?"

"Don't push it." Dobs swatted him again, this time against the back of his head, hard enough to ruffle dark hair.

"Alright, we're in position. Let's get a wiggle on." Chu scowled, hands on hips. "Instead of sitting here clucking like Ro is already onboard and ready to pop bubbles."

"Chulita's right." Gertrude stretched her arms, cracked her neck. "But before we waltz out into the void," she tapped the console, "looks like a pod of negs are closing in. I don't know what's calling them, but they're swimming fast." She drew up a holoscreen for all to see. "Chu, you smuggling some uncut prime we don't know about?"

"Yeah, up my dusty snatch."

"What's our window?" Dobs demanded.

"Thirty-seven minutes on the clock," Maverick warned. "You'll need to be off the *Challenger* in less than thirty-five."

"You heard him," Dobs spoke up, a general mustering her troops. "Unless you're aching to get gnawed on by a pod of negs, it's go time, ladies."

Nimah followed Dobs and the crew from the bridge down to the main airlock. It was a snug fit with the six of them crammed inside, and soon as the door sealed shut, the computerized operation system's voice rumbled through the speakers with a warning. Helmet on, her heart rippled a little faster once the lights flashed to red as air whooshed from the vents, depressurizing the space, and ended on steady green.

"As predicted, the Challenger*'s main shields are doing a fine job of clearing the course,"* Maverick spoke across the intercom. *"We're all green lights, Cadet."*

"Good. We're about to launch," Nimah answered, voice ragged. "Hold her steady as she goes."

"I've got her, Cadet. I've got you."

Dobs reached for the airlock handle and disengaged it with a hard twist. The doors split on a slanted angle, opening in a silent yawn. Overhead the belly of the *Challenger* stretched like a hull metal horizon, but beyond that the void spread—wild, dark, and grinning black with stars that glistened like the teeth of negs waiting to devour her whole.

Nimah recoiled a step, colliding with a solid body.

FLIGHT OF THE SPARROW

"Oi!"

"Sorry," she stammered, but the word came out garbled thanks to the fist of fear around her throat, strangling her stupid.

Don't be afraid.

Don't be afraid.

Don't be afraid.

"Gertrude, Boomer, you take the first leap," Dobs ordered. "Chu and Siggy, you're second." Dobs twisted around to Nimah, stern features lit blue from the nanite helm. "I'll follow with the kid."

She's clearing the airlock. She doesn't want them to see—to know . . . In case Nimah lost her nerve and panicked, which she freaking was. Tingling speared into her fingers. Her toes. A fuzzy hum danced in her head, churning and spinning and reeling as each of them dove without hesitation. Without an ounce of worry, as if jumping without a tether wasn't tantamount to suicide.

They quickly shrank into silver dots, racing like bullets for the flat underbelly of the *Challenger*, large enough to swallow the *Stormchaser* twenty times over. Even with Maverick tethered, there had to be at least a solid two hundred yards of open void to leap across.

Nimah pressed against the hull, wanting to melt into it and disappear as terror radiated through every nerve in her body, bright as a solar flare.

Dobs closed in before her, blocking her sight of the black, empty hole of oblivion. "Be stronger than that voice in your head. The hardest part is taking the first step. Letting go. After that, you'll do whatever has to be done." She thrust out a hand. "Y'ready to fly, Sparrow?"

"I have to be." Stiff as a newborn foal, she staggered to the doorway. Her toes brushed the edge—the edge between safety and nothing. Panic roared in her ears, built into a wave of pressure that whooshed in and out to the beat of her heart.

One step and she'd be out there without gravity or any sense of direction—up or down—it made no difference. Leaping was the same as swimming and flying but without the ability to steer or control. Once you were out there, the void had you in its grip. Once you were out there—you were at its mercy. And the void had none.

Eyes closed, heart thundering, lungs tight. "Face everything and rise," Nimah whispered—and shot out into the emptiness. Weightless.

192 FALLON DEMORNAY

Afloat and adrift, her heart beat in rapid, searing pulses that shook her ribs like barren twigs in a winter storm. Chu, Sigourney, and Gertrude were nothing but distant, shimmering pinpricks up ahead. Casting her gaze to her left, Dobs sailed smoothly, arms pinned at her sides.

"Whooo!" she cackled, her laughter breaking inside Nimah's helm like she was a figment of her imagination. "Last one to the *Challenger* is fish bait!"

Nimah tried to laugh but it came out in a wheeze. "Glad someone is enjoying themselves." The visor on Nimah's helm whizzed with flickering gauges reading distance, speed, and temperature, biometrics of both the void and herself. Her breathing was too fast, her oxygen levels stunted, so it was no surprise she was a little lightheaded.

Fifty yards stretched like an impossible distance, and if she missed her mark? The suit had thrusters, which she couldn't use until she'd broken through the shield, otherwise she'd trigger their sensors, warning of encroaching objects. She also had mag locks to anchor her to the ship but here, in this chasm of asteroids and chunks of broken rock, they were useless. This would work. It had to work.

Because the alternative was death . . . or death.

"Almost there, kid." Dobs cast her a wry grin from across twelve feet. "Steady on."

"Projectile!" Nimah screamed but her cautionary cry was lost in the punch of rock that fractured off the *Challenger*'s shield and collided with Dobs like a bullet, sending her reeling.

"Dobs has been hit!" Nimah screamed. "She's off course. I think she's unconscious."

Chu swore a filthy, searing curse.

"I have to get her."

"You can't activate thrusters," Gertrude warned. "Their sensors will read you."

Nimah's mind swam, thick as cold oil, as Dobs spun and spun and spun, spiraling farther away with every frantic second. "Only if I keep them engaged. Short pulses should be too brief. They'll think it's ricochet from debris impact."

"Nim—"

FLIGHT OF THE SPARROW
193

"I have to get her!" Arms locked to her sides, Nimah flattened her hands, and with a single thought, engaged her palm thrusters. Blue sparks emitted, flaring white and violet at the edges. She counted three seconds, and disengaged, using the first pulse to change direction.

Dobs reeled head over heels, arms limp, corkscrewing farther and farther away.

Again. Heat swam in her hands and she shot forward, swift and agile, whizzing through the scattered chunks of ore. "Three, two, one." Her acceleration ceased the instant the thrusters shut off, but velocity held steady. Dobs was still a good thirty yards out, careening out of control, and not slowing down.

Sweat rolled down the side of her nose, she blinked it from her eyes, and this time held the thrusters for five seconds before shutting it off. Dobs was close enough for Nimah to see the smear of blood inside her visor, cracked but holding. The nanites would repair the seal, but it would take another few minutes to solidify.

Nimah clawed between them. Reaching, grasping. So close. Her fingers brushed a boot, a knee, and finally found a hold on her harness. "Got her!" she called out, locked in a twisting, disorienting spin with Dobs in her arms.

"*Apurate—coño!* You're eating time we don't have."

It took several tries before Nimah was able to fasten the harness to hers. "Hold on," Nimah whispered, and pressing her arms to her sides, she engaged thrusters once more, steering beneath the wide belly of the *Challenger* in three-second pulses until she caught the side of the landing gear where Chu, Sigourney, Gertrude, and Boomer were anchored.

Chu held out a hand and helped Nimah find her feet on the ship. Her boots sealed with a firm grip, but beneath the soles she could feel the rumble of the ship's gravitational pull welcoming her. Holding her steady. It was working.

"Give 'er here." Chu waved a hand, and Nimah hobbled over, Dobs's weight bearing down with the engaged maglocks.

"Y' don't think she tripped any sensors?" Boomer asked as Chu uncoupled her harness and held Dobs steady.

"We shall find out soon enough," Sigourney answered.

"Wha'ppened?" Dobs groaned and blinked rapidly. "Head hurts like the devil taking a bath in holy water. The fuck hit me?"

"Chunk of an asteroid the size of Gertrude's nutsack," Chu answered. "Deflected off the main shield."

Sigourney tapped a fist to Dobs's shoulder. "Are you well, Dobrevnic?"

"Fuck me sideways." Dobs winced, frowned. "Yeah, Siggy, I'm alright. Might've knocked a couple screws loose, but what else is new?"

Boomer snorted a laugh. "Screws."

"Alright, hike up those panties and let's get moving." Chu clapped her hands together, rallying focus. "We're losing precious seconds fussing over this old bitch."

"Who you calling old?" Dobs grumbled into a back-twisting stretch. "At least I've still got all my teeth."

Chu beamed. "Not if I punch 'em out your smart mouth."

"Much as I love watching you two snipe at each other, we've got work to do." Gertrude shook her head and swept out an arm, indicating it was time to move along.

Removing her rucksack, Chu muttered and grumbled as she went to work with laser cutters. Custom ones, given their ad-hoc design, and any other time Nimah would've been horrified at how they made short work of the SIGA-grade bolts and steel. But as of this moment, her stomach was too busy migrating up her throat for her to think of anything other than getting *inside* the belly of the ship.

One after the other, they crawled inside and sealed the breach.

"We should move, quick," Chu warned, pressing the points on her throat to disengage her helmet once the pressure had stabilized. It slid away from her face, folding like the canvas in a pixelated fan. "If sensors reacted, the bridge might send a couple engies to do a looksee."

"Engies?"

"Engineers." Gertrude rested a hand on Nimah's shoulders. "Chu isn't one for syllables."

"Want me to deck you? Keep it up and I'll have you flat on your back so fast, you'll think me a cog."

"We should leave a pair of eyes behind," Dobs said, dabbing a hand to her brow. The bleeding had stopped but she was going to have a wicked bruise.

FLIGHT OF THE SPARROW 195

Sigourney tapped the gleaming axes fastened to her hips and a long, carbide shield slung across her back. "I'll hold position in case they do."

"Keep your comms active at all times." Dobs nodded to Sigourney. "Give it ten minutes. If no one pops by, consider the coast clear and come rejoin us. Gertrude will make sure you have our live location."

"This way." Gertrude gestured ahead with a raised holoscreen before her eyes. "This is a spec map of the entire ship, but we'll need to find a port to connect to the mainframe and access the prisoner logs to know where they're keeping Ro."

Nimah's eyes raced across the map. "Here." She tapped the screen, pulling up the level above them. "This one is used mainly by the ship's engineers, but they won't be down on this grid unless there's critical system failure or a major breach in the belly. Should let us get in without being interrupted."

"Works for me."

Following the map, the port wasn't hard to find. Chu made short work of opening it with her kit, and Gertrude even less to connect her holoscreen to the ship's mainframe.

"Here." Dobs stopped by the security panel and, removing a dagger from her holster, slid the blade beneath the thin steel plate and popped it open to reveal wires webbed over a computer board lit with racing lights.

"What are you doing?"

"Making sure we're covered." Dobs answered, removing twin glass orbs from her pocket. She tossed one to Chu, who snatched it with a deft snap of her wrist.

"This isn't the Academy. The system's designed to know when it's being tampered with," Nimah hissed. "Any attempts to loop or distort will—"

"Relax, kid. Don't let Chu's surly mood fool you. She's a genius."

Nimah frowned as Chu nestled the orb inside and, with a knife of her own, snipped and exposed wires that she crossed with others. Her methods were old school. Vintage. It shouldn't have worked, and yet, no screaming alarms or strobing lights.

"There. That oughta do it." Chu slapped the panel shut. "What's with the face?" She rammed a bony elbow into Nimah's hip. "You been sucking a lemon thinking it was a peach?"

196   **FALLON DEMORNAY**

"It's just . . . too easy." Nimah waved a bemused hand at the panel. "This is a SIGA-grade voidship with the most advanced defense systems and you're skipping through it like they're made of cardboard. It's disconcerting. Insulting, even."

Chu cackled around a raspy laugh. "Lemme tell you something: the more complicated the system," she wiggled fingers in the air, "the easier it is to walk right through the front door."

"Alright, kid." Hands on her shoulders, Dobs shifted Nimah to the forefront. "Time to go to work." Holding the orb between them, her hand fell away, and it winked awake with a silver shimmer, hovering in the naked air. "Beautiful, ain't it?"

It was. She'd been too drunk on Seawater to appreciate its luminous beauty at the Academy. "What do I do with it?"

"Just tell it where to go. With this." Dobs tapped the holoscreen where a blip on the specs pulsed and hummed. Above it, a search bar waited for her to run a request.

"What am I looking for?" Gertrude asked, eyes accented with glowing violet contacts.

Nimah pushed all thoughts of hesitation and doubt aside. As Dobs had said, it was time to cross the line. Commit. "Run a search through the command hierarchy. To access prisoner logs we'll need credentials, preferably someone with the highest clearance that's also low enough on the ladder that the system won't flag them with a secondary bypass command code to ensure the request is valid."

"Got it." Gertrude pulled up a short list of the command database with dizzying speed.

Nimah skimmed the names and titles and settled on one midway through. "Staff Sergeant Norris Hamell." She tapped the screen. "Can you locate his codes?"

Gertrude smirked around an eyeroll. "Ten seconds."

She only needed eight.

"This can't be right," Nimah whispered.

"What?" Dobs snapped, arching over her shoulder for a clearer view.

"The *Challenger* has the capacity to transport well over two hundred prisoners. This roster should be full, but it's not. There's only *one*."

"Only one I care to see," she huffed. "Where are they keeping her?"

"C-deck. It's not far."

FLIGHT OF THE SPARROW

"Then what are we waiting for?"

"I—I need a moment. I need to think."

"We don't have time for this," Dobs snapped. "What's the problem?"

"I was banking on a *full* ship of convicts to shuffle the deck." Nimah closed the roster. "Creating confusion would've allowed us a moment of distraction to get in and out, but I can't shuffle a deck of *one*." Fifty STARs agents were aboard the *Challenger*, plus another thirty in crew—and all eyes were locked on a single target: Captain Indira Roscoe. How were they going to sneak her off board with so many? "I don't know what to do."

Sighing, Dobs activated comms. "Valkyries to *Stormchaser*. What's our countdown?"

"Looking good at the moment," Maverick answered, his voice a little strained. *"If we maintain current thrust, I estimate twenty-two minutes till the* Challenger *reaches the hardburn barrier."*

Nimah swallowed a groan. If they weren't off the *Challenger* with enough time for Maverick to clear the ship's hardburn radius, they'd get swept into the undercurrent and dragged like a body across pavement. The *Stormchaser*, and everyone aboard, would never survive that.

"You think you can raise the flaps? Create a little friction for us down there and buy us a little wiggle?"

"Not unless I want them to know I'm down here."

"Heard." Snatching Nimah by the collar, Dobs yanked her forward and thrust her into a fast walk. "There you have it. Gonna have to think on your feet, kid. Let's get moving."

Sweat flashed across Nimah's brow but she pushed up her chin and had to trust that she'd find a way through the problem soon enough. Because if she didn't, and they failed to deboard the *Challenger* before it hardburned, she'd have handed all of them over to Hollow Point agents on a silver platter. Life behind bars in the most fortified prison in all the void would be the least of their problems.

Scanning her holoscreen, Gertrude skimmed and swiped until satisfied. "We're clear. C-deck is to the left. Let's go. I'll steer us past any sentries or moving bodies."

The corridors swept out in clean, almost sterile precision. All LED-paneled glass walls, smooth and glossy without a single divot or bolt, and fused to slick metal flooring that pulsed with track lights illuminating the path forward in beads of purple or dashes of red, depending on destination and directionality.

Well-worn treads on the plating gave away the vessel's age, but little else. It was impeccably maintained. Almost ruthlessly so. The only interruption in the elegant design was the occasional viewport that allowed for a staggering glimpse of the inner belly of the *Challenger* in all her majestic glory. A twisting chasm of slowly spinning rings interconnected by a core centrifuge that held a prime heart big enough to power a small planet for twenty-seven years.

She was a marvel. An engineering triumph.

There was a time when Nimah had considered it artful in its simplicity, but now, standing in it outside of a simulation, it just felt . . . cold. Heartless, without the charm and rickety character of the *Stormchaser*. Without its soul.

"This don't feel like a boat," Chu muttered, elbows bent and knees clicking. "Feels like the cutting room of a damn medbay."

"Definitely is a chill in the air, innit?" Gertrude agreed.

Nimah didn't have the heart to tell them they weren't wrong. When it came to military and medical centers—both were often coldly functional with little else to distinguish them.

They made it all the way to C-deck without issue, but there was no working around the sentry on post. One, mercifully, but still a problem.

"How are we going to move the statue?" Dobs reclined against the wall after peering around the corner to inspect the way. "Specs say the captain is behind that last door, there. No way to take him down without making a ruckus, and if he gets out a call, we'll be stormed in minutes. Seconds."

"What're we working with?" Gertrude examined her nails. "Young? Old? Does he look skittish or hard to bend? How are his shoes?"

"I was more interested in clocking his weapons than his boots."

"And that's why I'll forever be the beauty and you the brawn. Scoot, darling, let me take a looksee." Moving around Dobs, she flicked a quick glance out into the corridor, barely a third of a second at most, then spun back around with a grin. "Be still my heart. Mid-fifties, a slight bend in the shoulders, with worn shoes but ruthlessly polished. We've got ourselves a lamb still in fleece. Loyal trooper, desperate to please his superiors but malleable." Gertrude tossed a hand. "Relax, ladies, I've got this."

FLIGHT OF THE SPARROW 199

"Get your helmet on, *pendeja*. He'll take one look at you and know you're not an agent in that getup."

"Darling, I came prepared for a reason." Gertrude tossed her thick mane of dense curls tipped with neon blue highlights.

"Chu's right. We're not in your club," Dobs seethed through a grating whisper. "We don't have time for games. How do you know you can—?"

"Age and experience, darling. This is what I do." Gertrude set her shoulders and fluffed up her chest before sashaying out into the corridor like an actress gracing the stage in silks instead of body-hugging nanites.

The guard jolted in alarm, and even at this distance Nimah could see his white skin exploding with splotches of red against the silver sheen of his stubbly beard. "No one's authorized to be in this sector."

"Hush, lamb." She batted a hand. "I won't tell if you won't."

"Identify yourself."

"That'll take a long while, and a stiff drink. But I do love a man in uniform. Make me an offer, handsome, and I might accept." Whip fast, she pressed the searing end of a blaser under his chin. "What's your name, lamb?"

Large eyes bulging, he blinked rapidly. "Wilbur."

Gertrude cooed, lips pursed and eyes gleaming like a sharpened blade. "Wilbur. I do adore the name."

"Are you . . . are you . . . ?"

She tapped his chin. "Ah, an adoring fan. Yes, darling. The Minx of Sparta3, at your service."

Wilbur flushed crimson right up to his stark white hairline, and bobbed a drunken nod. "What're you doing here?"

"A daring rescue." And when she stroked his arm like an adoring pet, he almost purred. "It would be *razor* if you would put down your weapon and step aside. You've such a pretty head, I'd hate to blow holes in it."

Wilbur shifted on the spot, feet dancing with anxious hesitation. "I can't. I can't."

She cupped his face, nails cinching around the scruff of his jaw. "Did I give you permission to speak?"

"No," he panted.

"No, *what*?"

"No, mistress."

FALLON DEMORNAY

"Did I give you permission to *look* at me?"

His eyes fell away and the flush deepened. "No, mistress."

Gertrude released his face and cocked out her leg, the toe of her boot pressed with dramatic flair. "On your knees." And to Nimah's utter shock, he sank without a moment's question. "Go," she mouthed gently to them. "I'll keep this *worm* occupied."

CHAPTER NINETEEN

This is it." Dobs shoved Nimah's shoulder, jarring her back to focus, and removed her handgun from its holster. "You and Boomer get Ro. We'll hold the corridor in case of any passing sentries. Two minutes, Sparrow, any longer than that, we risk getting pinched."

Nimah's heart quickened, a throbbing pulse of panic twined with an unexpected burst of nervous excitement. All the hurdles they'd crossed to reach this moment and now it was happening. In a matter of moments, she'd have her grandmother in hand.

And hopefully her future, as well.

"Right. Boomer." Nimah cocked her head and, holstering his repeater across his shoulder, he followed as she burst into the cell. No, not a cell. It was an interrogation room. The walls lined with long sheets of mirrors, pristinely kept without a single crack or crevice so the target could see what was being done to them from all angles.

A long medical exam table sat at the edge of the room, surrounded by monitors and displays and a wheeled cart covered with everything you could think of to inflict pain and extract information.

Captain Ro hung, suspended by magnicuffs at her wrists, from a cable at the center of the room. The length of her spun in a slow, almost drunken, circle. Even in her golden years, every inch of her was strong. Tight with muscle, lithe and compact. A warrior. Sweat soaked through her black fitted t-shirt and blood splattered across the thighs of her cargo pants, rusted and dried but a few patches still red and damp. They'd left her boots on, laced tight, at least.

Nimah reached out, almost afraid to touch this image and find it was real. Her fingers closed around the toned bicep of her grandmother's arm and stopped the gentle spin, angling her so they were face to face.

Her skin was more weathered and wrinkled, but not much else about Indira Roscoe had changed. Her hair was still stark black, roped in a long braid, but with a single sweep of palest silver at the front, like foam cresting a wave—or a tsunami—depending on her mood.

Nimah cleared her throat. "Nana . . . ?"

It took a few groggy seconds for that head to lift, for the wing of bangs to slide away and reveal a pair of bloodshot eyes more gold than brown. They flickered to Nimah—blinked into focus—then widened. "Sparrow?"

A watery smile cut across Nimah's face. "It's me."

Captain Ro shook a despondent head. "Voiddamn idiot," she grunted, and collapsed back into unconsciousness.

Shock blistered into hurt, bubbling and vicious across Nimah's nerves, spreading like a black web until she was cocooned in shadows. She hadn't given much thought to what the first words out of her grandmother's mouth would be after all these years, but those hadn't been chief among them.

"Well . . ." Boomer's sucked in an awkward breath. "That's gotta ice."

It absolutely did. But with the clock running out, there was no time for bruised feelings or wounded pride.

"Hold her steady," Nimah ordered, and Boomer gathered Ro in his solid arms. He hoisted her a few inches, increasing the slack while Nimah dragged over a steel-framed chair and, boosting onto it, went to work.

Suspension cables were sturdy and resilient, but her fingers made fast work of the knots after years of practice in the Academy under Professor Brakkin, who'd walk the aisles of his classroom with a whip-thin reed in hand, inspecting each student's efforts under a ruthless eye. Anything less than perfection was not good enough or even tolerated. Those who failed to meet his unwavering standards had their knuckles struck.

For nearly six months Nimah had gone to sleep with tears in her eyes, unable to move her fingers for weeks at a time, the joints all swollen and purple. Scars, thin as an eyelash, ribboned across the length of her fingers, a constant reminder of her failings. But she'd learned—more importantly, she'd never forgotten.

"Last one," she warned, and when the knot released, Captain Ro slumped over Boomer's shoulder with a wheezing cry like a hundred-and-sixty-pound sack of rice. "Lay her on the table."

"What for?"

"I need to see how bad she is before we move her. There might be internal injuries—broken bones that could rupture organs."

Boomer grumbled but did as instructed and, despite his hulking size, laid her grandmother down with considerable gentleness. Ro grunted but didn't move, and Nimah quickly set to work with the bodyscan in her holodeck.

Bruises. Lots of them, both internal and external, not that she'd expected any less. Plus fractured ribs—two on the left and one on the right. Readings also revealed the telltale signs of waterboarding and sleep deprivation.

"How bad?"

"Bad." Tears clung to her lashes. The left arm had a broken radius, at least a day old, that hadn't been reset, but it was the dislocated right hip that made her hesitate. If Nimah didn't set the joint, getting her out would be a problem. "This is going to hurt and she's going to scream."

Understanding, Boomer planted his forearm across Ro's chest, bearing down just enough, and clamped his other hand over her mouth. "Do it."

Taking a sobering breath, Nimah raised the right leg, mindful of the litany of other injuries, and with the weight resting over her shoulder, she twisted it into position. Roused by searing pain, Ro jolted awake and struggled wildly, but Boomer was as immovable as a mountain. Her eyes flashed to Nimah, bright with alarm and waking agony.

"This is the worst part," she warned.

Ro mustered up a determined nod, nostrils flaring. Another twist—and with a hard thrust, Nimah leveraged her weight and the joint popped into place. Eyes rolling back, Ro screamed—the sound smothered beneath Boomer's palm.

"Sit her up. I've got to bind the arm, then we can move." Rummaging through the cart, Nimah found a set of cables and a long, flat roll of bandages.

Ro groaned, swayed on the table, her shoulders trembling with shock as a cold sweat bloomed on her skin. Folding her arm across her chest, Nimah wrapped the bandages around her torso and anchored it in place with the cables. "There. That should hold. Can you walk?"

"I'll manage." Ro winced. Sliding off the edge of the table, her knees buckled and she would've dropped had Boomer not looped her good arm around his shoulder. Thankfully she was tall, but even then, the strain made her gasp. "Ribs," she wheezed.

"We'll get you patched up properly once we're aboard the *Stormchaser*."

"Ship was impounded." Each word pulled out of her in ragged breaths.

"I know."

"You stole my ship?" Ro lurched through each halting step, favoring her right leg. "How'd you manage that?" Nimah didn't have a chance to answer as Ro, weakened, pitched over.

In a seamless, almost graceful move, Boomer swept her up in his arms. "Got her," he said, adjusting her weight. "Let's move."

Opening the door, Nimah rushed out, Boomer hot on her heels. Chu and Sigourney, who'd rejoined them while Nimah and Boomer had been tending to her grandmother, closed in from the far end of the corridor. Dobs held position at the other end, blaser in one hand and six-shooter in the other. "Good job, kid. Any issues below decks, Siggy?"

"The eyes of our enemies remain blind, but 'tis twelve minutes before the hour strikes," Sigourney warned. Her white skull-face glistened like exposed bone in the harsh fluorescent lighting.

"Must you always speak like you're running lines for a period play?" Dobs rolled her eyes.

Sigourney raised a bemused shoulder. "I live for the theatrical."

At that, Gertrude cut her a bright smile, still stroking the head of the unconscious agent slumped at her feet. "Don't we all, darling. Don't we all."

FLIGHT OF THE SPARROW   205

"Ya done?" Dobs snapped her fingers between them. "I'm ready to get off this boat." Without waiting for an answer, or an apology, Dobs spun on her heel and the group of them jogged for the lift.

They'd only just turned a corner when the doors whisked open at the end of the corridor and a group of agents poured out with a medical team in tow, returning to continue their interrogation.

They slowed. Paused. A breathless moment stretched taut between them—the enemy on one side, Sigourney with her skull face and battle axes and Boomer with Captain Ro in his arms on the other. Then time snapped back—sharp as an elastic band against the sensitive skin of Nimah's wrist—as Dobs fired quick shots to hold the agents at bay while the rest of them backtracked and ducked inside the interrogation room.

"We're about sixty seconds from pinched. Tell me we got another way out," Dobs demanded between firing off cover shots from the doorway.

Chu spun in a swaggering circle, hands on her hips, like an architect studying holo-schematics. "Walls are mirrored diamond glass, triple coated, fused to carbide steel, likely as thick as the blast doors they bolted on us by now. It's a tomb. We can't hold here for long."

Roaring a vicious curse, Dobs vented her fury with another series of rapid shots, emptying her chamber. "What's our contingency plan?"

Nimah recoiled under the heat of her glare. "I—I don't have one."

"Razor," Boomer snorted, adjusting Ro's dead weight.

"Might I suggest we think of one?" Gertrude cracked a flare and tossed it into the corridor, spitting smoke. "And quickly, if you don't mind."

"There wasn't time . . ." Nimah blanched as cold seeped into her and sent her mind into a chaotic whirl. Every class. Every simulation. Nothing had prepared her for this. "I didn't—I just—I can't . . ."

Dobs anchored Nimah by the shoulders and brought the whirl to a standstill. Grounding her. "Stop it. Breathe. Good. Another deep one." Nimah obeyed, sucking air into starved lungs until the pressure in her head settled. "Now think, kid. Think carefully. What's our next best way out? Give us a heading. You know this, I know you do."

206   FALLON DEMORNAY

There isn't—Nimah shoved the panic aside and reached for calm. For certainty. Just because she was terrified of deep space travel and void-ships didn't mean she'd neglected that area of her studies. Sinking into that calmness, she pushed through her fear, back to nights spent poring over textbooks and hours in exams. When a ship was overrun, regardless of class or model, the safest point for STARs personnel was always the same.

"The bridge," she said finally.

"You trying to get us all killed?" Chu blurted.

"Shut up, darling, and let the girl think."

"From the bridge we can access any part of the *Challenger*," Nimah repeated, more certain. "There's a turbo-lift that will take us straight to the lifeboats. It's a private channel, which means it can't be intercepted or stalled by anyone outside bridge command. We get in there, subdue the command team, and commandeer the lift—but only if Chu can run a bypass."

"I might be four-eleven on a good day, but I'm tall enough to throat punch you if you insult my skills again."

"Works for me," Dobs agreed. "Now how do we get there?"

Gertrude analyzed the *Challenger* schematics, her fingers working with determined swipes across the holoscreen. "Fastest route is via the service ladder."

"The one in the corridor?" Chu guffawed. "Same one that puts us in the direct path of those agents waiting to punch us full of smoking holes? *That* ladder?"

"Wait . . . no, we can't go through there." Nimah waved her hands in warning. "That icon indicates the airduct leads through the cooling system."

"So?" Dobs grunted.

"The air is minus *eighty* on the inside. You take a single breath in that and your lungs will immediately freeze."

"The suits'll protect us," Dobs dismissed. "We'll be fine."

"What about Ro?" Chu scratched her chin. "She ain't got one, and doubt she can hold it long enough to scale three decks."

Dobs narrowed her eyes to fine slits, and Nimah could almost see the gears in her head spinning through the problem for a solution. "Lay her down."

"Why?"

"Shut up and do it."

Nimah helped Boomer, and together they lowered Ro onto her back, stretching her out while Dobs rummaged through the drawers and cabinets. She returned with a large, silver syringe.

"Now what?" Nimah barely got the question out before Dobs plunged it like a blade into the center of her grandmother's chest. The stopper sank down, pumping milky liquid into her body.

Ro seized, spasmed. Then fell limp.

CHAPTER TWENTY

What did you do?" Frantic, Nimah searched for a pulse and nearly screamed when she couldn't find one. "She's not breathing. She's not *breathing*!"

Dobs removed the syringe. "That's kinda the point. Her lungs can't freeze if she's not breathing, heard?"

"You're killing her!"

"And this," Dobs waved another syringe under Nimah's nose, "will bring her back. Three minutes. That's how long her brain will last without oxygen. So, you wanna waste that time arguing, or should we get a hustle on?"

Tears seared like bile at the back of her throat. "Three minutes."

"Good. Get her up."

Boomer did as commanded, but from the expression on his face, he was equally at odds with matters, and positioned her over one brawny shoulder.

"There. Now all we need is to clear a path." Dobs swung her gaze to Sigourney. "Think you can manage that?"

The sputtering red flare washed across Sigourney's gruesome face. Drawing both axe and shield, she bared platinum fangs in a lethal grin. "To the void or Valhalla!" she roared, and charged.

Nimah wasn't given time to question or hesitate as they rushed into the corridor after her, firing for cover. Sigourney lunged into the fray, barreling forward in a weaving pattern. Her axe sank into the armored chest of a STARs agent like a hot knife through butter, and in a deft

FLIGHT OF THE SPARROW 209

jerk, her shield swung the legs out from the second as she heaved the weapon in a whooshing arc into the head of the third.

Every movement was brutal, vicious poetry. Blaserfire rang off carbide steel like a struck bell, raining a flurry of glowing gold sparks. "Now!" she bellowed.

"Move it, kid." Dobs shoved Nimah ahead.

Gertrude hit the ladder first and took position while Boomer came up behind her, Ro heavy over his shoulder.

"Can you manage with her?" Nimah shouted over the din.

Boomer grabbed hold of the rung, sweat rolling down the dark brown skin of his muscled neck. "I'll have to," he answered, and hauled himself up swiftly, Ro swaying like a rucksack.

"Chu." Nimah guided her to the ladder and joined Gertrude in cover fire while Chu struggled and swore over every incremental inch.

Nimah's visor pixelated across her face. Cold blistered across the edges of the suit before quickly warming as the nanites went to work, leveling out the temperature. Boomer grunted up ahead. Carting Ro was no easy feat, and Nimah worried the struggle and exposure to the cold would worsen her grandmother's injuries. Dressed only in a t-shirt, cargos, and boots, frostbite was a dangerous likelihood if they didn't move quickly.

Distant shouts and blaserfire rang beneath her, but soon was lost to the heavy pant of her labored breathing and the clanging of pipes within the ductwork. She'd only just passed the third level and exited the duct to find Boomer in the corridor, hunched over Ro. Steam rose from her exposed arms and legs, skin and clothing damp from the melting frost.

Clearing the duct behind her, Dobs removed the syringe from inside her nanosuit, and once again, plunged it into the center of Ro's unmoving chest.

Seconds bled into eternity.

"Gimme the screen." Dobs snatched it from Gertrude, quickly scanning Ro for vitals.

Revival process: INITIATED
Scanning . . .
Central nervous system: UNRESPONSIVE
Cardiovascular system: UNRESPONSIVE
Revival process: FAILED

FALLON DEMORNAY

"No!" Nimah latched onto her grandmother's hand, frantic. "What's wrong with her? Why isn't it working?"

Dobs's eyes shifted, quick with thought. "Gotta be the cold . . . *Move*." She shoved Nimah aside. "Fuck tech." Perched on her knees, Dobs planted both hands to Ro's chest and heaved down in rapid, sharp pumps. Pausing after several counts, she pinched her nose, blew twice into her mouth, then set back to vigorous pumping, then paused for two more sharp breaths.

Helpless, Nimah watched her repeat the sequence in determined silence.

"C'mon, Ro." Dobs slammed a balled fist over the wall of her grandmother's chest. Right over her heart. "Not today." Again. "Not fucking today." Again!

Ro seized, her eyes snapped open with a sharp intake of air met with heaving coughs.

"She lives!" Gertrude tossed up her hands with a theatrical cackle.

Dobs grinned, lopsided around a broken cigarette, digging into her breast pocket for her battered pack and lighter. "Welcome back, Cap."

"Cold," Ro grumbled, her lips faded blue.

"Yeah, that's gonna take some time. Boomer, get Cap on her feet. Keep her steady, heard?"

"Razor."

Sigourney pushed through the grate, emerging from the hole in the floor like a demon rising from the bowels of a frozen Hell. Her helmet retracted to reveal her white skull face splattered with blood-red droplets, and eyes bright as the glint of blue fluorescents on her fangs.

"So," Dobs cocked a hip as she sealed the duct behind her, "how'd it go?"

"Glorious," she purred, wiping her axe against her thigh before holstering it on her hip. "Seven to dine in Valhalla. Worthy opponents, all."

"If you're done with the chit-chat," Chu grumbled, shoulders hunched, "we've got a command bridge to storm and, case you haven't noticed, the door's been sealed."

"On it." Dobs rubbed rough palms together before removing her gun and fired three rapid shots into the control pad.

"Oi!" Gertrude barked. "Can you *please* stop firing *live* bullets inside the voidship?"

FLIGHT OF THE SPARROW 211

"Relax, I know what I'm doing." Dobs tapped the end of her gun to the smoking panel, where three slugs were flattened amidst sputtering wires. "Steel's too thick to breach, heard?" Rearing back, she drove a hard kick into the split and the doors whined apart, retracting into the walls like broken wings. "Ladies and gents—"

"And those somewhere in between," Gertrude quickly chimed in.

"—name's Dobs. Anyone out of diapers should know I'm as precise with a scalpel as I am with this here gun." She waved her six-shooter and swept from left to right. "Kindly keep hands where I can see 'em, or lose 'em at the wrist."

A short, tawny man with blue-tinted hair stood up; he wore the SIGA emblem on his chest, marking him as the major general of the bridge. Silver eyes haloed in iridescent green narrowed in a square face, shaved clean and marred with pocked craters. "I know who you are," he said confidently. "I am Major General Singh Nakamora, commanding officer of the *Challenger*, and I won't risk the lives of my crew for the sake of securing a single felon."

Dobs swiveled her six-shooter between his eyes. "Smart man. Now, if the rest of you would please form an orderly line so that we might expedite this process. We are on the clock, and would appreciate your complete cooperation, heard? Kid—if you wouldn't mind entertaining the major general while we secure his crew."

"What?"

"Did I stutter?" Dobs answered without looking her way.

No, she hadn't. Removing her blaser, Nimah primed the charge and stepped forward until she was close enough to count the pores dotting his cheek.

"Now in the event of a breach, two things happen." Dobs lowered her gun. "First, all pathways to the bridge are sealed. Failing that, all command codes are removed from the major's possession and given to a lucky contestant to guard with their lives." She turned on her heel with a grin. "So, who is gonna step on up and spin the wheel first?"

Silence answered her. Not that Nimah was surprised. Although these were intelligence operatives, they'd been cadets once. Every single one of them knew how to fight when backed into a corner, and right now—they were boxed in tight.

212   **FALLON DEMORNAY**

"Since we got no volunteers, guess we'll make it a game of chance." Popping out the chamber of her colt, she plucked out bullets and casings, leaving one round inside, spun the chamber once, and snapped it shut with a flick of her wrist, then pressed the muzzle to a bowed head. And pulled the trigger—*click*. "It's your lucky day. Let's give our first contestant a round of applause." Fingers in her mouth, Dobs whistled sharply. "Now that we get the gist, who's next?"

"Stop this!" the major general roared.

"Happy to oblige when you point out your second." Dobs swung the muzzle between the eyes of a glaring man. Her finger curled on the trigger. Slowly.

"Lieutenant, reveal yourself."

A surly blonde with vicious blue eyes and a stubborn chin stood up suddenly, blaser in hand—the weapon active and aimed at Nimah.

"Lo," Sigourney grinned, twisting her axe in hand, "the war drums sound."

"Lieutenant," the major general barked, "lower your weapon."

"We are charged with delivering Indira Roscoe to Hollow Point. She is a terrorist insurgent responsible for the deaths of government and UPN officials—I can't let them escape with her, sir."

"I gave you a direct order."

"As you've been compromised and are under the control of a pirate threat, according to code G46-21, section twelve, I am relieving you of command and assuming authority of this vessel."

"She's got a pair, don't she?" Dobs spun on her heel and offered a mocking round of applause of palm to pistol. "We got us a full-blown mutineer."

"Release Major General Nakamora," the lieutenant demanded, her voice steady and certain as her aim. "This is your final warning."

"Look around you." Dobs swaggered forward, six-shooter limp in her grip, but Nimah wasn't fooled. She'd seen how fast Dobs could move and for a woman rounding the bend of seventy, she hadn't lost the edge of youth. "Don't think you're in the position to be making demands."

The lieutenant swiveled her gaze as far as her sightlines would allow without shifting her head a fraction before snapping back to Nimah. The icy blue blazed cold as void-frost across Nimah's skin. "She won't do it.

FLIGHT OF THE SPARROW

She doesn't have the nerve to murder an elite military official in cold blood. She's no pirate."

"I am the granddaughter of Captain Indira Roscoe. Don't push me." Nimah tapped the muzzle of her blaser against the major general's temple. "On. Your. Knees."

Maybe it was something in her voice, or in the way Dobs swayed ever so casually where she stood, hipshot with easy confidence, or Sigourney's gore-splattered skull-painted face and fanged grin, but soon enough the lieutenant lowered her weapon and sank dutifully to the floor.

"You'll never get away with this."

"Heard that one before." Chu snatched her card with a smirk. The clear glass was embedded with a holograph of the SIGA star and, when activated, blue credentials splashed across it, everything from access codes to the history of her personal record. Credentials were more than identification; they were an entire encyclopedia on every achievement and mark on an individual's record.

Accepting the card, Nimah blanched. Lieutenant Mashid Ankur was a decorated officer with close ties to the Academy—and Chief Commander Wallace. The dots connected, and Nimah recalled the holograph on the chief commander's desk of the two women, freshly graduated, standing side by side.

"I'm sorry," Nimah mouthed, as Dobs finished securing the lieutenant with magnicuffs to the rest of her bound and subdued team.

"You will be," she vowed, blue eyes as certain and uncompromising as her tone.

"We're cutting close," Gertrude warned. "I suggest we get a hustle on."

After Nimah finished securing their bindings to the console, the *Stormchaser* crew crowded onto the lift, but Nimah breathed a little easier once the door swiveled shut.

Chu swiped the tag and then popped the panel, exposing the wires. "Five minutes," she muttered, "a distance of twenty-three yards . . ." The rest of her words got lost in a sloppy mumble of sliding dentures.

"What are you doing?" Nimah demanded.

"Makin' up lost time." With a wink, Chu ripped out the red and crossed it with the blue. "Hold onto your butts." She punched the button, and they plummeted.

214   FALLON DEMORNAY

Braced for impact, Nimah swallowed the searing burn of her scream as gravity rattled her teeth. Chu's head bobbed, a metronome swaying in time to an unheard melody.

"Anytime now!" Boomer shouted.

Chu flagged a gnarled finger, waited another half count before pushing the extended panel back into position. The lift screamed to a sudden, jarring halt that wrenched the air from Nimah's lungs and punched her feet into the floor. The muscles in her neck and shoulders groaned under the strain, shooting needles of pain into the nerves.

"Everyone good?" Dobs grumbled, straightening.

"Peachy." Gertrude cast Chu a reproachful glare. "Couldn't give us a bit of warning first?"

"Quit bellyaching." She stuck out a flailing hand. "Help me up, dammit."

Gertrude caught her by the wrist, yanked Chu to her feet. "Age is nothing but a state of mind, darling."

"Tell that to my hip," she groaned into a side-stretch.

"After we finish this, we'll steal you a new one," Dobs teased.

The ship rocked hard, tossing them in the chamber of the lift like dice in a cup.

Nimah righted herself with a gasp. "What was that?"

"Docking?"

"Collision?"

Dobs set her teeth in a grimace. "Maverick, you catching drag down there?"

"Affirmative. They're trying to shake me off. Whatever you're going to do, make it fast."

"Heard. C'mon, ladies, time to get off this boat."

"Age before beauty." Batting Dobs aside, Chu stepped out of the lift first and shuffled into the chamber. A narrow, oval-shaped room, glossy and sleek, with pods circling the perimeter made of smooth, tinted glass and carbide steel. She touched the panel. Slapped it. And grunted, hands set on her bony hips. "Pods are disabled. One of them must've wiggled loose from their bonds on the bridge to cut us off."

"Can you pop these tin cans?"

"'Course. But I'll need to prime 'em one at a time."

"How many do we need?"

FLIGHT OF THE SPARROW

"Three, unless you wanna ride shotgun in someone's lap."

Dobs laughed. "Anyone but Gertrude."

"Darling, you wish."

Chu only just turned on her heel when a shot rang out. The force of it struck her clean in the chest. She went one way. Her dentures—another.

"Chu! Chulita!" Dobs shouted over the spray of fire.

Chu reared up with a growl, a smoking crater in her nanite suit armor—the rest of her mercifully unscathed. "*Thonuvaweech!*"

"C'mon," Dobs tagged her shoulder, "get back for cover!"

"Nah wif'ou my wucking eef!" Belly down, Chu scrabbled forward and Dobs hauled her back by her skinny ankles, dentures in hand—seconds before blaserfire seared the walkway.

"You good?" Dobs shouted.

"Peachy," Chu snarled, snapping off a molar before she slapped her dentures back into her mouth and clenched firmly to keep her teeth from rolling around on her gums. "Which one shot me?"

"Middle right." Dobs answered, brows lowered in a deep scowl. "Why does that—?"

Clutching the molar like a baseball, Chu lobbed the ceramic tooth with an impressive throw and sent it sailing like a bullet that popped with a static blast the second it struck the middle agent between the eyes. Dazed, the man dropped like a stone.

"Was that a sonic?" Gertrude gasped then whisked disbelieving eyes to Chu, her expression a blend of awe and horror. "You've had grenades in your mouth this whole time?"

"Among other things. Keep 'em busy." Chu bounced onto her feet and stalked off, elbows swinging.

Dobs jerked a thumb over her shoulder. "You count. I'll keep them distracted."

Waiting for a break in blaserfire, Nimah twisted around and found a gap between the column and pods for visibility. Dobs bought her seconds, but seconds was all she needed. "Seven," she called out, drawing back for safety. "Three on the right. Four on the left."

"Blasers won't make much of a dent in nanite armor." Hands on her knees, Dobs glowered with determined focus. "Booms, you got live rounds in that repeater?"

"Damn straight."

"I could kiss you."

"Please don't. You're like . . . ancient."

Dobs winked and, accepting the weapon, cocked the gun, loading a round into the chamber. "I'll have you know sixty-nine is an *excellent* year."

"And here I thought you were the only one stupid enough to use ammo that could punch a hole through this ship and kill us all," Gertrude sighed.

"You'll thank me for it in a moment." Repeater braced on her shoulder, Dobs swaggered off like a baseball player approaching home plate, and with a sharp twist, fired three shots before pulling back for cover. "Now there's one on the right. Two on the left."

As she cracked open the chamber to reload, the blast doors parted and black-cloaked figures emerged—faces hidden behind liquid metal masks.

Cyber operatives. Three of them.

Nimah's heart lurched into a cold stop. "Oh no . . ."

"Hey, Chu," Dobs shouted over her shoulder, "you taking a nap, or what?"

"Five minutes!"

"Make it two."

Gertrude swallowed hard. "They'll carve us down in half that."

One of the cybers stepped forward, and beneath their liquid black visor, Nimah could almost feel their cold gaze sweeping across her.

"We have come for fugitives Roscoe and Dabo-124," they demanded in a voice that wasn't distinctly male or female, but a blend of the two.

Sigourney rose and stepped forward.

"What're you doing?" Gertrude shouted. "Fall back, you daft cow!"

Ignoring her, she drew her axe. Raised her shield.

"Drop your weapons and submit, or you will be met with lethal force." The cybers squared in an offensive stance. "This is your only warning."

"I am a Valkyrie of the *Stormchaser*. The Queen of Bones." Sigourney bared her fangs in a wild grin. "I fear no hell from you!" And bellowed

FLIGHT OF THE SPARROW 217

into a charge, all muscle and steel as she flew like shrapnel, meeting them with blade and fury.

"Stupid sodding fool!" Gertrude punctuated the curse with several rounds of blaserfire in an attempt to keep the other two off Sigourney.

Nimah joined her, but it was no use. If the blasers had been ineffective against agents, it was proving far less so for the cybers.

They rushed in, ducking and dodging each shot like they instinctively knew where the blows were set to land. Like they could see everything before it happened. And perhaps they could. Forged in a lab, they were weapons with human bodies, created with a singular purpose: complete the mission at all costs. One broke through the line of Gertrude's fire and came at Nimah when she paused to reload and kicked her blaser aside. Without wasting time to think, Nimah lunged head on. Her movements sharp and quick and fluid, a flurry of fists, elbows, and knees, driving her opponent back—but each blow was met or deflected.

Hand arcing, the cyber reached for their triple-folded carbonite sword with a laser edge, hot and sharp enough to slice through a body in a single stroke.

"Kid!" Dobs tossed Nimah her grandmother's cutlass, and with a bounding leap, she dove. Her fingers closed around the worn hilt, activating the laser with a stroke of her thumb, and using the momentum to her advantage, she spun on her knees—rolled her head beneath the stroke of steel, swung the wakening blade up just as the cyber spun, and drove down.

Lasers sparked, steel rang, and over the line of their crossed blades, Nimah sensed their surprise behind the liquid black visor.

And their anger.

A cyber's blade was stronger, the lasers designed to not only cut through carbide, but to disrupt energy. And her grandmother's cutlass hummed against her palm, the power cells desperately pumping out energy that each clash drained away. Soon she'd be empty and vulnerable.

Nimah settled into a defensive position, electricity crackling down her blade, and as the cyber lunged, she pivoted in the same breath. The line of her sword slashed across the liquid metal mask—breaking through armor to slice into skin. She swung around to parry, but was a little too slow on the draw as a cyber caught her from behind, arm around her throat. That arm cinched tight and her vision immediately grayed at the edges.

Nimah sank her teeth into muscle with all the strength she could muster, biting down until she thought her teeth would break. The cyber shouted a curse and, releasing her, they slammed a balled fist into her face. Nimah's head ricocheted off hull metal, and stars exploded behind her eyes in violent bursts of light brightening the rapidly encroaching darkness.

She shook her vision clear, staggering to her feet with back set to the wall, and took in the chaos around her. Everything slowed to a pause, like a grain of sand suspended in liquid. Gertrude had been subdued, Dobs disarmed, and Chu knocked off her feet. Ro, tucked behind Boomer, struggled against his broad back. Around them, cybers closed in for the kill.

Sigourney was the only one still on her feet, ready to fight with fire and fury, but she was fading and couldn't take them all on. Not for long.

Let us. The pendant hummed against her heart. *Let us . . .*

The panic that swelled in Nimah surged at the whisper of that alien voice resurging inside her—and grew—into something brighter, *hotter.* Confusion quickly vaporized into certainty. Her breath quickened, time snapped back and, no longer off-balance, she followed the beckoning of her instincts, that voice, driving her to do exactly what needed to be done.

However insane.

She shifted to the balls of her feet and swung up with her sword, knocking her opponent back, and, throttling the cutlass to maximum— blue blazed to white—Nimah drove it into the collection of wires snaking down the length of piping in the walls at her back.

One hand still on the hilt, she gripped the sparrow pendant with the other as electricity fractured, arced, vicious as lightning, and embraced the current juddering up her arm—*into* her—weaving into bone and marrow. Hot. Blazing. Brutal. Distant shouts carried through the chaos, but she couldn't focus on anything beyond the power swimming inside her. In the glowing haze of her mind's eyes, she homed in on the cybers that, unlike the *Stormchaser* crew who shimmered pale gold, were fathomless as black holes.

One swung for her, and she ducked beneath the blade. When it arced back around in a downward stroke meant to cleave her in two, she caught the blade between her palms. At the precise moment skin met steel, the pressure inside of Nimah—all that captured power and energy—exploded! Erupting in shocking, vibrant blue currents that surged, guided by her thoughts.

By her *will*.

Screams blistered around her. Electricity crackled and sizzled in her ears. Filled her eyes. Her mouth, her nose, her chest, before falling fatally silent. Shaken, sweat rolled down her throat, seared raw from the stench of smoke and singed flesh that hung in the air. Nimah blinked away the haze from her eyes, and was met with the staggering sight of the cybers. What was left of them lay in smoking wreckage, like charred logs in a fading fire.

The *Stormchaser* crew—gaping in disbelief—stood untouched.

"*Whooo!*" Boomer punched the air, fracturing the stunned silence. "That was fucking razor!"

Dobs pressed a hand to her chest. If she'd been wearing pearls, she might've been clutching them. "Kid . . . what was that?"

Nimah wiped her hands on her thighs—against muscles that quivered and flexed like she'd run ten miles, unable to rid herself of the sizzle and jolt still tingling in her fingers and palms. "I don't . . . I don't know."

Reaching for the sparrow pendant, Dobs raised it between them, and her expression darkened. A storm cloud blotting out summer sun.

"C'mon. Time to get off this boat."

CHAPTER TWENTY-ONE

Maverick drove hard against the yoke and swore against the strain as the belly of the *Challenger* gave a quarter roll in an effort to shake them off. "C'mon," he growled beneath his breath. "You guys taking a vacation or what? Hurry up and seal the hatch!"

"All aboard and accounted for," Dobs responded through *Stormchaser* comms.

"Good. Get Gertrude up here." Maverick engaged the switches and the ship shook again, this time as it detached. Sweat dripped into his eyes and he swiped it away, focused on the path before him. The ship groaned as he pushed past the sweep of the *Challenger*'s shields and into the treacherous minefield of the Gauntlet where negs roamed wildly. They were swimming and screaming. Drawn into a feeding frenzy. But by what? There was no time to take it in. Maverick focused on the clearest path he could see, and punched forward. Weaving and dodging like a needle through silk. Behind him, the *Challenger* loomed with her nose angled in his direction.

She was coming for him.

"I need a burnpoint," Maverick demanded as Gertrude flowed onto the bridge. "Find me something. Anything. *Quick!*" He heard the whisk of her chair and the swooshing of strokes across the control panel.

"I've got a heading, but we need to be out another hundred yards to burn."

Proximity sensors blared, but Maverick didn't need to glance at his navigation feed to know what was coming. He saw it—a shockwave of crackling light that flashed in an expanding ring from the prow of the *Challenger*. Rising like a tsunami, it roared toward them with absolute fury. "They've ripped the EMP."

"Sodding balls."

"Enter the coordinates based on where we are, right now. Go for a loop."

"Have you lost your mi—?"

The EMP wave struck a neg and the creature exploded into a static burst of prime and entrails that punched the *Stormchaser* like a fist to the belly. Maverick groaned, struggling to bring her back on course. "If that wave touches us, we're dead in the water. Do it!"

Gertrude muttered a scathing curse and went to task as Maverick activated ship comms, broadcasting across all levels. "We're about to hardburn. You've got three seconds to strap in by any means necessary."

The wave was so close he could barely see the way ahead, and the *Stormchaser* shuddered in its wake. *C'mon baby. Just a few more seconds.*

<Coordinates accepted. Commencing hardburn.>

Gravity punched Maverick back into his chair with the force of a sonic grenade. It melted through him. Moved through skin and bone, prickled across every nerve. Ordinarily he loved this moment, the instant breath vanished and the stars, fixed in space, went liquid. Bleeding across the viewport like rain across glass. A few seconds was all it took, and they were gone. So far away that finding them would be like trying to pinpoint a twinkle in the distant void.

Maverick collapsed back into his chair. Gertrude sagged in hers.

"Well done, darling." She clapped her hands together limply. "Well done."

"Let's hope it's enough." Uncoupling his harness, Maverick waved his wrist and his chair sped to him. Transferring into it, he followed Gertrude to the medbay, where the rest of the battle-worn crew were gathered.

Sigourney's face was a blood-splattered mess, but her silver eyes bright. Chu, her lips pinched more than usual, cast him a baleful glare. Given the wakening bruise on her brow, it didn't take much for him to

FALLON DEMORNAY

figure out why. Boomer was jabbering and bouncing off the walls like ricochet blaserfire, but Maverick's attention was on Nimah, stretched across one of the two examination tables. And Captain Indira Roscoe occupied the other. He'd heard stories of this formidable woman whose very name shook the void to its core. The reality of her did not disappoint. Even with her arm in a sling and freshly bandaged, she emitted authority.

"What happened up there?" Dobs demanded while suturing the captain's bicep.

"The *Challenger* tried to sink us. But I've burned clear of her radar."

"One of those skinny bastards must've got loose." Chu scowled. "One of us didn't rope 'em tight enough."

"Don't look at me, darling, my knots are impeccable." Gertrude flounced her curls.

Sigourney wiped blood from her face and hands, features grim and focused on Nimah, who lay far too still. If it weren't for the sharp rise and fall of her chest, Maverick would've thought her unconscious. Or worse. "How fares our Sparrow?"

"The kid? She's fine. Nothing a couple painkillers and a few solid hours of sleep won't cure."

Maverick doubted sleep was on the docket for quite some time. Not with Indira Roscoe officially onboard. And awake.

"Easy," Dobs warned as Ro pulled herself up to sit. "Just finished stitching you back together like a quilt."

"How bad is it?" Ro demanded, voice rasping like smoke and sandpaper.

"You're pretty banged up on the inside." Dobs cleaned her hand on a microcloth, removing blood with ease and without the waste of water. "Our med supply is pretty threadbare but I had enough provisions onboard to reduce swelling around your kidneys some. You'll have to keep an eye for blood in your urine."

"And the arm?"

"Reset the radius. Clean break. No splinters or fragments to worry about. A carbon-cast would be better, but the splint should suffice for now. As for the shoulder . . ." Dobs whistled, long and low. "Won't be swinging any punches for quite some time, but all will mend, so long as you're careful."

Ro nodded stiffly. "Good." She turned her gaze to Maverick, and inadvertently he shrank into his chair beneath the ferocity she exuded as easily as breath. "Who is this?"

"Our pilot," Dobs answered, and Maverick was supremely grateful she'd left out any mention of him being a skinner for Hatchett.

"Capsy! Capsy!" Mumbles raced onto the medbay, boots clomping with frantic beats as she wove around Gertrude and nearly steamrolled over Chu. Dobs, quick as lightning, caught Mumbles by the waist a second before she hug-tackled Ro off the table. "Goody-hi, Capsy!"

Even through the wince of pain, the stiffness rolled out of Captain Roscoe like a slow tide receding from the shore, and the tension in her features eased into tender affection. Her good arm closed around Mumbles, and for a moment, she sighed into that embrace. "Hello, you."

Reeling back, Mumbles beamed like a rising sun. "Blind 'em, I dooz it." She pressed the heel of a palm against one eye. "Blind 'em true-true."

"Well done. We'd be lost without you, as ever."

If possible, Mumbles brightened even more in the wake of the captain's praise.

Boomer bounced an elbow to the cap of Maverick's shoulder. "She actually made sense outta that?"

"Oh," Ro cocked a bare wrist, angling it as if to read an imaginary watch, "would you look at that? Time for bed." She arched a smiling brow. "Captain's orders."

Mumbles nodded vigorously, pigtails bouncing against the jowls of her cheeks. "Aye aye, Capsy. Aye aye." Arms stuck out like wings, she buzzed her lips and sailed from the medbay like a voidship breaking atmo, almost plowing into Boomer in her haste.

Soon as she was gone, the captain's expression shifted to stone and ice and quaking fury. The crew fell silent as Ro stepped down from the table and staggered forward with the focused steps of a body trying not to pitch over, leaning heavily on a rolling stand from which hung a dangling bag of fluid with a clear tube running into her elbow.

"Foolish morons." Dark golden eyes—so similar in shape and color to Nimah's—were searing as she looked to each of her crew, and lastly to Maverick. "What in the void possessed you to come after me?"

Seated on a rolling stool, Dobs shucked a wrapper off a fresh pack of smokes and popped one into her grinning mouth. "You're welcome."

"I didn't ask for a fucking rescue party, and I certainly didn't ask for *this*." She thrust her hand toward Nimah, still reclined on the examination table with an icepack draped over her eyes. "She could've been killed." Ro bared gleaming white teeth. "Or worse."

Dobs rose, stretching out her legs to face Roscoe head on. They were well matched for height with barely an inch between them swinging in Dobs's favor. "What's worse than dead?"

"Dissected. Now that they've seen what she can *do*."

Silence fell so heavy and thick even the hum of the ship seemed to sputter to a halt, hanging on every tense word.

"You heard Mumbles, Cap—the feeds were blind, and all witnesses to that . . . *event* are dead or on this boat." Chu scratched her elbow. "Sparrow is safe."

"You should've told us, Captain." Seated closest to Nimah, Gertrude stroked her hand with tender concern. "You should've told us what she *is*."

"She's my granddaughter," Ro snapped. "That's all any of you needed to know."

"What?" Maverick whisked his gaze to each of them. Lost in the shuffle of confusion. "Is someone going to tell *me* what's going on?"

"Oh, me! Let me! Mav, you're not gonna believe it." Boomer swung around, hands clenched as he shook them like a fanatic kid hopped up on helio-smoke, still buzzing off the experience, and told him the entire story while Dobs finished making her rounds, patching up the crew. "Fucking blue lasers, Mav! Lasers! *Shooting* lasers! From her *hands*!" Boomer bounced on his toes like a giddy child. The last time he'd seen Boomer this pumped, he'd been gifted his first gun—a trashpiece Maverick had pinched from a local pawn, enhanced and modified by a grifter.

"Lo," Sigourney whispered, "our little bird showed her talons, and we live to see another day."

FLIGHT OF THE SPARROW

"This isn't over for us. There's nowhere we can fly far enough, fast enough where SIGA won't follow," Ro snarled, but beneath the venom was genuine fear. "How long since I was captured?"

Dobs cocked a wrist. "Shy of three days."

"Three days," Ro repeated under her breath. "Then there's still time."

"Time for what?" Dobs demanded, arms crossed.

"To finish what *I* started."

"Captain," Gertrude adjusted a purple pashmina around her shoulders, "I think you need to bring us up to speed on what's *really* going on."

"No." Roscoe lifted her chin and sent the long rope of her braid swaying. "I won't drag you any further into this than you already are."

"We're beyond dragged into this." Nimah sat up, a melting bag of ice in her hands. The whites of her eyes were utterly bloodshot and the amber of her iris shone a terrifying gold. "To end this, we *need* Jonothan."

"Jono Shinoda isn't the issue. It's what he gave me that *is*. Something SIGA will kill for." Crossing to Nimah, she removed the sparrow dangling around her neck. As the crew closed in, Roscoe snapped off a wing, revealing a gleaming blue core that pulsed and shone like the heart of a trapped star.

"Razor." Boomer squinted. "What is it?"

Something like grief moved through Roscoe at the sight of the broken bird. "The future."

Liselle had never seen a charred body before. However jarring to behold, the stench was by far the worst part. Nearly a full hour after Nimah and the Valkyries escaped with Captain Indira Roscoe, both she and Wallace boarded to take full account of the carnage. At Wallace's careful instructions, the smoking husks that remained of the cybers were sealed in body bags and tagged for laboratory examination by SIGA technicians. What had happened to them remained a mystery, and the reconstructed footage from what analysts had pieced together in the disrupted feed created more questions than it gave answers.

Questions the SIGA board was about to hammer her with as soon as the chief commander returned to her vessel to lead a debrief. The

226   **FALLON DEMORNAY**

roundtable of faces sat in glowing silence as Chief Commander Wallace activated the icon on her wristband, pausing the feed.

"As you can see, we don't have clear visuals of *what* transpired, but the results are . . . puzzling."

"Indeed," one of the directors responded, but like it did with most of the faces projected into the conference room of the voidship, his name escaped her. Liselle rolled her eyes up as if hoping to find the answer written on the top of her skull. Bleeding void, she really needed to start paying attention to politics.

"Did any member of your team survive to witness the event, Chief Commander?"

"No, Director Suarez."

"According to this analysis, the bodies were burned to an inconceivable degree within seconds. This level of damage should've severely compromised the ship, yet the hull metal was virtually unscathed."

"Initial reports show an energy output of something akin to prime but stronger. Whatever the substance, we don't have a name for it. A weapon like this . . . simply does not exist."

"Who is that in the room with you?" a woman asked. This one she did know. Chair of the SIGA board, Annelise Aramir.

"Cadet Namsara." Wallace gestured to her left, and all eyes snapped to Liselle.

"A cadet? Is that wise?"

"She has offered key insights about Nimah Dabo-124 that have been critical in our recovery efforts."

"Well then, with this in mind, Cadet, know that what is discussed here is classified. Failure to adhere to protocol will result in severe consequences." The overhead lights caught the flat slope of her brow, highlighting the severity of her features. "Do you understand?"

"Yes, Chairwoman."

"Excellent. Now, Chief Commander, given your compelling status report, as chair I'm issuing a change in directives. You are to suspend Blackout Protocol immediately, subdue felons Nimah Dabo-124 and Captain Indira Roscoe, and bring them both in for . . . questioning."

Wallace shifted, like a tree trying to replant her roots. Grounding herself. Liselle couldn't recall a time when she'd ever seen the chief commander unsteady.

FLIGHT OF THE SPARROW 227

"You have something to say on that score?"

"Jonothan Shinoda is still unaccounted for, and presumed *alive*." Wallace pulled her shoulders back. "The focus of our efforts should remain his immediate recovery."

"If you are able to do so without compromising your directives, then you have board approval. But let me make myself clear." Aramir linked her hands and leaned in. The movement caused her holograph to shimmer before pixelating into focus. "Contrary to Cormack Shinoda's personal beliefs on the matter, he does not run this government. Our involvement was merely a courtesy, but circumstances have changed."

"Chairwo—"

"This might be difficult to process after so many years out of the field," Aramir cut through Wallace's protest with ruthless calm, "but ultimately the details surrounding my decision fall above your purview. Whether you hope to receive a commendation or a criminal citation when this is over, I suggest you stop asking questions and do as you're told."

The transmission ended with a snap of light, and Wallace stood quaking with rage. Before Liselle could muster the breath to form a single syllable, that rage exploded from her with a vicious stream of searing heat.

Holes smoked in the walls from where the lasers in Chief Commander Wallace's HWKeyes had blasted through in her anger, though mercifully not deep enough to breach the hull. The woman had a staggering temper but reined it in just enough to keep them all alive.

Liselle exhaled, hard to do considering her heart was wedged at the back of her throat, and approached the console. "May I speak freely?"

"Permission granted."

"We can't give them Nimah."

Wallace straightened and turned around, her eyes still searing and flickering with heat so intense the gold shone molten with warning. "This isn't up for debate."

"Well, it should be." Liselle licked her lips, mouth dry with apprehension, but she couldn't back down now. Not when it mattered most. "Aren't you concerned about why they want Nimah? What they'll *do* to her?"

"My job isn't to be concerned. It's to follow *orders.*"

"They'll kill her. Or—"

Wallace raised a gloved hand. "That's enough, Cadet. Don't forget who you're speaking to. Our directives are clear, so I suggest you fall in line. It's more than your star at risk, now. Someone is going to be collared for this mess. It's either Nimah—or you."

CHAPTER TWENTY-TWO

Nimah's breath stilled, her heart quickened, and something hummed across the surface of her skin—warm and soft. Energy. Life. It was everything she'd been experiencing since leaving the Academy, but stronger. Richer. Her instincts screamed at her to look away, but she couldn't. If anything, she wanted to get closer to this strange, familiar substance.

"Mother of pearl . . ." Dobs closed in. "Is that—?"

"One and the same," Ro answered.

"I thought it was all destroyed on Valhalla?"

Boomer thrust up a large hand, waved it obnoxiously. "Someone care to explain?"

"Unofficially, this little gem is known as elite core." Captain Ro raised the glowing bit of stone. "SIGA got wind of where to find more of this miraculous mineral six months ago."

"What happened six months ago?" Nimah pressed her hands together, but the tingling still hummed in her fingers. Itching for release.

"The Frontier collision," Boomer answered. "Bunch of comets blew through the barrier shield and obliterated an entire settlement on the farthest edge of the RIM. Total shitshow."

Ro nodded. "What they kept out of the newscasts was that the cleanup crew discovered this unusual compound and brought it into SIGA labs for tests. Less than a month later, a team was sent back to investigate. Turns out the entire asteroid belt is rich with it."

"What's so special 'bout it, though?" Boomer assessed it, nose wrinkled. "Aside from how it makes Nimah shoot laser beams from her hands?"

"To fuel the *Stormchaser*, we go through what? Eighteen tons of refined prime for twelve cycles?" Ro asked.

Hand to her mouth, Chu's eyes rolled up in swift calculation. "Thereabouts."

"This little two-ounce nugget could power the *Stormchaser* for ten years."

Curses and gasps exploded around Nimah, popping in her ears like small percussion grenades.

"No way." Boomer tossed a hand. "How could something *that powerful* be hidden out there and no one detect it?"

"Because it carries none of prime's radioactive and unstable properties."

"It carries something," Maverick commented as the ship jostled with a gliding thump. "Negs have been closing in from every quad since you jumped ship. Whatever Nimah activated up there—they've felt it, and they're coming in hot."

"Indeed." Ro sighed. "This will reshape the void as we know it. Extending our reach to the farthest corners of space, and unlike its far more volatile sister compound, elite can be *weaponized*." She weighed it in her hand, the glowing blue reflecting deep in her eyes like the wink of something at the bottom of a very dark pond. "Imagine the possibilities. The devastation. No planet will be safe from SIGA."

Dobs flicked an inch of ash from the end of her barely touched cigarette. "And it was under our noses all this time."

"What makes it all worse," Ro continued, "is that SIGA doesn't want Inner Circle citizens to know—but prime caches are at critical levels. Our reserves won't see us beyond the next twenty . . . maybe thirty years, if we're lucky, and I can guarantee, hundreds of billions won't be. We're talking mass starvation and loss of life."

Nimah gasped. "That can't be possible. Just last year President Doja said that we've got a century, maybe two, before we reach anywhere near critical."

"Total and utter bullshit. The Circle is destabilizing, and we're operating on borrowed time. Have been for a while."

Nimah frowned. "How could they keep something like this buried?"

FLIGHT OF THE SPARROW

"They couldn't. Not for long. But elite solves all their problems a hundred times over. There's millions of metric tons buried on the RIM, and whoever owns it will stand to make trillions of dollars a year. There's just one problem."

"What's that?" Boomer quirked a brow.

"The RIM is safeguarded by United Planetary Nations policy, deemed government-unaffiliated land, and given to all refugee descendants removed from home planets after the century long Zone Wars."

"Meaning?"

"Elite belongs to the *people*," Nimah whispered. "The government can't touch it."

Ro raised her hands in gentle applause. "Well done, Sparrow."

"Fuck they can't," Boomer interjected. "SIGA monopolized control of all life-sustaining resources following the cataclysmic destruction of Earth-Prior. Water. Food. Medical care." He listed off his fingers. "Can't even take a fucking *breath* in an Inner Circle spacity without paying a levy."

"All under the guise of not repeating the wasteful ways of '*our past*.'" Chu wiggled her bent fingers in air quotes. "If that ain't some fly-encrusted horseshit."

Boomer crossed his arms, biceps bulging. "You expect us to believe they can't just swoop in like they always do in this voidforsaken system?"

Nimah's thoughts spun wildly. Boomer wasn't wrong to have his doubts. Their history was riddled with the ruthlessness of SIGA. Barely a thousand years ago, humanity would've been doomed to extinction were it not for a miracle that fell from the sky when an asteroid crashed into Earth-Prior, leading their ancestors to the discovery of prime. A potent mineral turned into an exceptional power source they used to flee their decaying world in search of a new one among the stars.

The survivors were mostly comprised of society's most influential members, from celebrities to government, who could afford to buy their way off-world, along with a host of working-class families and near a million cryogenically frozen embryos. All fertilized in a lab, after extensive screening, to ensure maximum genetic diversity upon settling.

What began as a single spacity expanded to twenty that fanned out to explore the cosmos in search of more prime deposits, which led them to a trio of systems that hosted well over a thousand promising planets they could terraform. Depositing the working class to toil away while the newly formed SIGA appointed a committee to preside from above while key members went into cryo-sleep to await progress. The governing body observed for centuries, until those planets proved ripe enough to awaken the SIGA board to displace all those they deemed second- or third-class citizens to moons or lesser planets farther out. And lay claim to the established Inner Circle for themselves.

But those who'd settled onto these worlds had long-established roots that ran as deep as bedrock, and not all were willing to give up their homes so easily. The ensuing Integration Zone Wars had been brutal, and SIGA, with the superior advantage and advanced weaponry of a vast military, struck without mercy. Rebel survivors were initially sentenced to slaughter but the Zone Wars had left a foul taste in many mouths, and at the decree of beleaguered Inner Circle citizens calling for respite, SIGA decided they had to assuage the masses or risk losing control altogether. It was then decided instead of death, they would be stripped of citizenship and displaced to the RIM in punishment for their insurrection.

During this time the United Planetary Nations was established to broker terms for a ceasefire to end the bloodshed, and drafted a treaty to ensure that those displaced on the RIM would be free to carve out an existence outside of SIGA authority, to regain a semblance of life and dignity for themselves. Even though the RIM was a hostile environment few would have chosen for themselves, having lost their homes once already, under no circumstances did they want to face displacement ever again. So they demanded that the RIM belong to them. Seeing no value in relinquishing ownership over an asteroid belt they'd used more or less as a dumping ground, SIGA happily agreed—laughing at their good fortune.

And so the accord was struck.

"They can't try to claim elite. Not without serious retaliation from the UPN," Nimah said at last, emerging from her thoughts with stunned clarity. "The RIM's under diplomatic protection. If they try, it would start another civil war, and they barely held onto their seat of power after the last one."

FLIGHT OF THE SPARROW 233

Boomer sputtered a second at that, then leaned back with a heavy exhale. "Well, fuck."

"But this isn't just about wealth. It's about *status*, too," Ro continued. "Because if RIMers claim ownership of elite, they go from being lower-class noncitizens to having all the control. All the power."

Dazed, Nimah sat back. Her grandmother was right. SIGA would destroy anything and anyone who stood between them and maintaining the status quo.

Chu wiggled her jaw, eyes narrowed behind bifocals. "How'd the Shinoda boy get mixed up in all this?"

"After I disbanded the crew . . ." Ro lowered her head, sighed. "I went deep for a while—a long while—before I later returned to the RIM and grifted for things I could trade or sell for credits to survive. Kept a low profile and wore a mask when bartering to conceal my identity on the RIM. Not uncommon, as many are disfigured from prime exposure."

"La Voz tilling through trash cubes." Dobs scoffed around a smoky laugh. "As I live and breathe."

"I was in a brewhouse when this boy walks in—clearly from the wrong side of the circle, and I might've paid him no mind except that a group of bruisers were gearing to skin him of clothes and credits. So I intervened. That boy turned out to be Jonothan Shinoda. He recognized me, and given my history with SIGA, he knew I was the only one who'd listen." Ro swiveled her glass, spinning the square cube of ice in the malt liquor. "After working a midyear internship at one of SIGA's labs, he uncovered an encrypted missive following the Frontier collision. It outlined what they were calling the RIM Detach Protocol. SIGA planned to tamper with the gravity system, launching nearly one hundred and fifty billion noncitizen refugees into the void. A catastrophic accident that would lay the foundation for a *groundbreaking* discovery. Pun intended. Cormack Shinoda signed on to oversee extraction efforts, and would obtain all exclusive mining rights once the RIM was . . . cleared out—in perpetuity."

"Why didn't Jono just go straight to the newscasts?"

"Shortly before our meeting, the lab SIGA had set up to allow Shinoda's geologists to do some covert testing was destroyed. Jono had stolen hard drives containing some of the data beforehand, using clearance codes he stole from his father, and must've tripped backdoor security."

Dobs stubbed out a cigarette with one hand, and was already fishing out her pack with the other. "SIGA coverin' tracks."

"Undoubtedly. If we were going to expose the matter, we needed a platform. That's where the Forum came into play. But soon as it went sideways, I got Jono out and hardburned from the quadrant before I turned myself in."

Dobs sparked a fresh cigarette. "You coulda just handed him over to authorities, Ro. Mighta used him to barter your way outta this whole mess."

"The only thing Cormack is obsessed with more than wealth is *immortality*, and his legacy—his son—is all he has to secure that. As long as Jono is missing, Cormack's focus is on everything but the RIMers, which keeps them safe while we expose the truth as planned. But we're running out of time."

"Wait . . . just to be sure I'm following all this correctly . . ." Nimah waved her hands, interrupting the exchange between her grandmother and Dobs. "If you're saying you and Jono were collaborating all this time does that mean—" Her eyes widened. "—*you* set those bombs? *Live* bombs?"

"They were never meant to go off." Ro released a heavy breath. "I couldn't bluff my way in there with duds, Sparrow, the threat had to be real so we could gain uninterrupted access to the Forum floor. The plan was to deactivate them on the way out, but someone knew of our efforts and tampered with the trigger. They wanted the matter silenced. They wanted *us* silenced."

"I don't care what your intentions were—you're a *murderer*."

"And I'll carry that with me unto my dying day," Ro agreed, her eyes rising as Nimah pushed from her seat, quaking with barely restrained rage. "But we're talking about nearly two hundred billion souls. Families. People with no protection or hope for survival."

Fury gripped Nimah by the throat, made it hard to breathe. To think. Her mind spun over all the things she'd done in the hopes of saving her life and proving Ro's innocence. Only to discover her grandmother wasn't innocent at all. Not even close.

FLIGHT OF THE SPARROW

She freed a terrorist, and for what? Ro's justifications didn't matter—she'd played a dangerous game for attention. Exposure. People were dead. Countless injured. And now Nimah was just as culpable. Their blood on her hands, a stain she'd never be able to scrub clean.

"Our government is a parasite," Ro continued. "They take and they take. Now they're out to take more. I won't stand for it. I won't watch another genocide. We knew my death would make intergalactic headlines." She shrugged. "Perhaps not as much as the Forum, but enough to spread the word worlds over. Before my execution, I'd be broadcast across the Circle with my last words. I intended to make them count."

"You still can," Maverick interjected, far too calm in the wake of this damning revelation. "You might've failed at the Forum—but we have something now that you lacked before."

Intrigued, Ro eased forward. "What's that?"

"Their undivided attention, and not just of a few, but everyone," Maverick carried on as if Nimah wasn't fit to explode right in the middle of it all.

Where is your outrage? she wanted to scream. *Where is your horror and disgust?* In fact, when she looked around the bridge, no one appeared sickened by any of it. They were fascinated.

"It's smart." Dobs swiped away fading smoke circles, bleeding into a filmy cloud over her head. "Every reporter across the span of a million parsecs is gabbing about Jonothan Shinoda. Soon as he resurfaces, all eyes of the Inner Circle and Outer RIM will be on him. Cormack couldn't even buy that kind of coverage."

"Not unless you're willing to sell your soul," Nimah countered, a muscle ticking in the corner of her left eye.

Chu whistled. "What d'we do now?"

"Only one thing to do." Ro clapped a hand to her thigh. "Hardburn for Tortuga. Soon as you're all off the *Stormchaser*, I'll take care of the rest."

"But Captain—"

"Someone was onto us at the Forum, and until I know who, I can't risk this mission. Too many lives are at stake."

"It's pretty obvious that Cormack knew your plans," Nimah answered. "He's the only one who stood to gain from silencing you."

"It's possible," Ro agreed. "Either way, I do this alone." She cut an uncompromising glare across the ring of bodies gathered around the navigation console. "That's final."

"No." Nimah silenced her grandmother with a glare. "Plot a course for the RIM."

"Belay that order." Ro battled to her feet. Swayed. It was pure determination keeping her standing, but the strain of trauma and exhaustion distorted the hard edge of her composure like waves pounding against a cliffside. "Have you not listened to a word I said?"

"We're done listening to you." Nimah shook a disgusted head. "Not only can you barely stand, you're a self-professed terrorist. *I* am captaining this ship. So you either toe the line, or I'll have you sequestered in medbay." She closed her hand around the hilt of the cutlass on her hip. The symbol of her authority. Ro's eyes tracked the movement and held there with grim understanding.

Chu gaped in wide-eyed disbelief and Dobs pressed a hand under her chin, snapping her mouth shut. No one spoke to Captain Indira Rosco in such a manner, but Nimah was all out of fucks—just as Dobs had once suggested.

Boomer waved a hand. "Why're we headed for the RIM?"

"That's where she stashed him." Nimah glared at Ro. "My guess is somewhere near the same outpost she deposited me fifteen years ago. Never set a foot in the unknown without keeping the other rooted in the familiar, right?"

The silence on the bridge cracked with tension and Ro's throat tightened, revealing the pulsing throb of a vein, the only indication of any emotion in her expressionless face, confirming Nimah's suspicions.

"Ain't that fucking poetic?" Dobs cackled, the sound heavy with phlegm.

"Fine, Sparrow, we'll do as you command. I'll take you to him." Ro grimaced as she stood. "Perhaps once you've had a chance to speak with Jono you'll come to hear sense."

"I already have. Which is why once I have Jono in hand, I will disembark with the shuttle for the nearest spacity and turn him in. The rest of you," Nimah dashed a hand, numb with indifference, "can make your own way from there."

FLIGHT OF THE SPARROW 237

"I don't understand. What about the reward?" Gertrude raised a finger with a wiggle.

"Don't you get it? We freed a terrorist—there is no reward now. Not for any of us. Whoever hands over Jono they'll thank by slapping in magnicuffs for our trouble. Or worse."

"Unacceptable." Gertrude folded her arms across her chest. "We had an accord, Sparrow. I expect to collect what is mine."

"You mean *our* reward," Boomer jerked a thumb between him and Maverick. "The one she promised Mav, here, to fly first chair? *That* reward?"

She shifted a cutting gaze to Nimah. "You double-roped us?"

"I did what I had to."

"For someone looking down her nose at the likes of us," Gertrude's lip curled with a sneer, "you handled that like a true sodding pirate."

"So that's it?" Boomer scoffed. "No one's getting paid for shitbuckets around here?"

"No," Nimah answered. "Because the only way we'd live to see any credits would be by handing over terrorists responsible for a crime she has just admitted to committing. Now our best chance for survival . . . our *only* chance . . . is to go our separate ways."

Dobs puffed out smoke. "And what are you gonna do, kid?"

"Face the consequences. For everything. Everyone. Once I'm off ship, I'll hail Chief Commander Wallace and turn Jono over with the data. I know I can trust her to do the right thing. And right now, that's all I care about."

"She'll string you up for your efforts."

"Maybe." Nimah nodded. "Maybe that's what I deserve."

"I won't let you die for this, Sparrow."

"You don't get to have a say. You forfeited that right when you dumped me in an orphanage." Nimah thrust up her chin. "When this is over, I don't care where you go, so long as it's far from me. Go deep as you can." She hesitated on the threshold. Looking back only so that her grandmother could see the truth in her eyes. That she meant every cold word. "Disappear like the ghost you are. Because, after this, if I see you again . . . I'll collar you myself."

Disappointment and despair twisted the lines along her grandmother's mouth, aging her. Breaking her. She dipped her chin. "Understood."

Loneliness. The hollow ache gripped behind her eyes like the skittering legs of a spider. Clinging. Waiting to release violent pulses of tears. That sensation crept downward, unspooling in her chest, winding and expanding until her breathing became rough and shallow. Every inch of her heavy with sadness.

Don't go. Not again.

Love me. Want me. Choose me.

But she buried the words and the acrid poison of them sunk into her bones. No. She wouldn't cry. She wouldn't plead or beg. Not this time. This time, it was Nimah who would do the walking.

CHAPTER TWENTY-THREE

Nimah stalked from the bridge before her rage could give way to heartbroken tears. She held herself together until she reached her cabin, then ripped apart at the seams. Arms hugged around her waist, she rocked with a gasping sob. No tears, but the agony of grief washed over her all the same.

All those people.

Nimah sat in the silence, knees drawn to her chest, and let the shadows swell in around her, an encroaching tide to swallow her whole. Submerging her in the dark. In anguish. In hopelessness. She heard the hiss of her cabin door opening and the spin of wheels crossing the threshold moments before the lights flickered on.

Nimah raised her brow from her knees. "What do you want?"

"I wanted to make sure you were alright."

"I'm fine." She pressed the heels of her hands into her eyes. Hard. "Now go away." But he didn't. Instead, his hand closed around her elbow and with a gentle pull, she was in his lap. Cradled close against him, the tears suddenly came, and Nimah wept pitifully into his shoulder. "She's guilty, Mav." More tears, and hiccupping sobs. "I'll never get my life back."

"Then make a new life." His hand stroked in easy circles, tracing up her spine to the nape of her neck. "This doesn't have to be the end for you. It can be a new beginning, Nimah."

Her name rolled off his tongue, warm and soft, and hearing it did something inside of her. Almost like electricity crackling across her skin,

240   FALLON DEMORNAY

but this wasn't painful. This was vibrant and stirring. Nimah angled back so she could meet his gaze with wet eyes. "At least I know I can count on you."

Maverick's expression shifted from concerned to pained, and Nimah's face glowed hotter than hull metal breaking atmo. That clearly had been the wrong thing to say. Eager to put distance between them before she said another word she'd live to regret, she leaned away, bracing to stand when his hand caught hers.

Maverick hauled her close, eyes burning. "I don't make promises I don't intend to keep." He cupped her face gently, wiping away tears from her chin with a stroke of his thumb. "But I promise you can count on me. Always."

His touch, warm and solid, drove through her skin like a solar flare, radiating liquid fire, and something inside her rose to meet it. A wild blend of emotions so strong that Nimah was drowning in them, tumbling through confusion, guilt, fear, and finally wanting—a wanting so potent she almost reached for his face with her other hand.

"Sparrow to cargo hold," Dobs's voice crackled across the intercom.

Maverick pressed his lips to her shoulder. Held there. "You sure you want to do this?"

Nimah nodded. "I have to."

Fifteen years evaporated in a matter of seconds as Nimah stepped off the gangway, and the RIM spread before her like a dream become reality. The surface was craggy and rough and crammed with discarded scrap, moving bodies and patchwork vessels. Overhead, the net of the ozone shield shimmered, casting ripples of light and energy to spread out like waves of luminescent light. Purple, blue, pink, and green. It was never dark on the RIM and those dancing lights had often soothed her to sleep as a child.

The vaguest sensation of warmth radiated from the net, but otherwise every creeping shadow came with a brisk reminder that the only thing that killed you quicker than starvation or thirst on the RIM was the brutal frost of voidburn.

They'd docked off Quay-Z37 in Port Fibris, a preferred station for grifters who came with a haul to sell and went nearly as fast. No one would stop them to ask questions or request registration. No sensors. No

FLIGHT OF THE SPARROW 241

security. This was the farthest edge of civilization, which meant you always kept a sharp eye and a ready hand, at all times.

"Boomer, Sigourney," Nimah called out. "You're our most intimidating members. Hold the ship until we get back. Anyone gives you trouble—you have full permission to take them down by any means necessary."

Boomer shrugged his brawny arms like a gladiator entering the holo-ring. "Razor."

Sigourney tapped two fingers to her sheathed axes. "None shall dare pass."

"Chu, Gertrude—load fuel cells on a hovercart and find a charging station. We'll need them primed to capacity to burn back to the core of the Inner Circle."

"Where d'you suggest we do that?"

Nimah pointed off to the distance to where a squat village spread. It was erected when the RIM had first been established, with the intent of developing into a military stronghold, before the project had been abandoned and the RIM later became little more than a dumping ground for Inner Circle trash and non-class citizens.

Anyone who'd been shipped out to live in such a desolate landscape should've withered into dust, but the RIMers were not privileged members of the Inner Circle, they were hardworking and innovative descendants of the underappreciated working class, and what they'd managed to create was nothing short of exemplary.

Using gravity dampeners, the asteroids were packed so tightly together they formed a solid plateau, shaped like a hooked grin, that spread hundreds of thousands of miles long. All encased in an atmo-netting with self-sustaining generators that recycled water and air to a near-impressive quality. Aided by the cultivation of cross-genetic breeding of plant and animal life, it allowed for the growth of asteroid trees, silver moon grass, and a smattering of fuzzy critters that supplemented the population's food.

By no means was it beautiful, but it was *thriving*.

"Aye," Gertrude tipped her brow. "Don't have much in the way of credits, mind you."

"Strip what you can from the *Stormchaser* that's of value to trade," Nimah said. "Whatever we can spare that won't compromise flight integrity." Chu exchanged a hollow look with Gertrude, but neither of them said a word as they strode off to complete her orders. Good. Nimah wasn't in the mood for further argument or insubordination. She'd played second chair for far too long in this mission, and it cost her everything. "How far is Jono from here?"

"About half a mile. Stationed at a makeshift medbay." Ro thrust her chin toward the high mounds of trash heaped together so thick the belt was no longer visible.

Shipped out mostly from the Inner Circle, garbage was dumped by the ton. A blessing more than a bane, as it was the reason so many survived at all. Fabric. Real leather. Fragments of gold and precious ore, broken microchips and scrap carbide—all had value in the right hands. The rich were always throwing things away.

Narrow pathways carved through the trash mountains, their slopes dotted with rough structures erected from whatever material could be scavenged. But those who'd lived here knew the best way to navigate the streets was from above.

"Is your chair fully charged?"

Maverick rolled up to her side. "Yeah, why?"

"She's too injured to make the jaunt on foot." Nimah nodded to her grandmother. "She'll ride with you and lead the way. Dobs and I will take the scenic route."

"What's the scenic route, kid?"

Nimah gestured to the heaping mounds staggering up in towering walls. She smirked at Dobs. "Think you can keep up?"

Dobs clapped her hands together, palms grating. "Kid, you're about to eat my dust."

It was strange how it all came back so effortlessly, the hauling climb as Nimah scaled up the side of the trash wall, hands and feet finding snug little holds with the ease of muscle memory. Behind her, she heard the whirring hum of Maverick gliding away in his chair to the tunnels. Dobs panted at her side, but with little shock or surprise—for a woman nearing her deathbed, Dobs certainly put Nimah through her paces. In full health, she'd have smoked her for sure.

"*Wooeee!*" At the top, Dobs set her hands on her knees, wincing. "That put some fire in my lungs."

FLIGHT OF THE SPARROW 243

"Need a break?"

"Yeah. Just a quick breather." Lowering to a squat, Dobs whisked the cap off her flask and took a long, heavy swallow, restoring that red color to her cheeks. "Fuck me, I'm getting old."

"It was a hundred-foot climb." Nimah sank down next to her and barely suppressed a violent shudder at the waft of Seawater on her breath. "Should be easier from here. May need to jump a gap or two, but the hardest part is always the climb topside."

"Ah," Dobs dashed a hand. "When I was your age I'd've cleared that faster than a star could wink." Sighing, she capped the flask and tucked it away. "But far as aches and pains go, how you holding up?"

"There were plenty of hand and footholds so . . . I'm fine."

"Ain't talking about the hike, kid." Dobs arched a brow. "I've been riding you hard this whole venture about Ro and, well . . . I was wrong and I'm sorry." She rubbed at her throat as if those final words were gathering like thorns she couldn't pry free.

"You don't have to apologize. I chose this. I gambled my life, my future. All of it." Casting her gaze to the veil, Nimah watched the dance of webbed lights with a heavy heart. "I've lost everything. It's over."

"Doesn't have to be." Dobs sank against the protruding mound of cubed trash with a freshly lit cigarette in her hand. "It's a vast sea out there, Sparrow. Plenty of quads for you to get lost in."

"Even if I wanted to, they're going to collar me as soon as I turn over Jono."

"Then let me do it." Dobs expelled a thick stream of smoke. "I'll take him back."

Nimah frowned. "That's a death sentence."

"I'm already dying, remember?" Dobs smirked. "But I'm also slippery. What do you say?" She nudged Nimah with an elbow, sucking hard on her cigarette; paper and tobacco burned like a setting sun. "I make the run, ditch the Shinoda boy, and then who knows, say I come get you and we sail off on our own somewhere. Hear the Astral rings are pretty slick."

"You'd do that?" Nimah's smile went watery. "Spend your last few months with me?"

"Mumbles, too."

Now Nimah laughed and her tender heart gave a hopeful squeeze. Why not? Why shouldn't she walk away from all of this and claim what was left of her life? There were people out there she could still help in so many other ways. She could join a band of mercenaries hired by off-world planets or perhaps be stationed as a spacity sheriff somewhere too remote for SIGA to patrol. But suddenly that spark of hope in her flickered before it faded beneath the weight of responsibility.

"I'd love nothing more, Dobs, truly. But I still believe in the system. I can't escape my fate." Returning Jono was essential not only to mitigate some of what she'd done, but also to ensure that the information about the elite was delivered into the hands of leadership who could save not only the RIM but all of humanity. "Whatever is waiting for me . . . I'll face it proudly. With honor and dignity."

Dobs assessed her for a moment, then flicked the stub of the cigarette over the edge of the wall with a nod. "Well then, you ain't going back alone, heard?"

"Dobs—"

"To the void or Valhalla, kid." She clapped a hand to Nimah's shoulder with an affectionate squeeze. "We're gonna finish what we started. Together."

Blinking away tears, Nimah shot to her feet. "We should get moving again, if you're good."

"Good as I'm gonna get." On her feet, Dobs cocked the flat of her hand to her brow and skimmed the horizon. "Looks like we lost eyes on Ro and the skinbag. You know which way to go from here?"

"No, but someone down there can easily point the way. Just be careful where you step," Nimah cautioned. "People tunnel through the mounds like miners hunting for prime." Plucking up a bent rod, she tossed it to Dobs. "Test each step before you take it."

Dobs planted the rod against the packed trash at her feet. "Never set a foot in the unknown without leaving the other rooted in the familiar."

"Exactly."

The hospital wasn't hard to find. It only took stopping a couple of vagrants and offering sealed packets of food to loosen tongues to point them on. From there all Nimah needed to follow was the endless line of weary bodies waiting their turn to enter the rusted-out hulk of a far too ambitiously built facility made from panels of welded carbide scraps,

FLIGHT OF THE SPARROW 245

broken glass, and hunks of rock fused with nanite-cement. Asteroid dust pooled in the deep shadows and a stiff solar wind would rip the roof right off come the late season.

Nimah wove past the waiting queue of bodies—broken men, sore-infested women, children so gaunt, so hollow, she could count every bone. And the smell . . . whatever she'd remembered from her own childhood, this was worse. So much worse.

Ro waited for them at the front, Maverick at her side, and gestured to the doors leading into the makeshift facility. "We should find Jono inside. People who run this place are solids of mine, and offered to keep him hid and his hands busy. As you can see the need is great."

"Do they know he's Cormack's son?" Nimah arched a brow.

Ro's jaw tensed and her tone went to ice. "I'd never ask them to put out their necks without all the facts."

"Very well." Nimah adjusted the line of her shoulders, drawing them back with certainty. "Everyone, follow me. If we're met with resistance—"

"We know the drill." Dobs tapped her holstered gun and tossed Nimah a smiling wink. "Lead the way, captain."

Nimah pushed her way through the doors and past attendants who stammered at her heels, calling her back. Not that they could stop her, even before Dobs drew her gun, bringing all commotion to an immediate halt.

"I'm here for Jono Shinoda," Nimah called out, voice carrying over the din of agony, sickness, and death. "Where is he?"

"No one is here by that name." One of the attendants rounded on her, a short woman with blue curls and skin dusted with hyperpigmentation. "Now if you'd please—"

"You seem pretty certain of that," Dobs interrupted. "But we never mentioned if he was a patient or worker and by my estimate there be well over a hundred beds, and near half that in staff with a line growing like a weed out the front door. You saying you know everyone in the books by rote?"

The woman shifted on uncertain feet. "I'll ask you kindly one more time to please leave. This is a hospital."

"And we'll do so," Dobs cocked the hammer of her gun, "when we have Jono Shinoda."

246   **FALLON DEMORNAY**

"It's alright," a cool voice answered. Young, but cultured with unmistakable Inner Circle refinement. Nimah turned to face a skinny youth with a mop of dark, straight hair hanging in sweaty hanks over his eyes as he wiped his hands on a microcloth, bloody to the elbow.

Nimah gave a quick glance over his shoulder into a narrow surgery, where a body lay unmoving atop an operating table. "I didn't know you were a surgeon."

"I'm not," Jono answered. "But I did receive enough medical training to be of assistance, thanks to my robust education within the very best institutions of the Inner Circle. You must be Nimah."

"How do you know my name?"

"Indira said if all else failed I could trust you." His eyes scanned across their entourage and the ensuing gathering of curious bodies, to land on her grandmother, and narrowed beneath a line of black brows. "Forgive me for being indelicate, Captain, but aren't you supposed to be dead?"

"Change of plans," her grandmother answered.

Jono tensed. "Why?"

"I'll explain it all aboard the *Stormchaser*." Nimah tipped her head back toward the general direction of the ship. "If you'd be so kind."

"I can't just pick up and leave."

"Maybe I'm not being clear." She stepped forward, voice low with warning. "I have been shot like a meteor across every corner of this voidforsaken system with almost no rest. I'm exhausted, battered, starving, and my veritable limit for bullshit is stretched about as thin as it's ever going to get, so you're coming with me of your own volition, right now, or I'll have you bound and carried from the premises."

Jono raised his hands, his stubborn shoulders easing with resignation. "In an hour I can—"

"We don't have five minutes," Nimah growled between clenched teeth, "let alone an hour."

"Well, you'll have to make time," Jono answered with an imperious lift of his chin that made Nimah want to knock him down on his ass. "I have important data and research I need to download and bring with me."

"Research on what?"

"Elite core, and my father's plans for it."

Nimah hooked her tongue along the edge of her teeth and looked to the others. "Can we carve an hour, somehow?"

FLIGHT OF THE SPARROW

"I think so." Maverick swiped a hand across the back of his neck. "But I'll need to head back to the ship to keep eyes on the skies."

"My lab's not far." Jono pushed his spectacles up his nose. "I have a two-person rover. The download won't be more than thirty minutes, and it'll take fifteen there and back."

Nimah nodded. "Alright, everyone head back to the *Stormchaser*. I'll take Jono to get what he needs."

"Kid," Dobs said under her breath so only Nimah could hear. "I should come with you."

"No. I need you on that ship making sure everyone's aboard and ready when we get back." Nimah glanced at her grandmother. "The sooner we're off the belt, the better."

CHAPTER TWENTY-FOUR

ab was far too sophisticated a word for the slanted shack Jono parked the rover beside, flanked by the petrified husk of an asteroid tree. Not that Nimah had expected much better on the RIM, but whatever his lab lacked in appearance on the outside, the inside more than made up for it with the same SIGA-grade consoles she'd seen at the Academy.

Tech like this shouldn't exist beyond the Inner Circle, let alone in the Outer RIM.

"Where did you get all this?"

"From my shuttle." Jono stroked the console, almost lovingly. "Plus a few other pilfered items. I've always loved science and exploration, but my father was raising me to be a man of business, to follow in his footsteps and become another legacy CEO in our generational line."

"You did all this in less than *three* days?"

"It's pretty rudimentary." Jono's grin swam sunny with pride. "But the locals here are nothing if not resourceful, and grifters often bring in all kinds of things for which I thankfully had the credits in a shadow account my father doesn't know about." He swept his bangs off his face as it tightened with a scowl. "I've been seeding money into it since I was old enough to understand that his vision for the future and mine did not align."

"And what is your vision?"

"Let me initiate this download and then I'll show you." Hunched over the console, Jono swiped through commands and in less than five

FLIGHT OF THE SPARROW 249

minutes, the download of data commenced onto a holodisk the size of a cherry. She'd never seen one so small.

"Systems analysis—pull up portfolio performance for IESO Mining." The images on the holoscreen faded into one large display with bar charts and graphs surrounding a glowing map of the Inner Circle, specifically IESO's mining territory. "My father is a focused man," Jono continued. "He comes from a long and proud line that can trace their ancestry to the days of Earth-Prior. Few can make such a boast, even inside some of the most affluent families of the Inner Circle." Jono gestured to the shimmering blue lines running across the graph.

"This charts IESO's prime yields for the last hundred years. While the graph may show a rise in production of extracted ore, truth is their mines are tapped and yields are diminishing rapidly. Not just for them—other mining companies are struggling to make quotas. Analysts have been padding the numbers to make it look like we're ramping up production, but in actuality we have maybe another four years left before all of our mines run dry. News hasn't broken yet, but when it does, frankly, our share value will plummet overnight. And not only ours." He swiped across one portion of the screen, where the line reached a precipitous drop. "Which is why my father launched deepvoid explorations to hunt for new asteroids carrying prime veins, but our geologists haven't been able to locate any floating within our galaxy. And any that might be outside of it are too far for our ships to reach. You see?" Jono arched a brow. "A future without prime has left my father desperate to save a dynasty that traces back a thousand years. Once the RIM is cleared, and he swoops in to claim ownership of the wreckage, he will hold all the power. The key to everyone's future."

And if Cormack Shinoda didn't have a god complex before, he certainly would after this. A hero offering triumph in the wake of destruction and despair.

"I have one more thing to show you. This way." Jono crossed the lab to the door, in all of five paces, and removed a lab kit from the hook by the door before exiting, holding it open for Nimah to follow. "I chose this site, specifically, given that the Frontier collision happened about three miles east of here. But the readings were strongest from just over there." He gestured up ahead to a clearing in the field of wasteland and rubble, marked with a bent pole lashed with a bit of fabricated wood into a crude X stamped into the ground.

Nimah toed the pebbled earth. "This is a grave."

"*Graves*," Jono amended. He stopped by the marker and sank to his haunches before it. "There's two bodies down there."

"What does this have to do with your research into elite?"

"Look for yourself." Removing the docuslate from his lab kit, he pulled up a report and handed it over.

Nimah frowned at the screen working through a series of subterranean images, illuminating the bones beneath her feet. She swiped through them, pausing and expanding on the details. The first body was most definitely male, and very large. Huge, even. But the proportions were all wrong. Torso too long, shoulders too wide . . .

"He would've stood at least eight feet." Jono smirked as if he'd read Nimah's very thoughts. "A giant among men. Clearly humanoid but most definitely not a descendant of Earth-Prior."

"Who is he?"

Jono shrugged. "A mystery I don't think we'll ever solve, but whoever they are—they were related. He, the father, was the first laid to ground here. She, the daughter, based on the decomposition readings of the soil samples, joined him somewhere between nineteen or twenty years later. That's when the *magic* happened. Swipe to the next file."

As instructed, Nimah scrolled through the file list and opened the next sequence. This time the images shone with an additional layer showing a vivid network of gilded blue light that fractured from the bones and radiated in glowing pulses, like roots through soil in search of water. A glistening web caught in moonlight.

"You see?" His eyes gleamed with excitement. "Elite *grew* here. And this is the origin point. He, more or less, seeded the ground, and the female, once laid to rest, fertilized it."

Nimah lowered next to him. "I don't understand."

"I didn't at first, either, but after running a series of tests, I discovered rather quickly that while elite is a mineral compound it's also organic in nature. It moves. It spreads. It *reacts* and wants to bond to living matter, but I can't make rhyme or reason of how or why. Not yet." Jono touched his hand to the ground, almost reverently. "Whoever was buried here was someone truly special. They brought elite to the RIM in their bones and through their passing it has taken root across almost the *entire* belt in under two decades. If you're calm enough, in mind and body, you can feel it."

"What?"

"A heartbeat. Here." Taking her hand, he pressed it to the ground and set his over it. "Close your eyes. Let it come to you."

Nimah did as instructed. For a while there was nothing except the waves of orbit breeze and milky breaths but then . . . *there*. Steady. Soft. A pulse against her skin, slow and even, as if of someone asleep.

At peace.

Excited by whatever he saw on her face, Jono beamed a wide grin. "I know. It all sounds mad. A lot of what I have at this point is theory and conjecture. I was planning to exhume the bodies next and run more invasive tests on their remains, but . . ." He paused with an aggrieved sigh. "This is why I need more time."

"Time is a luxury we don't have." But before Nimah could lift her hand away, it seized her. Tendrils of sensation that snaked through her palm and over the skin of her wrist, a visceral touch, rooting her to the earth.

Time is all we have. The voice shocked between her ears, not into her but through her—so much louder than ever before. The same voice that had haunted her every step since the start of this entire ordeal, but where it had once been only a whisper, it now spoke with rich, vivid texture. Deep. Commanding. Powerful. And not just one voice, she realized, but two woven into one.

Open your eyes, Sparrow. This is the key. Lead us. Lead us home . . .

"Stop it." Nimah ripped her hand away.

Jono shook lank hair from his eyes. "Stop what?"

"Nothing." She scrubbed her palm clean over her chest. "Gather your data."

"Please, Nimah," Jono rose with her, trotting at her heels like a determined puppy. "This is important work. Galaxy-changing. Think of what a discovery like this could yield. What it could do for the survival of humanity. Give me a month, or at least a couple of weeks. I could—"

Nimah turned and Jono skittered to an abrupt halt, nearly losing his footing. "You're down to thirty-three minutes." She lanced Jono with a glare. "And not a second more."

Palm still singing, Nimah boarded the *Stormchaser* with a sulking Jono in tow. To his credit he hadn't bothered trying to sway her mind any further on the trip back, made brief thanks to the rover's thick wheels and sturdy engine. It plowed over rubbled wasteland and cubed trash with barely a jostle along the way.

Dobs, seated on the stairway of the cargo hold, rose at their approach. A small mountain of cigarette stubs lay between the wide stance of her boots. "Mr. Shinoda," she exhaled around a thick stream of smoke. "Pleased to make your acquaint."

Gripping the strap of his lab kit like a shield, Jono swept his gaze across the crew, paling visibly at the sight of Sigourney with her fangs bared in a grin.

"Take him to one of the empty cabins and make sure our guest is comfortable." Nimah gave Jono a not-so-gentle nudge forward and Gertrude sashayed in, taking him by the arm.

"Now, now, dear lamb," she stroked his arm, "don't look so fleeced."

"You're making a mistake!" Jono called out to Nimah as he was led away. Nimah ignored him, along with the doubt ringing between her ears like a sonic blast.

Time is all we have—open your eyes, Sparrow.

"You alright, Cadet?"

Nimah pinched her nose, breathing deeply until the wave of nausea passed nearly as quickly as it came. "Yeah. Fine."

"You look about as pale as a stretched neck." Dobs braced her shoulders.

"I'll be better once we're off this belt."

"Heard. Mav, go haul in the gangway while I get our captain off her feet."

"Sure." He whisked around on his wheels and went to work.

"Where's my grandmother?" Nimah lowered to the steps of the stairway, hating this sudden rise of weakness that left her limp and heavy. Fatigue. Stress. Depression. Anxiety. All of it gathering into a single oppressive wave, hammering her to the ground. Of course she felt like

FLIGHT OF THE SPARROW

crap. But even as she tried to convince herself of the fact, the tug in her stomach coiled and yanked. Calling her back. Those voices . . .

Open your eyes, Sparrow.

"In her bunk." Dobs steered Nimah to the steps. "Been there since we brought her back, like you asked."

"Good." Grabbing the rail, Nimah hauled herself up to stand on shaking legs. "Then if we're all done here, I want us voidborne in ten minutes."

"Almost. Just gotta deal with a pest control problem."

Nimah halted, gripping the rail. "Pest control?"

"Someone sent off a wave with our coordinates. Real subtle like. I was able to kill the transmission before it bled too far out to sea." Dobs sparked a fresh cigarette. Sucked hard. "But it's clear we got a fly on the wall."

Chu scuttled over and spat a gobby wad at her feet. "I hate flies."

"A spy? That's not possible . . . Who?"

"Thought you'd never ask." Dobs drew her gun with a swift stroke and fired a clean shot for Maverick's chair. The wheel sputtered and rolled, pitching him out at her feet. She swung her aim for Boomer just as he snapped his repeater off his shoulder and cocked the hammer.

"You lost your damn mind?" he roared. "The fuck's wrong with you?"

"Put the gun down," Maverick grunted and Boomer shot him a galled look. "She's got you dead to rights, man. Put it down."

Aggrieved, Boomer lowered his weapon and Sigourney snatched it from him, pressing the blunt edge of her axe to his throat. "I loathe having to draw steel against my own. Speak sense, and quickly, Dobrevnic."

"Gladly." Though Dobs lowered her gun she didn't put it away, and she planted her boot in the center of Maverick's back, pinning him down. "I had my suspicions after the rescue nearly went sideways. Got to thinking—I know, not my forte," she winked at Nimah, "but you don't send cybers to escort a prisoner—even one as illustrious as our dear Captain Ro, heard? They're to assassinate extreme threats. In this case, us." She exhaled a thick stream of smoke and tossed her smoking butt. "SIGA's been one step behind us the entire way. Always one step behind. And for an organization with two left feet, that's awful

254   **FALLON DEMORNAY**

coincidental, if you ask me, unless someone's feeding them intel. So while you were waitin' on Jono, I dug into the matter and it seems our boy here had a clandestine meet with none other than Chief Commander Wallace at Tortuga."

"He couldn't have." The words flaked to ash on her tongue. "He had an errand. For his chair."

"Bet he did." She pressed down harder, and Maverick barked in pain.

"You're going to break my arm. Can't pilot this boat one-handed."

"We'll manage." Dobs bent over with a sneer. "So I'd start talking, unless you want me to pop this out of joint and shred your tendons."

Maverick ground his teeth, struggled against her weight, but Dobs was a formidable woman and not easy to shake off. Not when he was prone and flat on his belly.

"Wallace would never consort with a felon . . ." But doubt swirled in Nimah's throat, spinning and sloshing around her vocal cords like spindrifts in the air.

"Oh, my apologies. My mistake. I don't know how I got that idea in my head, except for maybe this pretty bit of brass." Dropping to one knee, Dobs dug out something from the cuff of Maverick's sleeve and tossed it to Nimah.

In her shock, she nearly fumbled it, and cupped the badge in her trembling hands. "A Star of Valor." And not just any Star of Valor. The slight chip in the blue enamel in one of the points made it unmistakable. This belonged to Wallace. She'd seen it pinned on the chief commander's lapel many times. Admired it. Hungered for it.

Nimah swept watering eyes to Maverick.

His own closed in shame.

"You set us up. You set *me* up."

"I had no choice. Either I helped her or she'd hand me over to Hatchett to be flayed alive. But I destroyed the tracker," Maverick added quickly. "About an hour before we hardburned for the *Challenger*. I chose my side."

"Told you, kid." Dobs clicked her tongue. "Never trust a skinner. Liars and cheats to the bone, heard? It's all about the long con. The big score."

FLIGHT OF THE SPARROW 255

"Cadet—Nimah—listen to me," Maverick shouted as Dobs wrenched him to his knees, hands anchored behind his head. "I didn't do this. I didn't *do* this!"

Nimah swayed and had to lean against the banister for support. "Can you manage without a first chair, Dobs?" Her grandmother was certainly the stronger pilot but with her injuries, she wouldn't be able to handle the yoke.

"With Gertrude mapping the way, I just gotta point and shoot."

"Good. Put him in the airlock until I figure out what to do with him."

"Walking the plank sounds about right." Dobs smirked. "What about his buddy?"

Boomer grimaced, hands curled into fists but otherwise holding steady, knowing full well Sigourney wouldn't hesitate to slice his head clean off with the smallest provocation.

"Boomer didn't know," Nimah decided after a moment of reflection. "Secure him in his bunk. Best to keep these two apart. Centauri is the nearest outpost and poorly manned. You can deposit me there with Jono. Once we land, *Stormchaser* is yours."

Nimah stalked to her cabin and once inside her bathroom, splashed water over her face. Cold, and shocking. Maverick had betrayed her. All this time, he'd looked her straight in the eyes and lied. Twisting and playing with her emotions. She wanted to scream but her heart wanted to weep.

Nimah refused to succumb to either. As she dried her face, the door to her cabin whisked open, and the footfalls of entry were firm but too even to be Dobs.

"May I have a word, Captain?"

Nimah tossed the microcloth to her bunk. "I've said all I care to say to you."

"Then listen," Ro offered, dragging the length of her braid across her left, uninjured, shoulder. "This is hard for you, I get that."

"You know nothing about me."

"That's not true." Ro smiled. "I was like you, once. A soldier. Not sharp enough for STARs, mind you." Her grin broadened. "But I was good at my job. Loyal."

"Until you went rogue. Turned against everything you believed in and became a pirate."

"You would've too, if you saw what I did. SIGA learned from the mistakes of our ancestors—don't reap the resources of your own world; plunder from others. Once the Inner Circle was established, it was our job to venture deepvoid to find new worlds to strip bare."

"I know, Dobs told me."

"Then you see? What happened on Valhalla was my fault. I led them to it." Ro bounced a fist at her side. "Planet after planet, home after home—SIGA pillaged everything in the Zone Wars and pushed anyone they deemed unworthy out to the RIM—our ancestors—like they were doing them a favor. But now that the RIM isn't as worthless as they thought, they're going to do it all over again. Only this time there won't *be* any survivors." She cut her eyes to Nimah, jaw high and proud. "I failed Valhalla but I won't fail our people. RIMers deserve reparations for harm done. They deserve to come home to the worlds their ancestors were used like chattel to build and then forced to vacate. They deserve to *live*."

"How is SIGA supposed to do that? By uprooting hundreds of billions of families who've occupied these planets for centuries? That's impossible."

"No, that's colonization. Perhaps a hard notion for you to grasp since you don't know what it's like to have your home ripped away from you—destroyed—but I've witnessed it firsthand, and despite what SIGA would have everyone believe, the truth, Nimah, is that the discovery of elite means no one has to die. There's more than enough room within the Inner Circle for all of us."

For all of us. Those words released shockwaves of anguish to cascade down her spine. Because "all of us" should've meant her, too. And yet, this same woman abandoned her own granddaughter with an easy conscience and a light step because it served the greater good. Caring more for strangers than she ever had her own flesh and blood.

"Sparrow—"

"Enough," Nimah whispered. "I risked everything for you. And you know what kills me? You weren't even worth it."

"I didn't want this for you. You shouldn't be here."

FLIGHT OF THE SPARROW 257

"Then why did you send for me?" Nimah handed over the shards of the sparrow.

Ro stared down at the remains of the broken bird. "I *didn't*."

"I did." Both women turned as Dobs swaggered across the threshold, cigarette in one hand, gun in the other. "Needed to stir up old ghosts, so to speak. But if I'd known what that bit of shine was worth, I'd have sent a replica instead of the real deal."

"You . . ." The word slid out of Nimah, low and slow. "What are you doing?"

"Mutiny. Ain't it obvious?" She prodded the barrel of the gun against Nimah's temple. "Out into the hall, if you please, and I expect you to be on your best." Dobs scraped a thumbnail across her furrowed brow. "Otherwise . . ." She cocked the hammer and the sound tore through Nimah's heart, splitting it wide open.

Ro spread her hands, nodded.

"Good. You." She prodded Nimah. "Start walking."

She brought them to the bridge, Ro leading the way, hands visible at all times. Inside, the crew was bound. Chu was unconscious; Gertrude, calm as stone. Sigourney, making an effort to free herself of her bonds, stopped and glared with venomous fury as Dobs entered the bridge. Magtape had chafed her wrists raw. Maybe in another hour she'd have worked herself free but she didn't have another hour.

She didn't have another second.

Shoving Nimah forward, Dobs stopped by her chair. Clucked her tongue. "Can't leave you children unsupervised for five minutes." She slammed the butt of her gun against Sigourney's temple. She crumpled over, blood seeping from a nick in the skin.

"Stop it!"

"Easy, kid, she's still breathing. Siggy's too tough a nut to crack with one blow." Dobs swaggered to the command deck where she drew up the system controls for the lifeboat.

"Maverick didn't send out the wave, did he?"

"Nope. But he made for a good smokescreen. Didn't expect him to go all soft on you, though. Doesn't matter, it all worked out and I got what I needed."

"You can't hand over Jono to Cormack, Dobs. He won't pay you."

"Oh, that's adorable, Cap. You think I've done all this for chump fucking change?"

"Then what do you want?"

"You tell me. Come on, kid." Dobs grinned, pleased to soak up her moment of glory. "Now that the shock's worn off, show me all the fine Academy training. Tell me . . . what's my angle? We talked enough. Any cadet worth her brass should be able to put it together by now."

Nimah worked her thoughts backward through every moment. Every exchange. *You weren't the only one who got dumped, kid.* "Revenge."

"Too easy."

"She abandoned you," Nimah added. "Just like she did me. You weren't just her crew. Her friend. You were family."

"That's the best you got, kid?"

"No. You're also sick. Really sick." *Blood in the lungs, nausea, disorientation.* How had she not seen it before? "You've got prime poisoning."

"Ding, ding, ding, we got ourselves a winner." Dobs grinned, teeth scoring across her bottom lip. "After Ro dumped us, I took up with a flea-bitten crew, got busted in a raid and shipped out to a prime mine. Spent almost three years chipping away on a toxic chunk of ore. Now I'm riddled with so many tumors, stick me under a bodyscan—I light up like a damn galaxy." The blue of her eyes went laser sharp. "And I'm not ready to die. Not even close." Hiking up a boot to the console, Dobs draped her elbow across her knee. "While I was laid up in a medbay, news broke about the Frontier collision. Injured survivors were reeled in, and we got to talking 'bout that strange bit o' blue flash on the RIM. No one knew what they were looking at. Except me. So I got in close with Cormack, told him what he stood to gain, and we struck a deal. I'd help him clear the RIM, make it accidental-like, and he'd haul the shine from the ground. Just had to close some loose ends first."

Ro is the brains. I just blow shit up.

"The forum explosion . . ."

"Now she's catching on," Dobs cackled. "Cormack knew his son intended to expose his plans, and ordered me to silence the matter before it got out. Didn't account for the boy being such a slippery little gizzard." She laughed again and paused to spit blood. "With him in the wind, forced me to find another way to get the wheel spinning."

FLIGHT OF THE SPARROW 259

"I don't understand. This. All of this. The rescue, everything—was all *your* idea."

"That's the fucking genius bit. You'd never see it coming this way. Probably could've hired a bunch of mercs and come after Ro by my lonesome, but I knew I'd never squeeze anything out of her without leverage." She gestured to Nimah with the barrel of her gun. "You're her only weakness, kid. Always have been. Getting you outside of the Academy took a bit of rusty gear churning, but then it clicked. Exposing your kinship to Ro, as a newly unmasked terrorist, not only got you the boot, it made you malleable as butter on a warm biscuit."

Eyes closed, Nimah pushed down the rise of shame and anger and frustration. Dobs had outplayed and outmaneuvered her every step of the way, even earned her trust and respect while pushing all focus of doubt and uncertainty onto Maverick's shoulders to keep Nimah's attention on him. It was so transparent—so . . . obvious, and yet she had been so mired in her past and pain she couldn't see what was right under her nose until it was too late.

"I should've known. I should've seen it."

"Yeah," Dobs agreed. "And you were right, Cap—SIGA would kill for this bit of shine." Reaching into her pocket, she tossed the elite into the air and caught it with a clean snap of her wrist. "And I'm gonna make sure they pay a premium for it before they do. I'll have more credits than I can spend in a dozen lifetimes."

Ro blanched. "It'll be mass genocide. Billions dead. *Again*. And for what? At what cost?"

"Not all of us have the luxury of fighting the good fight. Altruism is for the rich or stupid. If I did things your way the only ones getting paid would be the RIMers and last I checked, I ain't one." Dobs swayed with a smirk. "Ma!"

<Yes, Lieutenant Second-in-Command?>

"Initiate change of command to captain, on my authority, Dorothy Dobrevnic, *Stormchaser* SIC, voice access code—aces over kings."

<Confirmed. Captain's authentication required to complete override.>

Dobs tapped Nimah with the barrel of her gun, arched a brow. "I ain't got all day, kid."

Nimah held her tongue.

260   **FALLON DEMORNAY**

"Very well." She swung left and fired a shot to Ro's thigh. The punch of gunfire swept Ro's leg back. Her curse was lost in the scream that shattered in Nimah's chest. "Don't worry. I'm not gonna kill her. That's too easy." Dobs swiveled the smoking barrel back to Nimah. "But I got five more, heard? And there's lots of other parts I can punch holes in and still keep her breathing. At least a while longer."

"Mother," Nimah forced steel into her wavering voice. "Complete override, on my authority, Nimah Dabo-124, flight of the sparrow."

The system hummed and chirped.

<Override accepted. Dorothy Dobrevnic, you are now primary in command and captain of the Stormchaser.*>*

"I'll take that." She drew the cutlass sheathed at Nimah's waist. "Now that we got the messy particulars out of the way, what say you about being my second?" Dobs ripped the magtape from Gertrude's mouth and chuckled at her dark curse.

"Oh, I would, darling, if mutiny were my color."

"You got half a million credits hidden in your bra I don't know about?" Dobs fastened the sword to her belt. "Last I checked, being in debt to the blackbooks puts a countdown over your head every bit as much as mine. What I'm offering is enough to buy not only a ship—but your own voiddamn *planet.*"

Gertrude pushed up her chin.

"Alright, let's up the stakes. What about you, Siggy? Same offer. Forget queen, you'd have enough credits to build an empire."

"Sweet lies from a blackened tongue." Sigourney raised searing eyes, blood trickling down her temple. "Save it for summer ears. Mine have weathered far too many storms."

"I may lie about a lot of things, but never about a score. Do your part and you'll get a fair cut. My word on it." Dobs planted hands to hips. "Last chance, ladies. Only got a seat for one at the table."

Sigourney bared her fangs. Both women held true, but it wasn't long before the proud line of Gertrude's shoulders slumped and Nimah knew they'd lost her.

"Gertrude . . . no."

"I'm sorry, Sparrow." Her eyes glistened with apology. "I have no choice."

FLIGHT OF THE SPARROW 261

"Zip it, kid. Just wasting air." Dobs cut through her restraints and tossed Gertrude the roll of magtape. "Make sure those two are nice and secure, and then take the helm." She shoved Nimah by the shoulder toward the entryway. "Move."

"Where are you taking us?" Nimah demanded as Dobs drove them at gunpoint down the corridor.

"That'll be a sweet surprise. Don't wanna spoil it when you'll find out soon enough."

CHAPTER TWENTY-FIVE

Ro supported herself as much as possible, arm draped over Nimah's shoulder, but she struggled through each heavy step that reverberated off the grated floor and into Nimah like the shock of a heartbeat. Ticking down to their doom.

"What are we going to do?"

"Don't know yet." Ro set her jaw. "Just gotta keep her talking."

They reached the cargo hold and swung left. The lone shuttle hummed awake at their approach.

"Here we are." Dobs slapped a hand against the hull metal. "Now before you get all excited, I took the liberty of making a few mods so she'll get you to ground, but not much farther." She wiggled a beckoning hand. "In you go, Cap."

"What is this hatred for me born from?" Ro demanded as Nimah propped her against the wall for support, then tied off the wound on her thigh with her belt. "We had thirty-seven years, Dobs. Was it all a lie?"

Dobs's smile melted from her face, slow as a sun sinking below the edge of a winter horizon. "No. It wasn't."

"Then why? What happened between us?"

"What happened is I gave you my life, Ro. Four decades of devotion and loyalty sailing the void by your side. I would've followed you anywhere to the end of my days, and what did I get for it, hm? Nothing but scars, and a handful of credits to last me a week while my brain erodes in my skull. Thanks to you. So now I'm gonna take everything you have. Starting with the *Stormchaser*."

FLIGHT OF THE SPARROW   263

"This old bitch?" Drawing away from Nimah, Ro planted herself before Dobs and though she grimaced with the effort to stand, she held strong. "She's all rust and wear, couldn't sell her for scrap."

"Fucking A." Dobs smirked. "Her true value lies within her legacy, and that's something money can't buy. But it's not enough, I deserve more. I deserve glory and riches and the kind of wealth that will extend my years another fifty—another *hundred*. I deserve to be a legend, revered through the ages while all memory of you fades into dust."

A blur of movement—brown coat and flapping braids—was all Nimah saw before Mumbles latched onto Dobs like a feral cat, all teeth and claws and a violent roar. A sound Nimah never heard her make until this moment of spitting rage. Dobs barked a cry as Mumbles's few remaining teeth sank into her arm by the wrist, but with all her vigor, Mumbles was no match for Dobs's size and strength, and a hard shove was all it took to have Mumbles stumbling over her own feet.

"The fuck is wrong with you?" Dobs shouted, rubbing her bleeding wrist.

"Go shoot and bang on Capsy." Mumbles righted herself, shaken but otherwise unharmed. "Dobsy bee tray all. Dobsy bee tray *all*!"

"Betray? I am setting us free."

"Nay nay I say." She slapped a hand to her temple, beat it there three times with a sob. "Hail the stars and make them fall, head and brains to broken eggs—smush under boot. Dob make broke fool tongue. But stand I *still*. Stand for Capsy. For Nimsy."

"Step aside, Mumbles." Dobs tapped her gun impatiently against the side of her thigh. "Don't make me hit you again."

Unafraid, Mumbles spread her arms. A shield between Dobs and Ro. "With sword and wing, I be valcree. To Halla. To void." She bared bloody teeth. "Dobsy be yellow."

Dobs wiggled her jaw, grinding the caps of her molars as a hint of something shimmered in her glare.

Hurt? Guilt?

"Suit yourself." In a swift movement she seized Mumbles by the scruff of her neck and tossed her bodily into a locker, then snapped the door shut.

"Don't!" Nimah shouted. "She's afraid of the dark. You know that!"

"Won't keep her in there for long." Dobs sighed against it, the torrent of beating fists and muffled cries reverberating at her back. "Mumbles has a good heart and worships our captain like she shits prime. Then again, can't blame her—she ain't exactly all *there*. She'll cool off in twenty."

Beneath the wailing cries, Mumbles's words echoed back to Nimah. *Hail the stars. Make them fall.*

Hail the stars.

The way home . . .

"Hail the stars and make them fall," she repeated. Dobs's eyes shot to her. "Mumbles kept saying it to me, over and over, on Tortuga. I didn't understand what she meant but : . . not actual stars. Agents. STARs agents." Nimah's voice hardened. "She was trying to warn me. She wanted me to stop you."

"Wouldn't be the first time she tried."

"Mumbles didn't fall off that escarpment in Valhalla, did she? The night of SIGA's assault before the planet was destroyed . . . you pushed her. Didn't you?" Nimah shook a disgusted head. *Broken brain. Fool tongue.* "And that's why you went back to get her out. Guilt."

"I might be a backstabbing cur, but I got a heart, kid. Just don't fill it with much these days."

"How long?" Ro set her teeth. Horrified understanding pushed raw color into her cheeks, infusing the tawny gold with vicious red. "How long have you played the turncoat?"

"Got some nerve calling me that." Dobs rolled her tongue across her teeth. "I did what needed doing to get us home. Which should've been your responsibility, *Captain*, but you would've left us there to rot all because you were twisting limbs with a local instead of looking out for your crew."

"I loved him!" Her grandmother's anguished roar rang across hull metal.

"And I loved *you*," Dobs bellowed back. "We all did. But you didn't give a damn about us, about what we wanted. Did you really think I was happy to be grounded? To never sail the void again? I knew SIGA would

FLIGHT OF THE SPARROW   265

never come for us. We were expendable. So I gave the bastards a reason to come running. Elite was our ticket home and more credits than you could imagine, but then you had to go all noble and warn the locals to blow up the fucking *planet*!"

Ro lunged with a war cry and her fist caught Dobs in a clean strike across her jaw but in her condition, she was no match, and when her second swing missed, bouncing off the hull, Dobs swept her legs out from under her.

Struggling to her knees, Ro clutched her hand to her chest. "They welcomed us. Trusted us!"

"We were prisoners."

"Maybe we began that way. But not at the end."

"We were always prisoners, Ro, just hidden under the guise of friendship." Dobs ground through clenched teeth. "You know the single thing that has kept me from putting this gun to my head and emptying my skull? This." She swept out her arms. "This moment. Giving you a taste of your own venom." Dobs looked to Nimah, her eyes bright with a kind of manic joy. "What say you, kid? Can't unwind the clock—there's no going back to life at the Academy, but this doesn't have to be the last page in your book. Join me."

"What?"

"Think about it. Think carefully. She abandoned you—just as she did all of us. Family. Blood. Loyalty. None of that meant a single solitary damn. You owe her nothing."

Nimah shook her head, breathless with disbelief. "No. I don't, but I won't stand by you, either."

Dobs scoffed under her breath, held it in a moment of sobering silence. "Well, can't fault you for having more pride than sense, given your roots. I'm disappointed, though. Saw real potential in you for greatness, but if you be so eager to die for your convictions, who am I to stand in your way?"

The ship rolled, and in the halfmoon viewport, a scattered field of ore and steel swept out for miles amidst a hazy cloud of shimmering opalescent purple.

Ro's gaze narrowed. "The Boneyard?"

"It ain't Valhalla, but it'll have to do."

266   **FALLON DEMORNAY**

Nimah's heart plummeted to her knees. The Boneyard—a wasteland of scattered remains from the Zone Wars. Destroyed ships, burntout drones, ejected bodies, and obliterated husks of mined asteroids hauled out and dumped to clear voidways for travel to and from the Inner Circle.

It was a sea of death.

Ro released an easy laugh, like she wasn't the least bit terrified of being stranded in a busted lifeboat without any hope of hailing for rescue, left to suffocate among the dead. "Didn't take you for sentimental."

"This ain't about sentiment. It's eye for an eye and now we're even." She wiggled her gun at Nimah, then at the entry of the lifeboat. "Get in."

"She's not part of this," Ro snapped, clutching the wound on her thigh. Blood seeping through her fingers. "I'm the one you want."

"You're right." Dobs shook her head, sighed. "But the kid chose her bed, now it's time to lie the fuck down. If she'd just handed Jono over to me like I'd suggested while out on the RIM, that would've been the end of her part in it. But no. Had to go all noble, for what? Now here we are. It's messier than I planned but so be it. At least this way I get to cast you off."

"You can't do this." Nimah's voice broke and terror flashed across her skin, wrapping her in ice so thick her teeth wanted to shatter.

"Wallace won't be pleased about it," Dobs admitted. "She wants you both something fierce. Probably to do with that incident aboard the *Challenger*, but can't have you breaking word of my plans to save your necks, heard?"

"We'll die!"

Drawing the cutlass, Dobs leaned against it like a cane with casual, unaffected arrogance, and shrugged. "Dead men tell no tales."

Maverick struggled against his restraints. Against the magtape glued tight to his furious mouth.

Sonofabitch, sonofabitch, sonofabitch—a desperate refrain that roared violently in his head. He, of all people, should've seen this coming. The careful play, the gentle prods and slick maneuvers as Dobs fleeced him like a lamb in spring. Skinned to the bone, she'd beat him at a game he'd practiced for most of his life.

Because you got stupid, a voice inside of him chastised. A voice that sounded irritatingly close to Boomer in a snit. *Wallace dangled a clean slate, Nimah batted brown eyes—and you lost sight of what* mattered. *Yourself.*

First rule of the skingame—work alone.

Trust no one, a hard second.

And never, ever drop the con—the irrefutable third. Skinners were trained to hold on to the lie with their dying breath, but the look in Nimah's face, the abject hurt, had compelled him to give it all up. To bare his soul.

What soul?

He'd done horrible things. Dangerous and depraved things to good, honest people, all to keep Hatchet from skinning Maverick's quota out of his own back should he fail to meet it. Whatever soul he'd been born with was long gone.

The *Stormchaser* rumbled and Maverick stilled. That was a docking tremor, and since they weren't moving and hadn't hardburned—he would've been plastered to a wall like a squashed insect if they had—something had come to them. Something *big*.

The hiss of the airlock broke through his panic and Maverick swiveled around to glare as Dobs crossed the threshold, cutlass on her hip. His heart stopped, then surged violently into his throat. There was only one reason for her to be carrying the captain's sword.

Mutiny.

Dobs pried the magtape off in a single, deft *rip*, and Maverick swallowed a brilliant curse as lights of pain sparked behind his eyes.

"Where is she?" he panted, lips searing like he'd kissed the devil's asshole. "Where's Nimah?"

Dobs flashed white teeth smeared with red. A bloody grin. "Should be more concerned with your own neck."

The whispered groan of the hatch disengaging interrupted them, and Maverick's mouth fell open as four cybers flowed into the cargo hold with Liselle and Chief Commander Wallace behind, her military whites dazzling, arms tucked behind her back. HWKeyes swept the hold, scanning and searching, before landing on Dobs.

"Maverick Ethos-333." Dobs nodded toward him. "Djimon Boomer Omunye, and what remains of the crew, are also subdued, as promised. Got 'em hogtied on the bridge."

"What *remains* of them?" Wallace angled her head. "Where is Dabo-124?"

"Deceased."

"Indira Roscoe?"

"Also deceased."

Maverick swallowed his gasp, but the sound spun out of Liselle's chest and she clasped hands over her mouth. Eyes watering.

"I'd asked for both Dabo-124 and Indira Roscoe to be remanded, unharmed."

"Didn't give me a choice. Besides, what's it matter if a couple of criminals are put down in the dirt?" Dobs shifted her stance, widening her feet. An easy gesture, but Maverick saw the intent behind it. She was spreading her weight, expanding her center of gravity for possible defense. Or attack.

It was clear Wallace noted the subtle shift as well, but didn't give an inch. She remained in the relaxed pose of a commander facing an adversary in negotiations. Arms at her side. Chin high. But even she was far from calm. Storms surged inside of her. Bright and violent, charged with electricity that sizzled in the air over her shoulders.

"Criminals or otherwise, their fate was not for you to decide."

"As I said," Dobs stabbed her tongue against the corner of her lip, "they didn't give me a choice."

"Their bodies?" Liselle demanded, her words broken with grief. "Where are their bodies?"

"Ejected."

"What about the stone Nimah carried?" Wallace demanded. "Were you able to secure it?"

"Nope."

Wallace's jaw tensed. "I thought I made the new directives clear."

"What can I say?" Dobs hooked the cutlass across her shoulders, shrugged. "Things don't always go according to plan, but the Shinoda boy is alive and well. If you're done dallying, I'd say it's high time we fetch him home."

FLIGHT OF THE SPARROW   269

Wallace set her shoulders, posture rigid with displeasure, but eventually the tension eased and resignation softened her edges. "Secure the prisoners and have them loaded aboard the *Challenger*. Starting with Ethos-333." Wallace cast her flickering gaze to him. "Hatchett is waiting."

Liselle raised her hand in a sharp salute, then dropped it when Wallace and Dobs were out of earshot, headed toward the bridge. Or the crew deck. Whatever. It didn't matter. Nothing mattered.

Dead. Nimah was dead.

Liselle stepped in before a cyber could take hold of his chair. "Stay aboard with the chief commander. I'll ensure the prisoner is transported to the holding cells, immediately."

The cyber held their ground a moment longer, then dipped their chin a fraction in a nod. The liquid nanite helmet, slick as a mirror across its face, obscured any trace of gender or identity. Or emotion.

Dead. The word jolted through Maverick with each skipping beat of his heart as Liselle pushed his chair from the cargo hold into the airlock of the *Challenger*. Riveted walls gave way to backlit glowing panels and sweeping corridors, seamless and glossy, that flowed to a lift—he barely registered any of it as the door whispered open and Liselle steered them inside.

Bleeding void, he was going mad. The blackest edges of insanity rolled in like fog against his senses. Smothering him. Drowning him.

Dead. Nimah was dead.

Dead.

Gone.

Dead.

"Hey!" Liselle scrubbed a hand before his face. "Focus, Maverick. I need you to focus."

Maverick blinked at her, a little dazed, and the same hand she'd waved before his face cracked hard against his cheek. Hard enough to make his ears ring.

"I said *focus!*"

"Fuck!"

"There." She smiled thinly. "That put the fire back in your eyes. Listen, I was with Chief Commander Wallace when she received new directives from the board," Liselle continued, expression grim. "Whatever happened during the rescue mission . . . they've lost interest in Captain Roscoe—or even Jonothan Shinoda. Nimah's the target now."

"What're you going on about?"

"Detach Protocol. I don't know what it all means, but it sounded bad."

"It's worse than bad, unless you think destroying the gravity grid on the RIM and subjecting every living soul to a swift and brutal death is kittens and rainbows."

"Why would they want to do that?"

"Why else?" Maverick cut her a glare. "Greed. That stone Wallace asked about is an elite power source and there's millions of metric tons of it on the RIM."

Liselle's features morphed from horrified disbelief to livid fury. "Those self-important assholes. We have to find her before SIGA does."

"You heard Dobs." Maverick hung a despondent head. Weary. "She's dead."

"I don't believe that." Liselle gripped his shoulders and shook him steady. "Do you?"

His eyes lifted to meet her gaze, and something—something—inside of him warmed with refusal. "No. No I don't."

"Great. Now, we're going to have to move quickly. If we wait until the moment of detach from the *Stormchaser*, we should be able to avoid detection on their radars and be long gone before Chief Commander Wallace notices."

She was talking so quick—nerves, apparent in the clenching and unclenching of her hands—that Maverick's head spun on his shoulders. "Wait . . . what?"

"Try to keep up. I'm getting you off this ship. This turbolift will take us to the STARjets below the half-deck. You can fly one of those, right?"

Maverick jolted in his chair. "I can't leave Boomer."

"I know it's hard to leave someone you care about behind, but Boomer isn't in immediate danger," Liselle interrupted sternly, though her eyes shone with understanding. "Nimah *is*. Once we

FLIGHT OF THE SPARROW

have her, we can come back for the others. This is the only way to save everyone."

Maverick knew she was right, but guilt gnawed at him all the same. Boomer was his oldest friend and partner. The two of them had been snatched by Hatchett near the same time and it was Boomer who'd pulled him from the wreckage of his voidcraft and patched him up. Boomer who helped source the parts to make his first chair. Boomer who'd shared his rations so Maverick wouldn't starve and bloodied his fists when the other kids thought him an easy mark to skin just to stay alive in those hard, terrible years of training.

Forgive me, Booms. "Alright. Okay. I'm in."

"Excellent." Swerving around behind him, she gripped the handles on the back of his chair. "Now that we both agree Nimah's alive—where do you propose we look for her?"

"How would I know? I was stuffed in an airlock." Fury rolled through him, dark and thick. *When I get my hands on Dobs . . .*

"C'mon—" Liselle slapped him again, this time over the back of the head, "use that big skinner brain of yours and think! Where would Dobs dump them?"

Maybe it was the searing frustration in Liselle's voice, or the jolt that shuddered through the belly of the *Challenger*, but something inside of Maverick clicked. "The Boneyard."

"What?"

"The Boneyard," he repeated. "It's just offside of the RIM. Nothing out there but rubble and debris for miles—makes for a hellish no-fly zone. We passed through turbulence. Lots of it. Dobs must've marooned them there. Perfect dump spot to ensure they won't be found." And to die slowly, but Maverick held that to himself.

"Can you pilot us there?"

"In a single-chair fighter jet?" An x-shaped, polished carbide thing of absolute beauty? "Fuck yes, I can."

Liselle brightened. "Then let's get out there and find her. Let's find our girl."

The lift countdown chimed for their floor, and Liselle braced to push him out onto the *Challenger*'s lower flight deck when the doors whisked open to reveal Dobs, Chief Commander Wallace, and a retinue of cybers waiting on the other side.

"Told you." Dobs plucked her cigarette from her lips, exhaled with a grin. "Can't trust kids these days."

"Cadet Namsara. To say I'm disappointed is an understatement." Wallace set her jaw. "Seize them."

CHAPTER TWENTY-SIX

The shuttle released from the *Stormchaser* like a stone being thrown from a hand—hard, violent, and in that breathless instant of release—without control.

Nimah clenched against the violent shudder as the shuttle plummeted through the void like a stone dropped down an endless chasm. Each rattle and hard jolt tore a cry from her chest, each one trapped behind her teeth, and sent tears streaming down her cheeks.

I can't breathe. I can't breathe!

Ro struggled against the force, battling toward the console.

"What are you doing?" Nimah shouted. "You can't fly without power cells."

"No, but I can steer." Ro gripped the yoke, one-handed. "Brace yourself," she shouted over the emergency sensors screaming "proximity warning," and gave a firm yank, adjusting course to avoid collision. Her movements weren't smooth or graceful, but she wove around the largest mounds of debris, grunting and cursing her way through until she found a clearing in the chaos. A large flat slat of weathered ore that spread like a landing strip.

Ro punched the yoke forward, driving toward it, and slapped buttons across the console. Thrusters engaged, abruptly halting momentum, and Nimah's ribs groaned and lungs struggled as she was wrenched forward against her harness.

The shuttle bounced twice against the surface before gravity boosters took root and they finally staggered to a violent, firm stop. The alarms shut down, and the overhead strobing lights switched from searing red to calm white.

All fell silent.

Ro unfastened her harness and boosted from her seat, her face sallow and eyes glassy as she wrenched a med kit from an overhead compartment. The crimson smear on her thigh had grown wide, a damp eye blooming at the center, and blood splattered from her cuffed hem in a tempo that matched Nimah's scattered heartbeat.

Her hand shook as she rooted around, digging out a hooked knife she used to cut open the fabric of her pants, exposing the raw wound beneath.

"Clean exit," she rasped. "No fabric or debris. Good." Flushing it out with sterilized water, she sealed it with a thin sheet of second-skin. Over time it would dissolve as the wound knit beneath. Ro punched the needle of an antibiotic syringe into her thigh and cursed a vicious stream in a language Nimah didn't understand—and she spoke the Core Twelve fluently. They'd been implanted into her after her fifth year.

Casting the empty syringe to the floor, Ro closed her eyes, her breathing eased, and color returned to her skin, spilling across the hard edge of her cheekbones. "There," she sighed. "Sparrow, you alright?" When Nimah didn't answer, she cracked open an eye.

"Yeah . . . I'm . . . I'm not injured."

"Right, then let's get suited."

Nimah unbuckled her harness with numb fingers and struggled to stand on weak legs. "Why?"

"This was a rough ride. Best make sure we're not breached." Ro stood again, this time far steadier on her feet than she had been a moment ago, and from another overhead compartment, plucked out suits made of silver synth-fiber. She tossed one to Nimah before battling her way into the other with her splinted arm and injured leg, but thanks to the emergency med kit, she managed without so much as a grunt. Soon as Nimah fixed on her visor, Ro released the hatch and the air from the closet-sized airlock rushed out in a gasping *woosh*.

She followed her grandmother off the lifeboat. The suit, unsophisticated in its design, did little to anchor her, so her steps were bouncing and slow, each bob punching her heart higher into her throat. One hard leap—just one—and she'd launch from the corpse of an asteroid.

She'd be lost.

FLIGHT OF THE SPARROW 275

But I'm already lost. Grief rolled through Nimah, a blanket of fog smothering a waking sunrise. Snuffing out light, diffusing color and joy as the world went gray before her eyes. Vast and empty and stark. Cold. So cold.

Don't be afraid . . .

"She looks sound, albeit bruised." Ro stroked the battered hull like a beloved child. "Roughest waters I've endured in a lifeboat. Don't think it would've held fast if Chu hadn't worked her magic ages ago." She dropped her hand to her hip, turned in a full limping circle as if on the bridge of the *Stormchaser*, gauging the weather on the horizon. "What a terrible joke. To die here." Ro kicked a lump of broken rock and it launched into the void like a slow-moving bullet. Buoyant in zero gravity. "Surrounded by the bones of various civilizations obliterated beneath the punishing blow of a hammer. All that it was and could've been—smashed into dust."

Nimah flinched, as if the very hammer her grandmother spoke of found her most delicate nerves and proceeded to pound where it hurt most.

Five things you can see . . . See? What was there to see? Her teeth rattled. Her hands shook. Focus wavered. Everywhere she saw only death, emptiness, and desolation.

Smashed to dust.

Four things you can touch . . . but she couldn't touch anything! Couldn't smell or taste. Trapped in her suit. Trapped in a graveyard. *Trapped.*

Her breath rushed out, fast and uneven, creating clouds of steam on her visor. In the distance, the rumble and roar of negs. And . . . stars above . . . was that the shimmering tentacle of a kraken?

"I can't . . . I can't . . ."

"Easy." Ro stroked her shoulder.

"Don't touch me!" She shrugged her away with a high-pitched whine and staggered for the lifeboat, up the tier of narrow steps into the airlock. Ro, close behind, sealed the door and engaged the pressure valve to restore gravity and oxygen.

Nimah shook out trembling hands, itching to rip off her visor as the numbers ascended far too slowly. Soon as the light flashed green, she wrenched open the second door into the lifeboat—all but yanking her visor off in the same breath. But even here she was still trapped in a bubble, barely ten feet across in either direction, it was little more than a coffin to bury them in the blackest of waters.

"You have to stay calm. Slow your breathing." Ro approached her cautiously. "You're having a—"

"I know what I'm having," Nimah shouted. Each word vicious and barbed after a decade and a half of loss steeped in blood-soaked misery. Tears blistered in the corners of her eyes, gathered in a knot at the hollow of her throat. Rising. Scorching, like flames funneling furiously from an engaged thruster. "I've had them for as long as I can remember—*thanks to you!*"

Her grandmother actually had the gall—the temerity—to look surprised. "Me?"

Nimah rounded on her. Hands in fists, shoulders drawn so tight her spine wanted to snap under the strain. "You think I don't know what it feels like to watch as my home—*my life*—was destroyed? Well, I do. Because it was destroyed the day you dumped me like trash and took off into the void. Do you have any idea how many nights I cried myself to sleep wondering what I did that was terrible enough to make you stop loving me?"

Ro's shoulders—a proud line—sagged. "Sparrow . . ."

"Don't call me that." Nimah swiped at tears, but more came, blurring it all into a viscous mess—a fractured mosaic of so many years mired in anguish and hope. "I nearly died because of you. Do you understand that?"

"I'm sorry."

"Keep your sorrys. I begged you to take me. To love me."

"The only way I could love you was to leave you. I was protecting you."

"Liar!" Nimah shoved her grandmother hard, forcing her back a step. "I hate you." She shoved her again, harder. "Do you hear me? I hate you!" *Again.* "I should've let you rot at Hollow Point so you could feel alone and helpless and scared—feel everything I did. All of it."

Ro absorbed every vicious blow and violent scream as pain rippled through her, like glass in a shattered viewport—the cracks and breaks spiderwebbed toward the edges, touching every corner. Igniting every nerve. There wasn't a single inch that wasn't throbbing and aware. She was all rawness and feeling. Too much. Too damn much.

FLIGHT OF THE SPARROW 277

Nimah's vision blurred, her legs wavered, and with a sob, she broke. Utterly, completely broke. Sinking to her knees, Nimah hugged them to her chest and let the torrent pour through her, violent and bright and heaving in hard, frantic gulps.

"Sparrow." Ro gathered her close and this time she didn't fight back, didn't pull away. She sank into that embrace, and a strong arm folded around her, held her tight and warm until the torrent slowed. Eased. Lulled by the stroke of her grandmother's hand across her head and down her back. "I wish you could've known your mother," she said, so quietly Nimah almost doubted she'd heard her speak, but that hand continued stroking, slow and easy. "That's my fault. For not speaking of Zoraida more . . . *after*. It was too painful, but I failed you there, too. I failed you in so many ways." Sinking into the chair behind the console, Ro gazed out the viewport at the sea of bones like it was a painting from Earth-Prior hung on display in the Illyrio Museum.

Reverent and filled with regret.

"The pendant you're wearing is called *s'ahaelou*. Your grandfather carved it, knowing even before I did that I was pregnant. Every Valhallan was given one at birth, created by the hands of their elders and worn for life. It's an energy source not just for their technology, but for themselves as well. A precious gift and responsibility they safeguarded fiercely. When Zory turned twenty, I finally gave it to her. Initially, I kept it from her to hide the truth of her parentage after the planet was destroyed, but later changed my mind. I wanted her to have a piece of him—of her ancestry, even if she didn't know what it meant." Ro scored her teeth across her bottom lip, eyes fixed on some unseen horizon among the milky swath of silent stars and scattered rubble. They welled with grief.

Responsibility.

"Three years after you were born, we were set upon by SIGA enforcers. They'd caught up with us after a raid on one of their transport ships, and Zory was cornered. Outnumbered. Scared, I imagine, that she wouldn't make it back to you—the intensity of that maternal instinct . . . She couldn't control it. What mother could?"

Nimah swallowed hard. "Control what?"

"Soulfire." Ro shook her head, the gesture weary. "You saw what elite is capable of under duress. Valhallans could channel it—like a conduit—but your mother had never been taught. There was no one to show her *how*."

"Because they're all dead."

"Your grandfather gave his final breath to save his people." She scraped a weary hand across the back of her neck. "I buried what was left of him on the RIM, and your mother next to him."

He seeded the earth. She gave it life.

"It's them," Nimah whispered. "The gravesite."

"Ah . . . Jono proved his theory then, I take it?" Ro nodded at some absent thought before continuing. "Zory was plagued with nightmares, too. It took me a long time to realize it was the *s'ahaelou* calling her home to Valhalla. So when I saw the stone calling out to you, I realized you carried the same affinity. As I had feared. I knew I had to keep you safe. Secret. For a long time, I stubbornly believed I could," she spoke gently into the silence and Nimah held her breath for a beat as she listened. Truly listened. "But her death raised many questions within SIGA, and the dangers were proving to be too great, so I deposited you at the orphanage to bury all ties to me. After that, I disbanded the crew and went deepvoid to throw SIGA off my scent. If anyone was to come hunting, I wouldn't have it on their heads. No one else was going to die for my mistakes."

Dead men tell no tales, as Dobs would say, and this would've certainly been a sort of death for her. To lose it all in one fell swoop. She'd given up everything. Her crew. Her family. All for Nimah's safety. For love. A sacrifice beyond measure.

All this time . . . "I didn't know."

"You weren't ever supposed to. I figured you'd resent me for it. Hate me, even. But I was prepared to weather that storm rather than mourn your death. I failed your mother, Sparrow; I refused to fail you, too. But when I'd heard you'd been sold by that bitch warden, you'd already been found and shipped to a medcenter for treatment. I dealt with her first." Captain Ro's eyes seared cold as deepvoid. "In the only way she deserved. And after it was clear you'd recover, I called in every favor I had to grease the right wheels, so to speak, and get you through Academy doors."

"But I was found by the former chief commander during a site inspection of Hollow Point."

"And who do you think sent him on that inspection?" Ro's eyes twinkled with devious glee. "It's not just the poor who are criminals,

FLIGHT OF THE SPARROW 279

Sparrow. Plenty of rich folk sign their name to the blackbooks. Perk of being a pirate is, I encounter both. And I wasn't shipping you back to the RIM only to risk you being sold again." She tucked a strand behind Nimah's ear. Cupped her face. "Just because you haven't seen me, doesn't mean I haven't been paying attention. You've made me proud. Prouder than I've a right to be, and for what it's worth, I'm sorry that it's come to this. Run aground in the Boneyard. If I could spare you this terrible end—I would. You shouldn't have to die for my sins. So young and in your prime."

Nimah jolted, her heart leaping at a thought. "Prime . . ."

"What?" Ro's brows furrowed. "What is it?"

"Prime," she repeated. Her excitement growing. "Elite is stronger. You said the pendant could power the *Stormchaser* for ten years."

"Yeah . . . ?"

"Well, the lifeboat is sound, it's just out of juice."

"And we're not likely to find a refueling station here," Ro chuckled, and pressed the flat of her hand to Nimah's brow. "You bump your head in that ride?"

Nimah swatted her away. "We don't need a refueling station." Reaching into her pocket, she removed the shard, hands shaking. "Dobs dropped it when Mumbles lunged for her. I picked it up when she was too busy fending her off."

Ro barked a brittle laugh. "I'll be damned."

"Can you make it work in its raw state?"

"I don't have Chu's gift with engines." Ro accepted the fragment of glowing stone, the light of it catching in her eyes. "But I absolutely paid attention. Though once she's live again, I can't fly this bird out of here, Sparrow." She nodded toward her splinted arm, then toward the grave-yard. "Not through all that. Not with one hand. You'll have to take the yoke."

"I know." Nimah's belly seized. "But we're not dying here. Not today, and if we do, it'll be fighting."

Dark brows disappeared behind the sweep of white bangs. "Aye, Captain." Ro weighed the stone. "Guess I best be getting to work on put-ting this boat back in the water." Ro grunted as she lowered to her knees and crawled beneath the console to pry out the panel. There was a flash of sparks and more than a few curses.

280 **FALLON DEMORNAY**

Nimah plunked down in the piloting chair and scanned ahead through the viewport. The flight space was a minefield of floating debris—most the size of softballs—and deactivated drones. It would make for a bumpy ride. Lifeboats weren't designed to hold up against strenuous wear, and they'd taken a few hits on the way down.

The way out was going to prove far more challenging.

A final grunt and curse followed by a flash of brilliant blue sparks—and the lifeboat shuddered awake.

Ro emerged from beneath the console, her face a mess of blackened soot. "Bleeding void, if we make it off this heap, remind me to give Chu a raise." She plunked into the passenger seat behind Nimah.

"What now?"

"There's an abandoned outpost two clicks from here. Little more than a squatting station, but there'll be a comms tower to hail for aid from a nearby spacity or passing transport vessels."

"You're a wanted fugitive. They'd arrest you on sight."

"That's a problem for later." Ro deflected with a shrug. "Right now, we need to focus on getting voidborne."

"No. No. We can't let Dobs get away with what she's done. What she's about to do." Nimah gripped the yoke. "Chief Commander Wallace won't waste time with deepvoid travel. She'll burn for the closest Eye to thread Jono back to the Inner City. That's Higazi2. It's not far from us."

"Sparrow, while I admire your grit, you want to chase them down in a lifeboat? *Alone?*" Ro cocked her head with an *are you high* expression twisting her features. "Even if we could catch up, we'll never get the drop on them. Not in the open. Radars will detect us from miles off and proton cannons will blow us out of the water."

Nimah drummed her fingers on her thigh. "Unless we give them something else to chew on." Maybe it was the elite, but suddenly Nimah's mind was clear. So clear.

Once, when the sea had been thick with negs and krakens, mining companies had developed drones to extract the ore, but over time they decided shipping out people—convicts and RIMers—to do the work was easier. Machines cost far too much to maintain, but the dead and dying cost nothing. Now the drones lay discarded and forgotten. Floating spheres that quietly spun like dust moats caught in a sunbeam. There were hundreds of them. Maybe thousands.

FLIGHT OF THE SPARROW 281

All they needed was a charge.

Ro followed her granddaughter's gaze. "Do you think you can?"

"Only one way to find out." She looked to her grandmother. "Tell me what to do."

"I only saw your grandfather do this once." Ro set the remaining shard of stone on the console and ground it into powder with the pommel of the hooked knife from the med kit.

"What happens next?"

"You need to wake it."

"Wake it?"

"It's a bonding element, remember? This is raw and unrefined. It needs *you*."

Nimah frowned. "How do I do that?"

"Feel it. Like a heartbeat inside you. Let it take you somewhere . . . somewhere deep. After that I'm not sure." Scraping the dust into her cupped hands, she held it under Nimah's nose. "Close your eyes," she whispered. "And breathe . . ."

Swirling vapor, almost like steam, rose over the iridescent powder. Was it a trick of her eyes, or did the light within it pulse, timed to her heartbeat? She felt it shimmering across her skin like a caress, and with it, the distant echo of voices that had also carried hallucinations. The strange, bone-deep pull that vibrated right into her soul and seized control over her senses on the lunar outpost the night she'd fought Senior Agent Gallani.

Nimah recoiled. "What if I can't control it?"

"You will. Don't be afraid of who you are. Who you were *born* to be." Her grandmother smiled gently. "Trust it. Trust *yourself*. Be brave, Sparrow."

Don't be afraid . . .

Nimah closed her eyes. Breathed deep. Warmth and cold flashed in waves and she gasped as the force of it filled her. So much, so vibrant, it shot through her arms into her fingers, down her legs into her toes, and exploded in her chest like the birth of a new star.

"There," Ro whispered, her voice thick at the edges. "Take it in. Embrace it. Follow it."

Head tipped back, Nimah released all hesitation. It was like diving into an Eye and threading across the known galaxy, she shot so fast, so

282 FALLON DEMORNAY

dizzyingly fast through a chasm of blue and white. Blinding! Pulling her deep into memories and despair, into the blood-soaked darkness she'd struggled to escape from.

Don't be afraid . . .

Blackness took shape. Became solid and steel. Light and blood. Miranda's voice pushed around her, a stray wind, but louder and crisp. Back within the halls of the *Avenger*, Nimah stood before Miranda, blood seeping from her side. Skin wane and eyes glassy.

"Don't be afraid."

Nimah reached out a hand, and found her touch was cool and solid. Real.

Miranda's fingers tightened with a reassuring squeeze. "She's waiting for you."

The distant weeping answered Nimah's unspoken question, and it reverberated in her own chest as if pouring from her body. She was tethered to the pain and harrowing fear. It filled her like water in an urn, pressing into every crevice and nook, but this time, she wasn't scared of it. "Take me to her."

Hand in hand, they walked the darkened corridors of the *Avenger*, weaving around bodies and blood-smeared walls that shone black in the flashes of light. Miranda stood a few inches shorter than Nimah, her straight black hair tied back in a blunt ponytail, strands escaping around her oval face that waved like stalks of hay in a soft breeze.

"I'm so sorry you had to see all this."

"It's not your fault."

"Yes, it is." Before Nimah could question her answer, Miranda stopped outside a doorway and winced as instead of letting go of Nimah, she released her injured side to press a bloody palm to the entry panel. "Dr. Miranda Zhang." The locks disengaged and the door split into diagonal sections that retracted into the walls. Miranda swayed, blanched, and Nimah held her steady as she sank to her knees. "I'm dying . . ."

"Don't," Nimah whispered. "Please don't go. I can't be in there without you."

"Yes, you can. She's waiting for you. She's always been waiting for you." Miranda cupped Nimah's cheek. Brown eyes fading. "Forgive . . . me. Please."

FLIGHT OF THE SPARROW 283

And then she saw it. What Miranda had meant. A truth filtered through the eyes of a child who couldn't process or understand, but she understood now. Nimah struggled around the thickness in her throat, against the cold in her heart. The misery in her bones. But beneath it all? A simmering anger she didn't even know she'd been carrying. A quiet rage that grew louder and hotter and more hostile by the second.

Miranda was right. This was *her* fault.

"Adults are supposed to protect children." Nimah's voice hoarsened. "Not sell us to corporations like chattel."

"Yes," Miranda croaked.

And that was the brutal heart of it. She'd hero-worshipped this woman for what? For putting a bandage on a skinned knee and telling her a funny story? Miranda's job as a doctor on the *Avenger* was to keep Nimah healthy and docile until they reached their destination, all the while knowing that she was going to be shipped off to a mining colony to dig toxic ore out of an asteroid until she died of radiation poisoning.

A horrible, slow, and decaying end.

Nimah's voice trembled. "All these years, I carried your death inside of me—the guilt of it, leaving you behind to die alone, slowly strangling me. I thought you were my friend, but that's not true." This woman had made her choices and paid the price for the consequences that followed. She and the entire crew.

In her final moments Miranda may have done the right thing—but that didn't negate the years and countless lives she'd helped destroy as a tacit accomplice to the money-hungry corporations who profited off the capture and enslavement of RIMers.

"I'm not responsible for what happened to you," Nimah said, the truth releasing something inside of her. A weight. An anchor. And finally, she could *breathe.*

"Please . . ."

Nimah closed her eyes and released the emotions, the pain and the rage until it all went quiet, and when she opened them again, Miranda's tear-streaked face was clear as moonlight. "I forgive you," Nimah said. "But more importantly, I forgive myself."

Miranda's gentle smile faded into a dying breath, head falling back. Limp as her hand against Nimah's arm. Laying her down, Nimah stroked her brow, her cheek. Then rose with a steady heart.

284   **FALLON DEMORNAY**

Crossing the threshold, she stepped out of the *Avenger* and into the ejected pod. Red light strobed like a dying heartbeat, like blood pumping weakly from an artery, spilling across the huddled shape of a little girl with short dark hair and pale brown skin dressed in a white jumpsuit. Knees tucked to her chest, she wept softly, but beneath the sobbing Nimah caught the edges of a song. A song she hadn't heard or sung in such a long time she'd nearly forgotten it.

But the words returned to her now, vivid and filled with so much emotion.

> *Light on the wind, little sparrow takes wing*
> *Filled with morning song, listen to her sing—*
> *Bright as a jewel, sweet as morning dew,*
> *Little sparrow, little sparrow—*

"Fly straight," Nimah sang into the dark, "fly true."

The weeping stopped, and the child's head lifted at the sound of her voice. Her child-self blinked up at her, struggling to see clearly through tears and shadow. "It's so cold," she whispered, voice tender from hours of panicked screaming.

Nimah lowered next to her, breath misting in hazy puffs. "We'll keep each other warm."

"I'm alone. I'm always alone."

"No." Nimah gathered her close, and hugged tight. "Never. Never again. I'm here now."

Her child-self swiveled around, arms tangling around Nimah's neck. They lay together, and Nimah lost herself to the pulse of flashing red and the soothing rhythm of a trusting heart, beating in tandem with her own.

"Nimah . . ."

Nimah jerked in the quiet, and woke to find herself alone in the emptiness. Her child-self was gone—no, she pressed a hand to her heart—not gone. Here. Always here. Safe and protected and loved. No matter what happened, what came next, Nimah would never be alone.

Could never be alone.

"Nimah . . ."

A man stood over her. Skin tinged blue with vivid silver eyes and glowing white hair, he was starlight made flesh, and powerfully built. A

FLIGHT OF THE SPARROW   285

giant that descended to kneel, and at his side, a woman Nimah had only ever seen in holoimages, with golden skin and molten brown eyes.

"You've come home to us, at last."

Nimah rose to her feet, shaking. "Are you real?"

Zory nodded. "*S'ahaelou* connects us in life and in death. All of us. Everywhere."

"Everywhere?"

"Listen."

Nimah closed her eyes, held on to her mother's hand, and beneath the vibrating undercurrent of life were so many others and around them . . . something took shape. Solidified. Nimah gasped. *Valhalla.* "It's alive."

"The planet was never destroyed." Her grandfather grinned. "It was *moved.*"

Nimah squinted. "How can you move an entire planet?"

"With love," he answered. "And great sacrifice. It waits for you, but for now you must go back."

"I don't want to leave you."

"You won't. You carry us with you. Here." Zory touched her chest. "Listen to your heart, and you will find your way to us. Now go."

Zory clasped hands with her father, and in a sharp burst of light, Nimah was thrust from the darkness and into her body. When she opened her eyes, everything was vivid. Dazzling through a sheen of white light emitting from within her. She looked to her grandmother and saw the ache of familiarity. Of love.

"They're inside me . . ." Energy simmered in the palms of her hands. Pulses of light that shone in the power racing beneath her skin like webs of starfire. "I've always known. I've always known . . ."

"Yes, Sparrow." Ro wiped away her tears. "Listen to it. Follow it. Let it show you the way."

And she did. Craning her head to the whispers of something deep inside of her. Reaching out, she felt them, one after the other, hundreds of them, and Nimah closed her hand around those distant orbs. Fingers of energy weaving through fuel cells, silent as a dead heart in the cavity of a chest. She gripped each one tight, and in a single, violent breath, the Boneyard roared awake and shone, fully primed. A sentient energy that circled and looped—breathing life into the steel. Nimah flexed her fingers where the echo of it pulsed and hummed within skin and bone. A current. A tether, connecting her to the drones. Giving her sway and control.

An army of stardust and steel at her fingertips.

"Initiating flight sequence." Nimah punched buttons and flipped switches. "Engage thrusters." The console hummed and pulsed, lights strobing in concentric circles.

<Accepted—thrusters engaged. Prepare for launch.>

"You know what to do." A hand closed over her shoulder, the grip tight. Sure. "You were born for this. You were always born to fly."

Nimah gripped the yoke with hands that for once trembled from adrenaline more than fear. She understood the mechanics, the theory, well enough to plot a course as well as the best of them, but taking the yoke—that was something she'd never found the nerve to do.

Until now.

"Light on the wind, little sparrow takes wing," Nimah sang below her breath. "Filled with morning song, listen to her sing—" The shuttle rattled, thrusters fired awake, pitching her heart into a faster beat. Part panic. Part joy. "Bright as a jewel, sweet as morning dew—" The countdown sequence initiated, panic bled away, and calmness enveloped her. Steady. Warm.

I'm not afraid.

"Little sparrow, little sparrow." Smiling, Nimah released the throttle. "Fly straight. Fly true."

CHAPTER TWENTY-SEVEN

Maverick was getting more than tired of cages. Collared three times in the span of four days? Bleeding void, he was slipping.

"Look who decided to finally join us. Come," Boomer tapped the open stretch of bench at his side, "pull up a chair."

"Shut up, Booms."

"See Gertrude ain't wit'cha." Chu crossed stick-thin arms over her flat chest. "She and Dobs can roast in the fiery pits, far as I'm concerned. Yellow-bellied gobshites." But her tone lacked the depth of venom for spite.

It was hurt. Pure hurt.

"We have been betrayed by brethren most dear." Sigourney paced, restless with rage. Even stripped of her weapons, shield, and warpaint, she was still terrifyingly fierce. "I shall break open the bones of her back with mine own hands, fold bloody lungs over her shoulders like red wings, and watch the light of breath fade in her eyes."

"And who be this one?" Chu scowled at Liselle. "You look familiar, and I ain't never forgotten a face that crossed me 'fore." She boosted to her feet and Liselle dropped her chin, hands tucked behind her back. "You one of them who blew up my house?"

Liselle held her ground, but hesitation fluttered in the pulse at her throat. "Yes, ma'am. I was there."

Chu, spewing furious Spantonese, drew back a fist but Sigourney caught her by the elbow before she managed to let it fly. "Stay yourself. She is but a child."

"A child who blew up my fucking house!" Gathering herself, Chu paced on rickety knees. "So if you be one of them, why you tossed in here with us?"

"Because she was trying to make it right," Maverick answered. "By trying to find and save Nimah. But Dobs figured it out and had us both collared."

"The captain and her Sparrow are gone." Sigourney sighed. "Dobs's words were clear."

"No." Liselle shook her head. "I know they're still out there. And so long as Nimah is alive there's hope."

"Even if she isn't dead," Boomer scoffed, arms crossed and eyes closed, resigned to his fate, "anyone with sense would go deep to get out of this mess. We're on our own."

"You don't know Nimah like I do." Liselle planted a forearm to the viewport and stared into the glittering inky horizon. "She'll come for us. Even if she is scared to the bone, that girl doesn't know how to quit."

The entryway sputtered, a flash of sparks emitting from between the crevice of the doors before they split open with a groan. Mumbles stood on the threshold, an orb of limned glass hovering over her left shoulder. She wiggled stubby fingers with a gummy grin.

"Goody-hi."

"Bravo, darling, bravo." Gertrude swept into the cell and dropped a heavy bag at her feet. "Come, children, and collect your effects. Dobs is on the main bridge with the chief commander. If we're quick, we can get off this boat before they realize we've popped your collars." She clapped hands together sharply when no one moved a single inch. "Well?"

Chu crossed her arms. "I'd rather be keelhauled than slither into the gutter with a traitor."

"Darling, we don't have time for this."

"You traded your crew for credits." Chu pushed her glasses down to the tip of her wide nose. "Expect me to believe you suddenly regrew your spine?"

"Stars above you have a skull thick as your pride." Gertrude sighed, but her smile didn't diminish. "If I hadn't played turncoat, I'd be in this cell with you—then who was going to save your skinny butt from the noose, hm? Did you stop to think about that while you were cursing my name into the blue yonder?" She cocked a hip. "As for my

FLIGHT OF THE SPARROW 289

debt, I'm sure I can scrub my name clean from the blackbooks by calling in a favor or twenty." Gertrude threaded a curl between her fingers with a chuckle. "One day I'll have my ship. For now, I'd prefer my crew."

Chu harrumphed and clapped a hand to Gertrude's shoulder with a shove . . . but didn't let go. "Good," she grumbled. "Really didn't want to have to gut you on sight."

"As I happen to prefer my entrails to be inside my glorious body, I'm pleased to know they'll stay there. Now can we *please* make haste?" Gertrude swung her arm out in a sweeping circle. "I'll be sorely disappointed if my grand efforts of rescue are wasted due to stubborn pride and—" The rest of her words were lost in the blaring whoop of alarms.

"Didn't think to cut the damn security feed before you sprung us?" Chu snarled, hands cupped to her ears.

"Those alarms aren't for us," Liselle answered.

"How the heck d'you know?"

Liselle stood speechless with shock. Following her gaze, Gertrude's hand fluttered to her chest while the other gestured vaguely to the viewport. "Is that . . . is that what I think it is?"

Chu tapped a finger to the frame of her bifocals and the lenses shot out, expanding like dual telescopes. Hands to the viewport, her lips puckered in concentration. "I'll be damned." She jerked straight. "It's Nimah."

"Are you sure?" Maverick demanded.

"I'd know that lifeboat anywhere." Chu retracted her lenses. "And she ain't alone."

Everyone pressed in against the diamond glass. The lifeboat charged toward them, surrounded by a cloud of glimmering drones, hundreds of them. The *Challenger* shook from the blast of her guns and the drones sped forward, intercepting the whiz of blaserfire. Popping like dying stars.

Nimah was closing in fast. Negs swanned at her side and, *bleeding void*—a kraken!

"She's using 'em like decoys to clear the way," Boomer's normally loud voice was whisper soft. "How she even controlling 'em?"

"Lo!" Sigourney bared her fangs in a laughing roar. "Sparrow has taken flight—and see how she soars!"

"Soars is a bit generous," Gertrude snickered. "Our little bird flies like a drunken insect."

But she was flying, and what she lacked in finesse, she made up for with determination. With fearlessness. Nimah swung hard left and the lifeboat barrel-rolled in an insane blur, diving away from the lightning storm of blaserfire that corkscrewed after her. Finesse? No, but it sure as fuck was impressive.

Maverick picked up his jaw. "She's making for the dock."

Liselle bounced on her feet. "We have to help her!"

"And we will." Gertrude snatched up her discarded bag and pulled open the cord. "Suit up, children." She tossed a blaser to Chu, the repeater to Boomer.

"To the void or Valhalla," Sigourney purred, retrieving her axes. Her shield.

Liselle helped herself to an electroblade. "Come on."

Nimah had flown various simulations—a hundred and four to be exact—but for an inexperienced pilot having never touched a real yoke, breaking the barrier of the *Challenger*'s shield-line was like belly flopping from the highest point of the Academy towers. The shuttle pitched and screamed just loud enough for her to cast a prayer to the forgotten gods of Earth-Prior as something jostled loose and flew past her line of sight.

"What was that?"

"Might've been a buffing panel or two, but nothing major."

Not unless they wanted to break atmo, but Nimah saved that for herself. Soon as they boarded the *Challenger*, they'd reclaim the *Stormchaser*, but not before getting the data Jono Shinoda had downloaded back on the RIM to Chief Commander Wallace.

What if it didn't convince her? What if it wasn't enough? Nimah pushed the voice of doubt aside.

Ro clutched at her harness and cursed as Nimah wove around whizzing drones, swimming negs, and the shimmering tendrils of a hundred-foot kraken. "They're getting rowdy."

"The elite is fading from my system. I'm losing control." What was left of it sizzled at the edges of her vision, and through it she could feel their minds struggling to pull away, eager to tear into the drones and

FLIGHT OF THE SPARROW 291

feed on the remnants of energy lingering in their fuel cells like addicts feral for crumbs.

"Then let 'em go, Sparrow. We're in their shield-line and flying too close for *Challenger* cannons to shoot us down. All we got to do now is dock."

"Easier said than done." The *Challenger* was on high alert, and all three flight decks were bound to be swarming with agents. All she could hope was to pick one that held the fewest and punch through there.

"Nimah? Nimah, do you copy?"

Nimah snapped her eyes to her grandmother in disbelief. *It can't be.* "Maverick?"

"Head for the third quay. You see it?"

"Yes! Yes, I see it."

"Dock there. We'll clear your path."

"We?"

"Yo-ho, yo-ho," Gertrude sang. *"All Valkyries and two skinners accounted for, darling. Now shake those feathers and move!"*

Nimah's answering laugh shimmered with tears. "Copy!" Driving the yoke, she pushed for the third quay and after two attempts managed to connect to the dock.

"Well done, Sparrow." Her grandmother clapped a hand to Nimah's shoulder. "Well done."

Nimah uncoupled her harness. "How's the leg?"

"Still holding. Figure I got maybe another forty minutes before the pain relievers wear off. Plenty of time."

"Right. Then we'd better move." Releasing the airlock, Nimah hurried off the lifeboat, her grandmother limping at her side, and reached the hatch just as Maverick turned in his chair. Their eyes connected—a second stretched between them, an endless breath—before a smile broke across his face, dazzling as the sun. And her heart . . . stars above, her heart nearly exploded with joy at the sight of it. She pressed a hand to the glass. "Maverick."

He set his own to join it.

Boomer hit the hatch at his side, clip in his teeth and sweat on his brow. He winked at Nimah. "May wanna step back, if you catch my drift." Rooting around in a pocket near the front of his vest, he pulled out a slender tube, not much larger than a shotgun shell. Slapping it to the wall, he gave Nimah a nod for clearance before priming the charge.

The blast was small but vicious, and the pintsized grenade punched through six inches of carbide steel with ease. Reaching inside, Boomer ripped out a wad of sputtering wires, and the hatch hissed open, doors retracting into the sidewall.

"Cad—"

That was as far as he got before Nimah's mouth was on his in a firm, fast kiss. Maverick jolted against her, and Nimah smiled down at the stuck speechless expression on his face. "Hi."

His finger traced a gentle path from her cheek to chin. "Hey."

"Nims!" Nimah rose and turned just in time to catch Liselle in a flying hug-tackle that nearly took her off her feet. "I knew you'd make it! I knew it!"

Nimah swallowed joyful tears. "I'm sorry. I'm sorry for everything."

"You're alive." Liselle hugged her tighter. "That's all I care about."

"Look lively." Gertrude rushed over to them, repeater hugged to her chest. "We have company." She fired into the distance as agents swarmed through the rounded entryway of the flight deck.

By Nimah's brisk count, she estimated twenty before the deck erupted in chaos and the crew whisked behind the broad stern of the *Stormchaser*, her wings tethered with grounding chains meant to keep anyone from boosting her and flying away. The chains weren't impossible to remove, but they would require serious gear and time to cut through.

"Captain," Gertrude tipped her chin. "I believe this is yours." And drawing a sheathed blade from her rucksack, she tossed it to Ro, who caught it with her good hand. "Do try not to lose it this time."

"How did you get it back?" Nimah laughed and accepted a twin pair of blasers.

"With great difficulty." Gertrude smirked. "But I'm not without my ways."

"There's too many of them." Chu reclined against the hull. "We need to free our wings and blow off this boat. Go deepvoid."

"No. We can't leave." They'd come too far to turn back now. "Not without me getting to Wallace. I have to warn her about the Detach Protocol."

FLIGHT OF THE SPARROW 293

"Sparrow's right," her grandmother agreed.

"What's the plan, then?" Gertrude peered around the edge of the *Stormchaser*.

"Our enemy gains ground," Sigourney warned. "We have a minute, perhaps two."

"Let them. We have to draw Wallace to us." Nimah scraped a hand over her neck. "The more noise we make down here, the greater the chances she'll intervene if she's not headed for us already. Then it's up to me to get her to listen."

"That don't sound like much of a plan," Chu spat. "Not one to keep us breathin'."

Gertrude pumped her repeater. "Thirty seconds."

"Cap, you seriously s'pect us to hold out against fifty-some odd agents out there?"

"Ladies," Ro cast them a ferocious grin, "there is not a STAR in this galaxy who has not been weaned on our stories. Our legends. And by the glory of our fallen ancestors, may we live to extend that legacy, but if we must die—let it be like this." Captain Roscoe sparked her cutlass, and raised its blazing blue edge to burn between her eyes before planting the point to the grated flooring.

The women angled their weapons to meet in a circle, and Nimah could feel it rising between them, gathering like a storm—their strength, their determination, their bond. These were the fierce Valkyries of lore. The pirates who had shaken the void and rattled the stars; women who had forged a legacy that would reign long after their last breath.

The family that Nimah cherished, and was proud to call her own.

"Sparrow." Ro tossed the cutlass and Nimah caught it by the hilt. "This belongs to you now."

Gripping it, she held the glowing length of charged steel as her grandmother raised the proud line of her chin. And, taking Liselle's hand, joined the circle of women. "To the void," she intoned.

"Or Valhalla," they answered.

Grinning, Sigourney spun her axes and bellowed into the fray—a berserker gone wild. Gertrude and Chu roared at her side. With a toss of her shield, Sigourney knocked three agents clean off their feet. It returned to her arm with a raise of her fist, and without missing a breath, she charged into another volley. Blaserfire rained, quickly answered by Maverick and Ro, still positioned behind the *Stormchaser* for cover.

Three charged for Nimah, and in a single breath, she pivoted to the right and slashed her first opponent in the face, shattering the left side of his headguard, then dropped to her knees and swept low for her second opponent, sending his blaser to fly from his hand before sweeping his legs out from under him with her foot. A solid heel to the face kept him down.

Movement, instinct—Nimah surrendered to both, her strokes searing through armor and slicing flesh but with just enough restraint to disarm, not kill. These weren't her enemy, they were obstacles to be climbed or avoided—struck down only if there was no other recourse.

The ring of steel and screams echoed around her like a deadly song, and Nimah was growing all too familiar with the melody. A cluster closed in, forming the circle meant to cage her as they charged her in a sequence she knew how to dance in her sleep.

Nimah worked the points of that circle, meeting them with unexpected counters that threw them off balance. Feigning attacks and saving her most brutal responses for the strongest of the group, while wielding the momentum of the less skilled, pushing them off balance so they collided with other agents, injuring each other. She just had to wear them down. But her breath was sharpening, her arms growing heavy, and determination was only going to fuel her for so long . . .

"Sonic!" An agent shouted, seeing the arc of Boomer's arm as he lobbed a puck-sized grenade. Five dropped from the blast, but most reacted with enough time to brace behind disrupter shields, rebounding the stun waves to ricochet off carbide steel. Anything set to a higher frequency would compromise the hull metal, killing them all. The walls of the hangar rang like an ominous bell, and tethered jets rattled against restraints.

"Cease fire!" Wallace roared. "All agents, stand down immediately."

Without hesitation, the chaos drew to an immediate halt and agents eased back from their quarry, weapons lowered but still primed as she strode forward. Nimah held her guard but relief surged in her chest, refreshing as the first sip of water after a hard session of training.

Wallace reached the heart of the hangar, her mouth grim, hair less than pristine from the frustrated glide of gloved fingers. Dobs swaggered

FLIGHT OF THE SPARROW 295

in behind her, flanked by yet more agents, but her features registered none of the chief commander's alarm. Or shock.

"You're alive." Wallace snapped HWKeyes from Nimah to beyond her where her grandmother braced against the hull of the *Stormchaser.* "Both of you."

"Yes." Satisfied the fight was behind her, Nimah powered down her cutlass. "Dobs marooned us in the Boneyard to cover her ass."

"Shut up, kid."

"That's an egregious charge." Wallace angled her head. "Why would she do that?"

"Because she's running a skingame with Cormack." Dobs's face, schooled after decades of deceit, gave nothing away. "And for a skinner, there's no such thing as enough."

"Dorothy Dobrevnic." Wallace raised her chin, golden HWKeyes swirling—activated to their fullest capacity for scanning vitals. "How do you respond to these charges?"

Dobs skimmed her teeth across her bottom lip, sucked hard. "Utter bullshit."

Tension coiled around them, tenuous beats that pulsed in the silence as Chief Commander Wallace weighed the integrity of Dobs's words. Dissected them. "I sense no deceit."

"That doesn't mean she's not lying, and I can prove it to you." Nimah withdrew a disk from her deck, and raised the SIGA-encrypted holocard Jono had downloaded the data onto. "Everything is recorded on this. Five seconds, Chief Commander. That's all I'm asking for. Please."

Wallace assessed the coin-sized disk in Nimah's hand a moment before she accepted it, then docked the disk in a reader embedded into her palm. Her head twitched the barest fraction—a jumpstart from the download sequence. Although Nimah often turned up her nose at the process of retrofitting, there were times when she thanked the void for its development, as what would've taken her hours to process and absorb, Wallace's brain did in a series of quick blinks.

If at all possible, Wallace's already porcelain skin went whiter still.

"Chief—"

She silenced Nimah with the lift of a gloved finger. "Seize her."

A moment of confusion, as agents hesitated between which *her* to seize, was all it took. Fast. So fast. Nimah saw little more than a blur as Dobs took aim, eyes burning with fury. Regret. And fired.

The crack of a bullet, a horrible, deafening ring in her ears—Nimah's vision blackened in the clench of her eyes. But no pain. *Shock?* And opened them as Sigourney, braced in the line of gunfire, slumped to her knees.

"No!" Nimah dropped with her, catching Sigourney before she collapsed, and lowered her onto her back, screaming for a med kit. Blood. So much blood. Another thing Nimah had trained for, endless hours in simulation, but the shocking reality shook her numb.

"Press down, hard as you can," Ro ordered, already at her side, and gathered Sigourney's head into her lap. "Stay with me, Siggy. Hold on."

Spurred into action, Nimah did as she was told and perched on her knees for leverage, but the wound gaped wide and angry with blood that spurted between her fingers and streamed around the edges of her palm. A crimson flood she couldn't staunch. "There's too much. I can't stop it!" She couldn't even slow it down. "Where's the med kit?"

Wallace lowered to a graceful knee, HWKeyes whirling in assessment until finally they lifted to Nimah and the apology in them said what she already knew. What she feared.

Given Sigourney's horrific wet rasp, the bullet had obliterated her left lung. She was drowning in her own blood and a med kit would only buy her minutes. Without immediate surgical intervention, there was nothing they could do.

Nothing except watch.

"Look at me." Ro cupped Sigourney's face. "To me, Siggy." Silver eyes wheeled, drawn by her commanding voice, and focused on Ro with a warrior's gleam. "You have been my sister in combat and blood. The battles we fought together. The tales we forged. None shall ever again know the likes of Sigourney, Queen of Bones, the fiercest pirate there ever was or will be. Sailing the void by your side has been my life's greatest honor."

Sigourney's lips parted, a crimson smile. "Va . . . hal . . ."

Ro nodded, an ocean of tears in her eyes waiting to be shed as Sigourney seized, a sudden and violent shudder wracked her a body with fitful spasms. Her grin fell away, the light in her eyes brightening with alarm, and with a final sodden gasp, Sigourney was gone.

FLIGHT OF THE SPARROW 297

Sorrow gave birth to rage. It blistered through Nimah, so sharp and bright that even the walls around her seemed to vibrate. Perhaps it was a mark of naivete to think that in the presence of the chief commander no one would've been able to get the drop on her. Or that no one would've dared try. But she'd forgotten an important lesson: nothing was more deadly than a pirate with nothing to lose. There had only been a second of confusion, but a second was all Dobs needed. And Sigourney died for it.

Nimah rose on shaky legs. "Where is she?"

"Gone." Gertrude lowered cupped hands from her mouth. "In the confusion. We . . . I couldn't."

Ro caught Nimah by the wrist, damp with Sigourney's blood. "Don't. I won't risk losing you, too."

"She can't get away with this." *Not this.*

Ro's grip tightened but at the glare in Nimah's eyes, she slackened her hold. Sighed. "Be careful."

"Citizen, I forbid you." Wallace dusted her knees. "You will remain on this deck while I—stop!"

Nimah charged for the corridor and once through the doors she fried the panel beside the bulkhead door with two blasts from her blaser. The door snapped shut with a mechanical groan, sealing everyone inside the deck. It wouldn't hold for long, but it would slow Wallace down long enough for Nimah to make headway. Pressing the comm behind her ear, Nimah raced for the lift and the grated floor rang beneath the heavy beat of her boots.

"Gertrude, give me a trace on Dobs. Concentrate on lower decks. Look for heat signatures. She'll be moving fast."

"On it." Gertrude answered, her voice hushed, but in the background Nimah could hear Wallace's vehement orders before the comms hummed with heavy silence. *"Scanners show she's a level down near the secondary flight deck, but looks like she's swung for the reactor."*

"Copy." Nimah pushed harder into her legs, gaining speed. There was only one reason for Dobs to go there.

She was going to blow the ship.

CHAPTER TWENTY-EIGHT

The doors to the main turbolift hung ajar and the control panel sputtered with fragmented wires. Peering down the shaft, Nimah found the lift shattered at the bottom—a bubble of glass on fire. She tapped the comms button behind her ear. "Gertrude."

"This is she."

"I need another route to the reactor. The lift is destroyed."

Gertrude's answering weary sigh confirmed Nimah's worst fear. *"That's the only lift you can reach without diverting up four decks and swinging hard to port."*

Which would take far too long. Dobs would have blown the *Challenger* and been well on her way in a lifeboat before Nimah could cover half that ground.

"Great. Thanks." Eyes closed, she pressed a hand to her chest. "Come on." She reached for the distant foggy remnants of elite in her system—but it sputtered through her fingers with a final whisper. She was tapped. Everything had been used up in activating the drones and luring the negs into battle. She had nothing left.

No. She had plenty left—her wits and her training.

A length of cable swung like a dying pendulum and beyond it, the open mouth of an air duct. Nimah gripped the cable firmly and swung across into the mouth of the shaft, just large enough for her to crouch inside. Peering down, she could see the hard spin of a turbine fan directing airflow like a heart pumping blood through an artery.

FLIGHT OF THE SPARROW 299

The reactor chamber was three levels down and the shaft ran much farther than that with branches connecting to each level. She estimated a thirty-foot drop to the reactor chamber. If she couldn't control her descent, or missed her mark by an inch, she'd drop into the churning gears of the engine fan below and be ground into mush within seconds.

Bracing against either side of the air duct, arms and legs wide, and feet anchoring her in position, Nimah zeroed in on that ledge—and dropped. Sliding down the cable like the brass pole on the *Stormchaser*. Teeth clenched in a growling scream, rubber burned against steel and friction seared through the leather—a dizzying fall. At the final moment she reached out, clawing with both hands for the ledge. Dangling by her fingertips, Nimah grunted as sweat poured in rivulets down her brow and neck. Arms straining, she planted the soles of her boots to the riveted wall and battled for every inch, hauling herself up and over the ledge. At the top, Nimah rolled onto the flat of her back and laughed through a shaky breath.

"Move, Nimah. Get up." Legs soft as jelly, she swiveled around feet first and slammed her heels into the narrow slates. It took three solid kicks before it buckled loose and she poured herself out, landing on her hands and feet with a solid *thunk*.

Sweat in her eyes, she scanned for movement. The reactor chamber was oblong with a bilateral catwalk running across its length over the vent shaft, a smooth shell scorched from the heavy blast of reactor flames.

Above it was the heart, a massive fuel cell comprised of nearly fourteen tons of highly radioactive prime encased behind diamond glass a meter thick. Unlike elite, prime shone with a dull luster of washed-out sunlight fighting to break through a storm, encased with anchors and fusion wires that funneled up into the control room, independently managed by the operating systems. The pressure monitor splayed on a large screen gave a readout of ninety-four percent.

Nimah estimated roughly fifteen minutes, perhaps less, before the next venting, when the dual hatches would open, releasing all the highly radioactive primefire out into the void. And unless she wanted to be scorched to death by flames and radiation, she would have to clear the chamber before that.

The punch of gunfire off to one side sent Nimah diving into a roll behind the u-bend of a coolant pipe. Drawing her blaser, she swept for a target. Visible through the waves of steam breaking through the pipes from evaporating coolant, Dobs holstered her gun after blowing open the locked engineering cabinet loaded with an array of tools and replacement parts for the reactor. In an emergency, seconds were critical, and engineers couldn't afford to waste time hauling in heavy equipment.

She's going to disable the vent hatch, Nimah realized. And when the system next tried to purge, all that pressurized energy would rip through the *Challenger*'s belly like a knife gutting a fish. They'd be sunk within minutes.

"Stop!" Nimah boosted from behind the coolant pipe and vaulted onto the catwalk. "It's over."

Dobs nodded thoughtfully. Turned. "Is it?" With blurring speed, she drew her gun, hammer cocked.

But Nimah didn't flinch. "You're out of bullets."

"Am I?"

"You'd have put three in me already, otherwise."

Dobs's smoky laugh reverberated across the catwalk. "Bet your ass." Smirking, she returned the gun to its holster and widened her stance. "Siggy dead?"

"Yes." Nimah waited—for the spark of emotion. For remorse to break through her stoic shell. But Dobs kept her chin high and eyes clear; a stone-cold mask Nimah longed to shatter beneath angry fists. "You're not even sorry, are you?"

"She always wanted a warrior's death." Dobs shrugged. "Gave her what she prayed for, I reckon."

Nimah's jaw stiffened with fresh grief. This was not the woman she'd grown to respect and love. How could she be so cold? So unaffected? "I should kill you where you stand." Her hand trembled with restrained emotion. It would be so easy to pull the trigger and blow a searing hole between her eyes. Vaporizing the contents of her skull.

But Nimah didn't want *easy.*

Lowering her aim, she fired two simultaneous blasts into the vent shaft, and sparks rained against the fireproof hull metal. A hot flash that

FLIGHT OF THE SPARROW

quickly fizzled out. "One more left in the clip." She tossed the blaser and it clattered in the center of the catwalk, a foot in Dobs's favor.

Eyeing it like a starved wolf, Dobs licked her teeth. "That was stupid."

"Maybe," Nimah agreed. "Now you have a choice. Go for the weapon, and hope you reach it before I kill you. Or you can do the right thing and surrender." She drew the cutlass with one hand and tapped the magnicuffs looped on her belt with the other. "What's it going to be?"

Tongue in her cheek, Dobs made a show of weighing the air with her hands before she yanked a wrench free from its cradle in the cabinet. Nearly half the length of her body, it was made from the same SIGA-grade carbide steel as the rest of the *Challenger*'s hull.

She hooked it over her shoulders like a baseball bat.

Nimah sparked the cutlass. "So be it."

Steam rose in billowing clouds through the grated flooring on the catwalk between them, alternating blasts that punctuated the silence like the warning hiss of a cobra about to strike.

Dobs charged like a demon blazing through the mists, and Nimah surged to meet her. They clashed in the center of the catwalk and blade met bar with the jarring clang of steel against steel. The force of it shocked through Nimah like an EMP. Dobs was taller. Stronger. And the wrench, though without a lethal edge, was still capable of crushing bone.

One blow, just one, and Nimah's arm would shatter. Or her skull.

Teeth clenched, she battled against Dobs's punishing weight as she hammered down with devastating force, too fast for her to dodge. Every muscle in her arms ached, her back seared, and sweat formed on her skin, slick as grease. Sparks rained, and with another vicious strike, the lasered edge of Nimah's cutlass sputtered. Died.

"Ha!" Dobs's eyes shone with glorious triumph. "Give it up, kid."

"I'll die first."

"Heard."

Nimah roared into a lunge, driving her back enough to catch her breath, but she couldn't hide the shaking in her arms, muscles spasming with fatigue. Exhaustion—the weight of the last three days was catching up with her, and Nimah was nearly as depleted as the cells of her cutlass.

She ducked the swing of the wrench but moved right into the path of Dobs's fist. A straight jab followed by an uppercut slammed her teeth together and nearly took her off her feet. Dazed, she dropped her cutlass, and Dobs grabbed Nimah by the collar of her jacket, tossing her in the other direction. Putting distance between her and her weapon.

"Scared little Sparrow not yet grown into her wings—" Dobs cackled. "Afraid of everything. Even her own shadow."

Nimah deflected the first blow but the second caught her deep in the solar plexus. She wheezed, buckling to her knees. *Hold your guard. Arms up.* Reeling, she cradled her head against more fists.

"Stupid." Dobs cuffed her again, so hard her ears rang. "Fucking stupid," she bellowed.

Nimah shook her head clear. "You won't get away with this."

"Already have, kid." Rearing back, Dobs kicked Nimah straight in the chest, knocking her flat.

Winded, Nimah blinked above at the heart of the ship's engine beating madly overhead—a massive prism of prime core that pumped energy into the vessel. Her vision grew dull around the edges, her lungs whined for air, and she fought the wave of unconsciousness that hungered to pull her into shadows as Dobs settled on top of her. Fingers curled in the collar of her shirt, the older woman lifted her an inch off the ground and drove knuckles into her teeth. Blood swam in Nimah's mouth and pain arched like a bullet behind her eyes.

"You shoulda just stayed out of my way."

"Never." Turning her chin, she spat her mouth clear and a loose tooth fell between the grating and clattered below.

"Well, now you can give Siggy my regards." Dobs pressed the blaser between Nimah's eyes. Pulled the trigger. *Click.* Nothing.

"Tell her yourself." Twisting her arm free, Nimah snatched Dobs by the neck with both hands, yanked her down and cracked the dome of her skull right into Dobs's nose. Cartilage crunched against the slope of her brow, followed by the hot burst of blood. Dobs reared back with a violent curse, lifting just enough for Nimah to buck her off and flip back onto her knees.

"Fucking shit." Dobs pinched her nose and with a brutal twist, cracked it back into alignment, then glared at Nimah. Tears and blood streaming down her face. "I'm gonna gut you like a—" She gathered onto her haunches and lunged, but her momentum snapped to an abrupt halt and she slammed hard onto her hands. Confused, Dobs tugged at her ankle only to find it tethered by a magnicuff to the rail of the catwalk. She turned searing eyes back to Nimah. "When did you—how?"

Cradling her tender ribs, Nimah retrieved her cutlass and sparked the lasered edge.

Shock washed across Dobs's face. "You bluffed me?"

It had been a risky strategy, allowing Dobs a false sense of security as a means of distraction until Nimah found the right moment to gain the upper hand against a stronger opponent. But it had worked so well with Maverick.

"Never set a foot in the unknown," Nimah twisted the cutlass, "without keeping another rooted in the familiar."

Dobs eyed the glowing length of steel with an apprehensive swallow quickly chased by a dry laugh. "You won't kill me, kid." Her grin turned cold. "You ain't got the ice in you."

"No," Nimah agreed. "I won't kill you. But I won't save you, either." Clearing the walkway, Nimah vaulted back onto the platform, seconds before the energy shields rose, sealing Dobs in the vent shaft. The countdown meter flashed to ninety-nine percent.

Dobs spat out a wad of bloody phlegm, and swept a hand over her pockets, freeing a pack of smokes. "Well played, kid." She sparked the end with a lighter, hands steady, and sucked hard. "Guess you learned a thing or two from me, after all."

"I'm nothing like you." Nimah ground between teeth clenched as tight as her fist.

Dobs exhaled a thick stream of smoke, smiled. "And that's why you didn't see me coming."

<Twenty seconds to vent evacuation.>

"I'm not sorry." Nimah bounced her fist against the energy shield. "I'm not." But tears and grief welled inside of her all the same.

"Good." Dobs faced the reactor as the hatch creaked open. Nodded with acceptance. "To the void," she whispered. And though she had time left, she did not finish the refrain. *There's no heaven waiting for me*, the lift of her chin seemed to say. *I welcome hell.*

<Five.>

The beating heart of the *Challenger* shimmered with violent waves of blinding white that snaked around the chamber, weaving in fast, lapping circles.

<Four.>

Dobs cried out, folding in on herself as those waves seared across her skin.

<Three.>

Clothing wilted in the heat. Bubbles formed on flesh, angry red welts that oozed and bled. And burst.

<Two.>

Those cries sharpened, a deafening ring of profound agony, and Nimah pressed a helpless hand to the steaming glass. "Dobs . . ."

<One.>

The vent hatch released, and a turbulent force wrenched what was left of Dobs from the chamber—spitting a violent tornado of radiation and flames into the void like a streak of comet fire. The hatch closed, and the alarms stopped in a sudden blast of silence that descended upon Nimah like a thousand-foot tsunami.

<Venting complete. Stand by for shaft decontamination.>

Nimah released a tearful breath as dots of blaserpoints splashed across the chamber from behind her. Dozens of them. Little pale blue pinpricks that flashed like wakening stars across the energy shield.

"Citizen Dabo-124," a gruff male voice barked. "Raise your hands and get on your knees. Slowly."

Hands tucked behind her head, ribs screaming across her left side, Nimah lowered complacently to her knees as footsteps approached. She knew the stride long before Chief Commander Wallace stopped before Nimah and snapped her heels together.

"Where's Dobrevnic?"

Nimah inclined her head toward the vent shaft. "You just missed her, I'm afraid."

"Well . . ." Wallace sighed heavily. "That's one less pirate to wrangle, I suppose."

"Dobs may be dead, but this isn't over. You know it isn't. I've shown you the truth, and now you have an obligation to do the right thing

FLIGHT OF THE SPARROW

even though it compromises your orders. Or you can be a puppet and cuff me." Dropping her hands from behind her head, Nimah offered her wrists to the chief commander in supplication. "What do you want to do?"

"The only thing I can do, it seems." Wallace removed magnicuffs from her belt. "I'm taking you in."

CHAPTER TWENTY-NINE

Cormack Shinoda's estate swam in the viewport of the cruiser and hovered high in the clouds over Elysium—one of the most prestigious planets in all the Inner Circle. It was large as a spacity and shaped like a bubble of glass with a smooth terraformed base that split across the middle behind revolving bands that spun in a concentric dance like an armillary sphere.

True to her word, Wallace had come straight to his personal estate to deliver Captain Indira Roscoe and Citizen Nimah Dabo-124, along with his son. Unfortunately, she had the profound misfortune of arriving at the commencement of his corporate soiree, which resulted in hovering on the boarders of his estate's airspace for forty minutes, awaiting approval to enter.

Chief Commander Kimora Wallace hated waiting. Within the wings of the Academy, time bent at the sheer force of her will, but here her authority and merits didn't carry the same weight. And the reality of that fact rankled as the timer ticked down another minute to forty-one.

Nimah bounced a listless foot against the leg of her chair.

"Stop fidgeting," Wallace snapped, and that restless foot ceased immediately. Captain Indira Roscoe sat dutifully next to her granddaughter, shoulders drawn military straight and eyes hard as granite. She hadn't said a word since they'd broken atmo on Elysium.

Side by side, she saw the clear resemblance between them now. Almost as close as mother and daughter, one might even say. Staggering to think she hadn't noticed it beforehand.

FLIGHT OF THE SPARROW   307

Jonothan, seated opposite Nimah, had fallen asleep sometime during the long wait, and would've tumbled out headfirst were it not for the harness holding him in.

The comms hummed before a woman's voice slid out. *"Good evening, Chief Commander, we apologize for the delay. We have a lot of guests docking this evening and were required to clear the queue. Mr. Shinoda has given you clearance to dock at his private flight deck. Please adjust your heading to the coordinates provided, and a member of his security will escort you from there."*

The cruiser veered left, away from the patrons milling below. Hundreds—no, thousands of them. Media and the wealthiest members of government dressed in their finest. Music and extravagant food. Fireworks crackled across the atmosphere, taking the shapes of fabled creatures. In a few short moments, they came to an easy stop as docking cables engaged, anchoring them.

"Welcome, Chief Commander," a synth-guard intoned as Wallace exited the vehicle. "And Jonothan Shinoda, we are pleased to receive you." The synth blinked at Nimah and her grandmother. "I'm sorry . . . my systems do not know who you are."

"They are criminals in my custody," Wallace answered. "And here at Mr. Shinoda's request."

The guard settled into a deep bow. "Please follow me," it intoned, then turned in a smooth whirl, leading them through the massive oak doors into a marble foyer where a tiny young woman waited in a dress suit made of real cotton, flat black shoes, and red-framed specs.

"Chief Commander, apologies for the inexcusably long wait. I am Vivienne Tanaka, Mr. Shinoda's primary assistant," she said with a respectful bow.

"Where's my father?" Jonothan pushed lank hair from his eyes.

"Waiting in his study to receive you." Vivienne swept out a steady hand. "Please, follow me. And do not touch anything," she added. "He does not like fingerprints."

Wallace crooked a gloved finger and Nimah quickly followed. Captain Indira did as well, but with far less urgency.

The long corridor of white glass backlit in soft gold stained the white marble and made flecks of crystal shimmer like stardust. At the end of the winding corridor, they were met with the clear glass tube of a lift rising to the floating sphere of Cormack Shinoda's office. The lift rose, smooth and whisper soft, docking outside the circled archway of red-lacquered doors studded with wide brass disks.

Vivienne bowed before the doorway and a flash of lasers scanned her retinas. The doors parted at the center, pushing inward to reveal a spherical glass office. Shinoda stood behind his desk, gazing out at his vast estate, hands tucked into his pockets. He turned as they entered, Vivienne lingering on the threshold.

"Mr. Shinoda, I have—"

"Introductions are not necessary." Shinoda's lips set into a smug line framed by a trim black goatee. The dome of his head, shaved clean, bore the intricate design of a bold blue tattoo that enhanced the pale silver of his retrofit eyes. "Three days without a second to spare, as promised. I'm pleased to see your reputation isn't built on air, Chief Commander Wallace, as has been my experience in most cases."

"I always meet my objectives. I would not be in my position otherwise." Wallace brushed a hand across her lapel, clearing away nonexistent dirt. Standing in his presence made her feel foul. Tainted. "I have kept to the terms of our agreement. I trust you will hold to yours."

"Indeed, Chief Commander. Or, rather, *Admiral* Wallace." Whisking out the tails of his tailored jacket, he tucked his hands back into the pockets of his charcoal slacks made from real silk. As were his blood-red tie and crisp white dress shirt. He favored the ancient styles of Earth-Prior. Exemplified in his taste for expensive antiquities, including jade figurines, Dynasty vases, and abstract artwork she'd studied as a child. Priceless objects that should've been kept safe behind diamond glass in the Illyrio Museum instead of so casually flaunted.

She imagined there wasn't a skinner the void over who wouldn't kill to get into this office—fortified with more security than SIGA headquarters—to fleece him of his precious collection. And likely the only thing that kept his collection safe from their hands was that there wasn't anyone else wealthy enough to afford them. The black-book market for reliquaries was too niche. Too narrow.

Crossing the office, he handed Wallace a badge case. "Your new credentials."

FLIGHT OF THE SPARROW 309

Opening the case, Wallace's heart gave a tremulous squeeze. "Sir." The download was nearly instantaneous. A series of sharp blinks and every department door within SIGA that had been barred shut suddenly snapped open.

"Admiral Kimora Wallace," her comms sighed. *"Approved for active duty."*

"There." Shinoda clapped his hands together and turned to Jonothan. "Now. Let me take a look at you." He reached for his son—but instead of embracing him, as Wallace expected, Shinoda struck Jono across the face with the back of his hand. "Idiot boy," he seethed. "You nearly destroyed our family. Betrayed everything our predecessors have built. I am ashamed to call you my son."

Jono straightened, cheek flaming red, and adjusted his glasses so they were no longer askance. "I take that as the highest praise."

"Sir," Vivienne interrupted before Shinoda could strike him a second time. "Might I remind you that the speech is scheduled to commence shortly? President Doja—"

"This won't take long." Shinoda bared his teeth. "In the meantime, see that my son is returned to his room. And make sure he stays there."

"Yes, of course." Bobbing anxiously, she steered Jono from the study, and with a wave of her hand, the doors sealed shut behind her.

"What Jonothan fails to understand is that to be the hero in our own story means we all become the villain in someone else's." Shinoda skimmed his teeth across his lower lip. His attention flickered to Nimah, then to the formidable woman at her side, and a grin spread wide across his face. "So this is the infamous Captain Indira Roscoe," he said, stopping when he was toe to toe with Indira.

"Why am I here?" Indira demanded.

"You're here because I could use a pirate of your skillset," he spread his hands, "since I've apparently lost the one I had on payroll."

"You'd hire an enemy?"

"I'm a businessman, Captain, and you don't create an empire like mine by wasting talent or resources. Besides, it would be more fun to own you than break you."

"I'd rather spend what's left of my years rotting in a cell on Hollow Point."

310　　　　　FALLON DEMORNAY

His answering laugh was soft but brittle with hatred and pleasure. "Oh, that's not where you'd be going. You see, an hour from now, a broadcast will be released stating that the *Stormchaser* and all aboard her were destroyed in a strenuous battle led by Admiral Wallace." He swept a hand toward Wallace, and had the temerity to wink for good measure, as if she were a co-conspirator in his insidious plot. "To the public, you will be dead. Both of you."

"And where will I really be?" Indira demanded.

"If not working for me, chained in the bowels of a dead prime ore mine. While the mineral might be fully extracted from the asteroid, the radiation levels there remain quite extreme." Shinoda removed the stopper from a crystal decanter and poured out two fingers of a clear liquid into a tumbler. "And don't worry, I'll make sure you have company." Rounding the desk, tumbler in hand, he stopped before Nimah and stroked the edge of his pinky down the side of her face, skimming a stray lock of hair behind her ear. "So fresh. So young. Can you imagine watching her beautiful little face melt from her bones? Seeing the blood she'd spray into the air with each agonizing breath? The palest pink mist— warm as a sunset."

When Indira prepared to lunge, Wallace struck her behind the knees and she dropped with a pained grunt.

"Sir, I think it's time I escort the prisoners from the premises."

"That won't be necessary, Admiral."

Wallace stepped back a pace, careful to keep her eyes trained on them both.

"You're a sick, twisted excuse of a human being," Indira seethed through tears of pain as she struggled back to her feet. Hard to manage with her hands behind her back. "And I would expect no less from the man who plans to slaughter a hundred and fifty billion innocent people so he can get his greedy hands on an energy source more powerful than prime."

Shinoda rocked on his heels, eyes narrowed and features calm. But Wallace caught the tightening of his knuckles, the surge in his pulse, and the flush of sweat infusing his skin.

"Progress demands sacrifice. I'm merely providing a public service." He clasped his hands together. "Taking out the trash, if you will. I suppose I do have you to credit for its initial discovery, though you

FLIGHT OF THE SPARROW 311

cost me many, many years of frustration over its loss on Valhalla. But now—the RIM offers a rich cache, and with this new mineral, the limitations of retrofitting will be obsolete. I'll extend my life cycle as many times as I wish." Shinoda's eyes gleamed wildly. "Immortality, can you imagine? No one has ever been so close to becoming a god until this moment. I'll live a thousand years over, the master of an empire so great, so vast—there won't be a star left untouched by my reach."

"What about your son?" Indira snapped. "You can kill me, but you won't be able to muzzle him. Unlike his father, he has a soul."

Shinoda nodded around a sigh. "Ah yes, my son, useless, pathetic excuse that he is—while he is mine, and I protect what is mine, I fear you're right. Jonothan has forgotten where his loyalties reside, but he will either come to see reason or I'll squeeze the air from his lungs myself."

"You'd murder your own son?" Nimah gasped.

"With elite, I can make another. Lab-grown and engineered to possess none of his . . . less-desirable qualities. His weaknesses."

"It doesn't have to be this way," Nimah pressed. "Elite can save all of us."

"Not everyone is worth saving. Noncitizens have been a scourge on our system for two hundred years. Draining resources we should never have had to spare. Feeding into the dregs of criminal society. Pirates, skinners—vermin, all of you. The time has come to crush the weak under the heel of your betters."

The door pixelated open, and his assistant, face ashen, rushed inside. "Sir! Mr. Shinoda, there's been a—"

"Stupid, insipid clod! I said no interruptions!" Cormack snatched a vase off the corner of his desk, the same priceless beauty Wallace had admired so fondly—and heaved it at her.

The assistant ducked with practiced ease a second before it would have struck her head, and smoothed her hands across her stomach. "Sir, I thought it should be brought to your immediate attention that an emergency broadcast just went live across all channels throughout the entirety of the Inner Circle and Outer RIM."

"So?" Spittle flew from his mouth, eyes wide as his splayed hands. "You dare to waltz in here with that?"

312   FALLON DEMORNAY

Calmly, his assistant crossed to the lake-sized glass conference table and raised the remote, activating the holoscreen that shone like a mirror to reflect Shinoda's startled face. And beneath it, a banner splayed with looping script that read:

IESO Mining CEO Cormack Shinoda admits to conspiring to commit act of terrorism and mass murder—is subject to immediate arrest.

"As I was trying to say," Vivienne's voice trailed from behind the screen, "it appears that you are, effective immediately, number one on the STARs Most Wanted list." Removing her headset, she dropped it at his feet before dusting her hands. "Given the circumstances, I am tendering my resignation."

"I . . . how—?"

Wallace tapped a finger just below her left eye as the assistant walked out of the office. "Sixth generation HWKeyes, along with the admiral-level clearance codes you graciously provided, allowed for access to top-priority feeds to livestream an emergency broadcast of any extreme threat to public safety. I believe that conspiracy to murder one hundred and fifty billion non-class citizens falls within those parameters."

Indira Roscoe withdrew her hands from behind her back.

As did Nimah.

"You—you're not cuffed?"

"No," Nimah answered, her grin sharp. "And in your arrogance you never thought to check."

Shinoda's eyes blazed to Wallace. "You don't know what you've done. Your career—your life—is over. I'll make sure of it."

Wallace set her shoulders. "All my life I was raised never to defy my superiors, to bleed silver and blue, but if protecting the lives of innocents comes at the cost of my brass, so be it. At least I will have done this one thing right." Removing the magnicuffs from her belt, she held them out to Nimah. "You've earned the privilege, Agent Dabo. This collar is yours."

Nimah had a moment, a single breath of awe, before she gathered herself. Shoulders drawn, she turned to Shinoda. "Cormack Shinoda, on behalf of SIGA authority, I am placing you under arrest."

"No . . ."

"Anything you say or do is being recorded for evidence and that evidence will be brought to trial against you. Due to the nature of

FLIGHT OF THE SPARROW   313

your transgressions, all assets will be seized under Section Code R567. Therefore, should you require an attorney, you will be given access to public resources to procure one. Please stand and keep your hands where I can see them. Any attempts to resist or movements interpreted as signs of aggression will be met with force—lethal if necessary. Do you understand?"

"You can't!" Shinoda recoiled. "I'm an honorary member of the SIGA board! I *won't* be cuffed like a common criminal. I want my attorney! I demand *counsel!*"

Nimah caught his arm, and with a brutal twist, slammed him face-down on his desk and snapped on the magnicuffs as the doors to his office pixelated open, admitting a flood of agents and officers to process the scene. Whirling media drones hovered beyond the sphere of glass walls, capturing every angle of his humiliation as Cormack Shinoda—stripped of his wealth, privilege, and status—did the only thing left in his power to do.

He burst into tears.

"Identity tag, please."

Boomer and Maverick brushed their wrists against the scanner and the projected image of their faces swam on the screen.

"Thank you, Idris Reid-619 and Hunter Devere-818. You are approved for entry to the Namsara residence in the Enola Towers. Lift 42B will take you to their quarters."

Maverick shook a bemused head. It was going to take some getting used to, but at last he was free. It was a strange feeling. When he left the medcenter, rolling out into the busy afternoon streets without a disrupter on his chair or a camo-mask over his face, somehow everything felt sweeter. His senses were confused by it all, and the pale whisper of instinct telling him not to linger for too long was hard to shake. But he had time to learn.

Maverick drummed a steady beat with his thumbs on the wheels of his chair as the doors of the lift sealed, and within a moment, it rose with stomach-dropping speed.

"The Namsara penthouse is at the summit of tower one hundred and fifteen," the synth spoke in crisp, blunted syllables of automation. "We shall arrive in approximately forty-seven seconds."

Sweeping left in an ascending arch, the lift became transparent and the entire city of Lysandis spread below, white spires that stretched like a forest of marble-hewn trees. Wide windows cleaved in intricate patterns, decorating their lengths, and elegant open arches spanned between them like the bridges cascading over the body of the jade sea at their base.

At the top of the tower, the turbolift walls went dark again, and the doors slid open to reveal a foyer large enough to dock the *Stormchaser*. Grand double doors stood opposite the lift and an attendant waited for them to disembark. His black goatee and sideburns were streaked with gray that matched his silver uniform.

"Welcome." He inclined his head. "Wait here, I will announce your arrival."

The walls of the great room curved and arched to meld seamlessly with glass that wrapped around one entire side, drawing in what was left of the late afternoon light. Beneath the wash of searing orange and pink, every beautiful piece of furniture was arranged with purpose and an eye to aesthetics. Blue edged with gold accented with white in a mixture of wood and leather and chrome. All authentic and very valuable.

Hovering over the stretch of the city, a newscast splayed on a hundred-foot holoscreen, and even from the perch of the Namsara penthouse it was easy to make out amid the slender buildings towered in columns so high they were lost in the whirl of early-morning air traffic.

IESO Mining chairman and CEO Cormack Shinoda, charged with conspiracy to commit genocide and terrorism, has been sentenced to life without parole. His son, Jonothan Shinoda, has assumed control over the company and announced its dissolution. He plans to return to the RIM, where he will further study this astounding new mineral—elite.

Lysandis was one of the most prominent hubs of the Inner Circle and home to the wealthiest citizens of Atreyes, who he now imagined felt a very vulnerable tremble at what was to come.

It was barely three days since Shinoda's arrest, and the collective rush of emotions was thick as smog. To say the Inner Circle was less than thrilled was putting it mildly. Every newscast station was broadcasting its own spin, but most were centered on what financial experts were

FLIGHT OF THE SPARROW 315

calling "the collapse of civilization as we know it." The UPN, upon receiving all documents that Jono had in his possession, drafted a policy stating that the RIMers, and their future descendants, would share equal ownership of the elite core.

Maverick was about to come into more money than he knew what to do with.

"Look at 'em scatter." Boomer was planted at his side, his feet spread wide and arms crossed over his barrel chest. And grinning like a pig in shit. "Like roaches when you turn on the light."

"It's something."

"Something! Ha! Everyone always treated RIMers like trash. Now we're the ones with all the power and credits. Never have to feel worthless again." He scraped a hand overtop his dense curls, freshly cut in a fade. "This is the most razor week of my life. And this . . ." He turned to take in the foyer once again and whistled low. "Imagine we own a spot like this when reparations are paid out?"

Maverick shook a dazed head. "Not even in my wildest dreams." But as crazy as it was to imagine, it was possible. Finally. After a lifetime of struggle and scraping through trash, anything and everything was right at his fingertips. He was free. *Free* . . . at least from being hunted by STARs. Hatchett was a whole other concern, but for now he would celebrate this moment for however long it might last.

"You're here."

Maverick spun on his wheels and tried not to swallow his tongue. Nimah stood in the wash of sunlight, dressed in a crisp navy suit with polished brass on her shoulders and braided filigree down the front, caging her waist. Heeled black boots lengthened her legs and highlighted their strength, and dark hair hung loose in waves around golden-skinned cheeks flush with joy from her dazzling smile.

Maverick dipped his chin in greeting. "Agent."

"Not yet." Smirking down at her toes, Nimah scraped her heel across the smooth marble floor. "Not officially."

"Already looking the part," Boomer commented. "Brass suits you."

Her cheeks glowed from the unexpected praise. "Thank you."

"Best give you two a moment." He clapped a hand to Maverick's shoulder. "I'll be at the lift."

316   FALLON DEMORNAY

"He's right, you know," Maverick added once they were alone. "You look good, Nimah. Happy."

"We were just doing final adjustments." Nimah joined him on the terrace, restless fingers touching the brass detailing on her lapel. "Liselle and I graduate the day after tomorrow. Special honors. Admiral Wallace assures me my grandmother will be released from the hospital in time for the ceremony. I was told even President Doja will be there."

"I'd expect nothing less for a couple of heroes."

Nimah glanced down at him. "You should be there, too. You deserve to be acknowledged for what we've done."

"I'm not one for trophies. Besides," Maverick swatted a hand, "according to newscasts, I died out there. Showing up at an event like that defeats the purpose of getting a whole new identity."

"Right. Of course." She planted her forearms against the stone balustrade. "Well, now that you have a new name, what are you going to do with your hard-earned freedom?"

Mimicking her pose, elbows to his knees, Maverick gazed off into the distance, where blue sky bled into the horizon. "Find a ship and join a crew eager to explore." A wistful smile stretched across the width of his face. "For as long as I can remember I've dreamed of the stars, wondering what was out there beyond them. Now I get to find out."

"I can't wait to hear about what you discover out there."

Neither could he. But when their eyes met, tears shimmered in the fringe of her lashes. As much as she would miss him, and he could see it in her face, she understood the power of dreams. Of finally achieving them.

"I guess this is goodbye, then." And his chest ached with sudden realization. After this moment he'd likely never see her face again, and suddenly he wanted to memorize the shape and pattern of every freckle scattered across gold-dusted skin. The way her eyes brightened seconds before a laugh rolled up her throat. Or to feel the soft, silken texture of her hair curling around his finger one last time . . .

She thrust out a hand. "Thank you," she added as he clasped hers and shook, warm and slow. "For everything."

"None of it would've happened if you hadn't collared me. So, thank yourself, I guess."

FLIGHT OF THE SPARROW

Nimah tucked her hands away with a thin-lipped smile, a tear breaking free and as she walked away, her shoulders proud and stride steady. Maverick sighed, pensive and deep. She had touched his heart and would remain there now. Part of him. A beautiful scar that would ache to touch, but one he was glad to carry.

Nimah belonged to the STARs. Maverick belonged to the void.

This was how their story was always meant to end.

CHAPTER THIRTY

Damn, Nims." Liselle pursed her lips with a soft whistle. "You clean up real good in agent blue. Melanin all crisp."

"So do you."

"I can't wait to see the look on Trolltega's face when he sees us on stage wearing our stars before the entire school body. Bet he'll puke with jealousy."

"Or pass out."

Both girls burst into excited and equally nervous laughter that faded into silence.

"Nims?" Liselle whispered, eyes downcast. "I never got a chance to say . . . I'm sorry. I'm so sorry. I hope you understand why I had to come after you."

"I would've done the same if you'd been equally as boneheaded." Grasping Liselle's shoulders, she urged her to look up. "Wallace would've killed me half a dozen times over if it wasn't for you. You had my back, even though it meant you could lose all of this." She gestured around them. "You're my best friend, Lis. You've always been my best friend. Always will be."

Liselle blinked her eyes clear. "At least we made it here. Together."

"Ladies, are you decent?" A gentle knock at the door interrupted them seconds before Madam Isabeau Namsara floated into the room wearing a flowing suit-gown of plum that verged on black and was trimmed in elegant brass platework. She was equal parts queen and warrior. Her long locs were curled and styled loose, faded to palest silver at the ends,

FLIGHT OF THE SPARROW 319

matching the shade of her retrofit eyes. "Oh." She pressed a gentle hand to her heart. "You two are a sight to behold."

Side by side, Liselle and Nimah exchanged smiling glances.

Gliding as if her feet never touched the ground, she hugged Liselle first and kissed her brow, then followed suit with Nimah. "My girls. I'm so incredibly proud of you both. This is a wondrous day."

Nimah's cheeks warmed to the bone. "Thank you, Madam Namsara." The Namsaras had always been kind to her, despite the brand on her wrist and the numbers formally hitched to her last name. She'd joined them several times a year during the Academy holidays, as one of three students without family—they hadn't wanted to see their daughter's bunkmate left alone.

They'd never treated her like a RIM-rat. Not once. Not ever.

"No need to be so formal, even if I am wearing my crest." Isabeau winked. "I came to let you know that you have a visitor waiting for you in the lounge." She squeezed Nimah's shoulders. "Please be quick. Our escort will be here in fifteen minutes to take us to the ceremony."

"Who is it?"

"Someone I think you'll be very happy to see."

Captain Indira Roscoe turned from the windows, her hair roped into a single braid down the length of her strong back. She was dressed in fatigues, crisp white shirt buttoned low on a neck lined with tattoos and layered silver chains that matched the rings adorning her blunt fingers. A fierce figure against the sunset backdrop of Lysandis. She smiled as Nimah joined her on the terrace, a sly grin, and she surveyed her granddaughter from head to toe. "Look at you."

Nimah flushed. "You like it?"

Ro circled her with a nod, hand on the hilt of her cutlass. After a week in the medbay, her bones were set and she moved with the fluid grace of a warrior. "Military blue is definitely your color."

Nimah tugged at the waist of the jacket. The uniform was snug and stiff, the material blended with nanites. It hugged like a perfectly tailored second skin, and would adapt with her body over time, auto-repair rips, and gather important data to sync with her medical records. It was part of her now. She'd dreamt of this for the better part of a decade, so

320   **FALLON DEMORNAY**

why did it feel so alien compared to the weight of her grandmother's leather trench she'd been told to keep?

"Where's the crew?"

"They wanted to come say their goodbyes—but rich folk tend to get jumpy when there's more than one pirate in their midst."

"Goodbyes?" She blinked away the sharp sting of emotion. "You're leaving?"

Ro tucked a stray stubborn curl behind Nimah's ear. "I'll be clearing atmo this afternoon. I need to be out there." She pointed toward the stars. "For the people."

"But it's over now . . ."

"We won a tremendous victory, it's true, but that was only the battle. A war is coming. Something ugly and fierce. Feel it in my bones like a damp cold."

"You could stay . . ." *Stay with me.* "For the ceremony, at least."

"I'll just steal your thunder. And I've never been good with goodbyes, but I wanted to do better this time around." Ro rolled the proud line of her shoulders before removing a small box from a pocket inside her jacket. She popped the lid.

"What's this?"

"Something to remember who you are. Where you come from." Inside the box, on a bed of black velvet, sat a sparrow, this one made from silver with opal eyes and wings spread in glorious flight. Lifting it out, Ro pinned it to the lapel of Nimah's suit. "There." She crossed her arms. "You deserve this, Sparrow. Is it true the president herself will be anointing you?"

"And Admiral Wallace, who is receiving her second Star of Valor today. Awarded in honor of her heroic leadership efforts in saving two hundred billion lives." Nimah shook a despondent head. "You're the one who deserves to be accredited. And the crew."

Laughter shimmered through Ro like stardust. Then her grandmother sighed. "I'm just a pirate. I have no need for bits of shine."

"No," Nimah whispered, letting tears fall. "You're a hero. And I am so proud to be your granddaughter."

She gathered Nimah close and held her tight for a slow, tense breath. "You sure you want to hand your life away to the brass? You could come with me, Sparrow. Come sail the void. I can show you things." Drawing

FLIGHT OF THE SPARROW

back, she cupped Nimah's shoulders. "Things you couldn't even begin to imagine. There's so much you haven't seen."

Nimah's gaze wandered to the swath of sun in a fading orange sky. Somewhere out there, the lure of Valhalla beckoned like fingers plucking at strings. The sensation reverberated through every limb, begging her to answer.

Could she walk away from it all?

"I've worked my whole life for this. *This*." Nimah's throat tightened. "I can't give it up when I fought so hard to get it all back."

"No." Ro sighed. Smiled. "I guess not." Eyes shimmering with unshed tears, she captured Nimah in another hug. This one hard and bone cracking. "Between Shinoda's takedown and implications of government-sanctioned genocide, we bruised a lot of toes." She spoke against Nimah's temple, breath warming her skin. "Powerful brass will want retaliation. Be vigilant. Be ready." Drawing back, she cupped Nimah's face in rough hands, and didn't wait for a response before letting go.

For the second time in her life, Nimah watched her grandmother walk away, but as she climbed into the cockpit of the shuttle, Captain Indira Roscoe gave her one last look—one last smile—before launching into the clouds and disappearing from sight.

A Valkyrie on wing, returning to the sky.

CHAPTER THIRTY-ONE

Saying goodbye was never easy, especially not when said to two people she cared about greatly. Nimah swiped her eyes clear. This was as it should be. Everyone heading off into the horizon of their destinies. Her grandmother, the voice of the people; Maverick, discovering new worlds; and Nimah, at long last a STARs agent.

"Miss Dabo-124?" The synth-guard hummed onto the terrace and teetered before her on its uniwheel base. "The escort is an estimated three minutes away from arrival. Madam Namsara has requested your presence on the main landing pad."

"Yes. Of course."

"Do you require any assistance in getting there?"

Nimah steadied her breathing. Three minutes was just enough time to stop by the bathroom at the end of the corridor to clean her face. "No. I'll manage on my own, thank you."

The synth rolled away to attend to other household tasks delegated to its system mainframe. Now that she'd been checked off as complete, Nimah might as well not even exist unless she flagged it for service.

Though it was hard seeing her grandmother leave, she didn't feel the expected weight in her chest, the cloying sadness. This wasn't goodbye forever. Somehow she knew they'd see each other again. Perhaps in the void, with Nimah leading a crew of her own, or while she patrolled the busy streets of a jostling spacity in a rogue sector.

"—agree that the RIM Accord is a problem that must be prioritized above all else."

FLIGHT OF THE SPARROW 323

Nimah eased to a halt as she reached the fringes of the west wing of the Namsara home—a three-story office that included a library, gym, kitchen, and even a set of bedrooms for the nights when either or both parents were locked in pressing government business.

The door, usually sealed shut for complete noise cancellation, was cracked open the barest sliver, allowing the distressed voices of whoever was engaged with Chief Counsellor Lennox Namsara to seep through.

Peering through the crevice, her eyes traced across the second level of the suite until she found Lennox returning to stand before the conference table, where the holoimages of the SIGA board members circled, waiting. At the head of the table was Chairwoman Annelise Aramir. Nimah recognized her sour, pinched expression and shrewd, large eyes. She looked like a shark without the grinning mouth and endless rows of teeth, but she still had a vicious bite. And never stopped moving.

"I understand this is of concern to the board," Lennox replied, his voice as weary as the set of his shoulders. He stood tall, with a straight back that carried his dark suit with absolute grace. His jaw shadowed with a trimmed, silver-studded beard and eyes the same shape and shade as Liselle's, and just as warm. "I've been on back-to-back commcasts across the Inner Circle since news broke and I'm afraid the damage of the livestream in Cormack's office is absolute. There's no getting ahead of this, Chairwoman. We're going to have to settle with the UPN on the Accord."

"Cormack Shinoda shit the bed, on that we can agree, but now that his assets have been seized there's little he can do to position himself against us. He's at our mercy and will fall on his sword. That's a powerful card we can play to help deflect public attention. They love splashy trials, and his crucifixion will keep them entertained for weeks. As for Kimora Wallace, her admiralship ensures we retain her as an ally, for now at least—beyond that, there's little we can do on that score until we put this inconvenience to bed, but I'd like to mark in the official minutes that we circle back on that point at next quarter's board meeting."

Nimah pressed in closer, careful not to touch the door panel or any part of the walls lest she trip the perimeter sensors. So long as she didn't breathe too harshly or move too quickly . . .

"What are our options to counter the RIM Accord?" another board member mused. "Can we play up the 'days of Earth-Prior' angle?

Resources left to public dissemination tend to fall into excess and waste. RIMers lacking the know-how to properly and effectively manage such responsibility, et cetera?"

"Or perhaps we offer incentive to those willing to relinquish ownership," Chairwoman Aramir suggested. "If we can secure majority share—"

"Our analysts predict less than a third will be swayed," another board member interjected. "What about the rest who won't?"

Chairwoman Aramir pinned her fellow director with a frosty glare that numbed Nimah all the way to her toes. "Then we press harder."

"The UPN's anti-coercion policy makes that prospect impossible," Lennox spoke up, drawing attention back to himself. "Along with the internal investigation, hence why we're holding this briefing in an isolated holosphere instead of at SIGA base. If Cormack was still in place, we'd have a leg to stand on, but without him—"

"Well, that's unacceptable. As our chief legal counsel, we expect you to fix this, Lennox. And fast."

"The law may be malleable." He leaned against the table with large, wide-palmed hands, rings clinking as they connected with the glass surface. "But I can only stretch parameters so far."

"Stretch them, break them, I don't really care what you do. But find a solution to this ordeal. The Circle is spiraling. If we lose our grip on this, we lose everything. And without us at the helm, we're facing anarchy. That cannot happen."

"I need time."

Chairwoman Aramir leaned forward, and her holo-projected body stuttered out of focus from the abrupt movement. "The RIM Accord goes to bed in eight weeks. You've got seven."

"Understood."

Nimah eased from the doorway an inch at a time until she was well out of sensor range, then picked up the pace, flying down the corridors for the main landing pad. Her grandmother was right. The battle might've been won, but many more loomed on the horizon before the war was over and the RIMers would see their due.

The thought haunted Nimah, looping through the tracks of her brain in endless circles as the chauffeured vehicle airlifted them to the Academy, the courtyard flooded with cadets and their families gathered for the ceremony. Nimah smiled and laughed, she joked and engaged, but it was all a careful pretense.

Chief Counselor Lennox was equally masked, but she saw past the proud gleam in his eyes to the worry rooted there. He was concerned. More than concerned; he was afraid.

"You alright?" Liselle nudged Nimah with her elbow.

"Yeah . . . I'm good." Nimah hadn't realized until that moment that she'd stopped walking. Her feet were cemented to the polished stone of the courtyard—shaped in a four-point star.

"We need to get up there." Liselle nodded toward the ceremony stage, flanked by the gilded hundred-foot-tall doors of the Academy. Admiral Wallace graced the stage, joined by Chairwoman Aramir and the rest of the SIGA board officials. The crowd erupted in applause. Liselle's parents were already seated on the stage. As government officials and proud charitable patrons of the Academy, they'd earned the privilege.

The RIM Accord goes to bed in eight weeks. You've got seven.

Nimah dug in her heels. "I have to go."

"Ha-ha, real funny." Liselle rolled her eyes.

"I'm not joking."

Liselle gaped at her like she'd grown a second head. "Nims, the ceremony is starting." She caught her hand. "This is everything we've ever wanted. Dreamed about."

"I know." Which is why Nimah had to disappear now. No one would ever expect her to run away, not when she was moments from achieving a dream she'd committed several major crimes to achieve.

"Then why?"

"I can't tell you." Because uttering a single word would not only put Liselle in a precarious position with her family but put her life in danger as well, and Nimah had done enough of that already. Liselle deserved to be happy. To live her dream. "I need you to trust me."

Emotions flitted across Liselle's face. Sadness. Understanding. Joy. Despair. But also love, and love was what mattered most. "I trust you, Nims. I'll always trust you." Liselle embraced her tearfully. Beyond her, Admiral Wallace approached the podium and raised her hands; the audience hushed. "You must be out of your mind."

326　　　　　　　**FALLON DEMORNAY**

"Must be," Nimah trembled with a laugh. "You're my sister. The sister I chose."

Sniffing, Liselle hugged her tighter. "I love you, too."

Nimah pressed her hands to her face, cleaning it of tears, and turned her head as a patrol sentry swung his leg off a jet-bike and kicked the stand, docking it with his helmet on the handlebar, before joining his comrades by the fountain. "How about a distraction, for old times' sake?"

"What did you have in mind?"

Nimah cast her a smirk. "Remember Professor Loran's class in third year?"

Liselle sighed. Then arched a devious brow. "Coming right up."

The *Stormchaser*, freshly washed and welded with new plate metal, gleamed like a STARship in her prime. Grounding on the dock near its broad, polished wing, Nimah leapt off the jet-bike and activated the hover stand as Captain Indira Roscoe barked commands at her crew and dock workers. She halted as Nimah approached, and tossed the length of her braid over her shoulder.

"I thought you'd be halfway across the void by now." Nimah smiled.

"Just waiting on our new pilot," she said with a thrust of her chin.

Nimah followed her grandmother's line of sight, and her heart quickened as Maverick rolled to a stop at the base of the gangway. "What happened to getting a ship? A crew?"

Maverick tapped his wheels, shrugged around a wide grin. "Looks like I found one."

"Can't believe I let you talk me into this," Boomer muttered, tossing people-sized bags into the cargo hold. "Hitching our wagon to a crew of crotchety old space grannies."

"You mean band of witty pirates," Gertrude amended, dark curls in an array of waist-length twists that matched her frosted-blue lashes and glittering lipstick.

"Plagued with arthritis and bum hips," Chu cackled.

"Yet glorious as ever, darling." Gertrude slapped Chu with a guffawing high-five.

"Settle down, and let's get her loaded. I want us voidborne in twenty." Ro shook a smiling head, then turned to Nimah, hands on her hips. "And you? Shouldn't you be at your graduation right now?"

FLIGHT OF THE SPARROW

"Yeah."

Ro angled her head, gazing past her, and a bemused expression crossed her face. "Did you steal someone's jet-bike?"

"Sorta."

"Why?"

Nimah scraped a hand across the back of her neck. "Guess I'm more like you than I thought."

"That's not what I meant, Sparrow." Ro chuckled, then quickly sobered. "Why are you *here*? What are you doing?"

"You're right. SIGA's going to fight back, so it's up to *us* to protect the people."

"Us?"

"Yes. Us." Nimah nodded. "As an agent, I'd be their puppet. But as a Valkyrie . . ."

"Told you." Chu ribbed Gertrude, both of them sunk into folding chairs, and an immensely pleased expression pulled across her wrinkled face. "Owe me fifty credits."

"You sure about this, Sparrow?"

Nimah's heartbeat quickened, not with fear, but thrill. Dark and glittering, it settled across her tongue and tasted like . . . purpose. "Yes," she answered. "This is where I belong."

A tender gleam shone in Ro's eyes. "Yo-ho, yo-ho." She thrust out a welcoming hand.

Nimah clasped it firmly. "A pirate's life for me."

ABOUT THE AUTHOR

Fallon DeMornay is the author of *Stiletto Sisterhood* and *Flight of the Sparrow*. Known for writing about powerful girls smashing the patriarchy with swords or stilettos, she was a finalist in *Harlequin*'s "So You Think You Can Write" contest, and her work has been featured on Cosmopolitan.com and reviewed by *RT Book Reviews*. Affectionately referred to as Wonder Woman by her own real-life Sisterhood, DeMornay can be found tearing up the dancefloor to salsa or bachata when she isn't writing. She currently resides in North York, Canada.

Podium

DISCOVER MORE
STORIES UNBOUND

PodiumEntertainment.com